Everything She Wanted

T0033931

By Jennifer Ryan

The Montana Men Series
Her Lucky Cowboy
When It's Right
At Wolf Ranch

The McBride Series
Dylan's Redemption
Falling for Owen
The Return of Brody McBride

The Hunted Series
Everything She Wanted
Chasing Morgan
The Right Bride
Lucky Like Us
Saved by the Rancher

Short Stories
"Can't Wait"
(appears in *All I Want for Christmas Is a Cowboy*)
"Waiting for You"
(appears in *Confessions of a Secret Admirer*)

Everything She Wanted

BOOK FIVE: THE HUNTED SERIES

JENNIFER RYAN

AVON IMPULSE
An Imprint of HarperCollinsPublishers

Excerpt from *Stone Cold Cowboy* copyright © 2016 by Jennifer Ryan.

Excerpt from *Dirty Deeds* copyright © 2015 by Megan Erickson.

Excerpt from *Montana Hearts: Sweet Talkin' Cowboy* copyright © 2015 by Darlene Panzera.

EPub Edition JANUARY 2016 ISBN: 9780062396426
Print Edition ISBN: 9780062396433

Avon, Avon Impulse, and the Avon Impulse logo are trademarks of HarperCollins Publishers.

HB 05.12.2023

For all the fans who loved The Hunted series and emailed me asking for Ben's story. I hope Everything She Wanted *lives up to your expectations. I loved revisiting the Turner-Shaw-Reed family. It's like visiting old friends. Thank you for your continued support.*

To my amazing agent, Suzie Townsend, thank you for having my back, teaching me about the business, reading for me at the very, very last minute, and answering all my many questions. I'm so excited about the future, knowing you'll be right beside me for all that is to come. This is just the beginning.

Everything She Wanted

Chapter One

"YOU HAVE TO kill him or we'll lose everything." Christina Faraday ignored her son's eye roll, too distressed about the earlier argument with her husband, Donald, to care about Evan's insolence.

"Mom, seriously, don't you think you're being overly dramatic, even for you?"

"Dramatic. Really? He's divorcing me."

"How many times have you or he threatened that over the last nearly thirty years? I mean, really, come on. He'll come around. He always does."

"Not this time."

"What now? You slept with your yoga instructor? The Pilates guy? The guy who always remembers your coffee order at Starbucks? The waiter you met at dinner last night? Did you finally up your taste in men and drop your young pups and go for one of the stiff suits Dad calls friends? What?"

"This isn't funny."

"Well, whatever it is, I'm sure you'll work it out. You always do. You'll go back to the usual indifference you have for each other and what you do."

"Not this time," Christina yelled. "He served me the papers. If this goes through, it will ruin everything."

"You'll be fine. It's not like you love him and can't live without him."

"The prenup I signed means I get next to nothing."

"Well, that's your own damn fault for signing it in the first place."

"How was I supposed to know he'd take on a partner the following year and build a multimillion-dollar business out of it?"

"Dad's smart, focused, and a workaholic. He probably had that partnership set up before he asked you to sign the prenup. That's what I would have done."

Christina tried not to think Donald had been that cunning before their marriage. He'd had plans and big dreams for the business. She'd never paid much attention—then or now—and it was coming back to bite her on the ass.

She desperately needed Evan's help to get out of this mess. With his volatile temper, it wouldn't take much to set him after his father. But would he come through for her? He'd have to if he wanted to keep his cushy lifestyle of drinking, gambling, partying, and playing.

"He swore he'd cut you off for good this time. You'll have nothing and neither will I."

"No, he won't. He always says he will, but he never

does. Not really. Well, not for long anyway. I know how to change his mind."

"You're not listening. It won't work this time." She fell onto the sofa and dropped her head in her hands. She stared at the plush carpet and her Jimmy Choo shoes. "Why did I sign that prenup? The one-million payout isn't even a drop in the bucket of the wealth we share now. The company is worth three hundred times that. This house is worth five times that. I'll lose my home, my money. Everything I've accumulated and helped that bastard achieve will all be taken away."

"Well, you shouldn't have been so blatant about cheating on him. I'm surprised he didn't leave you sooner."

Christina wagged her pointed finger. "Be careful, Evan. You side with him, you may find he's not on yours anymore."

Evan narrowed his eyes and leaned forward. "What the hell are you talking about?"

"You pushed him too far with that last bar fight. You nearly killed that man. Then you get a DUI and wreck your car and nearly kill yourself." She stared at the long scar on his neck. He'd nearly bled to death before help arrived.

"He deserved it. Fucking asshole thinks he can hit on my date."

"What do you care? You'd only met the woman that night. You probably don't even remember her name."

Evan's face took on a thoughtful, far-off look. He shook his head, indicating he really didn't remember the woman's name. What did it matter? Her son went from one woman to the next like he changed his shirts.

"It's the principle. She was with me."

"Sometimes you're like a spoiled child. Someone touches your toy and you punch them out."

"Maybe, but I'm never going to let my woman get away with looking at, let alone sleeping with, another man right under my nose. Not the way Dad let you get away with it."

Christina huffed out an exasperated breath and rolled her eyes. "Are you going to help me or not?"

"What the hell do you want me to do about this?"

"Kill him before he has a chance to do anything."

The silence grew between them as Evan finally understood that she meant it. They had no other choice.

A lopsided grin tilted his mouth. He shook his head, dismissing her again. "I'm not going to shoot him dead because you signed away a fortune. Hire a lawyer and fight him for more money. He's a good guy, he'll pay you just to make this go away."

She growled, then tried another tactic. "He has a girlfriend. Everything will go to her if he divorces me and marries her."

"Bullshit. Dad? A girlfriend? No way."

"He bought her a house ten months ago. That's where he spends his evenings now. Not here. Not with me."

"How long has this been going on?"

"I don't know. I found out about the property when we did our taxes. He doesn't think I read over those things, but I do. He thinks he can spend five point two million on a house and I'm not going to notice."

"You think you can spend thousands on dinner,

drinks, and hotel rooms and he won't notice. And watches. Seriously, you don't think he knows you buy those fucks gifts. He sees the credit card bill, you know?" Evan shook his head and downed the last of his Scotch. "You two are something."

"He's never had another woman in his life. She's special to him if he bought her a house and spends time with her. If he marries her, we lose everything. She'll inherit, not you."

"He won't do that."

"Yes, he will," she snapped. "He's already said as much."

"I'm calling him." Evan pulled his phone from his back pocket, frustrated his parents' fucked-up lives always screwed with his. He hit the speed dial for his father and put the phone to his ear, but kept his eyes trained on his distraught, and obviously mad, mother. "Dad, I'm with Mom. What is going on?"

"What did she tell you?"

"That you're divorcing her and have a new girlfriend."

"Not new. I've been with her over a year and a half. I'm happy. I can't do it anymore, Evan. I can't live a lie with your mother. Her deceit, your continued lack of motivation to get a job, build a decent life, and getting into trouble at every turn has pushed me too far. My life with you both has turned into a bad habit that eats away at who I am and the kind of man I want to be. I won't do it anymore. I'm done. She'll receive her settlement. I'll set up a trust for you that will pay a monthly allowance for your rent and utilities but nothing more. The next time you get arrested or need to pay someone off to keep them from pressing charges for whatever trouble and harm you cause, don't call me. I won't bail you out again."

"Dad, come on, you can't be serious."

"It's over. I will not pay both personally and financially for your debased lifestyles anymore. Believe me, under the circumstances, what I'm offering is generous. Push me on this and you'll get nothing. Unless and until you change your ways, we have nothing left to say to each other."

"What the hell do you mean by that?"

"Ask your mother. She obviously didn't tell you everything."

"You can't do this."

"Don't blame me. Your mother lied and cheated throughout our marriage. She got away with it right up until I discovered the real truth. A truth I never wanted to see, but stared me in the face every day. You never take responsibility for the things you do. You always blame others. So you want to blame someone for this outcome, blame her. She did this to me and to you. I'm sorry for that. Because I am, I'll set up the trust. Take it or leave it, but that's all you get."

Evan wanted to chuck the phone across the room, but held on to his temper. Barely. "Dad, this isn't fair. I don't understand what you're talking about."

"You want answers, get them from your mother. Let her explain why she did it. Why she does anything. The only things she cares about are herself and the money. I mistook her joy when I gave her things as love. She never loved me. She loved what I could give her. Now, I'm taking it all away."

Evan stared at his phone in disbelief. His father hung up on him.

"I told you. He won't be swayed this time. We're cut off."

Evan fisted his hands at his sides, the phone digging into his palm, and tried to control the welling anger in his gut. "What did you do?"

"Something that can't be undone."

"What did you do?" he demanded.

"What I had to do, but that isn't important. We need to fix this before it's too late."

Frustrated with her nonanswers, he growled under his breath and tried to think. Without his father's money, what the hell would he do? The lawyer he'd hired to keep him out of jail cost a fortune. His father paid off that fuck he assaulted at the bar, but he still had the DUI charges hanging over his head. If his father didn't pay for a top-notch lawyer, he might face some serious fines and jail time.

Furious his mother refused to give him answers and explain why he was about to lose everything, he tried to come up with a plan. Based on the call with his father, the way his father spoke, there was no use talking to him. He'd made up his mind. Evan had changed it many times, but something about the way he spoke, the deep hurt and anger laced in his words, set off alarms in Evan's mind. The rift in their relationship had turned into a tear that couldn't be mended with empty promises to change his ways.

"I'm telling you, Evan, there is only one way to fix this. If your father lives, we lose everything. You've got to make it look like an accident or murder. The insurance company won't pay out if it looks like a suicide."

Evan raised his hands, then let them fall and slap his thighs. "Do you hear yourself? Do you know what you're asking me to do? Kill my own father. It's beyond reason."

"You've killed before for a hell of a lot less than what you're about to lose."

Evan tried not to think about the man he beat to death and left in a dumpster behind a bar over a fucking five-hundred-dollar bet. The guy cheated. He needed to be taught a lesson. Evan was drunk and high and out of control. He barely made it home that night, too messed up to even remember how he drove home. His mother found him passed out in bed the next morning, his clothes covered in blood from beating the guy's face in. His memories of that night were more flashes of images than an actual play-by-play of what happened. They found the guy's body at the dumps four days later. By the time the cops came to question him as one of the last people who had contact with the guy, Evan had his shit together and his story straight. They played poker. Evan lost and went home to sleep off his night of drinking. His mother backed him up about what time he arrived home. She even helped hide the bruises on his knuckles with makeup before he went downstairs to meet with the cops.

That's it. The cops never came back or linked the murder to him. She always had his back.

Unlike his father, who always wanted him to take responsibility, do the right thing, and generally let him suffer whatever fate came his way. No thank you. He didn't deserve to spend his life rotting in a cell. If it came down to it, he'd go out in a blaze of glory before he let the cops lock him in a cage.

He liked his life. The freedom he had to do what he wanted, when he wanted. Now, his father wanted to take that all away. Make him responsible for earning the money he'd learned to enjoy his whole life. He'd never had to work for anything. Didn't really know how. Definitely didn't want to do the whole daily grind in an office or some other shit job. As far as he was concerned, his father made him this way. He couldn't just cut him off now. Evan didn't care about the reasons; he wanted what he'd always had, what he deserved as his father's son. But could he actually kill him? He needed to see his father, this woman, the other life they'd been secretly living.

"What's the address?"

His mother handed him a slip of paper she took from her pocket.

He walked out the front door without a word to his mother. He slid behind the wheel of the Range Rover she bought him for his birthday two months ago to replace the car he wrecked. It pissed his father off that she'd given him the gift. His father always wanted to pull back when his mother wanted to spoil him. Well, he'd take his mother being in control of all that money over his dad any day. This wasn't about killing his father but securing his future.

A thought flickered—maybe the Scotch might be fueling his outrage—before it burned out without really flaring to life inside his mind.

He checked the address and swore. What kind of person buys a house for his mistress this close to his own family? His parents were fucked up. No wonder he didn't turn out normal. Hell, normal was for all those stiffs working their lives away. Not him.

He was fucked up enough to know what needed to be done. To keep his life, he had to take his father's.

Chapter Two

"HE DID IT, Kate." Margo held her fisted hands up to her chest and bounced on her feet, excited like a child on Christmas morning.

Kate Morrison stared at her sister, trying to understand her enthusiasm. Nothing ever went this right in their world, so Kate waited for the hammer to drop.

"He left her. We're going to finally be together like we've wanted."

"Donald said he'd leave her when you met and practically every month since then. He swore it when Alex was born. What makes this time any different?"

Margo rolled her eyes. "You're such a pessimist."

"No, I'm a realist."

"The proof is in the safe downstairs. He had his lawyer draw up all these new papers. He told her today. It's done. He isn't going back there. He's staying with Alex and me."

She'd seen Donald downstairs sitting on the couch, a

drink in hand balanced on the sofa arm. The solemn look on his face piqued her interest. She'd thought he'd had a bad day at work. Instead, it appeared his two worlds collided and he'd had to pick a side. The miserable life he'd been living with a woman he didn't love, and in fact despised, or the woman he adored, who made him happy.

Kate hadn't always been on board with her sister dating a married man. In fact, Kate didn't find out Donald was married until after Alex was conceived. She didn't like Margo keeping secrets from her. It still irritated her. Margo wanted this family so bad, Kate overlooked the imperfections in the relationship and focused on her sister's hard-won happiness, because Margo deserved it after all she'd been through growing up. As her best friend, Kate wanted it for her.

Ever skeptical, Kate asked, "Why now? Why'd he finally do it?"

"For me and Alex. He wants to be with us."

"There's never been any doubt of that, except for the fact he didn't ask her for the divorce."

Margo huffed. "It's complicated."

"That's an excuse, Margo. You have a son."

"So does she."

"Their son is twenty-five. Yours is four months old."

Margo's eyes filled with resignation. "Donald had to think about the company, the money, everything else they share. It's not a simple thing to divorce when there is so much at stake. Breaking up the company like that, giving her a huge piece and a say in the company he spent his life building, makes it hard for him. I don't know what happened. We haven't had time to discuss it, but something changed, and he gets to keep everything."

"How is that possible? This is California. A community property state. She's entitled to half."

Margo raised her hands to the sides and let them fall back to her thighs. "She signed a prenup. Whatever stipulations are in there, she violated them and only gets a million dollars."

"I'd take the million and be happy."

"Would you? After nearly thirty years of marriage and living with the means to do and buy anything you want, you'd take a million and be happy? A house in most areas around here costs at least half that if not all of it. Look where she's lived and how and tell me a million is enough."

Kate tipped her head, acknowledging that truth. "So what did she have to say about all of this?"

"As you can imagine, she's pissed. I don't know all the details. Donald and I want to sit down and talk about it and what comes next."

Kate nodded, understanding dawning. "Which is why I'm here. You want me to babysit."

"Please. It's only for a few days."

Kate widened her eyes and held her breath. "Days? Margo—"

"He's nervous about what she'll do now that she knows about the divorce. He wants Alex away from here in case she does something."

"What does he think she'll do?"

Margo waved her hand. "Oh, mostly just throw a fit.

Maybe come here to cuss him out and demand he give her what she wants. He doesn't want Alex here if that happens."

"Does she know about you and Alex?"

"About me, yes. Not Alex. At least Donald and I don't think so."

Kate grimaced. "And you want to keep Alex a secret awhile longer."

"At least until Donald and I can be married. Please, Kate, will you take him for a few days? Four tops."

"I told you I needed time. I'm just settling in to seeing him with you when I visit."

"You never expected it to be this hard, did you?"

"No. But nothing is ever easy, is it?"

"Not for you and me." Margo put her hand over Kate's and squeezed. "If something happens, go to the safe deposit box. Everything you need is there. I set it up just like you taught me."

"Always have an escape plan."

"Everything is going to work out this time."

"If you believed that, you wouldn't ask me to take Alex and remind me that even now we need a way out."

Margo squeezed Kate's hand again. "I know everything will be okay. I'm being cautious and protective of what I love. When we had nothing, it was easy to walk away. Now, I have too much to lose to leave it to chance. Please, Kate. Do this for me, so I'll have peace of mind and can see Donald through this rough patch."

Kate gave in to need and picked up Alex from his crib and held him to her chest. She stared down into his beautiful blue eyes and frowned. "Your mother knows exactly how to get me to do her bidding."

"I know it's a lot to ask . . ."

Kate brushed her lips against Alex's forehead and smelled his sweet baby scent. Her heart softened and threatened to melt in her chest and reduce her to a teary-eyed mess. "I got this, Margo."

"You always do."

"Is everything okay?" Donald asked from the door.

"She said yes," Margo answered.

"Thank you, Kate. It's a lot to ask . . ."

"Both of you stop. I'm the aunt. I'm the perfect person to ask. You two enjoy a few days alone. Alex and I will hang at the bar, go dancing, you know, have some fun."

Margo laughed and touched Kate's shoulder. "You know he doesn't have ID to get into the bar."

Kate shrugged that off. "I could probably call some old contacts and get him a fake one."

"Okay, but cut him off after one bottle," Donald teased, holding up the baby bottle in his hand.

Kate took it and stuffed the nipple into Alex's mouth. He sucked greedily.

"You hear that, little man?" Margo said. "One bottle and you're done. Aunt Kate will take care of you. Maybe you can teach her to smile more often." Margo kissed Alex's head and gave Kate a look that clearly said, "You're too serious."

"I'll take the bags down to the car," Donald volunteered, grabbing the diaper bag and a small suitcase.

"I put two cans of formula and extra bottles in the

suitcase. More than enough for the few days you'll have him." Margo picked up the blanket from Alex's crib and a soft puppy. "These are his favorites. Donald will also put the playpen I left downstairs in your car. He can sleep in that." Margo scanned the room. "His pacifier is pinned to his shirt, but let me run downstairs and grab a spare just in case."

Kate sat in the rocking chair with Alex in her arms and let him finish his bottle. "Go. We're good here."

Margo stopped at the door and turned back. "You're going to be a wonderful mother someday."

Kate plastered on a smile for Margo's benefit. "You were always the sweeter, kinder, gentler one of us. Alex is in the best hands. I'm better by myself." The lie sounded convincing but tasted sour and made her heart ache.

"Anything is possible, Kate. Just look at what I have with Donald."

"You two seem happy together. I'm happy for you."

"I hope you have something even better than what I've found. You just have to learn to trust and have a little faith."

This from the woman who fell in love with a married man and went to extreme lengths to have his child and the family they never had growing up, including sharing him with his wife—though he swore he hadn't slept with Christina in the last few years, especially since he met Margo. Kate dropped her cynicism and admitted the couple seemed happy. Kate wanted them to get past the impending divorce, marry, and be a family. They deserved it. Alex deserved to have his two loving parents together and happy without all the hiding of their relationship and the drama.

"Come downstairs when he's finished."

Margo left the room. Kate sat in the waning sunlight and rocked Alex back and forth. She studied his sweet face from his wide forehead to his softly rounded cheeks. He caught her watching him and took time out of gorging on his milk to smile at her with his mouth still wrapped around the nipple.

"Charmer. You know I can't resist you. Don't tell your mother, but I really am looking forward to having you all to myself for a few days."

Dangerous, dangerous ground. Her heart might not be able to take letting him go again. She loved the little boy. He almost made her think dreams do actually come true and don't always turn into nightmares. Almost.

Kate put Alex up to her shoulder and patted his back. He let out a huge belch and settled his cheek back on her shoulder. "That's my big boy. You sound like every guy I've ever met in a bar."

Actually, it had been a long time since she'd been a part of that scene. She'd given up playing the party girl, the tough girl who liked even tougher guys, the girl who didn't care about anyone or anything and all she wanted to do was have a good time. Nothing about that scene or that girl seemed fun anymore.

At twenty-two, she'd turned a corner and got serious about herself and her life. For all her negativity about what happened to her in the past and the rotten way she'd been raised and treated, she'd never done a damn thing to change things for the better. A hard realization to wake up to on her birthday, look back at her life, and realize all she'd been doing is surviving. She wanted more. So she went back to school and got her degree in social work. Used the supervised hours she worked in the field to gain experience and hone her skills to work with teenagers. She worked during the day and attended school at night to finish her master's this past year. Twenty-eight now, she finally had a job and a purpose in life that filled her up most days, even as the daunting task of helping others who sometimes didn't necessarily want it dragged her down, but never knocked her out. She loved her clients. Most of them anyway. Teenagers had a way of making you work for every small achievement. They made her think and come up with creative ways to connect with them so she could get them to trust her and eventually try to change their lives.

Like she'd done with her own.

"Come on, let's go find your mom and dad. It's time to blow this joint and get you settled at my place. Don't get me wrong, kiddo—I'm happy to have you for a few days, but that's it. You're not staying."

She tickled Alex's belly, made him laugh, and rose and carried him out the bedroom door and across the landing to the stairs.

"It's going to be all right," Donald assured her sister. He reached up and cupped Margo's face in his hands, sweeping his thumbs over her cheeks and looking her right in the eye with so much love and devotion that Kate looked away. The tenderness in his affection for Margo stunned her every time. She'd rarely seen that depth of kindness and love between two people. She envied her sister that connection to Donald. It's why she'd agreed to help them. Why she believed in them even if she didn't admit as much to her sister.

"What's wrong?" she asked, stepping down the last few stair treads. "Did something else happen?"

"Evan called. He's upset about the divorce and what that means for him as well as his mother," Donald said in his usual diplomatic way.

"Donald is cutting off his unlimited supply of funds and putting him on a reasonable budget," Margo added, rolling her eyes. Margo may live in this big fancy house, but she still clipped coupons and bought items on sale. She didn't take what she had for granted.

Something about the worry clouding Donald's eyes about the call triggered a ripple of danger to skitter across Kate's nerves. Her gut went tight. As easygoing as Donald was, his son Evan's personality swung the other way. All the way to volatile. Rage mixed with antipathy and entitlement. Not a good combination when you just told a rich kid he'd been essentially cut off.

"How did you leave things with him?"

"I told him to speak to his mother to get the real truth of why I'm doing all of this. He deserves to know, then he'll understand that what I'm offering is generous under the circumstances."

"He's been in trouble in the past. Do you think he'll come here and cause trouble for the two of you? Is that why you want Alex out of the house?"

"No," Donald said definitively. "No." This time the word held traces of uncertainty and worry. "My concern is that these types of calls will go on for the next few days. It's going to be a stressful time, and I don't want my emotions and Margo's worry to upset Alex. It's better this way."

Kate read between the lines. Donald didn't want to upset Margo, but he expected trouble in some form from his wife and son. At the very least, he knew they wouldn't go away quietly.

"I promise, Kate, I'll take care of everything. I won't let anything happen to Margo."

"I hold you to that promise."

He smiled, released her sister, and came to stand in front of her. He put his hand on Alex's back and the other on her shoulder. "I know you will. Margo, Alex, *and you* are my family. This will all blow over, and we'll move on together and watch Alex grow into a wonderful and loved man. He is the gift we share. Nothing will make me happier than to have this business behind us and move on. I want to spend the rest of my life making Margo happy and raising our son. All of us together and happy."

Kate's inner pessimist shouted, "Yeah, right." But holding Alex in her arms, seeing his happy face and the innocence in his eyes, sparked the belief that maybe the life Donald described wasn't out of reach. They needed to work for it, and that included taking care of old business.

"Call me if anything more happens. Keep me in the loop."

"We will. I promise," Donald agreed.

Her sister and Donald walked her out to the car. Margo took Alex, hugged him close, and put him in the car seat in the back of her car. Margo settled Alex, then kissed him on the head. "Be good for Auntie. I'll miss you, sweetheart. I love you."

"I promise, I'll take good care of him."

"I know you will. It's just I've never been away from him, since he came home."

"Go with her," Donald suggested at the last minute.

Margo shook her head. "No. I'm staying with you and seeing you through this ordeal."

"That's just it, it is an ordeal. I'll handle it. It's not for you to work out, but for me to do."

Margo took Donald's hand. "We're a couple. Partners. We do things together. The fun things and the tedious."

"I much prefer the fun we have together." Donald hugged Margo close.

"Then Kate will take Alex, and you and I will have some fun." The sparkle in her sister's eyes when she said those words made Kate blush. These two were good for each other. Margo's fun nature balanced Donald's seriousness. Donald gave Margo the things she'd always done without and the love she deserved.

Donald set her sister aside, leaned in, and kissed Alex goodbye.

Margo's eyes shined brightly as she stared down at Alex in the back of Kate's car. "I'm going to miss him so much." Margo leaned down and kissed Alex again, brushing her hand over his head, then tapping his little nose. "Be good, my sweet boy."

Donald pulled Margo back and kissed her on the head. He patted Alex's arm, closed the back door, and opened Kate's door for her. Before Kate took her seat, he reached for her hand and held it tight. "Thank you for doing this." He pressed hard on the key he'd placed in her hand and whispered, "Just in case."

Chapter Three

BEN KNIGHT WALKED into Decadence restaurant and glanced around the elegant dining room. He'd eaten here more than two dozen times with Jenna and sometimes with her and Jack, but he'd never attended one of their legendary family dinners. He always found an excuse to get out of the invitation. He didn't do the whole family thing. And for good reason. Being around happy families made him think back to the anger, resentment, and yes, sadness he'd lived with as a child. Right up until his mother shot his father dead.

Best day of his life.

The cops arrested his distraught mother. A lawyer who worked in conjunction with the local church and a women's shelter stepped in, took the case pro bono, and got the murder charges dropped, proving his mother acted out of self-defense and a bone-deep belief that if she didn't shoot him, he'd kill her and Ben. The truth saved them. That lawyer understanding all his mother and he'd been through saved them. Ben never forgot that his mother and that lawyer saved him. So he became a lawyer who helped women like his mother. That's how he met Jenna Merrick. He helped save her, and now she'd taken him into the family fold, dismissing his wariness to fully join the group. Despite his many attempts to stay at arm's length, she kept tugging him in.

He could only say no or come up with an excuse so many times, so this time he agreed to meet the group for dinner and Morgan Reed's baby shower. She and her husband, Tyler, were expecting their son sometime in the next couple of weeks. He envied Tyler his beautiful wife and child on the way. They seemed happy the last few times he'd met them. The whole Turner-Shaw-Reed family seemed to have that thing everyone wanted. A partner who loved them and the happiness that came with that elusive gift.

"Ben." Jenna ran into his arms and hugged him close.

"Rabbit. I've missed you."

"You wouldn't miss me if you showed up even half the times I invite you to things."

"Point taken, which is why I'm here." He held up the light blue bag dangling from his fingers. "For a baby shower no less."

Jenna smiled up at him, her hands still on his chest. "You love kids."

He couldn't deny it. The best part about working at Haven House was getting to see the children. He organized baseball and soccer games on the weekend.

He opened the place years ago to help women like his mother, battered and in need of a safe place to hide. A place to find themselves again and start a new and better life. A safe place to bring their children, so they could play and be kids, not cower in fear every minute of their existence waiting for the next episode of violence to explode around them.

"Where's Jack?"

"Having a beer with the guys. Come on. I'll lead you back into the mayhem."

He followed her through the dining room toward the private dining area. "How's everything at Merrick?"

"Running smoothly thanks to your cousin, Cameron."

Funny how that worked out. He helped Jenna escape her abusive ex-husband, she took over his company, and hired Cameron Shaw to run it as president. Then Cameron discovered he was actually George Knight's son. Ben's and Cameron's great-great-granddads were brothers. Cameron's branched off to form the more successful side of the family with Knight Industries, while Ben's side straddled the line between decency and all-out debauchery. You can't pick your family, but he wished he'd been born to the other side of his.

"Are you still flying in and working three days a week?" he asked, hoping to avoid another lengthy conversation about his background compared to the one George Knight had provided his family and left most of that wealth to Cameron.

"Most weeks. You know how much I'd rather be with Jack and the kids on the ranch in Colorado."

"I can't blame you. That place suits Jack. He always liked his solitude."

"With three kids, the twin boys most especially, he only gets his quiet time when he's out working with the horses."

"The boys giving him a run for his money?"

"Of course, but it's Willow who has him wrapped around her little finger. He can't say no to her."

"Men have a hard time saying no to any of the women in their lives, but I imagine it's especially difficult to do with their daughters."

"Is there a woman in your life you can't say no to?"

Ben tapped his elbow to Jenna's arm. "As always, only you, Rabbit."

"You say no to me all the time." Jenna pouted.

"Only because you married Jack and not me." Ben gave her a fake frown. Jenna and Jack were beyond happy. That's what he wanted for his two good friends.

"Your loss, man." Jack smacked him on the shoulder when he walked into the back room. "You sent her to me. I kept her."

Ben accepted the beer from Jack as well as the handshake.

"How about you return the favor and send me a girl as great as her." If there was a girl out there as great as the women his friends had found, he sure as hell hadn't met her.

"You'll meet her tonight." Morgan stepped close and kissed him on the cheek. "Jack isn't sending her to you, but she's yours. You've met her before. You liked her." Morgan studied him. "She's tough. Difficult to read. She likes you, but doesn't want you to know it. You didn't see it before, but this time you'll look closer. She needs your help."

Ben stared at Morgan unable to speak. They all knew about her special gift, but he'd never actually seen her make a prediction about something, let alone be the target of that prediction.

"Don't sweat it, Ben. She does this all the time. You'll get used to it," Tyler said, wrapping his arm around his wife and holding his hand out to shake Ben's.

"Uh, so I'm supposed to meet her tonight? Here?"

"No. When you leave. She's worried. Has reason to be. A force is pushing the man to do things he doesn't necessarily want to do. She'll get in his way. She has a desperate need to protect what is hers. She'll give her life to do it. You want to see this man go down. You've gone up against him before and lost. You hate to lose."

Ben smiled. "Yes, I do."

"The truth is in the details. Things aren't always what they seem," Morgan said. "It's kind of a jumble right now, but she'll sort it out, or die trying. You'll stack the odds in her favor."

Ben went along, not really believing the woman of his dreams was out there, let alone about to walk into his life. Tonight.

"She walked into your life months ago, but you let her go after you shared a moment." Morgan shook her head. He could almost hear the *tsk, tsk*.

Ben opened his mouth but closed it when he didn't know what to say to her reading his mind.

"Eventually you'll get used to it," Tyler assured him. "Listen to her, Ben. She knows what she's talking about."

If he'd shared a moment with a woman in the last months, he couldn't remember it. "Anything else I should know?" he asked, paying closer attention, unable to deny her prediction intrigued him at the very least. The thought of finding the woman destined for him seemed more fantasy than reality, but wouldn't it be nice to have what his friends had found?

"The things we have to work for are often the things that bring us the most joy and satisfaction."

"Nothing is ever easy. Don't I know it?"

"Well, if it was easy, what fun would that be? You men love the chase. You helped Jenna take her life back. You help the women at the shelter do the same thing. This woman needs more than that from you."

"What if I can't give her what she needs?"

"You can. You both want the same thing, but neither of you wants to admit it, because you don't think it will ever exist for you.

"The question isn't can you give her what she needs, but will you take a leap of faith and believe in her. Not in what she says, but in what you know to be true about her."

"I don't even know her."

"You will. Trust me."

"The last time someone said that to me, Jack stole my girl."

Morgan laughed, so did the others because it was an old joke. Jenna was never really his. Once she met Jack, Ben never had a shot.

"That was meant to be," Morgan said. "This is meant to be."

"So is dinner," Jenna announced. "Elizabeth and the waiters just arrived with the food. I'm starving. Come on, let's take our seats."

Ben landed beside Sam with Cameron and his wife, Marti, on his other side. Their youngest, Camille, beside Marti. He glanced at all the faces around the table. Jenna's twin boys, Matt and Sam, sat with Cameron's daughter, Emma, across from him. Willow sat in her high chair next to Jack. Elizabeth's children, Grace and J.T., sat between her and Sam. So many young ones between the couples.

He stared at the head of the table where Morgan sat, round and beautiful in her pregnancy. Tyler sat beside her, saying something to his wife that made her smile. Tyler reached over and set his hand on Morgan's round belly, rubbing the baby bump with a huge smile on his face. Everyone knew they were having a son. Ben had even written "Noah" on the card. He wondered if Morgan knew exactly what day she'd give birth.

Her gaze met his and she gave him a mysterious smile. He shook his head and smiled back.

Sam's son, J.T., got bored jumping up and down on Sam's lap and leaped into his. Ben caught the toddler under the arms to balance him, then lifted him up and above his head like an airplane.

"I fly."

"Yes, you do, little man. Play with Uncle Ben for a while and give your old dad a break."

The "Uncle" warmed Ben's heart. He loved hanging out with these guys. They treated him like family. "Old dad? You're the same age as me," Ben said.

"And I've got two kids. You need to catch up, man."

"You guys took all the great women, so I'm left alone and envious, playing with your kids." Ben brought J.T. down to his chest, hugged him close, then tickled his sides, making him squirm and laugh.

"Stop, Uncle Ben."

Ben settled J.T. in his lap and handed him a slice of apple from the bowl the waiter set in front of him for J.T.

Sam leaned back and eyed him. "So, you're ready to settle down?"

"I have no objections to a less empty bed."

Sam laughed. "No man objects to that."

Ben thought of the mysterious woman about to come into his life tonight.

If he found her, would he have it in him to hold on to her?

Time to put up or shut up. If he wanted more in his life, he'd have to hold on. Now all he had to do was find the woman meant for him.

Chapter Four

MULTIMILLION-DOLLAR HOMES SPOKE to the wealth of the people who lived in the Los Altos Hills. Their children went to the best schools and wanted for nothing. He was one of those children, and he'd be damned before he lost all this to some bitch his father fucked.

The street was quiet. But wouldn't be for long with afternoon turning to evening. Evan had sat outside houses during the day, watching, noting what time the gardeners arrived and left along with the cleaning crews who kept these houses immaculately groomed and spotlessly clean. He might be reckless in his life, but not when it came to breaking into a house to supplement his income when his father grew stingy or cut him off for a few weeks. No one suspected the robber was one of them. The elite. Just because he didn't want a job didn't mean he was fucking stupid. He'd made good grades throughout school. But school hadn't been about learning for him. No, he enjoyed the social aspect. He'd partied hard in college, but always passed his classes. So he could stay and party. Good grades also kept the money from his father coming. Now, nothing would make his father pay up.

Evan slammed his hand on the steering wheel. "Fuck. What did you do, Mom?"

He didn't know, and she probably wouldn't give up that particular secret at this point. She did so love her little secrets and intrigues she played with his father. Too bad his father didn't fall for that shit anymore, which apparently made his mother do something to royally piss him off.

The house sat on the right side of a cul-de-sac, the property large enough to encompass half the circle. Bigger than his parents' home. With only four houses on the block, the houses set back from the street behind gates and mostly concealed by gardens and trees, he had the perfect cover. No one would notice his vehicle parked on the street. If they did, they'd think him a guest at one of the other properties. He parked so it wasn't obvious which house he was visiting, grabbed his gloves and mask from the backseat, and pulled the gun he kept tucked under the driver's seat out for those occasions he needed to show force to get someone to back off after a bad night gambling or a fight. He stood beside the car, tucked the gun at his back in the waistband of his pants, and covered it with his shirt. He slipped out of the car and walked up the drive like he had a right to be there. He ducked behind some bushes, pulled on the gloves and mask, tugged the gun from his waistband, and held it in his grasp. The weight of it made what he was about to do all the more real. He thought of the meager allowance his father was about to impose on him and what that meant to his life and pushed through the dense foliage and onto the property ready to see this through to the end.

He avoided the front windows and went around the back of the house. He cautiously walked across the patio to the back door. He tried the handle and pushed the door open. So easy. Too easy?

His heart raced. Hyped up, Scotch roiling in his gut, he walked into the house, entering through the dining room. White roses and lilies in a dark blue vase sat on the table. Their sweet scent filled the open space. He stopped and stared at the elegant home. Bright, cheerful, colorful with touches of blue, green, and lavender to offset the white walls, rustic wood beams running across the ceiling, and neutral furnishings. He actually liked it compared to his mother's drab autumn-colored home. That place always felt closed in and sad. This place seemed cheerful, and it pissed him off.

The door to the study stood open across the room. His father stood with his back to him, reading some papers. He paced, head down, eyes on the documents.

A cold sweat broke out over Evan's skin. Nerves tightened and soured his gut, but he didn't change his mind.

His father gave some bitch this nice house, and now she'd get everything else if Evan didn't do this now. He needed to find the woman. He walked away from the living room area toward what he suspected was the kitchen. He stood in the doorway, stunned by the beautiful woman in front of him. He expected her to be older, like his mother. Instead, she had to be in her early thirties. Not that much older than him. Long blond hair hung down to the middle of her back in soft waves. She wore a pair of white slacks and a soft blue top with sleeves that went to her elbows. She sliced an apple into wedges and added pieces to the two plates in front of her. She'd prepared a light dinner. A bowl of creamy soup and turkey sandwiches piled high with red onion and leafy green lettuce. Nice.

Fucking bitch.

He saw what was going on. This woman manipulated his father, fucked him into believing someone as young and pretty as her loved him. She slept with him, made him dinner they'd eat together on the sofa in their cozy living room, pretending to be happy and in love when all she fucking wanted was his father's money. She'd convinced his father to leave his mother. She caused this, and his father fell for it, cutting him and his mother off.

Evan held the gun to her back, right between her shoulders. "Don't move."

He expected her to go still. Instead, she flipped the knife in her hand, shifted sideways away from the gun, and swung the knife down at the same time. He shifted at the last second to avoid the sharp blade. The knife missed plunging into his thigh and skimmed along the outer edge, slicing a long gash that hurt like fucking hell.

"You bitch!"

He reached for her with his left hand before she got away, but she turned and punched him in the jaw. His head snapped back. She had a good jab. He worked his jaw to ease the sting, swung the gun, and clocked her on the side of the head, making her stumble, but not fall. She kept fighting, screaming out, "Donald," when he grabbed her by the neck and slammed her back against the counter, toppling the plate and soup bowls. She held on to his hand at her throat, her hazel eyes wide with shock.

"Be still."

"Fuck off." She slammed her foot down on his and brought both hands up, then crashed them down on his arm. He had no choice but to let her go when the pain shot up his arm and down his hand.

She leaned back against the counter, planted her foot in his gut, and tried to push him away, but he moved faster, twisting to the side, turning, and grabbing her around the neck, her back to his chest. He dug the barrel of the gun into her temple and shook her to get her attention.

"Don't. Move."

"Evan, stop," his father said from the doorway.

With the mask over his head and face, he didn't think his father would recognize him. He held perfectly still, waiting to see what his father would do.

"I know it's you. Your mother and I gave you that watch when you graduated college."

Evan glanced at the gold Rolex on his wrist, then the gun in his hand. He'd hoped his father wouldn't know it was him. Too late to do anything about it now, he needed to either finish this, or get away.

"Don't do this. She didn't do anything to you. I know you're upset. Put the gun down and let's talk about it."

His rage surged. "She ruined everything."

"No. That's not true. Your mother is responsible for her actions and the lies she told."

"You never cared what she did. Now, because of her"—he shook the blonde he held in a choke hold, her nails digging into his arm—"you want to toss us aside."

"I want nothing to do with your mother, but you and I can still have a relationship."

"You cut me off."

"No, I didn't. I'll pay to keep a roof over your head, but it's time you stood on your own two feet and made a living at whatever you want to do with your life besides drinking, gambling, and fighting your days away. You're smart. You graduated college without ever really having to try. All I'm asking is that you grow up and take some responsibility for your choices.

"Things don't have to end this way. If you do this, if you kill her, your life will be over. You don't want that."

"My life won't be over. It'll be better. Without her. Without you." Evan slowly lowered the gun from the woman's head and extended his arm, pointing the gun directly at his father. "Murder-suicide. She kills you after you fight here in the kitchen." He made a point of looking at the mess around them from his fight with the bitch. "She kills you, then herself."

His father held up both hands and pleaded, "Don't do this, Evan. Please."

"It's the only way." He believed that now. When he arrived, he wasn't so sure. But after this, seeing the way his father looked at the woman and pleaded for her life, his father would have him arrested. He'd cut him off for sure. He'd leave him to rot in a cell.

"I love you, Donald. I love you so much."

Evan squeezed her neck and shook her again. "Shut up."

"I love you too, sweetheart. Be still. It's okay." He took a step closer, his hands still up in front of him. "Evan, please, we can work this out. No one needs to know about this. I'll give you whatever money you want. Please, don't hurt her."

Evan vibrated from the inside out with the rage overtaking the last glimmer of indecision in his heart. "You lie."

Evan fired. Blood spread across his father's chest over his heart. His eyes went wide with shock and surprise, then blank as he dropped to his knees and fell forward onto the floor. A red pool of blood oozed out from underneath his father's body and spread across the tiles. The crimson color vivid against the white marble. His father's body tensed, then went lax.

The woman screamed. The sharp sound pierced his eardrums and made his ears ring. She struggled to get free and run to his father's dead body. She jerked against his arm and body, bringing him out of his shock. She kicked at his leg and scratched at his arm. He held her to the side, put the gun to her head, and fired. The side of her head exploded, blood and brains splattering against the refrigerator and cabinets. A gruesome splotch of red against the wood and stainless steel. He released her. Her body dropped to the floor with a sickening thud. Her head lay only two feet from his father's, their hands outstretched, fingertips nearly touching.

The gun hung at his side, his hand numb of the weight. He didn't move. Couldn't. He stood frozen, staring down at what he'd done, wondering what to do now. He thought he'd feel happy or relieved. Maybe remorse. Something. But he didn't feel anything. In fact, he couldn't believe he'd done it.

He quickly scanned the kitchen and the two bodies. Everything looked exactly as it should for the cops to see what he wanted them to see. There'd been a scuffle, she shot his father in the chest, then turned the gun on herself. He kneeled beside her, sucking back a hiss of pain. The cut along the outside of his thigh bled profusely, soaking his black pants down to his ankle. The intense, throbbing pain became a part of him, but he ignored it. He needed to be quick and get the hell out of there in case someone heard the shots and called the cops.

His hand shook when he reached for the woman's hand. He didn't touch her, but stared at his shaking hand hovering over hers with blood splattered over his glove. The need to run overtook him, but he held it together. He picked up her hand, put the gun in it with her finger on the trigger, turned her hand and pressed the back to his glove to transfer the blood and gunshot residue—thank you to every CSI show he'd ever seen. He scraped her hand on the floor to smear the blood, so it looked like that's how her hand landed, the gun slipping from her grasp to lie just out of reach.

The metallic scent of blood filled the air as well as the pungent smell of gunfire. He stood and took a few steps away from the bodies, staring until his eyes watered. He blinked to clear his vision, then turned and walked back to the patio doors. The sunset painted the sky in pinks, oranges, and purples. The pleasant scene didn't erase the bright red blood in his mind. He sucked in a deep breath of the cool fresh air and sighed it out. He tore the mask from his head and walked around the house to the front, keeping to the trees and bushes for cover. He went back past the gate and down the street to his car. He bit back the pain and walked as normal as he could on his bad leg. Every step pulled at the cut and made it bleed more. The last thing he wanted was some nosy neighbor saying they saw some guy limping down the street.

He opened his car door and slid behind the wheel. His hands still shook, even when he grabbed the wheel and held on tight. The shiver rippled over and through him.

He'd left his cell phone in between the seats in the console. It beeped with four missed calls. He reached for it, jumping when it rang a split second before he picked it up.

"Evan, honey, what's going on?" his mother asked, panic and desperation in her voice.

He choked out only one thing before he hung up. "It's done."

EVAN TOSSED HIS bloodied shirt into the fireplace behind him. The chill that took over his body the moment he'd gotten into his car and drove to his parents' place went bone-deep. Even the fire's heat didn't penetrate to his altered soul. He couldn't take it back. He couldn't tell his father how sorry he was it ended this way.

"You had no choice. We had no other way to solve this problem. Now, it's done. We'll get through this and everything will be ours. It will be okay." The tremor and the trace of disbelief in her voice sank into his mind and made him doubt too.

How could anything be right again?

The man he beat to death left a black mark on his soul, but not like killing the woman and especially his father did. The man's death had been an unfortunate accident. Sometimes, he didn't know his own strength, especially when he was blind drunk. Tonight, he'd known exactly what he was doing.

The shirt turned to ashes. He tossed in his bloody pants, smothering the flames for a moment before they flared back to life and consumed the bloody slacks. Would the nightmare in his mind consume every bit of happiness from his life from now on?

"Once we get through the next few weeks, everything will get back to normal."

Normal? He didn't know what normal was anymore.

"Evan! I'm talking to you."

"It's done. What more do you want?" he snapped.

"I want to know what happened, so I'm prepared for when the police show up to inform me of my husband's death."

Evan hung his head and stared at his bare feet on the hardwood floor. He sat on the stone hearth in nothing but his boxer briefs. Bloody bandages, gauze, cotton pads, and medical tape lay scattered at his feet. He pressed his hand to his bandaged and wrapped thigh, remembering the deep gash he'd cleaned and dressed when he got home. He picked up the glass of Scotch off the floor and drank deep, hoping the burn would wake him up and make him feel again. Nothing.

Evan gave his mother the bare bones version of what happened, refusing to elaborate as she tried to ask questions.

"I'm not sure how long it will take the cops to find them. I imagine they've got a maid and gardening service. Someone from Dad's work will wonder where he is when he doesn't show up to work. It might take a few days."

"Plenty of time for you to shake this off."

Like his mother did so easily. She sat there like he'd just told her nothing more serious than he'd gone out to run some errands.

"We'll act surprised and horrified by what's happened. I'll tell the police that your father and I had quietly decided on a separation. We'll keep it simple. I'll be your alibi. You'll be mine. We had dinner here together. You stayed the night as you often do. It's that simple and straightforward. We don't know who that woman was. Your father kept her a secret from both of us."

"Who she was," he repeated. "I still don't know who she was." Except the woman his father looked at with something in his eyes he'd never seen there when he looked at Evan's mother.

"She doesn't matter. She can't hurt us anymore."

"Are you sure about that?" He'd gotten lucky when she attacked him. If he hadn't gotten her in that choke hold, she'd have kicked his ass. "He cared about her. I think he really loved her. Somehow, that makes this worse."

"It would have been worse, because she'd have taken everything. You think she'd have put up with you always asking him for money to bail you out of one jam after the next, not to mention jail? She'd have influenced him and made sure he drew further and further away from us. All she wanted was his money. She wanted it all for herself, so don't grow a conscience on me now. It's done. End of story. From here, we put this behind us and move on. Nothing and no one will get in our way."

Chapter Five

THE DARK WINDOWS loomed like evil eyes in the big house. Not a single light welcomed her, setting off another round of chills up her spine. She'd left several messages for her sister this evening. Concerned by her silence, Kate packed up Alex in his car seat and drove back here to check on Margo and Donald. Something about the look in Donald's eyes when she left hours ago, and the way he secretly handed her that key, disturbed her on a deep level. That deep dark place inside everyone where monsters exist and evil is a presence that makes your bones go cold.

Kate parked in the driveway behind Donald's BMW. The quiet wrapped around her. She didn't like it.

She pulled Alex from the backseat and carried him by the car seat handle around the car to the walkway. Two steps toward the front door, the garden lights went on, along with the motion lights by the front door. Donald must not have reset them for the earlier sunsets this time of year. Nearly eight o'clock, she wondered for the hundredth time if Donald and Margo took her Mercedes and went out to enjoy a quiet dinner at a local restaurant and spend some quality time alone together. She hoped that's what they were doing. A romantic evening out that would make her sour gut seem ridiculous. Margo would chastise her for being overprotective. Like always.

She unlocked the door, walked into the dark foyer, and flipped the switch on the wall, lighting up the entry and part of the living room. Something alerted her to danger, but she couldn't say what. Maybe it was the quiet, or the darkness that kept everything beyond the overhead light masked in shadows.

She closed the door behind her and called out, "Margo, Donald, are you home?"

No answer. Not even a surprised, "We'll be down in a minute," from her sister as she lay locked in Donald's arms in a rumpled bed upstairs. She didn't really expect an answer, but not getting one set off another round of alarms in her head.

Alex whimpered and sucked harder on his pacifier. Even he sensed something wasn't right. Afraid to leave him alone by the door, she grabbed the car seat handle and carried Alex with her through the living room toward the dark kitchen. Some kind of sixth sense drew her in that direction. She stopped short before crossing the dining room when the scent registered and her mind filled with past images of her mother, bruised and bloody, on the floor at her father's feet. The unique metallic scent would never be forgotten. Imprinted on her soul, she'd recognize the smell of blood anywhere.

Fear stole her breath. She set Alex down on the floor, not wanting to take him with her into the kitchen to discover whatever lay beyond the darkness. She turned on a lamp by a side chair to keep him in the light, though it wouldn't change the nightmare of what she suspected she'd find in the kitchen.

Alex reached for her hand. She gave him her finger. He squeezed tight, like even he didn't want her to go in there. She didn't want to either, but had to know what happened to her sister and Donald. She didn't want to believe what her senses told her.

"I'll be right back, sweetheart."

Kate dropped her purse beside Alex, dug out her cell phone and the switch blade she kept for protection when she met clients in a bad neighborhood. She flipped open the knife, leaned down, and kissed Alex on the forehead, took a deep breath to muster her courage, and stood and walked through the dining room.

Donald's feet were highlighted just inside the kitchen entrance in the soft light barely making it this far into the house. She stopped and gave herself a moment to take it in. Dead. Lying on the kitchen floor. She couldn't help him. No one could. But she'd make the bastard responsible pay.

Her heart pounded against her ribs. She continued on and stood at Donald's feet. She spotted her sister, lying dead on the floor in front of Donald in the dark. She reached for the light switch, stalling for only a second before she turned it on and illuminated the gruesome scene in front of her.

Her heart stopped and a scream rose to her throat, but got choked off by the gush of tears that ran down her cheeks in a torrent. No sound escaped her lips, but the scream of outrage and grief rang out in her head. The depth of her grief squeezed her heart until it shattered, tore her insides to shreds, and she couldn't breathe.

The scene didn't seem real. The blood a mocking kind of horror to her mind's denial of what lay before her. She swiped the tears from her eyes with the backs of her hands. Noting the knife and phone in her hands, she closed the knife and stuffed it in her pocket. The phone she held on to until she could collect herself. She sucked in a ragged breath and tried to think through her pain and see what really happened here, because what it looked like couldn't be the truth. The gun near her sister's hand lied about the sweet, gentle sister she knew and loved. Margo would never shoot Donald. She detested guns. She loved Donald.

The scattered and broken dishes on the counter and floor told her there'd been a struggle. She and Margo were expert kickboxers. They'd studied together for the last ten years. Kate taught classes, so a struggle seemed normal if someone tried to hurt her sister. Margo wouldn't hesitate to fight back.

Soup smeared down the cabinet and puddled on the floor. Apple slices lay scattered around both bodies. A bloody steak knife lay just under the cabinet lip on the tile. She studied Donald's face and body. No slice marks that she could see. Unless Margo stabbed him in the gut, he hadn't defended himself and gotten sliced on the hands or arms. Blood pooled at his middle, making it more likely Margo shot him. But why? How did she get the gun? Where did she get the gun? Did Donald try to shoot her and she took it from him? Not possible.

She hated to look at Margo with her head a bloody mess, her skull blasted open. No way Margo shot herself. She wouldn't do that. She loved Donald. She loved Alex. She had every reason to live, especially now that Donald had left his wife and they were going to be married and be a real family.

Something nagged at Kate. She made herself look, think, find the things that lay beyond the obvious picture. Margo's knuckles were red and swollen. She'd gotten in a few punches. Donald's face didn't show any bruising or swelling. She hadn't hit him. She'd go for the face, the ribs.

Kate's eyes settled on the bloody knife again. Away and across from Margo, someone must have knocked it from her hand and it skittered across the floor. The small splatters of blood led back toward Margo and the counter where she'd been making the food. Someone surprised her. Kate scanned the floor and spotted it. Small drops of blood on the other side of Margo, a splatter on the drawers, another on the refrigerator. Cast off from the knife after Margo sliced someone open.

Satisfied she'd seen everything, she turned her back and called the police.

"Nine-one-one. What is your emergency?"

"My sister and her fiancé are dead. They . . . they're d-dead," she rambled. "Someone shot them."

"What is the address?"

Kate absently rattled off the address, her eyes glued to Alex in the other room. His mother and father were dead. Everything they'd tried so hard to build together gone in the blink of an eye. He'd never remember them.

"Ma'am, what is your name?" the operator asked, like she'd had to repeat the question several times.

"Kate Morrison. I . . . I'm Margo's sister."

"The police are on the way. Please stay on the line and . . ."

Kate dropped the phone, unable to do this. She'd wait for the police, but right now, she needed to sit and hold Alex. He needed her. He'd keep the grief from sucking her under. Margo dead. It couldn't be real. She didn't know how to live without her sister. They'd seen each other through so many bad times. They'd made each other better, competing to always be better than the other. They'd promised each other they'd never be alone.

Alex stared up at her. It hit her hard. Margo kept her promise. Kate wasn't alone. She had Alex. He needed her. He was hers. She'd make sure he got everything coming to him, and the man who did this to her beautiful sister and Alex's father would pay.

Chapter Six

Ben thought about what Sam said about settling down. He never minded sharing his bed. In fact, he'd gone too long sleeping alone. The thing was, he enjoyed the sex, but not the sleepover. He had no trouble connecting with a woman on a sexual level. He went out of his way to treat them right, because his dad had been a prick to his mother, degrading everything she did from her cooking to her looks, even though she didn't deserve a single insult. He made sure the women who came into his life had nothing to complain about his behavior. Except one thing. The distance he kept emotionally.

J.T. seemed content to eat his dinner from Ben's lap, so Ben grabbed his fork and took a bite of his favorite fettuccini Alfredo with spinach and broccoli. J.T. stole a long noodle and sucked it into his mouth, a huge smile on his sauce-covered mouth.

J.T. ate half of Ben's dinner, ignoring his own chicken

nuggets and fruit. Ben ate half the apples and coaxed J.T. to eat more of them. He only wanted the noodles. At least he ate a bunch of spinach drenched in the sauce without even knowing it.

"I can't believe you got him to eat that," Elizabeth whispered across Sam.

"Got him? Who could stop him?" Ben laughed with Elizabeth and gave J.T. a hug. He liked the little boy and couldn't help wondering what it would be like to have his own son. He didn't really have to think too hard. All he had to do was look at the other men around the table sitting with their kids. Tyler would find out soon enough when Noah came into the world.

Waiters cleared the dinner dishes and Morgan opened her presents with a lot of help from Emma. As the oldest child in the group, she took charge, holding up each present for everyone to see and repacking it for Morgan, so she could open more gifts.

Morgan opened his gift last.

"Ben, I love the books. Thank you."

"You're welcome. No one should trust me to buy baby clothes. Books seemed an easy alternative choice."

"And the spa day?" Morgan asked.

"After what you're about to go through, you deserve a spa day. I'll even come over and hang out with Tyler and help take care of Noah while you get your facial, mani, pedi, and massage."

"You're on," Tyler said, raising his beer in salute.

"I'll hold you to that," Morgan said.

"It's a promise."

Grace, Sam and Elizabeth's daughter, didn't want to be outdone by her little brother and climbed into Ben's lap for dessert. Sam tried to pluck J.T. out of his lap, but J.T. whined and struggled to stay put.

"Leave him, Sam. I've got them."

"Dog pile on Ben," Jack teased.

"At least let him have some dessert," Jenna said, a laugh in her voice.

"My hands are too full of kids. It's cool, let them eat."

"I helped Aunt Elizabeth frost the cake," Emma announced.

"You did a great job, Sugar Bug," Marti praised her daughter.

As much as Ben liked being with the family, the large group overwhelmed him. The noise, the comradery, and the laughs made all the things he'd longed for as a kid surface along with the bad memories.

Family get-togethers were a time to fear and endure. His uncles drank as much as his father. Seemed that their fun lay in one-upping the other in how mean they could be to each other, the women, and even the children. His older cousins joined in, having learned it's better to be a part of their so-called fun than to be on the receiving end of their sharp tongues and backhanded smacks on the shoulder or cracks to the head that only elicited more laughs. His mother and aunts either joined in the drinking, or ended up trying to reason with unreasonable drunks until the inevitable fight broke out. Someone always left bloody, whether it be man, woman, or child. It never ended well. The end of the party was never the end of the fight. No, his father would pick and pick at his mother, him, until his father lost his temper and hit one or both of them. The good nights were when he passed out. Ben thanked God every day he didn't inherit his father's addictions. To booze. To drugs. To hurting others for sport, thinking it made him feel better when all it really did was prove he was a colossal heartless asshole.

Grace pulled him out of his dark thoughts, leaning up and holding his neck and kissing the side of his face. "Want some?" She held up a bite of cake at the ends of her fingers, poised to fall in his lap at any second. Chocolate frosting covered her tiny fingers.

He smiled, knowing this was going to make a mess and not caring one bit. He couldn't resist the girl. "Gimme." He opened his mouth and she crammed the piece of cake in and against his lips.

She smiled and licked her fingers. "You have chocolate on your face."

He tickled her ribs and made her giggle. "You have chocolate everywhere."

Sam grabbed Grace under the arms, avoiding letting her put her hands on him, and handed her to Elizabeth. "You take care of her. I've got the boy." Sam plucked J.T. from Ben's lap and set him on the empty chair beside him.

"Thanks," Ben said, wiping his face with a napkin.

"You've got more chocolate on you than in you," Sam teased. "Thanks for distracting them. They love playing with you."

"I like them. They're good kids."

"Despite the chocolate on your dress shirt?"

Ben looked down at his chest and the perfect imprint of Grace's hand in smudged chocolate against the white with navy blue pinstripe fabric.

"Yes, despite that."

"I'll buy you a new shirt," Sam offered.

"Don't worry about it. No big deal."

"You're going to make a really great father someday," Marti said from across Cameron on his other side.

"Well, if I keep hanging out with you guys, I'll get a lot of practice."

"That's for sure," Cameron said, scanning the table and all the small faces staring back at them.

Four couples had produced eight kids, counting Noah, who would be a welcome addition to this bunch of fun-loving kids. They really did seem happy and carefree. So unlike how he felt growing up. Maybe that was why he liked playing with kids so much.

Ben wiped the worst of Grace's sticky handprint from his chest, knowing he'd never get the stain out and not caring one bit. He tossed the napkin on the dessert the kids ate the majority of without him and stood.

"Thanks, everyone, for a great night, but I've got work to do on a pending case."

It took him five minutes to say goodbye, shake hands with the guys, and hug the ladies. The kids gave him hugs too. Grace gave him another kiss on the cheek. He loved that little angel. J.T. gave him a high five.

"Good luck and be well," he said to Morgan, hugging her goodbye.

Morgan held him close and whispered, "I know what

it feels like to want to be a part of a family like this. All you have to do is accept this is your family too. When you need help, come to us. We'll always be here."

He didn't know what to say, so held her away and stared into her eyes, knowing she spoke the truth, but unable to accept it and take it in.

He walked away, but Jenna caught up to him by the door. "Hey, are you okay?"

"Fine. I really do have work to do."

"I'm glad you came."

"So am I." He meant it. "I'll see you soon, Rabbit." He hugged her close and held on longer than normal because they shared a special bond. He needed her warmth and friendship.

He let her go and ducked out the door quicker than needed, but he had to get away from the things she made him want and the feelings he didn't want to feel. He loved Jenna, but not in that way for all the joking and razzing he gave Jack about stealing her away. He and Jenna would always be friends. But he saw all too clearly what she'd overcome to find the love and happiness she had with Jack and their kids. It was possible to be happy. He didn't know how she did it. Maybe all it took was finding the right person. So much harder than it sounded.

He drove home with one nagging thought that refused to leave his mind. *Is Morgan right? Is the woman meant for me about to crash into my life? Does she even exist?* He hoped so, but was he ready? Did he have it in him to be a friend, lover, partner to a woman like he'd never been to anyone else?

Would his worst fear come to pass and he'd end up being his father's son?

He swore it would never happen, which is why he'd never allowed himself to forge a deep and lasting relationship with anyone. All it got him was lonely and alone in his quiet apartment, staring at a stack of endless work. Work he used to fill his time and the hole inside of him he never filled.

His phone rang. He checked caller ID and hit the button on his steering wheel to accept the call. Detective Raynott's voice replaced Bruno Mars singing "Uptown Funk" coming through the speakers.

"Guess who's in trouble again?"

"Evan Faraday." Easy guess. His hands tightened on the steering wheel.

"Get here as fast as you can." The detective rattled off the address and hung up.

Ben punched it into his GPS at a red light, gripped the steering wheel tighter, and looked forward to finally getting another chance to take Evan down.

BEN PULLED IN behind several police cars nearly thirty minutes later, their red and blue lights flashing. He turned off the car's engine and sat staring up at the massive house. Morgan's prediction played in his mind. This late at night, the woman meant for him had to be in that house. He hoped she wasn't the dead woman Detective Raynott called him about.

Evan Faraday hit Ben's radar when Detective Raynott

caught the case of a man found beaten to death in an alley after gambling with some guys in the bar, including Evan. That man was the son of one of his Haven House clients. Ben stepped in as a legal advocate for the family. The guy was only trying to scrape together extra money for his mother and sister. Evan played cards with the guy, but Raynott couldn't link him to the murder. Not with any actual evidence, but the circumstantial kind added up to Evan drunk and pissed off about losing to the guy. Evan killed him; they just couldn't prove it.

More recently, Evan got into another bar fight. Donald Faraday paid off the guy with a heavy heart. He knew what and who his son was, but that didn't stop him from getting Evan out of trouble. Again.

Detective Raynott caught that case too. Ben asked the detective to call him if Evan got in trouble again. Ben wanted to take the selfish, smart-mouthed prick down. Then came the DUI arrest. Now he'd killed again.

Ben got out of the car, tucked in his shirt, and straightened his tie.

"What am I doing?" He was at a murder scene, not meeting a date for drinks and dinner.

But she was in there. He knew it. Anticipated it. And hoped he wasn't a fool for believing in Morgan.

The anticipation and hope swamping his system surprised him more than a little. He hadn't realized how much he wanted a woman in his life. Not just any woman, but the right woman.

"I'm sorry, sir, this is an active crime scene. Law enforcement only," the officer guarding the police line said. Ben noted the neighbors' interest. They lined the street, whispering to each other and staring at him. Some in their bathrobes, others in lounge clothes. This late at night the sirens got most of them up out of their beds. In this neighborhood, a murder was the last thing they expected.

"My name is Ben Knight. Detective Raynott called and asked me to come."

The officer held the tape up for him to pass. "He's in the living room. Give your name to the officer at the door."

Ben did and stepped into the elegant home and surveyed the officers and crime scene techs working the scene at the back of the house and what looked like the entrance to the kitchen. He spotted Detective Raynott standing over a woman with long brown wavy hair, a baby sleeping in a car seat at her feet. With her back to him, he couldn't see her face, but something about her seemed familiar. A strange tug pulled him toward her.

"Ben, you made it. Thanks for coming," Detective Raynott said, waving him forward.

"Anything to nail Evan Faraday and see him behind bars."

The woman turned and raised her face to look up at him. He stopped midstride and stared into her beautiful blue eyes. Like a deep lake the soft outer color darkened toward the center. "Kate?"

He never expected her. Morgan had been right though—they'd shared a moment at a wedding reception for a mutual friend and colleague. That had been more than a year ago now. They sat at the same table and talked, mostly about work and how out of place they felt at the event, made even more uncomfortable when they realized they were seated at a table full of singles and the bride had arranged them as couples, playing match-maker. They shared some laughs and danced, deciding to make the awkward situation fun. They fell under the spell—the music, champagne, the celebration of love—and Ben enjoyed himself more that night than any other date. He kissed her right there on the dance floor during a particularly slow, sweet song. He remembered it per-fectly. The way she stared up at him with those blue eyes. The way her mouth parted slightly as she exhaled and he leaned in. The softness of her lips against his. The way she gave in to the kiss with a soft sigh. The tremble that rocked his body and hers when the sparks flew and siz-zled through his system.

The startled look on her face when he pulled back just enough to see the desire flaming in her eyes. A split second later she bolted for the door.

He went after her, but didn't find her. She didn't answer his calls over the next two days. He still didn't know if he'd overstepped, done something wrong, or simply scared her.

"Ben." Her soft voice, filled with surprise, startled him out of his thoughts. "What are you doing here?" Her sad eyes narrowed on him.

"I called him," Detective Raynott said. "If this is Evan's doing, there's no one besides yourself who wants to take that man down more than Ben."

"Why?"

"I hate assholes who think they can get away with hurting people for no other reason than they can."

"Put him in front of me and I'll see to it he doesn't get away with anything ever again," Kate swore.

Ben admired her conviction. He believed her. She wanted Evan dead. He wanted Evan to pay for his many sins, but he didn't want Kate to get hurt or end up in a cell herself.

"Tell me what's going on here."

Kate jumped up from the couch, her face contorting with rage. "That fucker killed my sister and her fiancé."

"This is your sister's place?"

"Yes. Donald bought it for her last year."

Ben held up his hand, palm up. "Wait, your sister's fiancé is Donald Faraday?"

"Yes."

Ben grimaced. "He's married."

"He wasn't going to be for long. He asked his wife for a divorce today and now he's dead. They're both dead."

"And you believe Evan Faraday killed them?"

She waved one hand in front of her palm up. "Now you're all caught up."

"Why would he do that? It's too obvious if Donald asked Christina for a divorce."

Detective Raynott stepped forward to fill him in. "The scene's been staged to look like a murder-suicide. Kate schooled the responding officers and the crime scene guys to look deeper at the bloody knife and blood drops unrelated to the shootings. We can't confirm a third person, but the lab tests will tell us if the blood is from our victims or someone else. We don't have Evan Faraday's DNA in the system, so getting a sample may be tricky."

"Have the police notified Christina and Evan that Donald is dead?"

"Not yet."

"So Evan could have left the country by now." Ben hated to think Evan might get away with this after all.

"That would only make him look guiltier," Kate pointed out. "They want the money. Donald had a prenup. Christina got next to nothing for cheating on him. Donald and Evan fought on the phone today."

"Did you overhear this conversation?" the detective asked.

"No. When I left with Alex . . ."

"The baby?" Ben asked.

She sighed heavily. "Yes. Donald was upset. He said he spoke with Evan on the phone. They argued. Evan wasn't happy his father essentially cut him off. I sensed there was something more, but I'm not sure what. Donald was uneasy when I left. He handed me a key without my sister knowing."

"A key to what?" Ben asked.

"I think the safe. He tried to convince me and Margo that everything was okay, but deep down, I think he worried something like this might happen. That's why they asked me to take Alex for a few days."

"Wait. Alex is Donald and Margo's child, not yours?"

"He was, but now he's mine."

She didn't wear a ring, which made his assumption that she hadn't gotten married in the last year plausible. But the baby made him think she was in a committed relationship and he didn't have a chance with her despite Morgan's prediction. Now he breathed easier.

Ben thought through all the facts. "So Donald asked for a divorce from his wife to be with your sister, who has been his mistress for at least two years if they have a child. There's a prenup that leaves Christina Faraday with a settlement, but the bulk of the estate would go to Evan and Alex."

"Essentially, if Donald and Christina divorced. He served her the papers, but it's not final or anything, so I don't know if a judge would say they're technically still married. So now, the Faradays will fight to keep everything and exclude Alex." Kate raked her hand through her hair and held it away from her pretty face. Grief dragged her shoulders down and made the depths of her eyes flat.

"That's why I called Ben," Detective Raynott said. "If you're going up against the Faradays, you'll need an attorney who's dealt with them before and has a personal interest in taking them down."

"Why do you hate them?" She narrowed her eyes, the ever present suspicion still there despite the fact they had a common foe.

"Just Evan. Pricks with money who think they can get away with anything and everything because their victims don't have the same resources to fight back."

"The reason you founded Haven House," she guessed.

"Is that how you two met?" Detective Raynott eyed Ben, then Kate, silently asking Ben if they had a past.

"Kate is a social worker down in San Jose. She works with teens, but sometimes gets cases of abused women. She's sent a few to Haven House when they needed help and a safe place to hide outside of San Jose."

Ben didn't offer up any other information. Like every time he saw her in the past, no matter how short the visit to her offices to pick up someone in need, he'd been drawn to her and her quiet intensity. Smart and kind with an underlying strength that told you she didn't take shit from anyone. She'd always kept things on a professional level, sending out don't-touch, don't-even-ask vibes. Still, he'd always sensed interest in her that she didn't give in to—except that one time. The few times he saw her after the wedding reception, he could have pushed, tried harder, showed more interest, but he pulled back to save himself from a polite rejection. The attraction was there, thrumming through his system even now. The lost and devastated look in her eyes drew him in and made him want to wrap his arms around her and hug her close. He wanted to comfort her. The need to keep her close surprised him.

He wanted to fight it, dismiss it, and move on before she ran out on him again, but Morgan's prediction played in his head. What if Kate was the woman meant for him? What if he walked away from her without really trying and he never got another shot? What if he missed his chance for the kind of happiness Jenna and his other friends had found because he let it slip right through his fingers because he was too stubborn, afraid, lazy to hold on tight to it?

She'd brushed him off before, held back when he sensed she wanted to leap. He'd let her. Not this time.

"Ben, I thank you for coming tonight, but there's nothing you can do. I'll go through my sister's and Donald's papers, see what's what, and go from there. The police will nail Evan. He staged the scene, but he made mistakes. Those mistakes will land him in jail."

He placed his hand on her shoulder and slid it down to her arm. She didn't back away. He held it there, offering comfort.

"You're not dismissing me that easily. I can help with the papers and make sure Alex gets what's his. As far as Evan is concerned, don't think this is a slam dunk. Evan will hire a top attorney to defend him. He'll try to squirm his way out of this mess. If he can't, he'll use his money and status and the fact he's never been convicted of a crime to get out of serving any real time. He'll find any hole he can escape through to get out of this mess. Let me help you, and I'll keep the pressure on the DA to make sure he pays."

Her sad gaze met his. "Why? Why do you want to help me?"

"No matter what, you're going to need a lawyer to go up against them. You and I have worked together in the past. Better the lawyer you know, the one who is going to put everything I have into this case, than the one who will run up a huge bill. You don't want the DA handing out a plea that gets Evan out in a few years. You want him locked up for good. I will advocate for you and Alex to make sure that happens. I know Evan and what makes him tick. I've gone after him in the past."

"But you didn't win."

Ben felt the jab right in the gut. He tried not to take it personally. Still, the loss pissed him off. Having her point it out embarrassed him, but he'd done everything he could to advocate for the family of the man Evan beat to death and get them justice. The DA couldn't prove the case and there wasn't a shred of credible evidence to file a civil suit. Not the case for the man Evan beat in a bar brawl. That civil suit ended in a settlement, the criminal charges plead down to a measly misdemeanor. He couldn't fault his client for taking the money. Still, Ben didn't want to see Evan get away with yet another murder. He wanted to see Alex get his due.

"If you're right and the evidence puts Evan in that kitchen and the gun in his hand, he'll go to jail, but you'll still have to go up against Christina Faraday to get Alex's share of the estate. I can help you with that."

"As a social worker, you know I don't make a lot of money. I probably—no, I definitely can't afford you."

Ah, so that's why she hesitated. Not because she didn't think he could win this time, or do his best not to lose. The hope she squashed earlier that she had some faith in him rose up again.

"Kate, I don't want or need your money. I'm not asking you to hire me. I'm telling you that I will help you make this right."

Kate fell onto the sofa and landed with her back against the cushions. She covered her face with both hands and scrubbed them up and over her head. "I don't know what to do first. I need to bury my sister and Donald, figure out what to do with this house, and Alex's inheritance. I have to figure out a way to explain all of this to him one day. I have to figure out how I'm going to take care of him."

"Kate, one step at a time. I can help with all of that."

"You can help me take care of Alex?" One of Kate's eyebrows shot up.

"Well, everything but that. Though kids usually love me."

"Do you have kids?" She cocked her head, her eyes filled with accusation that maybe he'd kept something from her.

"No."

"What's with the handprint on your shirt?"

"Dinner out with friends included eight children. Grace loves chocolate cake and me."

The suspicion left her eyes. Her lips tilted. Not exactly a smile, but he'd take it. He hated seeing her this devastated and upset.

"That's sweet."

"She's a sweet girl." He thought fondly back to how much he enjoyed dinner with the family tonight.

"They do exist."

He didn't quite understand the reference. "Sweet kids?"

"No. Nice guys."

Maybe that's why she ran off that night. She thought he was taking advantage. "You're looking at one, Kate." He wanted her to believe good men existed, that he was one of them. He had to admit, the way he grew up, surrounded by men like his father, he'd often wondered that himself. He questioned his own goodness on many occasions. As a small boy, acting out his anger and frustration because of his depressing and scary home life, he'd feared he'd end up just like his father and uncles.

"Ben's the best," Detective Raynott agreed. Ben's eyebrow shot up, surprised by the compliment. "If you like those do-gooder types. I mean, he's a top notch attorney, rich, and helps women and children, for God's sake. He makes the rest of us look like asshole losers."

Ben couldn't hide the smirk. "I'm sure you can find at least a half dozen women who will tell you what an asshole loser I am and a hundred times that of people who have lost to me in court who will tell you I'm a total dick."

Kate met his steady gaze. "Well, lucky for me Ben the dick lawyer is exactly who I need to go up against the Faradays. Evan may think he'll get away with killing my sister, but there is no fucking way I let the Faradays get away with taking anything more from Alex."

"Then let's get started on taking down the Faradays," Ben suggested. "Detective, when will you notify them of the murders and question them?"

"The crime scene techs will finish up here. I'm heading over to see Mrs. Faraday now."

"Great, I'm coming with you," Ben said.

"Me too." Kate stood and straightened her purple

blouse. The deep color made her blue eyes that much more striking.

"Sorry, Kate, but I can't allow that." Detective Raynott held Kate's shoulder.

A friendly gesture meant to comfort and make the refusal easier for her to take. It set off something inside Ben. He wanted to tear Raynott's hand right off his body and stuff it down his throat. He'd never been the jealous sort. Well, not like this. He stuffed his hands in his pockets to keep from following through on impulse and tried to drag in a soothing breath. It calmed him, barely.

"Ben can go on your behalf as your attorney to inform them that you intend to get Alex's inheritance, but I can't allow you to interfere in the investigation. Plus, I don't want to tip my hat too soon about the bloody knife and other blood evidence. We'll wait for confirmation from the lab results. They'll take time. We'll use it to build a solid case against Evan. Right now, all we have is speculation that he did it. Let's see how confident Evan is about getting away with murder."

Ben walked the few steps to Kate and sat beside her on the sofa. He stared down at Alex sleeping peacefully. He saw bits of Donald in the boy's face. The shape of his chin. The slant of his nose. He had the same shade of brown hair as Kate. Ben wondered if he had blue eyes, or maybe a different color, more like Donald's dark brown. He'd met Donald on several occasions, but had no idea what Margo looked like. Did the two sisters look alike? Or were they as different as Kate seemed to all other women?

He could never quite put his finger on it, but something separated her from others. She wasn't better than anyone, just different.

"He looks so peaceful when he sleeps," Kate said. "Like nothing and no one bothers him. He has no idea his father and mother are dead in the other room. He has no idea the life he could have had with them is gone. He'll only know the life he'll have with me." She sighed so heavily he felt the depth of her spent emotions reverberate through him where their thighs touched. "It's not fair. This isn't how it was supposed to be."

Ben put his hand over Kate's in her lap and squeezed to offer what little comfort he could, knowing nothing he said or did would change what was and what would be. "If you ask me, he's lucky to have you. You love him. That's all anyone really needs."

"I don't know if I can be everything he needs." The whispered words held a trace of fear.

"That's the same thing I imagine every parent faces when they have a child. You'll be great, Kate. Because it matters to you, you'll do your best to be everything he needs."

"You're an optimist."

"Most of the time, but in this case, I know a sure thing when I see it." Before things got too weird, he asked, "Will you be okay here until I get back?"

She eyed him curiously.

"I'll come back after we see the Faradays and fill you in on what happened. Then I'll drive you home."

"I can get home on my own."

Ben pulled out his phone. "What's your number? I'll call you when we're finished and meet you at your place."

Kate kept her head down, her fingers tracing the back of his hand she held in her other as she rattled off her cell phone number. He punched it into his phone and set it up on speed dial. He liked the absent way she touched him. Not practiced or flirtatious, but genuine comfort in holding on to him during this difficult time. A sense of trust built between them. Something he'd never felt from her before because she didn't seem to trust anyone.

"Let's head out and get this done," Detective Raynott said.

Ben waited to see how long it took for Kate to let him go. She stared at his hand, softly rubbing, lost in her own thoughts. He couldn't sit here all night, but he wanted to if it gave her any sense of comfort.

"Kate."

"Yeah?"

"I have to go."

"Yeah, I'll talk to you later. I want to know all the details. I need to know for sure he's the one who did this."

"I'll tell you everything. I promise."

Her gaze came up to meet his. "Okay."

"Okay. But you have to let go so I can leave."

Her head snapped down. She stared at their joined hands like she had no idea of what she'd been doing. When he asked her to let him go, she'd actually held on tighter. Now, she quickly released him and scooted a few inches away from him on the couch.

Alex fussed in his car seat, squirming to get out. His

bottom lip trembled and his eyes filled with tears. Kate leaned forward and smoothed her hand over his head. "There now, you're okay."

"I think he needs a diaper change. I'll leave you to that and call you as soon as I can."

Ben gave in to impulse and rubbed his hand up and down Kate's back. She turned and stared at him, but didn't say anything. He tugged a lock of her hair. "See you soon."

He rose and walked with the detective to the front door. Chaos still reigned in the house. Flashes went off as the techs took pictures. Officers came and went from the scene. Unable to help himself, Ben turned back and stared at Kate, sitting on the sofa with Alex in her arms. The lost look in her eyes made his gut tight and his heart clench. He vowed he'd see Evan Faraday in a cell or dead for hurting her.

Chapter Seven

BEN WALKED UP the path beside Detective Raynott to the Faradays' front door surprised to see lights on inside this late at night. Just after midnight, he expected everyone to be asleep. Were they expecting the police to come and notify them of Donald's death?

"That's Evan's Range Rover in the driveway," Detective Raynott pointed out.

"Yeah. They're going to cover for each other."

"How long have you and Kate been a thing?"

Ben stopped in his tracks and stared at the detective. "We're not a thing."

The detective grinned. "It's not often sparks fly the way they did between you two. You going to do something about that? 'Cause if you're not, I'm thinking of asking her out."

Ben's green monster roared inside of him. "She just

lost her sister. You're supposed to investigate the case and arrest the bastard who did this. Stick to business."

"She's upset, in need of comfort. All I'm saying is I'd like to be there for her, you know?"

Yeah, Ben got the innuendo and the flash of lust in the detective's eyes. "Back off. Do your job and leave her the hell alone."

Detective Raynott laughed and continued on up the path to the front door. "That's what I thought."

Ben walked right into that one.

He usually kept his emotions in check. People said he was hard to read. It worked to his advantage in court. He chalked up the detective's remarks and seeing far too much Ben wasn't even sure about himself to the fact the detective was trained to see what others tried to hide. Ben wasn't necessarily ready to admit Kate got to him on a deep level. Maybe she wouldn't have gotten under his skin so quickly if Morgan hadn't prompted him that she was meant for him. He couldn't say, didn't know, and at this point didn't care. Kate needed his help. Evan needed to go down for what he'd done before he hurt or killed anyone else.

Ben's train of thought came to an abrupt halt when Mrs. Faraday opened the door with a glass of wine in her hand, her eyes bleary with too much alcohol.

"Mrs. Faraday, I'm Detective Raynott. This is Ben Knight. May we come in?"

"What's this about?"

"Your husband."

"He's not here-er," she slurred, her bloodshot eyes

darting from the detective to Ben and back again. She picked and pulled at the hem of her short red silk robe gaping open at her chest. If she bent forward even the slightest bit, her ample breasts would fall out of the bodice barely holding her in. She'd gotten ready for bed, but hadn't actually gone yet, judging by the nearly full glass of wine in her hand. The lights were on in the living room. A fire burned bright in the fireplace. He couldn't see more than the sofa and fireplace, but he bet there was a near empty bottle, or two, of wine on the coffee table.

Detective Raynott stepped forward, getting Mrs. Faraday to move back and let them in. She didn't so much invite them as had no choice but to stand her ground or move out of the way.

"Are you home alone, Mrs. Faraday?" the detective asked, knowing Evan had to be here with his car parked outside.

"My son and I had dinner together. He's asleep in his room upstairs."

"Will you please get him for us?"

"You said this is about my husband, not Evan. Why do you need to see him?"

"We have news about your husband and it might be easier if you have your son with you when we tell it."

"What's happened to Donald? He's dead, isn't he?"

"Yes, ma'am, I'm sorry to say he is."

Tears welled in her eyes, but didn't spill over. The surprise Ben expected, even if faked, didn't show through her drunk-hazed gaze.

"He's really gone." The words sounded far off, like she didn't really speak to them, but more herself.

Interesting. Telling.

"Yes. I'm sorry to say he is." The detective answered the statement that wasn't a question.

"I'll get Evan." She turned for the stairs, wobbly on her unsteady legs. She reached out to the round table in the middle of the massive foyer to steady herself, shaking the huge glass vase filled with orange, yellow, and red flowers. Their sweet scent filled the air. Christina actually put the wineglass down and headed up the stairs, lost in her thoughts and not particularly in a hurry to get Evan.

"She didn't ask how he died," Ben pointed out.

"I'm guessing she already knows. But yeah, that's not normal. Most people want to know how it happened. Why. When. Who's responsible."

Ben grimaced. "She's so drunk, she's about ready to pass out."

"Let's see if sonny-boy is any better off."

Ben and the detective waited in silence for nearly ten minutes for the Faradays to appear. They strained to hear even a murmur from the two upstairs, but heard nothing. Mrs. Faraday must have had a devil of a time getting Evan out of bed. The man looked wrecked, his eyes red-rimmed and swollen. He pulled a white T-shirt over his head and down his torso, covering the bruises on his side.

Detective Raynott glanced at Ben to see if he'd seen them too.

Evan walked down the stairs behind his mother. His

eyes squinted with pain with each step though he tried to hide it. Ben kept a close study, not missing anything. Even the smallest detail could be the key to taking the scumbag down.

"What's going on? My mother said you're here because my father is dead," Evan said, raking his fingers through his disheveled hair.

"I'm sorry to inform you that your father was found murdered tonight," the detective said, pausing to watch their response.

Both Faradays' eyes went wide with surprise a second before they exchanged a look.

"Murdered?" Mrs. Faraday asked.

"I'm afraid so."

"Maybe we should sit down and you can explain what happened," Evan said, walking away from them and straight into the living room. He practically fell into a chair facing the couch and stretched out his right leg, slouching against the back of the chair and staring up at them. "Don't I know you?" he asked Ben.

"Ben Knight. I represented Chris—"

"Burg. You're the fucking lawyer from the civil suit who tried to shake me down for all that money when all I did was defend myself against that asshole."

"Witnesses said you threw the first punch. Chris ended up in the hospital with a concussion, two broken ribs, a bruised spleen, and a broken cheekbone. The DA may have plead you down to a shit misdemeanor with a suspended sentence thanks to your father's lawyers and influence, but you still needed to pay for your crimes.

Daddy paid for you, but he's not here to get you out of this."

Evan dismissed all that and demanded, "What the fuck are you doing here?"

"I represent Kate Morrison and Alex Faraday for your father's estate."

"What?" both Christina and Evan said together.

"Who the hell is Alex Faraday?" Evan asked, leaning forward now, his forearms planted on his knees, eyes intent on Ben.

Ben glanced at the detective. The surprise in the detective's eyes matched exactly how Ben felt. They didn't know about the baby.

"Alex Faraday is your father's four-month-old son."

"He didn't have a child," Mrs. Faraday said.

The detective took over the explanation. "Mrs. Faraday, your husband and his fiancée, Margo Dexter, were shot at her home this evening. Although the scene was set up to appear as a murder-suicide, we have evidence that another person was in the home and committed the crime."

"What evidence?" Evan asked, his eyes narrowed with concern.

They had their attention now.

"I'm not at liberty to say. We're still investigating. Kate Morrison is Margo's sister. She returned to the house tonight after becoming concerned that she couldn't reach her sister or your husband, Donald. When she checked the house, she discovered the bodies and called the police."

"Where is the baby now?" Mrs. Faraday asked.

"Margo left the baby in his aunt's care earlier today. The baby is with her," the detective answered.

"How can you be sure this baby is Donald's child? I mean, he's having an affair with some slut. She probably passed off the kid as his just to get his money." Mrs. Faraday spat out the words like venom spilling from her lips.

"It won't be hard to prove with a simple DNA test," the detective pointed out.

"Not to worry, Mrs. Faraday, you can trust that I will make sure Alex gets everything that's coming to him from his father," Ben added.

Evan and his mother stared at each other for a long moment, broken only by the detective's next question.

"Where were both of you tonight from about four o'clock until we arrived?"

Mrs. Faraday jumped. "You think we had something to do with this?"

Ben had to give her credit. The outrage in her voice almost sounded genuine. More than likely she resented all these tedious details that kept her from getting control of her husband's money.

"Standard procedure, ma'am. When someone is murdered, it's usually the spouse who did it. Or a close family member." The detective made a point of staring at Evan.

"Well, look at someone else," Mrs. Faraday snapped. "We've been here all night. Together."

The detective expected that answer. So did Ben unfortunately. Too much to hope they'd simply confess and this would all be over. He'd like to spare Kate the pain and hardship of going through all this.

"When is the last time you saw Donald?" the detective asked both of them.

"Today," Mrs. Faraday confessed. "Early afternoon. He arrived with another man to serve me divorce papers."

Ben perked up. "He actually served you the papers today?"

"Yes. Not that I was surprised. We've been living separate lives for some time even though we share a roof. Obviously, he'd decided to move on with his slut."

"Did you know about Margo?" the detective asked.

"Of course I knew. A wife always knows when her husband strays."

"I find it very coincidental that your husband is murdered the day he serves you with divorce papers," Ben said.

"Don't you think it would be stupid of me to kill my husband on the very day he asks for a divorce?"

"Sometimes the obvious is the right answer," the detective shot back. "It's a simple matter to rule you out. Provide your fingerprints and a DNA sample."

Alert now, Mrs. Faraday eyed the detective. "Of course we will, as soon as you present a warrant to my lawyer. We're done here. Please leave."

The detective stood and handed her his business card. "I'll be in touch. If you have questions or information related to your husband's murder, please let me know." The detective took two steps away before turning back. "Those are some nasty bruises on your jaw and ribs, Evan. How did you get those?"

"Bar fight." Evan didn't even blink, but turned and stared down Ben, daring him with a look to contradict that's how he got the bruises.

"I bet they hurt like hell." Detective Raynott cocked his head and plastered on a thoughtful look. "Kate told me her sister, Margo, was an expert kickboxer. I bet she got a few licks in before that bastard shot her in the head."

"Maybe if she'd been better, my father would still be alive," Evan said under his breath.

Mrs. Faraday snapped her head in Evan's direction and glared.

Detective Raynott gave Ben a look. The show of remorse surprised even Ben. He expected the cocky, arrogant asshole who'd done everything, including buying off Ben's clients to get out of going to jail, not someone with . . . feelings. Killing his father went far beyond a drunken brawl.

How long would Evan's remorse last? Would he confess? Not likely. Not with all that money on the line. Not with the possibility of life in prison and the death penalty looming over his head if he couldn't pull off a miracle. No way he bought his way out of this mess if they found evidence that proved he killed his father and Margo.

"About the child. Alex?" Mrs. Faraday asked, and the detective nodded she got the name right. "If he's my husband's son, then perhaps it's best if he's here with Evan and me. Evan is his brother after all."

"Alex will remain with his aunt. She will take care of him and oversee his inheritance until he comes of age," Ben swore.

"Well, we'll see about that." Mrs. Faraday tilted her chin up. "If he is my husband's son, then Evan and I will want to protect his interests as they are ours as well."

"Be assured, Kate and I will protect Alex. Someone already took his parents." Ben stared down Evan, then turned his glare back to Mrs. Faraday. "No one will take anything more from him." He echoed Kate's earlier vow.

Evan leaned forward. "So, it's you and Kate, huh? I can't wait to meet her."

The implied threat in those innocuous words sent a bolt of rage through Ben's system. "Stay away from her."

"I'd like to meet my brother." Evan's cocky grin said he really wanted to meet Kate just to piss off Ben.

"I doubt Kate will bring him to see you in jail."

"I'm slick, man, nothing sticks to me. Ask my lawyers. Oh, wait, you already know that."

"We'll see about that. Your father isn't here to make it all go away anymore."

Evan fell back into his seat and plastered on a fake air of arrogance with his arms crossed over his chest in a defensive gesture Ben relished.

"There's nothing to make go away," Mrs. Faraday defended her son. "Evan had nothing to do with what happened to Donald and that woman." She turned her cold eyes on Detective Raynott. "Shouldn't you be out looking for the person or persons responsible for this heinous crime?"

Detective Raynott smiled. "I'll contact you once I have

that warrant for your prints and DNA." He eyed Evan again. "Of course, we already have your prints from the numerous times you were arrested."

"Get out." The deadly tone in Evan's quiet words brought a smile to Ben's lips he couldn't contain. They'd made Evan nervous. Good. He'd botched the cover-up of the murder-suicide. Ben couldn't wait to see how his overconfidence and arrogance nipped him in the ass next.

Ben walked out the door with Detective Raynott. Evan slammed it at their backs.

"He's guilty as hell." The detective shook his head and stuffed his hands in his pockets.

They stood on the path. Ben turned and stared back at the front door. "Margo gave him those bruises. He tried to hide it, but he's favoring his right leg. I'll bet that's where she cut or stabbed him."

"Without the blood evidence back, prints, something to prove he was in that house, I'll have a hard time getting a judge to sign a warrant to get his DNA and a look at his person."

"His lawyer will do everything possible to keep you from getting it. You need to find something, however small, linking him to the crime besides the obvious motive."

"I'm working on it."

"Test Donald's blood against the blood on the knife. See if it's a familial match. That will get you the warrant for Evan's blood."

"The lab guys will test everything, but it could take weeks."

"Put a rush on it. If Evan leaves the country, we're screwed."

"God, he's an asshole." The detective rolled his eyes.

"Assholes with money always think they can get away with anything. Let's prove him wrong." Ben headed back down the path to their car. "Drive me back to Margo's. If Kate's not there, I'll call her and fill her in."

Ben stared out the car window on the short drive, thinking about Kate and all she'd been through tonight. The next few days and weeks wouldn't be easy. One thought nagged at him.

"They don't want Alex to get anything," he said, thinking out loud.

"They hinted they'd like to take control of him and whatever inheritance he might get."

"Never going to happen."

"It might if Kate's not in the picture." The detective pointed out Ben's worst fear.

They'd already killed Donald and Margo to ensure their financial future. Ben's gut soured knowing they'd remove any obstacle in their way. Kate's sad eyes and tear-streaked face came to mind. He'd protect her. Nothing and no one would harm her or Alex.

Was he this determined to protect her simply because of what Morgan told him? The building urge to help her said otherwise. The overwhelming need to see her again came from a deeper place. One he didn't know existed. One no other woman had sparked to life.

EVAN LEANED HIS back against the door and hung his head. "Fuck."

"We will be if we don't control this situation. I'll contact our lawyer first thing in the morning. Is there any possible way they can tie you to this directly?"

Evan rubbed his hand over his aching thigh. The cut stung and throbbed under his palm. "I forgot to pick up the fucking knife."

"What? No! How could you be so stupid?" his mother spat out.

"I'd just killed my own father and blown that woman's head off," he yelled back. "I wasn't thinking straight. I thought it would be easy, but it wasn't." He held his hands up and stared at them. "My hands were shaking, I tried to set up the scene to look the way I wanted between the two of them, and I forgot she'd cut me." He dropped his hands back to his sides. "I didn't really feel it until I was on my way back here."

"This is a mess."

"Only if they get my DNA. Otherwise, they can't link the blood to me."

"Maybe we can get someone in the police department to destroy the evidence."

"Seriously, how are you going to do that?"

"Pay them off."

"You think that won't be traced back to you?" Evan shook his head and tried to think. "If they do pin this on me, I'll leave the country before they lock me in a cage. You'll still get the bulk of the estate. You can send me money to live on."

"Your father's bastard is going to get half the estate, if not all."

"How do you figure that?"

"Your father served me with divorce papers. My lawyer will fight that I am still his legal wife and entitled to the estate, but if your father signed papers saying he left everything to that boy . . ."

Evan came to the inevitable conclusion. "We're fucked."

Chapter Eight

BEN PULLED UP in front of Kate's condo. He got her address from Detective Raynott and drove over, deciding not to call her this late at night. After the day she had, he expected her to be crashed out in bed. Instead, the downstairs windows showed all the lights on. If they'd been out, he'd have driven home and called her first thing in the morning. Those lights drew him in like a beacon.

He parked in the visitor parking area, got out of the car, and dragged his tired ass to her front door. He liked the pots of yellow pansies flanking the dark green door.

Alex cried at the top of his lungs. The sound made Ben's chest tight. Anxious and nervous, he knocked. His gut knotted with anticipation at seeing Kate's pretty face again. He liked her. They had a lot in common. They both spent their lives trying to help others in their own ways. She as a social worker, helping teen runaways and foster kids. Him working with abused women and their children. He wanted to get to know her better. He wished they didn't have her sister's murder and Alex's inheritance to deal with while he did that.

If she was even interested in getting to know him better. She'd never given him any indication she liked him more than an acquaintance and colleague, except for that kiss. It played in his mind and made him want. He wanted that feeling she evoked in him back.

He'd play it by ear.

Kate opened the door with Alex in her arms. Her gaze met his and the relief he saw there unknotted his stomach. "Thank God you're here. I didn't hear from you and got worried."

"What's wrong with him?" Ben tilted his head toward Alex.

"I think he knows his mother is gone. He wants her. Nothing I do is good enough. He just keeps crying." Tears shimmered in her red-rimmed eyes and spilled over. "I don't know what to do."

Ben stepped into her apartment, making her back up. She didn't exactly invite him in, but the desperation in her voice prompted him to act. He closed the door behind him. Kate stood close, looking up at him, waiting for him to do something. He wanted to kiss her and make this all go away. A crazy thought he didn't act on.

"Give him to me." Ben held out his hands.

Kate handed Alex over, sighing and shaking out her arms. The boy didn't weigh much, but she must have been holding and carrying him for quite some time. She'd changed out of her slacks and blouse from earlier into a simple navy blue tank dress. She'd pulled her long curls up into a messy knot at the back of her head. The fatigue etched lines on her forehead and made her shoulders sag. Nearly two in the morning, she and Alex should both be sleeping. Neither looked ready to call it a night, too wound up to relax into sleep.

Ben tucked Alex in the crook of his arm and held him close to his chest. He snagged the pacifier off the coffee table and pushed it into Alex's open mouth. He tried to spit it out, but Ben held it gently in place as Alex cried around it. He bounced the boy up and down. "Shh. It's time for you to sleep, buddy," he whispered.

Kate stood in the middle of the room, wiping the tears from her cheeks, a lost look in her eyes that tore at his insides. Alex's cries softened, but he wasn't quite ready to give up yet.

"Turn most of the lights off, Kate. The darkness will help him calm down and fall asleep."

Kate automatically started hitting switches on the kitchen wall and turning off one of the lamps in the living room space.

"Which one of those stuffed toys is his favorite?"

Kate picked up a black and white spotted puppy. "I gave him this in the hospital when he was born. Margo said he doesn't sleep without it." Kate placed the puppy on Alex's belly and fell into the corner of the sofa, sobbing out her grief.

Ben didn't think, just went with instinct. He sat beside her, bounced Alex in one arm, and held Kate to his side with the other. She came willingly and pressed her face into his shoulder. Alex held the puppy in his hands, sucked his pacifier, and slowly drifted off to sleep, hiccupping a few times after all those tears.

Kate's tears ran out, but she didn't pull away. Her head turned, and she laid her cheek against his chest and sighed. Though her body pressed against his, she kept her hands tucked between them at her side. She didn't really touch him, but he wanted her to. It felt so right to have her next to him, even with Alex tucked close in his arm. The baby's sweet face softened in sleep.

"It's going to be all right," he assured Kate. Comfortable with the two of them, he propped his feet on the coffee table and settled into the sofa, ready to stay as long as they needed him.

They needed him.

A warm glow flared to life inside of him that spread to all the cold abandoned places he'd hid deep within himself. He helped others who needed him, but it didn't feel like this.

"It wasn't supposed to be like this. Alex hates me. He wants his mother."

Ben smiled and leaned his cheek on top of Kate's head. "He doesn't hate you. He misses his mother like you miss her. He sees that you're upset and sad and he feels that too. He needs you, Kate."

"What happened tonight with Donald's wife and son? Did Detective Raynott arrest Evan?"

"I wish I could tell you that he did and this will all be over soon. Evan showed a few glimpses of remorse for his father, but he didn't confess anything, or really give anything away. I did see some bruises on his face and ribs. He's trying to hide a limp."

"Margo got a piece of him."

"Margo tried to kick his ass." Ben brushed his cheek over Kate's soft hair. He absently traced circles on her bare arm with his fingertips. He felt her awareness of him beside her. She didn't move away, so he kept touching her softly, hoping to comfort her and draw her closer to him. "I like your sister."

"She was amazing in her sweet way. You look at her and see all this softness in her hazel eyes, blond hair, and light complexion, but under it all she could be strong and tough."

"Not as tough as you though, right?" he guessed.

"We looked out for each other, but I took care of her more than she took care of me. I loved her for holding on to her optimism and dreaming for all those pretty things we didn't have growing up. That's all she wanted—a husband, a child, a happy home and life. She almost had it all and they took it away from her. I can't—I won't—let them get away with it."

"*We* won't let them get away with it."

"Why are you doing this? Why are you here? What do you want?"

Ben tried to sort out the many answers circling his mind. "You and I have a mutual enemy in Evan. I want to see him pay for his sins just as much as you do. I'm here to help you with whatever you need. We want the same thing, Kate, and if we work together maybe we can both get what we want." He meant Evan behind bars, but something deep inside of him whispered that he wanted a hell of a lot more from her.

"I've never really been good at being a team player. I look out for myself. With my background in the system, I am fully aware of my hang-ups about trusting others, let alone relying on them."

"You can trust me. I won't let you down. I want you and Alex to get everything that's coming to you, and that includes justice for your sister and Alex's father."

"I believe you. It's so unexpected and strange that you showed up tonight. After what happened before . . ."

The kiss. "That was the past. Someone I know would simply say this was meant to be."

"Whatever this is, I'm glad you're here. And that surprises me too."

No more than Morgan's prediction coming true surprised him. Where this thing went with Kate, he didn't know, but he was committed to seeing it through to the end.

"Speaking of surprises, Evan and Christina Faraday didn't know about Alex."

Kate tilted her head up to look at him. Her lips parted with surprise. Her soft breath washed over his skin. If he bent a few inches, he could kiss her. She kept her gaze locked on his, ignoring or oblivious to the pull between them.

"What?"

"They knew about your sister's affair with Donald, but not that they had a son."

"Huh. I assumed she knew about Alex even though

Margo didn't think so. Donald always said he and his wife hadn't been close in years. I hoped she knew the divorce was inevitable. Donald promised for over a year to make it happen, but put it off for one reason or another until he did it without really telling Margo his intentions."

"So, it came out of the blue."

"In a manner of speaking. Evan has gotten into trouble a couple of times over the last few months."

"The bar fight Donald paid to get him out of, then a DUI arrest."

"Right. Something happened that set Donald off. Maybe he'd just had enough with Evan and Christina dragging him down. You should have seen him with Margo and Alex. When they were all together, they looked so happy. Especially Donald. Sometimes I'd catch this look on his face that he felt lucky to have them and a second chance at a happy family. I wanted that for him and Margo both."

"At least they had that for a short time. Some people never get to experience that kind of love and happiness."

"Tell me about it. I sure didn't, but seeing Margo with Donald changed my mind about never having a husband or a family."

"You don't want to get married someday and have kids?"

"I didn't, but with Margo so happy, and the way Alex brought so much joy into their lives, I'd changed my mind. In fact, seeing Alex with them the last few months had been hard for me. It brought up so many feelings I never thought I'd have about being a mother. Now, he's all mine. I will be the only mother he ever knows." Kate raked her fingers into her hair, then dropped her hand. "Everything has changed and I feel so guilty that I want it to be this way. I want to be his mother."

"You don't have to feel guilty that Margo died and Alex is yours now."

"Yes, I do. There's something you don't know."

"What?"

"I am Alex's biological mother."

Shocked, Ben tried to process this new revelation. "Are you telling me Donald isn't Alex's father?"

"It's complicated."

If he was going to push for Alex's inheritance, he needed to know all the facts. "Uncomplicate it for me."

"Due to Margo's past, she couldn't carry a biological child of her own."

That sounded ominous, knowing both Margo and Kate grew up in the system. "Why?"

"Her father molested her as a child. He destroyed her reproductive system before they took Margo away from him for good."

"Christ," Ben swore.

"Exactly."

Another complication popped into his mind. "Wait. So you and Margo aren't blood sisters."

"No. Foster sisters. But that doesn't mean we aren't . . . weren't family."

He responded to the defensive tone in her words. "Hey, I get it. I had dinner tonight with a group of people who are family by blood and friendship. They are closer than any family I've ever known. Family goes beyond blood."

"And you're a part of that family."

"I've been avoiding it for the most part, but they keep pulling me in."

"That's what a real family does, right? You're accepted no matter what. You're included every time you show up. That's how it should be."

He'd never thought about it that way, but she was right. "I guess. I like being with them, but it reminds me too much of my messed-up past. I want what they have, but don't feel like I belong."

"You choose not to belong."

"Look who's talking," he said, pointing out that neither of them had close family, or believed in having one of their own. Funny, they'd both recently come to the point in their lives that they thought it possible for them too. Freaky.

"Margo wanted a child more than anything in this world. More than she wanted the husband and happy home, she wanted to be a mother. She met Donald and he wanted to give her anything and everything to make her happy.

"Margo came to me just a few months into their relationship and in her crazy, silly way said, 'Can I use your uterus? I mean, you're not using it, so I thought you'd let me borrow it.' Just like that." Kate wiped the fresh tears from her cheeks.

Ben laughed. "You two had a really great relationship if you agreed to do that for her."

"Well, I didn't exactly go along with it right away. At first I refused, but Margo wore me down. Abuse and neglect punctuated my childhood. Having a child, being a mother, never crossed my mind. In fact, I vehemently stated it would never happen. I believed that."

"Then you had Alex for her."

"I wanted her to be happy and have everything she wanted too. So Donald made a donation, and I was artificially inseminated. I got pregnant immediately. I thought I could carry him, then hand him over to her and Donald and be the aunt. Throughout the pregnancy, she kept asking me if I had second thoughts about giving up my child. I didn't. I wanted to do this amazing thing for her. I tucked my feelings and thoughts into a box. I added being pregnant and delivering him to my to-do list like grocery shopping, paying my bills, and taking my car in for a tune-up.

"I went into labor and something strange happened. It hit me all at once that he was real. The minute I saw him, this wave of emotion washed through me and for the first time in my life I really felt true and overwhelming love. I didn't want to let him go, but I had no choice. I'd promised him to her. Donald was his father. I liked the man, but I didn't want to raise a child with him. What could I do?

"So I distanced myself from them. Margo figured it out. I visited them and she saw it on my face. I resented her the happiness I saw in all of them. Alex was in her arms and loved her. He accepted her as his mother. She loved him as her son. I couldn't take that away from them."

"But you wanted to. You wanted Alex back."

"Now I have him. He's mine. He won't remember her. He'll only remember me." Another wave of tears overtook her. Her shoulders shook.

Ben hugged her close. "You'll tell him about her. He'll know that you did something amazing for your sister, and despite the fact you wanted Margo and Donald to raise him, you always wanted him. When the chance came for you to have him back, you took it. You loved him.

"I have no doubt that over the years if Margo had raised him, you'd have been like a second mother, a real and important presence in his life. Margo and Donald would have wanted to repay your gift by making sure Alex always knew the amazing person you are and that despite the fact they raised him you were always there for him."

"I would have been."

"You will be now."

"I'd do anything for him." She yawned so big he followed suit.

He leaned his cheek against her head again and relaxed into the sofa with her at his side. Alex slept peacefully across his belly and in the crook of his arm, sucking on his pacifier.

"I should put him to bed." Kate tried to move away, but he held her close.

"He's fine."

Kate yawned again. "It's late. I'm so tired. I should see you out and go to bed."

He held back a smile when she settled into him again and tucked her legs up on the couch.

"Yeah, you probably should."

Neither of them moved, content to sit close and let the quiet envelop them after such a difficult night. Her breathing evened out as her weight settled into his side. He waited for that part of himself that always pulled away to rear its head and tell him to go home and sleep in his own bed. Kate snuggled into his chest. Her soft hair brushed against his face. Her sweet rosy scent filled his nose and made him turn and inhale the heady scent again. He didn't want to go. In fact, he'd like to stay right here with her for as long as she'd let him.

BEN WOKE UP to Alex fussing and wiggling against his chest. He'd lost his pacifier sometime during the night. He needed a bottle and a diaper change. Happy to do both for him, but still Ben hesitated for one very good reason. Kate slept soundly curled at his side, her face in his neck, hand on his chest beside Alex. She had his full attention, but his focus remained on his hand planted smack over her ass, holding her close to him. He'd never actually slept with a woman. He'd never wanted that kind of intimacy. Yet here he was with a woman and a baby. He thought about having a family in the abstract, but this was reality up close.

Not even a hint of anxiety crept into his system. He didn't feel the urge to hurry up and get the hell out of there. In fact, if Alex didn't need anything, Ben would be happy to sleep another couple of hours.

Unfortunately, he had to see to Alex and get home to shower, change, and get to work. He needed to make plans with Kate for what was to come with her sister's and Donald's estates. He needed to be sure she'd be safe with Evan on the loose and looking to keep what belonged to Alex.

The baby planted his hands on Ben's chest and raised his head, staring right at him. "Hey, buddy, you hungry?"

Alex head-butted him in the chin and rubbed his forehead against him. He raised his head, smiled, and did it again. The kid liked his beard stubble.

Ben planted his right hand on the couch beside him, balanced Alex on his chest, and slid out from under Kate, slowly lowering her to the spot he vacated. Exhausted from staying up so late last night and crying herself to sleep, she barely stirred as she settled into the warmth he left behind on the sofa.

Stiff from sleeping with his legs out on the table and his head tilted back on the sofa, he stood and stretched his back, bending forward, then back and side to side with Alex pressed to his shoulder. The baby smiled and gurgled.

"You're easy, kid. Let's get you cleaned up." Ben dug through the diaper bag next to the playpen beside the side chair. He pulled out a diaper, the wipes, and a clean set of clothes for his little buddy. He laid Alex on the play mat on the floor and kneeled beside him. How hard could this be? He'd seen Cameron change a dozen diapers like it was nothing. Ben removed Alex's dirty clothes. Alex giggled and flapped his arms, kicking his legs ready to play. He grabbed hold of Ben's finger and tried to pull it to his mouth. Ben gently pulled free and tore the tabs on the diaper free. The smell hit him all at once.

Ben wrinkled his nose and shook his head. "Wow. That's deadly, buddy." Ben made quick work, holding his breath and using the wipes to clean Alex and rediaper him. Finished, he folded up the soiled diaper, secured it with the sticky tabs, and set it aside. Not bad. Easy. Alex rolled to his belly, planted his hands on the mat, and raised his head up to look around at everything. He kicked his little feet up and down. Not exactly steady, or in control of his head, he worked hard to move about the mat.

"Where are you going?" he whispered, eyeing Kate asleep on the sofa. Her hair fell over part of her face. Her eyes remained closed. She looked so pretty and soft in sleep.

Alex fell forward and nearly face planted on the blanket. Ben rolled him back over and stuffed his little feet into the dark blue sweatpants. He bunched the shirt in his hands to find the head opening. He sat Alex up on his butt, pulled the shirt over his head and tried to put his hand through the sleeve. Not as easy as it seemed with Alex struggling against him and falling over on his side. Ben left him on his back and worked the shirt over his belly, finally getting his hands to poke out the sleeves. Dressed and happily trying to grab at the toys hanging over him, Ben rubbed Alex's belly and left him to play.

He hated to take liberties in Kate's place. They barely knew each other, but Alex needed to eat before he started crying and woke his mother. Ben wondered how Kate would feel this morning knowing today was the first day she'd truly be Alex's mom.

The can of formula and several clean bottles and nipples sat on a dish towel on the kitchen counter. A tablet with notes and instructions sat beside the container of milk. Ben read through several of the items Margo instructed Kate to do, including how to make him a bottle. Ben followed the instructions, heated the water, poured in the scoops of milk, gently shook the bottle to mix it, and poured several drops on his wrist to test the temperature. Warm, but not hot. He went back to the living room to give it to Alex. He spun around at the last second and went back to the kitchen to make the coffee since Alex seemed content to stare at himself in the little mirror on a bear's belly.

Ben got over his trepidation about rummaging through the cupboards in search of the coffee and filters real quick. He'd only been up for twenty minutes, but he felt hungover and exhausted after only four hours of sleep. He dumped the old grounds in the garbage under the sink, fixed up a new pot, and hit the on switch. The machine hissed and spit, then gurgled to life, dripping coffee into the pot. Ben exhaled with relief, hoping the thing would hurry up with his caffeine fix.

The smell helped wake him up. Alex too, with his sudden cries for his bottle. Ben scooped him off the floor, sat in the soft oatmeal-colored chair next to the couch, and stuffed the bottle in Alex's mouth. Some of the milk dripped down his chin. The kid gorged, hungry after his crying jag and sleep. Ben leaned over and snagged a blue and white polka-dotted rag off the side table and wiped Alex's face, then tucked the towel under his chin to catch whatever else the kid spilled.

Ben studied Alex's face. He had his mother's blue eyes and even her eyebrows. Ben traced his finger over one, following the soft arch. Alex reached for his finger, grabbed it, and held tight, staring up at him, completely trusting and content to lie in Ben's arms and drink his breakfast.

"Sorry about your mom and dad, buddy. Kate loves you. She wants to be your mom. She'll settle into it today. She's strong and tough on the outside, but she's got an amazing heart. Once, I saw her break up a fight between two street punks who thought the only way to solve a fight was with guns, knives, and fists. She stood between them. They towered over her, but she didn't back down or show any sign of fear. They could have roughed her up, but instead she said something to them that made both of them take a step back. All the fight went out of them. She kept talking. I don't know what she said. The guys yelled at her, each other, tried to brawl once again, and went around and around like that for about ten minutes. In the end, she got them to shake hands and do garbage duty together at the group home.

"Another time, she called me in to help with a mother and her teenage daughter. The girl was beat up, hurting, crying, knowing her mother would never leave her abusive father. Your mom spoke to the mother, got through all the layers of her feeling like she caused all the problems, thinking her husband really loved her but he just needed a chance to change. He'd promised. She got through all those years of fear and self-doubt and convinced the woman that the best thing for her to do was take her daughter away from that man. One week at Haven House and the woman changed. She found her courage and strength and protected her daughter. Your mom did that for them.

"She'll do the same for you. She'll never let anything bad happen to you. I won't either. I'm going to work with your mom to make sure that asshole who killed your father and mother is locked behind bars for the rest of his life."

Maybe he shouldn't swear around the child, but hey, the kid didn't understand the words. He hoped he got the meaning. Ben meant every word. He admired Kate for the work she did and the amazing way she connected with the people who came to her needing help but not necessarily open to receiving it, or doing what they needed to do when it went against everything they'd ever known. Change scared people. Scared people feared the unknown. The promise of something good wasn't enough to get them to try sometimes, because not many good things happened to them. When they did, they were always waiting for the other shoe to drop. Kate got that and worked with her clients in a way that encouraged them to trust.

Ben hoped she'd trust him now to help her with the

Faradays and everything that came next. She'd let him past her walls last night. Her grief may have compromised her usual resolve to keep everyone at arm's length. When she woke up, would he find her walls up, the windows black, and the professional woman he'd known back to being all business? Or would she show him some of who she really was, like the night they danced and kissed, like the open and honest woman from last night? He really wanted to get to know her better. Explore the fluttering feeling living in his gut that made him want to stare at her and ask a million questions to discover what lay beneath Kate's surface. He liked the surface. Her pretty face, those blue eyes that saw far more than he wanted her to see. She did that. She delved deeper when she looked at a person, and summed that person up with astounding accuracy. What happened in her life that made her need to hone that skill? She'd hinted about her past last night. He wanted to know the whole story of where she'd come from. What made Kate the woman he knew now?

His gaze roamed over her from her cute feet, up her smooth legs, the curve of her hip, the dip in her side, the fullness of her breasts, the long column of her throat, and back to her face and that gorgeous dark wavy hair.

What really drew him to her?

Everything.

Chapter Nine

KATE FELT HIS gaze on her. She'd heard everything he said to Alex. She appreciated his vote of confidence in her taking on the role of Alex's mother. Actually, she *was* Alex's mother. It wasn't something she had to do, but what she was at the heart. He was her son. She loved him more than anything in this world. She hated to give him up and struggled every day since with the loneliness in her heart that opened a deep dark pit in her soul of wanting him back. Now, she had him. She hated the way he'd come back to her, but she'd spend every day from now on grateful to have him in her life permanently.

She'd rewrite the story of their lives and tell him that once she'd tried to give his aunt Margo the child she wanted and deserved. He'd have had a happy life with her and Donald with Kate a constant presence in his life. By the time he was old enough to understand what she'd tried to do for Margo and him, he'd know how much she loved him and didn't want to be without him. He'd understand she never wanted to give him up.

That fear resolved in her mind, she vowed to spend the rest of her life as the person Alex needed. As his mother. Someone he could always count on. She'd be the family he deserved and she never had.

She opened her eyes and stared across the room at Ben working in her kitchen. Alex sat strapped in his bouncy seat on the kitchen table. Ben walked over, tickled his belly, making Alex smile and shake his puppy and kick his feet with excitement. The smell of coffee and eggs filled the room. Her stomach grumbled. She'd missed dinner last night when she decided to go and check on Donald and Margo. She'd been too upset to eat last night when she got home.

Alex squealed with delight at Ben, who smiled down at him. Did Ben know how much she liked him? He made her nervous every time they met. Those brief encounters always set something off in her system that charged her nerves, made the butterflies in her stomach flutter to life, and her heart beat faster. She tried to hide it even now and wondered why. Something inside of her told her to reach out to him. Try for something more than colleagues or casual dating with no strings attached. She'd never relied on a man, never given herself permission to trust that she wouldn't end up like her mother—devoted to a man who only wanted to use that love against her and break her down until no matter what he did she'd never leave him.

The rational part of her knew that she had more

strength and conviction than that, but she'd never been in love, or experienced feelings and emotions like that for a man.

Except that one time with Ben. The kiss she shared with him rocked her. He'd tilted her world off balance, and she ran, afraid she didn't have anything to offer an amazing man like him.

She loved Margo and Alex. But that was very different than loving a man. Did she have that kind of love in her? A kind of love that wouldn't destroy her but fill her life with happiness?

The few times she felt even a glimmer of attraction for a man, she'd walked the other way. She enjoyed dating. She liked sex. On her terms.

Maybe she truly was ready for something more. She certainly didn't feel like running now—unless it was into Ben's arms.

The intense attraction she felt toward Ben eclipsed all the other times her hormones made her tingle with lust. Ben sent her body into overdrive. The ache deep inside her made her squeeze her thighs tight and imagine what it would feel like to have him cover her body with his and make love to her right here on the couch.

She needed Ben to help her with Donald's estate. He was a lawyer. A damn good one. He promised to help her. For free. Who would pass up free legal services and advice? She couldn't afford to turn him down just to avoid complications. Like the fact she wished he was still next to her, holding her close and making her feel safe. There had been too few times in her life she'd felt that way.

Her gaze swept up his lean legs, over his flat belly to his wide chest and shoulders, and up to his gorgeous face with that square jaw, perfect mouth, and intense brown eyes staring back at her. One side of his mouth quirked up in a slight grin.

"Breakfast is ready."

Great. Not only had she been caught ogling the guy, but did he have to look that damn perfect in the morning when she probably looked like a rag doll dragged through the yard?

His deep voice resonated through her like an echo of something long forgotten but still cherished. The tingling that swept over her skin settled in her chest and made her breasts heavy and her nipples harden. She tried not to squirm or press her arms to her aching breasts. In fact, she avoided eye contact, rolled up to sitting, and raked her hand through her messy hair, dislodging the band that most of the mass had fallen from as she slept. She shook out the strands. Ben's gaze narrowed on her. She swore he inhaled and leaned forward like he meant to come to her. A trick of the mind? Wishful thinking? Either way, she couldn't deny the effect he had on her. Judging by the way his eyes strayed to her breasts, she couldn't hide it either.

Ben's gaze met hers again. "Is there something you want, Kate?"

Avoiding the awkward answer that she wanted him to hold her, kiss her, make everything that happened yesterday disappear for a little while longer, she went with the practical. She was always practical. "Coffee."

His smile spread. "Sure. Anything you want."

So many naughty things flashed through her mind. Her fingers gripped in his dark hair as his mouth latched on and sucked her aching breast. His mouth kissing and hands caressing every inch of her naked body. His body, every sculpted muscle on display, pressed down on hers as he filled her, rocked against her, and made her pant out his name.

God, how she wanted to do all those things and more and avoid reality.

It had been far too long since she let a man that close to her. Way before she got pregnant with Alex. But this went deeper than the physical. Ben called to something deep inside of her. Something that answered only to him.

What was she going to do about it? What did she want?

She wanted her sister to still be alive. She wanted this to all be a dream. She wanted Alex to still have his father and Margo. She wanted to be the perfect mother to Alex. She wanted to know he'd always be happy and healthy. She wanted someone else to carry the load she faced.

She wanted life to finally be simple and not so complicated.

When Ben came toward her with a cup of steaming coffee, she admitted she wanted him to be the man she'd wished for as a little girl, scared and lonely locked in a dark closet, hoping that one day she'd find the one man who would love her and never hurt her. She'd long forgotten that hopeful girl existed. Life taught her some hard lessons. You had to work hard to get the things you wanted. You could never count on someone else to give you what you really needed.

You had to love yourself.

She'd been alone a long time. Since she was ten and spent some time in juvy before she got dumped in the foster care system and met Margo. It would be nice to have someone to help her. Someone to count on. Someone she trusted as much as she'd trusted her sister.

Tears shimmered in her eyes. She'd let her mind go there. The images of Margo lying dead on the floor, her head blown open, the blood everywhere.

"Kate, honey, breathe."

She responded to that sweet term with ridiculously too much longing to hear him call her that again.

She tried to suck in a breath, but only ended up hyperventilating. Not one to lose her shit, she shook her head and tried to erase the images in her mind, or at least change them back to her and Ben setting their bodies ablaze in passion. It didn't work.

"They're dead. The blood. She's gone. She's not coming back. I'm all alone." She admitted her worst fear. That for all her bravado and thinking she didn't need anyone, she'd always known Margo had her back. Someone cared. Someone loved her.

"You're not alone. I'm here. I'll see you through this. I'm not going anywhere."

She sucked in a ragged breath and let it out. Ben kneeled in front of her. He reached out and touched the side of her face, sweeping his fingers through her hair and holding the side of her head. She leaned into his touch, sucking in his warmth and kindness. She needed it right now, because the cold reality of all she'd lost when Margo died hit her hard.

"Why are you doing this?"

Ben looked her right in the eye. "Aside from the reasons I gave you last night, the same reason you haven't told me to go. I want to be here with you. You want me to stay. Let's at least admit that."

"I barely know you."

"We'll work on that while we set things right for Alex. Let's start with having breakfast together."

He made it seem so simple and easy. Why did she think it had to be complicated? Why couldn't she just have breakfast with him? Every friendship had to start somewhere. They'd start here, because he was right—she didn't want him to go.

"I've never had a man make me breakfast." She cocked her head and thought back over her "relationships." "I've never had a man stay overnight."

"See, something we have in common."

"You've never had a man stay over and make you breakfast either?" she teased.

"No." Ben laughed. "And I've never been the guy who does that either."

"But you did it for me," Kate pointed out, not letting him off the hook so easily. She wanted to know that he did it for her because it meant something, not because he felt bad about her sister and her circumstances.

"I wanted to."

Those words conveyed so much more than his simple truth. She appreciated his honesty.

"Let's eat before it gets cold," he coaxed.

Kate caught the nerves in his rushed words. He avoided looking at her, turned, and went back into her kitchen to plate up the eggs he'd left warming on the stove. She left him to rummage through her drawers to come up with forks and went to the table. She smiled down at Alex, picked up the puppy he'd dropped on the table, and pounced it up his belly to his nose all the while saying, "Ruff. Ruff. Ruff." Alex smiled up at her and just like that all the fun and joy disappeared, replaced with the overwhelming sadness that ebbed and flowed since last night.

Tears spilled down her face. Ben set the two plates on the table beside Alex's bouncy seat. His big hands pressed on her shoulders. He squeezed her tight and aching muscles. That and the warmth of his body at her back eased and reassured her.

"It's going to be okay, Kate. You'll get through this."

"I know. It's hard. I look at him and it hits me all at once."

"You need time to grieve. The shock will wear off and you'll settle into your new reality. You'll adjust to being a mother. In fact, I came up with a few things you need to do right away."

Ben pulled out her chair. She sat. He handed her a fork and stared down at her, waiting for her to eat. The man didn't just scramble up some eggs. He'd added cheese and some green onion. She didn't think she was hungry until the food touched her tongue. The taste, the yummy melted cheese, brought her stomach back to life.

Ben took the seat across from her. "You need to call work and take family leave. Time to sort out day care or a babysitter for Alex when you work, to figure out this mess with Margo's and Donald's estates and how that plays with his divorce. I'll help you with funeral arrangements for your sister and Donald. You'll want to go get her stuff before the Faradays swoop in and take over the property."

"They can't. It's in my sister's name. Donald gave it to her."

"Wow. That's quite a gift."

"To prove how much he loved her. To give her a sense of security. You know, she may lose him, but she'd get to keep her home."

"I bet that's important to the two of you after living in the foster care system."

"Yes, it is."

"Do you want to live in your sister's house, or stay here?"

She looked around her tiny place and sighed. She liked it here. The place belonged to her. It's the first real home she'd ever had that no one could take away. Still, she didn't have a yard for Alex to play in, or a room to make his.

"Even if I wanted to live in that mansion, I can't afford the utilities, taxes, and upkeep."

"Are you sure about that? What else did your sister leave you? We have no idea what Donald set up for Alex."

"If anything, right? He might not have done anything for Alex."

"He was a smart businessman. He didn't rush into asking his wife for a divorce even after he and Margo had Alex. He waited. Why? My guess is so that he could plan and make sure Christina and Evan didn't take more than he wanted them to have. He'd have protected Margo and Alex if anything happened to him. You said it yourself—he gave her the house to make her feel safe. To protect her."

"I'll call work, then go down to the bank. I'll see what Margo left in the safe deposit box for her go-bag."

"Excuse me, what?"

"Margo and I only shared two foster homes together. The other three were close by each other. We always kept a stash of what we'd need if we had to run."

"Damn, five different homes. In how many years?"

"About eight."

Ben shook his head, his eyes filled with sorrow. "Tough life."

"I got by. Margo and I got by together."

"Why'd you have to run?"

"You don't want to know."

Ben pressed his forearms on the table and leaned forward, intent on her. "Actually, I do."

"You like hearing about abusive fucks who get their kicks hitting kids, or worse, using them for their sick and twisted sexual fantasies? Or teenagers who prey on younger kids because they're so angry someone preyed on them they want to make someone else feel just as bad?

There are some good foster homes with people who give a shit, but those can be few and far between when you're a kid and all you want is someone to pay attention to you. You get stuck in a cycle of making poor choices and even worse mistakes just so someone will notice you. You get labeled *bad* and *difficult* and no one wants you, so they pass you from one foster home to the next until you never know when that social worker will show up and take you to the next place until they dump you out of the system on your eighteenth birthday."

"It's a shitty way to grow up," Ben agreed. "Do you have any other family?"

"None that wanted me after I shot my father."

"Why'd you do that?" His voice didn't hold a lick of censure or disgust. He genuinely wanted to know how a ten-year-old kid ended up with a gun in her hand and a dead man at her feet. Kate often wondered how it all came down to that sad but inevitable fact.

"He stabbed my mother two dozen times because she refused to bathe me and get me ready for bed. After years of putting up with his ugly mouth, foul behavior, and punishments for whatever slight he perceived, real or imagined, she put her foot down and stood up for me. So many times she'd turned her back, ignored the things he said or did, but that night she refused to back down." Lost in the past, she said, "I remember her crying and screaming. All the blood. On the floor, the walls, him." Her mother's image and Margo's lay separate in her mind, shifted, transposed, then vanished under all that red blood.

Ben settled his hand over hers. The warmth of his touch brought her back. She blinked the nightmares away and shook off the icy shiver racing up her spine.

"I don't even remember getting the gun. I just had it in my hand. My father sat on his knees on the floor beside my mother's dead body. He held the knife in both his bloody hands. His head was down and his chest heaved up and down as he breathed heavy from the exertion of killing her. He sat quiet after he'd jabbed that knife into her all those times. I stood in front of him, my mother dead on the scuffed linoleum. His head came up and his empty gaze met mine. I told him, 'I hate you,' and fired right into his chest. I kept firing even when the bullets were gone." The *click, click, click* of the hammer rang in her head and made her squint and jerk her head just like she did that long ago night.

"A neighbor heard the shots, called the cops, and they found me hiding in the closet my father used to lock me in when I was bad. I must have been really bad because I spent a lot of time in that dark hole.

"I spent some time in juvy, until the prosecutor had no choice but to render the case self-defense. I stuck to my story that he'd raised that knife to kill me after he killed my mother. But he didn't. Doesn't mean he didn't need to be dead."

"My mother killed my father. Shot him." Ben's deep voice came out flat and matter-of-fact, but she heard the underlying hurt and pain. "He liked to beat us. One day, she'd finally had enough. Like you, she knew he needed to be dead or he'd keep coming back to hurt us."

He'd used her words to show her that what she'd done didn't repulse him. A man of the law, he didn't judge her. He understood that what she'd done she had to do, because he understood what his mother had to do for him.

Kate found the courage to finish her tale. "My father had been prepping me for weeks. Hugs that lasted too long when he'd barely hugged me my whole life. He'd touch me, sweep his hand down my cheek and neck and across my chest. He'd pull me out of my seat at the dinner table, wrap his arm around my waist and put his other hand on my chest and ask me about school without caring one bit what I said. The way he looked at me creeped me out. I knew something was coming. The fear in my mother's eyes when she looked at me said all I needed to know. I tried to avoid him, but he went out of his way to find me all the time.

"I've never told anyone but Margo the truth about that night."

"I'm glad you trusted me with what happened. I understand how you felt about him. Scared, always looking over your shoulder, anticipating the next bad thing he'd do because you knew it was coming. I felt the same way about my father."

"What happened to your mother?"

"A very good lawyer got her off. She lives not too far from here. She works at a nonprofit animal rescue. She loves being with the dogs and cats. She married an accountant. He's a total nerd and loves her to death. They take a cruise once a year and barbecue in the backyard during the spring and summer. She's happy."

"So, you like the new guy."

"Anyone is better than my dad, but Tom is exactly what my mother needs. He's kind and thoughtful. He makes her feel special. Hell, the man worships her. That's all I ever wanted for her."

"That's all I wanted for Margo."

"And yourself?" Ben squeezed her hand. Sometime during their talk she'd pushed her empty plate aside and held his hand in both of hers. She stared at their joined hands. She didn't release his, but traced her finger over the veins in the back of it, giving in to her need to touch him, connect with him.

"I've been too busy being practical and working to really think about what I want."

"Until Alex. He opened the door to you believing you could have someone in your life."

"Not just someone. The right someone. I know not all men are bad people. I've just never given any of the good ones a chance. Too stubborn and set in my ways, I suppose."

"Too afraid to take a chance and have them disappoint or hurt you."

She didn't look at him, but nodded to let him know he'd pegged her right. Curious, she met his steady gaze and something in his eyes told her he'd done the same thing with the women in his life, never letting them get too close or attached.

"Things have changed again. I don't just have me to think about. I have Alex. Anyone interested in me has to accept him too."

Ben didn't miss a beat, or look away. "He's a great kid."

To change the subject to something easier for her to deal with, she threw out, "Donald handed me a secret key yesterday."

Ben's eyes narrowed on her. "You mentioned it last night. Did he say anything to you about it?"

" 'Just in case,' " she said, repeating Donald's ominous words.

She should have done what Donald suggested and made Margo come home with her. She should have told Donald if he was worried to take Margo and Alex away somewhere safe. Wishing for things to be different wouldn't change what happened. Too easy to look back and second-guess. All it did was make it harder to deal with reality.

"So, he thought Evan might do something."

"Evan or Christina. Or both of them. From all I've heard, she's not a nice woman. Very self-centered. She cheated on him practically their whole marriage. He turned a blind eye and built his business. He tried his best with Evan."

"Evan is nothing but a spoiled rich kid who thinks he should be given everything."

"Well, he can't have it this time. He doesn't deserve a dime if he killed them. Alex will get what he's due—the estate and justice for his parents' deaths."

"We'll get justice for him." Ben squeezed her hand. "I've got to get home, shower, and change. I'm due in my office by eight-thirty. Detective Raynott said there's an officer watching your sister's house until they clear it as a crime scene, which should be in the next day or so. You can go and pick up what you'll need for Alex. Get into whatever that key opens and find out what Donald left you. Get your sister's stash from the safe deposit box and come to my office. The address and all my phone numbers are programmed into your phone."

She cocked her head to the side. "Wow, you've been busy this morning."

"There's something else I'd like you to consider."

"What's that?"

"Moving into my place."

One of her eyebrows shot up. Her hands stilled on his. She'd continued to absently play with his hand and fingers without really thinking about it. Knowing it didn't make her stop.

"You want me to move in with you?"

"No. Yes." He shook his head. "That didn't come out right. I want you to move into Haven House. Just for a week, maybe longer. To keep you safe. Evan and Christina didn't know about Alex. They thought they'd gotten away with the murder-suicide. Now that they know Alex is due to inherit, they may come after you to get him."

"What?"

"They may even try to kill you to get control of him."

Kate fell back in her chair and raked both hands through her hair. She stared at Alex. Her little boy. So innocent and undeserving of all this turmoil in his life. She thanked God he had no real idea about what happened and all the changes coming to his life.

"I don't want to scare you, Kate, but we need to be careful. We need to protect Alex. I need to protect you."

"You need to protect me?" Did he mean that for his own personal reasons? The hope that he did rose up and made her heart flutter. *Stupid. You can protect yourself.*

"Alex needs his mother."

The answer didn't surprise her, but the disappointment did.

"Besides, if you're close by, we can work on the legal issues faster and . . ." He paused and looked away.

"And?" she prompted.

"I'll have a chance to get to know you better."

"Well, let's hope I come off a lot better in the coming days than I did this morning. I mean, so far all you know about me is that I killed my father and turned into a workaholic social worker."

"That's not all I know. You're a great sister and mother. You love your family. You'd do anything for them. That's important, Kate. That matters."

"Today is my first day being his mother."

"You'll do great." Ben wiped his mouth with his paper napkin and set it on his plate. "I cooked, you clean up. I'm late. I'll see you at my office later today. Call me if anything comes up." He rose and headed for the door. At the last second, he turned and walked back. He stood over her, leaned down, and said, "I know something else about you. You're damn sexy in the morning. You're killing me in that body-hugging dress."

Shocked, her mouth dropped open. Her, sexy? She

glanced down at the simple, comfortable tank dress that did in fact mold to her body.

He groaned, then kissed her on top of the head. "I mean it, be careful. If anything happens, you call me." He walked out the door, reached back in, and locked the handle. He pulled the door shut and tested it to be sure it held.

Nervous by his extra attention to her safety, she stifled the urge to call him back. His warning about Evan and Christina Faraday sent a chill through her. How far would they go to protect the Faraday fortune and cover up the murder? All the way. The simple answer worried her more.

She stood and plucked Alex from his bouncy seat. He whimpered and turned his head to the door.

"I know how you feel. I miss him too." A very hard admission to make, even to her son.

Her son. Alex belonged solely to her now. She'd never let anyone hurt him. She'd protect him to her dying breath. She hoped things with Evan didn't go that far, but if they did, Evan would find her a far more difficult adversary than any other to take down.

Chapter Ten

KATE SET ALEX on the floor inside the small alcove designated for safe deposit box customers inside the bank. She'd arrived just as they opened this morning. She wanted to get this out of the way, hand the papers over to Ben, settle this matter, and get on with her life.

Nothing is ever that easy.

"If there is anything you need, please let me know. When you're ready to return the box to the vault, I'll assist you, but please, take your time." The bank employee backed out of the alcove, allowing her the privacy she needed to sort through the meager belongings her sister left behind from a life cut short.

She tried not to let her mind get mired in all the things her sister would never do, the things she'd miss out on, the things that should have been but would never be. The wave of grief hit her again, but she sucked back the sob rising in her throat, stared at the wood-paneled wall, and blinked the tears away.

"Keep it together, Kate."

She stared down at Alex. He stared back at her. Such a sweet face, so trusting that she'd see to his every need. Well, he needed her to do this.

Kate opened the lid of the large box and stared inside. Several folders, envelopes, and stacks of cash. The money had to come from Donald. She'd hoarded it away for a rainy day. Kate had her own stash of cash, but nothing like this. She counted the bundles and came up with sixty-five thousand dollars.

"Well, you've got a college fund," she said to Alex.

She opened one envelope after another, discovering Alex's birth certificate, the deed to Margo's house, the pink slip to her Mercedes, and Margo's will. Her life reduced to what she owned and the money she saved. Nothing but papers locked away in a box.

Kate stuffed the papers into her leather satchel. She put most of the money back in the safe deposit box, but pulled out five thousand in cash just in case. Ben said he'd help her for free, but she wanted to give him something for all the help she'd need to go up against the Faraday lawyers. No doubt Christina and Evan would fight her for every last dime they could get their hands on.

Finished, she called out, "Excuse me, I'm done."

The bank employee walked over, took the box, and escorted Kate back into the vault to lock it back up. Ready to leave, but dreading her next task, she picked up Alex in his car seat and headed out of the bank to her car in the lot. She secured Alex in the backseat, slid into the driver's seat, and dumped her purse and satchel on the passenger's side.

Her phone chirped with a text message.

BEN: *Heading into court for at least an hour. Everything okay?*

KATE: *Finished at the bank. Heading to Margo's house, then the morgue to collect Margo's personal items. Funeral home after that.*

BEN: *Need any help?*

KATE: *I got this part. You get the legal papers.*

BEN: *Bring them to my office when you're done.*

KATE: *'K.*

Kate started the car and backed out of her parking space. Her phone chirped again.

BEN: *I liked having breakfast with you. See you soon.*

Kate stared at her phone and took those words into her fluttering heart. "I liked breakfast with you too," she said to her phone, but didn't type it back to him. Those simple words wouldn't tell him how much it meant to her that he stayed last night, a solid, protective presence to see her through the grief and keep the nightmares at bay. How could she tell him that his being there this morning had made it easier to face the day? Just knowing he was waiting for her, ready and willing to help her through all of this, comforted her. At the same time, her need to see him, her wanting to have him close, scared her.

She'd always had the strength and conviction to get through anything on her own. Relying on someone else went against everything she'd learned. She wanted to believe he'd come through for her. Maybe his help would make a difference. Maybe it would make things easier to share the burden. If he let her down, it would hurt. She knew that already, despite the fact they barely knew each other.

Someone blasted their horn behind her. She pulled forward to the parking lot exit and got out of their way. If she got out of her own way and let things happen naturally, maybe she and Ben would have a shot at . . . something. Their acquaintance had turned to friendship this morning. Maybe it could turn to something more. She'd like a shot at something more with the sexy lawyer, whose smile did something strange to her insides.

The forty-minute drive over to her sister's house gave her far too much time to think. About Ben mostly. She easily distracted herself with thoughts of him, because thinking of her sister ate at her insides and made her gut sour. She hated being sad. The empty pit in her stomach expanded every time she thought of her sister and all she should've, could've, would've done in her life. So she held back the pain building inside of her with thoughts of one hot lawyer and the multitude of tasks she needed to accomplish to put her life back in order now that everything had changed.

Alex slept peacefully in his car seat. God, what she wouldn't give to be too young to know and remember what was happening. It hit her hard again, all Alex would never know about his father and Margo.

Kate drove past the police car out front, pulled into

the driveway, and stared up at the big house. The home Margo planned to raise Alex. The embodiment of Margo's dreams. Kate's condo was great for her, but a little boy needed space, his own room, a yard to play in. So many things to think about and do. Not just to finalize Margo's estate, but to do and provide for Alex.

She snagged the satchel off the seat, stepped out of the car, opened the back door, and pulled Alex out. His eyes squinted at the bright sunlight. She quickly pulled the shade down on his car seat. He fussed and kicked, ready to be free of the restraints.

"Just a minute. I'll get you out of there and let you stretch out on the floor in your room with your toys."

She walked up the path and met the officer who got out of his squad car parked in front of the house.

"I'm sorry, ma'am, but this is a crime scene. You can't go inside."

"My name is Kate Morrison. Detective Raynott spoke with Ben Knight this morning and cleared me to pick up some things for my son." She took a deep breath and let that sink in. Her son. It got easier each time she said it, thought it, embraced it. Too easy. How could she ever think she'd get over or be okay letting Margo raise her child? She'd struggled so much these last months and distanced herself from Margo and Alex. The guilt overwhelmed her that a part of her was happy to have Alex back and Margo out of the picture.

"Miss Morrison, are you okay?" the officer asked.

Tears slid down both her cheeks. She swiped them

away with her free hand and glanced down at Alex in his seat. She sucked in a ragged breath and silently apologized for her dark thoughts and betraying her sister.

"Um, this is the first time I've been back since I found my sister's body. I'm sorry, it just hit me all at once."

"No problem. I'll just need to see your ID and you can go inside."

"Thank you." Kate dug her wallet out of her bag and showed her driver's license to the officer.

He nodded. "Um, the kitchen is . . . off-limits."

"I know." They'd removed the bodies, but the kitchen hadn't been scrubbed clean of the gruesome remains.

The officer eyed her. "Take your time. If you need anything, I'll be right out here."

"It's f-fine. I'm fine." She stuttered out the words with little reassurance behind them.

He turned, and went back down the path to his patrol car.

Kate trudged up the wide stone steps to the front door, inserted her key, and pushed the door open, but didn't go inside. She stared into the foyer and kitchen far beyond. In the daylight, she could see all the way to the back of the house to the dark bloodstained marble tile floor.

Oh, right, one more thing she needed to add to her list—schedule a crew to come and erase the reality that couldn't be scrubbed from her mind.

Just call 1-800-crime-scene-cleanup for all your crime scene needs.

Oh, God, I'm losing it.

Alex kicked and fussed. Maybe he knew he was home

and wanted to be amid his things. Either way, she needed to get moving and do what had to be done. She set the car seat on the floor, unstrapped Alex, and picked him up. She held him to her chest. He head-butted her and gurgled a bunch of nonsense. She hugged him close, rubbing her hand up and down his back.

"Come on, big guy, let's get this done."

She walked into the office to the left and dropped her satchel on Donald's desk, noting the many folders scattered on top. His briefcase sat on the floor beside the desk. It looked like he'd been working the night before, like he'd be back any second to sit down and finish. But he wouldn't. He was gone too.

She liked him, but had never given much thought to how she really felt about him. Alex's father. Now, she let the emotions come. How kind and generous he was to her and Margo. She wished she'd known him better. She wished she had a million little stories to tell Alex one day about the man who lit up whenever he looked at his son.

The picture on his desk drew her attention. She picked up the silver frame and stared down at the beautiful couple. Donald, dressed in a dark suit, stood beside Margo. Her sister looked lovely in a blue dress. Her favorite color. Donald held Margo close to his side with his arm around her waist. Margo stared up at him with a brilliant smile. Donald looked down at her, that same look of love and adoration she'd seen last night before she left.

God, had it only been last night? It felt like a lifetime ago. So much had changed in such a short time.

She turned the picture to Alex. "Look at them. They were happy and in love—the kind of love that lasts." She had to believe that whimsical thought. "I hope you find that one day." She hoped she found it for herself, for Alex's sake. He needed a man in his life. A good man to show him what one looked and acted like.

Ben popped into her mind. So, deep down she thought he was such a man. She must if she was willing to trust him to help her. Maybe she was just desperate for someone to get her through this, because the emptiness gnawing at her insides without her sister hurt too much to bear alone.

Kate stuffed the picture into her bag. She'd keep it for Alex. For herself. To remind her of all that could have been, all she was fighting for.

"Come on, let's go get some more of your things from your room."

Kate walked up the stairs, trying not to let herself feel the emptiness and quiet of the house. It spooked her. Like her sister's and Donald's ghosts were still here, pushing her to do something, fix this.

Alex's room seemed so peaceful and sweet. Light blue with painted birds flying across the walls. A happy little bunny stared out of a bunch of grass from the baseboard. This room was nothing like the dull, dingy places she and Margo grew up in.

"Here you go, lucky baby." She laid him down in his crib. He squealed and flapped his arms, trying to reach for the zoo animals spinning around on his mobile.

Unable to help herself, she smoothed her hand over his belly and smiled.

With Alex safe in his crib to play and stretch after being cooped up for over an hour, she went to his dark wood dresser and pulled out several more sets of clothes and bibs. The kid drooled as much as he spit up his food. She pulled a few books from the shelves. Snagged the baby book about what to expect the first year off the nightstand. "I'm definitely going to need this." She found a bag and several spare blankets in the closet. She stuffed everything into the oversized tote and turned back to the room.

"What am I doing?" She didn't know where they'd live, or what she really needed now versus for wherever they landed in the future.

She shook her head, pulled the tote strap up her arm to her shoulder, and went to the crib. Alex smiled up at her, happy to be in his house, his room, surrounded by his things, in his bed.

"Hi, happy baby. I promise I'll fix this and have you back to your routine." She didn't know much about raising a child, but in her line of work she'd learned one thing. Kids needed stability.

She carried Alex back downstairs to the office. She took one of the blankets from the tote and spread it on the floor, laying Alex down with a stuffed giraffe she'd also grabbed from his room. He held it by the neck and shook it, rattling the beads hidden inside. He smiled with delight and her heart felt lighter.

With Alex happy and settled next to her, she opened the double doors on the credenza and stared at the safe. She didn't know the combo, but pulled the key from her pocket, inserted it into the lock, and turned. She pushed the handle down and the door popped open. She sucked in a deep breath, opened the door wide, and stared at the contents.

Margo's jewelry. More cash. Lots of files. She pulled out the ones that appeared to have been hastily stuffed on top of several velvet jewelry boxes. She opened the first one. Divorce papers for Donald and Christina. The second contained a brand-new will dated two weeks ago. The third held the adoption papers she'd signed for Margo to become Alex's legal mother. She stared at the bottom of the page, a sense of dread coming over her. She flipped through the other folders, including the documents from the fertility clinic. One folder held a lab report that rocked her to the core.

"It can't be true."

She turned and stared at her son; his blue eyes stared back at her. Her blue eyes. She saw so many pieces of herself in him.

Lost in her dark thoughts, she jumped when her phone chirped.

BEN: *Find everything you need?*

KATE: *We have a big problem.*

BEN: *What's happened?*

What could Kate say? If this was true, she needed to show Ben the papers and figure out what it meant. How it happened? Who the fuck was responsible for this catastrophe?

KATE: *Unforeseen complication.*

BEN: *What does that mean?*

KATE: *I'll bring you the papers and maybe you can tell me.*

BEN: *Come now.*

KATE: *On my way.*

She'd go to the morgue and make arrangements for her sister after she showed Ben the papers. She needed to know what this meant for her and Alex. If they were true, the Faradays might just get everything.

The angry huff she let out startled Alex. He jumped, his eyes wide when she turned to him.

"It's okay, sweetheart. Mommy will take care of everything. Let's go see Ben."

Alex smiled and babbled, wiggling like he couldn't wait to go. Funny, the anticipation and trills rippling inside surprised her. She wanted to see Ben. She couldn't wait to see him, and it had nothing to do with needing his help.

Chapter Eleven

EVAN DIDN'T WANT to go back to the scene of the crime. His damn mother forced him. She didn't want to step foot in the other woman's house. So here he stood on the steps with a fucking cop beside him.

"I'm sorry, sir, but you aren't authorized to go inside."

"This is my father's house," he explained for the third time.

"No, it isn't," a woman said behind him, standing in the now-open doorway.

He turned to the sultry voice that snapped out those words. The woman was even better than the voice. Long dark hair, startlingly blue eyes dominating her heart-shaped face. The scowl only made her lush lips more appealing. Not that tall, maybe five-five, slender with just a hint of curve to her hips, and full breasts that would be more than a handful. The longer he stared, the harder she glared. He liked a woman with attitude.

"Who are you?" he asked, very interested in getting to know her better.

"Your worst fucking nightmare."

Her spunk only made him smile more. "Is that right? Well, do you have a name?"

"Kate Morrison. Margo was my sister."

"Who?"

"You don't even know the name of the woman you shot last night?"

Well, fuck. He didn't expect that. Luckily, he schooled his features and shut down his surprise with a good dose of anger. "Hold it right there." Evan took a menacing step toward her.

The cop planted a hand on his chest to stop him. "Stay where you are."

"She's fucking accusing me of killing her sister." He turned to Kate. "I had nothing to do with it. The police informed my mother and me late last night that my father and his mistress were killed."

"You mean your father's fiancé."

"He planned to marry her?" Evan should have guessed. The look in his father's eye when he looked at the woman told him how deeply his father cared for her. Didn't matter now.

"He gave her a ring and everything. He loved her. He wanted to make a life with her because she was warm and kind and sweet and thoughtful." Her voice cracked on those words. "She made him happy. Can your mother say the same?"

No. Evan didn't speak the word. What use was it to

defend his mother and a marriage neither of them participated in for years?

His gaze fell and landed on the car seat and the little boy dozing off with a giraffe in his hands. "Is that my brother?"

"He's mine now. And so is this house and everything in it. My sister's name is on the property, not your father's. You're trespassing. Leave."

The officer perked back up again. "Let's go, sir. This is a crime scene. No one is allowed in without permission from Detective Raynott."

"I need to get my father's papers."

"No," Kate snapped.

"You've already gone through them, haven't you?"

She didn't answer, but the gleam in her eyes was all he needed as confirmation.

"Hand them over."

"I have a meeting with my lawyer. Get off my property."

"Your property."

"That's right. Mine. My sister left this property to me and Alex."

Evan walked right up to her. He used his height to intimidate her. She stared up at him, not the least scared. In fact, the anger in her eyes flashed even hotter.

"You don't get to fucking tell me what to do at my father's home."

"Are you deaf or just stupid? This is my house."

Evan didn't think. He reacted and grabbed her by the throat. "Listen, you bitch . . ."

The officer put his hand on Evan's shoulder. "Let her go. Now."

Somehow she managed to slam her hand into his hand and make him lose his grip. She held his forearm, pulled it around and behind his back, kicked him in the back of the leg, sending him down to his knees and falling to the pavement. She landed on his back, her knee digging into his spine, his arm so high up his back he thought it might snap, or pull his shoulder right out of the socket.

"Miss Morrison, let him up." The officer stood over the two of them. "This has gone too far."

Kate leaned down next to his ear. "That's a nasty bruise on your jaw you've got. She hit you, didn't she? She cut you with that knife. You fucking touch me again, it'll be the last thing you ever do. You hear me?"

"Get her fuck off me before she breaks my arm," he yelled at the cop.

"Miss Morrison, please. Enough. Self-defense is one thing, but you're over the line. Back off."

"He started it." She glared down at Evan again. "I'm the one who's going to finish it. Count on it." She pushed her knee into his spine harder, then jumped off him, letting him go all at once. She went to the front door, grabbed the baby, and closed the door, locking it with her key.

It took Evan a second to gain his feet. Between her and her sister, he had enough aches and pains to make him forget he deserved them.

Right now, he wanted to make the bitch pay, but the

cop stepped between him and Kate and shook his head. "Touch her again and I will arrest you for assault."

Evan gained his head and thought twice about going after her again. For now.

"I want to see my brother."

"No. Stay away from this house, me, and Alex."

"He's my brother. I have a right to see him."

"You lost all rights the second you pulled that trigger and killed your father and my sister."

"I didn't kill them. I was at home with my mother."

"No one believes that bullshit story. Soon, the cops will prove you were here last night. You killed them. I will make you pay for that."

Evan hated to retreat. Not his style, but she had him by the balls. Nothing he could do with a cop standing between them. "Fuck this, I'm out of here as soon as you give me my father's papers." He held out his hand for her to give them over.

She smiled in a not so nice way. "I don't know what you're talking about. Excuse me, but I'm late to see my lawyer."

"Ben Knight, right? I beat him before, I'll do it again."

She looked him right in the eye. "You won't beat me."

"We'll see about that."

"You *will* see. I'm not some weak person you can trounce with your fists or your money. If you know what's good for you, stay away from me and Alex. If you don't, I'll have you on the ground again. Maybe next time, you won't get up."

"Threatening me in front of a cop. Not smart."

"I don't make threats. I make promises. I will keep the one I made to my sister and your father." She eyed the cop without a hint of trepidation she might actually get arrested for threatening him. "If he comes back, arrest him for trespassing."

If he didn't want to take a swing at her so bad and shut that smart mouth, he might like her. She had guts.

Why the hell did he even come here? His mother should go to his father's lawyers and get copies of whatever his father set up along with divorcing her. He needed to lie low before the cops did find evidence to put him behind bars for good.

He turned without another word and headed for his car, rolling his shoulder to work out the sore muscles and tendons after Kate laid him out. God, he needed a drink, or ten. She wouldn't get the better of him again. In fact, he planned to teach her a lesson. She wouldn't get away with speaking to him in that haughty tone, or besting him in a fight. She wouldn't take everything that belonged to him. He'd make sure of it. That was a promise he intended to keep.

Chapter Twelve

BEN SAT AT his desk, trying not to check the time again. Kate said she was on her way. She should have arrived twenty minutes ago even with traffic. According to the traffic alert on his computer, there were no accidents reported. Where the hell was she?

A knock sounded on his door a second before the door swung open and Jenna, Elizabeth, and Marti walked right in without his assistant announcing them. He loved seeing them, but never expected them to show up at his office.

"What are you doing here?" He might have snapped that out a bit too brusquely judging by the narrowed gazes he received.

Jenna smiled and came around his desk to hug him. "We are here to see how it went last night."

"What are you talking about?" Dumbfounded, he didn't follow, just stared in wonder as Jenna sat on the edge of his desk and Marti and Elizabeth took the two chairs in front like they owned the place.

"Morgan's premonition. You met her last night, right?" Marti asked.

"Her?" he asked, trying to play dumb. He should know better.

"Oh, come on. Don't leave us in suspense. What's her name?"

Ben checked the time, worried that another five minutes had passed with no word from Kate.

"What's wrong?" Jenna asked, reading the concern he couldn't hide.

"Her name is Kate Morrison. She's supposed to be here, but she's late."

"So, we'll get to meet her." Marti smiled.

"If she shows up."

"So, you don't mind introducing her to us?" Jenna asked. "Your family?"

"No. You'll like her. She's a lot like you guys. Strong. Independent. Tough, but nice. Beautiful."

"Just like us," Elizabeth teased, using his words.

He laughed under his breath. "Just like all of you. She's got a good heart she hides well. She doesn't trust easily. Not surprising since her background is in some ways like mine and in others a lot worse."

"She sounds fascinating," Jenna said. "How did you meet her last night?"

"I've actually met her several times. She's a social worker down in San Jose. I got a call from a detective I know that someone I tried to put behind bars may have killed a man and woman last night. Kate's sister was one of the victims. She pointed the finger at the man's son. Evan and I have gone a few rounds. He killed the son of one of my Haven House families and beat one of my clients near to death. His father settled the suit by paying off my client."

"Now, you think he killed his father and Kate's sister?" Marti's eyes filled with sadness.

"The evidence is circumstantial at the moment. We're waiting for some lab results. I've promised to help Kate settle the estate for her son."

"She has a child?" Jenna asked.

"A son. Alex. He looks just like her, right down to his blue eyes. Margo wasn't able to have a child of her own, so Kate agreed to be artificially inseminated. She gave birth to Alex four months ago. Alex is Evan's father's son. Donald had just filed for divorce from Evan's mother. He planned to marry Margo and they'd raise Alex."

"That's an amazing thing Kate did for her sister."

"She's an amazing woman." Ben hadn't really meant to say that out loud. To all of them.

"So, she's the one. Morgan was right," Elizabeth said.

"I don't know if what I feel for her is because of what Morgan said, or because it's how I really feel."

"You know." Jenna reached out and squeezed his shoulder. "You're just afraid to admit she means something to you because then you have to admit that Morgan was right. All of us have been wary of things Morgan knows, but she's never wrong."

"I'm not afraid Morgan is wrong. I'm afraid she's right. What do I do then? I don't do relationships. The longest one I've ever had lasted less than three months."

"That's only because they weren't Kate," Marti pointed out. "You've been waiting for her."

Ben shook his head. Leave it to the ladies to make this some grand romantic gesture. "The relationships never last because I'm not husband material."

"I call bullshit," Elizabeth said.

"Me too," Marti added.

"You're afraid that one day you'll wake up and find you are your father's son." Jenna spoke the truth he didn't want to admit to them or himself. "That simply isn't true. You are a kind and decent man who would never hurt anyone, let alone a woman. You care for the weakest, most vulnerable people with compassion. It simply isn't in you to hurt people just because you can. Look at all the lives you've changed at Haven House. You can't tell me that you look in the mirror and see anything but a good guy."

Elizabeth and Marti nodded, agreeing with everything Jenna said.

He sighed out his trepidation. He wanted something more with Kate, but with everything going on, now might not be the time to pursue something deeper. She needed his help.

"If not now, then when?" Jenna asked, reading his mind. "She's in your life now. Don't let her get away. If you like her, tell her. If you want to be with her, be with her. For once, Ben, don't go into a relationship with one foot in and one out the door. Go all in."

A baby cried outside his office door. He was up and striding for it before he consciously thought about going to get Kate. The door opened and she walked in with Alex in his car seat at her side.

"I'm going to kill that fucking bastard," she announced. The anger clouding her eyes said she meant every word.

Still worried that it took her so long to get here, he scanned her from the feet up, stopping on the red marks on her neck. "What the hell happened to you?" He reached out, laid his hand on her shoulder, and swept his thumb over one dark bruise.

"He fucking tried to choke me."

"Evan?" The anger exploded inside of him and made his chest swell and his hand fist.

"Don't worry, I laid him out on the ground. Next time, I'll kill him."

Alex let out a wail that made Ben squint his eyes against the pain in his ears. "What's wrong with him?"

"He needs a bottle, or a diaper, or a mother who knows what she's doing, because obviously I don't."

Ben laughed when Kate squatted to pick up Alex. "Lucky for you, I have three of the best mothers in the world right here."

Kate's head snapped up and her gaze went past him to all three very interested women.

"Hi," they said in unison.

Kate's eyes closed as she exhaled deeply. "Oh, God,

I am so sorry. I had no idea you were in a meeting. No one was outside, so I let myself in. I'm sorry, Ben, ladies, there's no excuse for my poor behavior."

Alex wailed even louder. Ben took him and bounced him in his arms. "Kate, relax. These are my very good friends." He held his hand out. "Jenna is . . . well, my friend, client, and partner in Haven House. We've known each other a long time. Elizabeth is her sister-in-law. They're married to twin brothers."

"Really?" Kate asked, interested.

"Identical twins," Jenna confirmed. "I have twin boys too."

"Wow."

"Last but not least, Marti is married to my cousin, Cameron, who is also the president of Jenna's company, Merrick International. Now, between these three ladies, they have seven children. Elizabeth's Grace left her hand-print on my shirt last night."

Kate smiled softly. "The little girl who's got you wrapped around her finger."

"She's not the only one. Ask these guys. I do their bidding too."

Kate laughed. "Really?"

"He's a tough one," Jenna said, "but we manage to get him to say yes most of the time."

Alex's crying softened, but he squirmed and whacked his hand into his mouth a couple of times. "I think he's hungry."

Elizabeth stood and came forward. "Kate, so nice to meet you. Do you have a bottle in the bag?"

"Uh, yeah." Kate dug it out along with the can of formula.

Elizabeth took both. "Great. How many ounces does he eat?"

"Six. I can do that."

"It's no trouble. I know where the kitchenette is. I'll warm some water, mix up the milk, and be back in a jiffy."

Jenna stole Alex right out of Ben's hands. "Come here, little one. What's all the fuss? We'll get you fixed up right away." Jenna didn't ask for the diaper bag, just picked it up off the floor and took it to the sofa with her. She pulled out a diaper and the pad and laid it and Alex out on the couch. "Let's get you clean and dry. Aunt Elizabeth will be back with your food and you'll be all set," Jenna crooned.

Kate stared up at him.

"They've got this. Tell me what happened at your sister's house."

Kate took a deep breath and let it out. "First, I got all the papers from Margo's safe deposit box. It's everything I expected. Alex's birth certificate, the deed to the house in her name, her will, stuff like that. Then I got the papers from the safe at the house. They don't make sense. It can't be. You have to find out who is responsible for this mistake and sue them."

"Wait. What are you talking about?"

Kate pulled the strap up and over her head. She set the heavy messenger bag on the chair Elizabeth vacated and pulled out the folders. She handed him several papers.

Ben read through them quickly, trying to understand

what it all meant. "This is a DNA test. Donor #1 is not a match to Donald Faraday."

"According to that, Alex isn't his son."

"That doesn't make sense. The papers from the fertility clinic clearly state you were inseminated with Donald Faraday's sperm."

"Someone made a huge mistake. If Alex isn't Donald's child, he gets nothing."

Jenna stepped up beside them with Alex in her arms. Kate touched her fingers to Alex's head. "If he's not Donald's son, who is his father?"

Ben hated seeing the tears in Kate's eyes.

"He just lost his mother and father. Now, I don't even know who his father is?"

"How could this happen?" Marti asked the question all of them were thinking.

"I don't know, but I'm going to find out. I'll contact the clinic. We need to know for sure what happened and whether or not Donald really is Alex's father."

"But the DNA test says he's not."

"It says Donor #1, not Alex Faraday. If I'm to prove anything in court, we'll need confirmation one way or another. Let's start there. Mistakes happen. Maybe the test is wrong. Maybe the lab that ran the DNA test made the mistake and not the clinic. Whatever the answer, we'll get it," he assured Kate.

"That's not all I found. Donald and Margo never filed the adoption papers. A judge never signed them. If Donald found out Alex wasn't his son, it explains why they never filed with the court."

"Maybe they didn't file the papers because Margo knew you were having trouble giving Alex up. Maybe she wanted to wait in case you changed your mind and wanted him back."

Kate bit her bottom lip, the tears spilling from her eyes. "The evidence points to the fact the clinic made a mistake. They didn't want him if he wasn't Donald's."

"Kate, honey, you know that's not true. They loved him. They wanted him." He held up Donald's will. "Donald had this drawn up only two weeks ago. After this DNA test was done. He left everything to Margo and his son Alex. What does that tell you?"

"I don't know. It's all so confusing now. Everything I thought was true is muddled with those other papers. One says one thing and the others say something completely different."

Ben gave in to his need to touch her. He cupped her cheek in his hand and rubbed his thumb over the soft slope, taking away her tears. "We'll sort it out. I promise."

Elizabeth arrived with Alex's bottle. "Here we go."

"We'll leave you two alone," Jenna said, handing Alex off to Kate, who took the bottle from Elizabeth and pushed the nipple into Alex's open mouth.

"So nice to meet you, Kate." Marti pressed her hand to Kate's shoulder. "If you need anything, we're all here to help."

"Thank you. I'm sorry for all the swearing and yelling. Everything is kind of a mess right now."

"Ben will help you sort it out. He's good at that kind of thing," Jenna said, hugging him goodbye. "Evan will wish

he never met either of you when you get done with him."
Jenna caught his eye. "Whatever you need, it's yours, all
you have to do is ask."

"Thank you, Jenna. I appreciate it."

The three ladies left his office without another word.

"What did she mean by that?"

"Exactly what she said, and a whole lot she didn't say.
Jenna has the means to provide us with whatever help we
need. Elizabeth's husband is an FBI agent, so we've got
some help there if we need it."

"You think we need a federal agent."

"No, but it's nice to have someone with a badge on
our side. Elizabeth's father is also a very prominent
judge."

"You hang out with some very well-connected people."

"They're my family." He really did mean that. Which
meant he needed to stop holding himself apart from
them. "I don't want to use them, but if we get into a jam,
they might come in handy."

Kate took the seat in front of his desk. She fed Alex
and stared up at him. "What do we do first?"

"You take a break. Let me call the clinic and set a fire
under them to figure this out." He brushed his hand over
her hair. Her eyes softened and she leaned into his hand.
"Did you eat anything for lunch?"

"No. I came straight here after my run-in with Evan."

"Does your neck hurt?"

"It's sore. Not as sore as his arm and shoulder are
though."

That made Ben smile and his chest swell with pride. It

also settled his tense gut. Kate could definitely take care of herself. "You should press charges."

"The cop watching the house saw the whole thing. He came at me first, but I put him in his place. Leave it alone for now. I want him to go down for murder, not get out of another assault charge. Besides, I threatened to kill him in front of the cop. The last thing we need is for him to press charges against me and leave Alex vulnerable."

"Kate . . ."

"I know. I lost my temper."

He rubbed his fingers deep into her hair and the back of her neck. He rubbed the tense muscles. "I hate seeing you hurt."

"It's nothing. You need to call the clinic."

"You need some food. You need to take care of yourself."

She leaned back into his hand. He rubbed harder and she groaned.

"You're doing a good job of taking care of me right now." Her gaze shot up to his. "That came out wrong."

"No. It didn't. Wait here, I'll be right back." Ben left his office, walked to the kitchenette, and rummaged through the refrigerator and cupboards. He made Kate lunch and took it back to his office along with a bottle of water.

"Here you go."

"You made me a peanut butter and jelly sandwich."

"I keep some staples here in the office for those days and nights I work right through lunch and dinner."

Kate popped a grape into her mouth. "Fresh fruit too."

"The grocery store delivers once a week for me and the staff."

"Lucky staff."

"It pays to keep them happy. They work harder and barely complain about the long hours." Ben took his seat and grabbed the papers Kate brought. "You eat. Let me take care of this." He picked up the phone, dialed the number on the clinic's form, and said the only thing he needed to say to get to the person who could help him. "This is Ben Knight. I'm filing a lawsuit against your clinic for impregnating my client with the wrong sperm. Who should I speak to . . . ?"

The person who answered transferred him, and he spent the next ten minutes explaining what he knew, what Kate and Donald had set up at the clinic, and the DNA test he held in his hands. He hung up and stared across at Kate. The fatigue and sadness in her eyes killed him.

"They'll review their records. I'll take you down there on the way to the morgue. They'll run a DNA test on Alex and compare it to our lab report."

"You asked them to verify it against the DNA test the police are running on the bloody knife that they'll compare to Donald also."

"Never hurts to cover all our bases."

Kate dumped her empty plate in the trash bin beside the desk. "Thanks for lunch."

"I'll do better than a sandwich next time."

"Don't worry about it. Raspberry jelly is my favorite."

He smiled. "Mine too."

"Shall we go?" she asked. The weariness in her voice matched the look in her eyes.

"Any chance I can send you to Tahiti for a few weeks until I sort this all out and Evan is behind bars?"

"Nope. But if he comes near me or Alex again, will you at least bail me out?"

Ben bobbed his head sideways. "Of course."

"Let's get this done."

They drove in near silence to the fertility clinic. Alex slept in the backseat of his Audi RS 7.

"I can't believe you put a car seat in the back of this sports car."

"Why?"

"I don't know. It doesn't seem right."

"I drive clients around in this all the time."

"I bet the speed and other bells and whistles impress, but let's face it, this isn't exactly a family car."

"Sure it is. This is a dad's kind of family car." That didn't earn him even the hint of a fake smile.

"When we conceived Alex, we all went to the clinic together. Margo and Donald disappeared into a room together. I don't know what they did in there, but a few minutes later, Donald came out with the sperm."

Ben laughed at her choice of words. Came. Hey, he was a guy, he couldn't help himself.

"Margo and I went into another room. I dropped my pants and they . . . you know." She cocked her head. "I teased Margo that she got all the fun, and I got all the work." She went quiet again. "I don't know how they could have messed it up."

"We'll get to the bottom of it. No matter what, Alex is your son. Margo left you the house and everything else. You've got more than enough to take care of him. You give him the only thing he really needs."

She rolled her head to look at him.

"You love him, Kate. It doesn't matter who his father is."

"It does matter. Evan and Christina don't deserve to take everything Donald left behind. Not after what they've done to him."

"Maybe that's exactly how he felt when he named Alex in his will. Maybe it didn't matter to him at all that Alex wasn't his biological son. He planned to leave him everything. He wanted to take care of him. You saw Donald and your sister with Alex. Did you ever get the feeling they didn't want him?"

"Never. They loved him so much."

"If I've learned anything from being around Jenna and her huge family, it isn't the blood you share but the bonds you create with the people who are closest to you."

"I liked them."

"They liked you."

"Why were they there? Seems strange they'd visit you at your office."

"They came to meet you."

"They did? Why?"

"Because of something Morgan said last night at dinner."

"Who's Morgan? What did Morgan say?"

"Another friend. It's not important."

"If it has to do with me, I want to know. I mean, they don't even know me."

Ben didn't want to sound like a lunatic. "Listen, Morgan is special. She isn't like other people."

"How do you mean?"

"She has a gift. Several actually."

"Are you trying not to tell me she's psychic?"

"Yes."

"Reeeally." Kate drew out the word with every ounce of skepticism he'd once had.

"She's the real deal. She works with her husband, Tyler, for the FBI. She's solved a lot of cases."

"Okay. You have my attention. So, what did she say about me?"

"Nothing. She just said I'd meet you last night."

"You met me a long time ago. What did she really say?"

Ben parked the car and shut off the engine. He stared out the window at the building, trying to decide what to say. Certainly not the truth. She'd think him crazy. He still didn't know if he believed it.

Liar, a voice in his head yelled out.

Kate's hand settled over his. "Ben, whatever she said, you can tell me."

"She made a prediction. I'll tell you exactly what she said when I'm certain it's come true."

"That's it. That's what you're leaving me with?"

He smiled at her incredulity. "Yes." With that, he

slipped from the car and took Alex out of the backseat. Kate met him at the front of the car.

It didn't take long for the director of the facility to make a dozen assurances that everything about the procedure had been standard practice and there couldn't possibly be a mistake. They didn't want to say or do anything that could be used against them in court. Ben assured them that at this point they only wanted the truth. A technician swabbed Alex's mouth and Ben escorted Kate back to his car. Inside, he took her hand and linked his fingers with hers.

"We'll have our answer in a couple of days."

Kate didn't say anything. She stared out the window as he drove to the morgue. She never let go of his hand. He settled into the drive, content to have her by his side.

The morgue attendant tried to make things smooth and easy for them, but Kate still fell into his car pale and exhausted, a plastic bag of her sister's personal items in her lap. He secured Alex in the back, making sure he had his pacifier and puppy for the ride to Haven House.

"You can make the final arrangements with the funeral home tomorrow."

"It shouldn't take long. I'll have her cremated. I don't know what Christina will have planned for Donald's body. I wish I could scatter their ashes together. They'd want that."

"I'll talk to Donald's lawyer and see if I can make that happen."

Kate took his offered hand again. "Thank you for doing all of this."

"I want to, Kate. Anything you need, I'm here for you."

She squeezed his hand, then pulled free and opened the plastic bag. She took out her sister's diamond engagement ring and slipped it on her right ring finger.

"That ring has got to be worth a small fortune."

"She'd want me to keep it to remember that dreams do come true. She kept trying to get me to believe. The thing is, I did believe because I saw how happy she was to be marrying the man she loved. A good man, despite the circumstances. She'd want me to remember the past doesn't have to be my future. I'm not that same little girl locked away in a closet." Kate held her hand up and stared at the sparkling solitaire. "She loved me. I'm worth loving."

The last words came out on a whisper, but he heard her. He'd felt the same way when he was a young boy, terrified, watching his father beat his mother while he stood by helpless. He felt that way every time he got beat. Maybe a part of him still felt that way.

He took her hand again and squeezed. "It's beautiful. You two shared a close bond. I've never had anyone in my life like you've had Margo." He'd been pushing people away the same way Kate did to him. She'd let Margo behind her walls. She'd opened the door for him to step through. Now all he needed to do was find a way to make her want him to stay, because for the first time in his life, he wanted to pull someone close. He wanted to let Kate into his life and share it with him.

"What about Jenna and the others?"

"I'm closer to Jenna than anyone, but I still hold her at a distance."

"You should stop doing that. It's so obvious those ladies love you. They came to your office to check on you."

Ben laughed. "Yeah, they did." He needed to stop pushing them away. Their invitations to be a part of the group could taper off until they stopped altogether if he made them feel like he didn't want to belong—even though that's not really what he wanted. He hated that he might make them feel that way and vowed to be a better friend. The kind they'd been to him.

"Does Jenna's husband mind that she's so close to you?"

Ben shrugged. "Not really. Jack and I were college roommates. We're still good friends. When Jenna needed a place to hide from her ex-husband, I sent her to Jack, hoping he could keep her safe. He did, then he just kept her. He owes me. They are very happy together."

"And you're happy for them. You love her, but you're not in love with her."

Ben took his eyes off the road and looked at her. "I'm glad you see the difference. Though when you meet the whole crew, you'll see there's a running gag that Jack stole Jenna from me."

"I'm meeting your family?" Surprise and trepidation filled her soft voice.

This time he didn't take his eyes from the road and said very softly, "I hope so."

"I'd like to meet them." An uncharacteristic shyness laced those softly spoken words.

Unable to speak, he brought their joined hands to his mouth and kissed the back of hers. Neither of them found it easy to share their feelings, or commit to a relationship. This thing between them—it seemed so easy to just go along and see where it took them. Neither of them resisted. Why would he? He wanted to be with her. Even as he drove toward San Francisco and Haven House, he regretted having to leave her there. He wanted to take her to his place. But then what? Uncharted territory. He'd take things slow and steady, knowing that when he did bring her to see his "family" she'd belong. She'd be a part of him. Hell, she already was a part of him.

He'd spent his whole day thinking about her, anticipating when he'd get to see her again. He'd felt something similar with other women, but not like this. Not this deep. Not this all-consuming. He waited for the need to distance himself to grow inside of him. It didn't. In fact, he wanted to pull her out of her seat and into his lap so he could kiss her.

"Ben."

His name on her lips did something to him. His gut went tight. His mind conjured one dirty dream after another, all of them including Kate naked in his bed.

"Ben."

"Yeah."

"Isn't that Haven House back there on the other corner?"

He took the next right and went around the block. "Yeah, we'll park in back."

Nice cover, idiot.

He chanced a glance at her when he killed the engine. She gave him a soft smile. Yeah, she knew he'd blown that.

He reached for the door handle, but didn't open the door. "I'll get Alex."

"We didn't stop at your office to get my car. I'll need our bags."

"I already took care of it. Your car will stay at my office, but I had my assistant bring over your bags."

"You did?"

"I told you I'd take care of things. You'll be safe here. If Evan comes looking for you, he won't find your car. If he tries to get inside, well, I've got state of the art security on the building."

"Keeping people safe is what you do." The confidence in her voice touched him.

"Keeping you safe is my top priority. I won't let that asshole hurt you again." He reached over and traced the bruises on her neck with his fingertips in a light caress. She sucked in a surprised gasp, then exhaled and settled into his touch. Their eyes met. Hers dipped to stare at his mouth before they shot back up to meet his gaze again. His hand slipped around her neck and pulled her closer. Did she lean in first? Did he? Didn't matter. All he cared about was the way his body sighed with relief when his lips met hers. The way his pulse quickened, his heart jumped, then settled like it finally found the right rhythm. The one that matched hers.

He kept the kiss soft, light, an exploration of her full lips, the taste of her, the way his mouth fit perfectly to hers. She pulled back first, but only a few inches. Her hand came up and cupped his jaw. Her thumb pressed to his bottom lip, then swept away as she leaned in and kissed him again. Her tongue smoothed along his in a long sweep that remained slow and sultry.

Everything about her drew him in, from her sweet taste to her rosy scent. He became aware of so many things at once. The softness of her hair sliding beneath his fingers at the back of her neck. The way she took her time kissing him, finding just the right angle to deepen the kiss and bring him closer to her. The way she breathed him in.

She ended the kiss, softly pulling away until their lips parted and her hands slid over his face and cupped his jaw in both her hands. He stared into her desire-filled eyes. She didn't hide how much she wanted him in that look.

"I want to rush and hold back all at the same time," she admitted.

"Just don't run away this time."

With the way things were going, he understood that maybe she didn't think this thing was real. He'd had his moments wondering if everything he felt for her was because of what Morgan predicted. Kate had been through a traumatic event. He didn't want to be just someone she held on to because she didn't want to be alone. She needed the connection.

But he felt everything in that kiss. Neither of them could hide what they truly felt when they kissed like that.

"This is real, Kate. Whether we take it slow or fast or somewhere in between, it will still feel like this." He kissed her again to show her and prove to himself that the truth lay in those words and between them. She was

meant for him. It hit him all at once. He was meant for
her. That thought took on a whole new meaning. The
urge to protect her and be the man she needed and deserved swelled inside of him until his chest ached. His
kisses grew hungry with the need to show her, prove to
her, that he could be everything she wanted. Everything
she'd dreamed, but never truly believed could be for her.

He could be the man his father never was.

She matched his urgency, then pressed her lips hard
to his to slow him down. She kissed him several times,
breaking the kiss and pressing her forehead to his. She
still held his face. He didn't move, except to slide his fingers through her hair and up to cover the back of her head
and hold her close. With her eyes closed, she breathed
in and out a few times, evening out her breath. He did
the same, but watched her. How could he not? This close
to her, she took his breath away. Her dark lashes rested
on her pale cheek. When her eyes finally opened and
stared into his, he saw the depth of her need for him. Not
just for the physical connection that still raced over his
nerves even now, but for that something deeper he felt
but couldn't name. What he saw in her eyes matched that
unique feeling she gave him.

Alex stirred in the backseat and let out a soft whimper
of distress. Now that the car stopped, he woke up, wondering what was going on.

Kate fell back into her seat. He let her go, but wanted
her back in his arms. Well, not in the car. Somewhere
more private. And soft.

"Does it bother you?" she asked.

"Not kissing you bothers me a lot."

She smiled and let out a nervous laugh. "No, I mean Alex."

"He doesn't bother me at all."

"You and me, we've kind of avoided the whole complicated relationship thing for a long time. If we explore this thing between us, well, it includes him."

"First, what I feel for you isn't complicated at all. I want to be with you, Kate. I don't know what it is, why it feels different, but it is that simple for me."

Her eyes narrowed and her lips pressed tight. Then she admitted, "It is for me too."

"Alex is your son. He's a piece of you. I know a relationship with you means a relationship with Alex. I can't have you without including him. I'm perfectly fine with that." She eyed him again. "Really, I like kids. I like him. I don't mind sharing you with him."

"You have no choice, really."

"I wouldn't change it even if I could. I see the way you are with him. The love you have for him and Margo. It makes me like you all the more, Kate. I know you want me to see how strong you are, that you can take this on and you're fine. Giving in to your feelings and leaning on me . . . it's not weak, Kate. You could never be weak."

"I want to hide away with Alex and pretend none of this happened, that all the bad things were just another nightmare. What does it say that I want to let you handle it, so I don't have to face it?"

The grief in her eyes and riddled through her words tore at his heart. He didn't like the way she wanted to push this off on others to handle. That wasn't her way at all and spoke of how deep her grief and exhaustion ran. It worried him, but he knew she'd rally, because she'd never take a backseat when something needed to be done.

He reached for her again, sliding his hand along her cheek and cupping her face. She leaned into his touch and he smiled softly at her. "It says you trust me." Her eyes went wide with surprise. "That's not something you do easily, so I'm glad we've got that between us. It's a very good start. You're grieving. Let me handle the case, you take the time you need to process what happened and where you go from here."

She closed her eyes and leaned into his palm. "I'm so tired."

"Come inside. I'll show you to your room. You can rest. In a few days, we'll have more answers. You'll be safe here."

Chapter Thirteen

SAFE SEEMED RELATIVE. In the two days since Ben dropped her off at Haven House, someone had set off the security alarms in the middle of the night four times in different areas of the building. Each time, Ben arrived in a near panic despite her assurances over the phone that she was fine and no one got into the building. The fear in his eyes washed away with relief when he finally saw her. The tremble that rocked through him when he pulled her into his arms for a hug touched her more deeply than if that shiver came from pure lust. He cared.

The belief that he had real and deep feelings for her scared her, but didn't stop her from growing more and more accustomed to having him around. He stopped by in the early morning on his way to work and had breakfast with her. He came by after work to meet with Jill, the person running the center for him until he hired a new director, then he had dinner with Kate. They'd kicked back and watched a movie each night with Alex falling asleep on Ben's chest. Seeing him with Alex, holding him, feeding him, playing and making silly sounds to make Alex smile, made that fear inside of her ease and grow in a different way. The more she needed him, wanted him in her life, the more she feared losing him.

"Kate?"

She looked up from where she sat on the floor with Alex, playing on his mat, batting at the toys hanging over his head with one hand. In the other he waved a bright green ring around that he sometimes managed to get in his mouth to suck on.

"Hi, Jill. What's up?"

"If you're not busy, I wondered if you'd help me out with one of the girls."

"Let me guess—Mariana." The fourteen-year-old was all attitude and defiance. Everyone who stayed at Haven House was required to pitch in and help. Though Ben had a full-time staff that included everything from a janitor and chef to counselors and job placement coordinators, residents chipped in with setting the tables for meals, washing dishes, and cleaning up the children's playroom, the TV room, and the computer lab. Older kids were expected to oversee the little ones on the playground out back and help pick up the toys.

Jill smiled and nodded. "She's having a difficult time adjusting. She doesn't believe her mother will stick with the program."

"Valentina attends her classes. She's working with the counselor."

"Her husband is in an anger management class. She's been sneaking calls to him. Mariana isn't convinced this time her mother will leave him."

"What does Valentina's counselor say?"

"She hasn't quite hit that point where the success she's achieving in her computer classes translates to a better life for herself without her abusive husband."

"Her self-esteem will improve over time."

"Mariana is tough, but she's scared," Jill said.

"She's got good reason to be. Unless her father really embraces anger management, it's just a means to an end in getting his wife back and the authorities off his back. For now."

"Which is why I hoped you'd work with Mariana. She watches you in the gym. I thought maybe you could teach her some kickboxing moves. Work with her to build her confidence."

"Sure. Where is she?"

Jill smiled and tilted her head to indicate the hallway. "Pretending to be you in the gym."

That made Kate smile. She picked up Alex and held him close. He grabbed fistfuls of her hair and pulled, rubbing his face against her neck.

"Tired baby," Jill crooned, patting Alex on the back. "Give him to me. I'll grab his bouncy seat from your room and bring him to my office."

"Are you sure?"

"You help me out with Mariana, I'll watch this little man for you."

"He needs a diaper change before his nap."

"I'm on it. He likes the puppy to sleep with, right?"

Kate appreciated Jill's attention and friendship these last two days. "Yes. And the blue blanket on my bed."

Jill held her hands out and Kate transferred Alex to her arms. She hated to be without him, even for a short time. Funny how that happened without her realizing it. Every second of the day she grew closer to him and the guilt that Margo wasn't here dissipated. Margo would want her to raise Alex without constantly beating herself up for loving every second she had with him.

Kate kissed Alex on the head, patted his back, and watched Jill walk away with a smile on her face and in her heart. The last two days she'd let herself grieve for her sister, but not think too much about the future. She needed to make plans and decide what came next.

Soon. Right now, she could fall back on what she knew how to do. Help teenage girls direct and overcome their anger.

Kate stood in the gym doorway, spying on the little girl punching the heavy bag. Mariana had some moves. The tears in the young girl's eyes tore at Kate's heart. She knew each one cost her. As much as she hated her father, she hated that he made her cry even more.

Been there. Done that. Kate understood all too well.

Dressed in black leggings and a pink short-sleeved tunic, Kate walked into the room ready to lend a hand. First, she'd need to get the girl's attention.

"You'll never hurt him that way."

The girl punched the bag harder, but it barely moved. She flinched with the impact and held her hand against her chest.

Kate stood next to the bag, crouched, and held her hands up, fists ready for a fight. In slow motion, she moved her right hand into the bag. "You need to plant your feet wide. Bend your knees to keep your balance and your center of gravity low. When you swing, follow through with your body, keeping your stomach tight."

Kate made the move a couple more times in slow motion, then went full force with the third punch.

"Come on, crouch like me. Show me what you've got," she taunted, because a girl like Mariana couldn't back down from a challenge. She needed to be tough. She'd been taught to be tough, or left bloody and bruised on the floor.

Mariana didn't say a word, just mimicked Kate's moves. Kate moved in behind her. Mariana jumped out of the way, spinning to face off with Kate.

Kate held up her hands. "I'm not going to hurt you."

"But you could."

Kate nodded. "I've spent many years learning how to protect myself. I'll teach you the basics."

"I need more than the basics. I need to be able to fight."

Kate understood that all too well too. "I can teach you how to fight. First lesson. Be smart. A guy who is ten inches taller and a hundred pounds heavier will always win."

"Then what is the point of even trying?"

"Survival. You don't have a chance if you try to stand

and fight. What you want to do is block and counter so you can get away."

"I'm not scared. I can fight."

"You should be scared. Fear can either get you killed, or keep you alive. If you let that fear freeze you in the moment, you're dead. If you learn to think through the fear, you can save yourself. It is more important to save yourself, than win the fight."

"But I want to hurt him."

Kate sighed. "I know you do. I want you to live. I know it doesn't seem like it right now, but there is so much more out there for you than the life you think you'll never escape."

Mariana's sad gaze fell to the floor. "She'll go back to him. I'll have no choice but to go with her." The misery in Mariana's voice tore Kate's heart and made it bleed. It took her back to when she was young.

"Then I'll teach you to survive until you do have a choice."

Mariana nodded, then waited for Kate to begin the lesson.

"Be smart. Never be a stationary target. Keep moving. If he can't catch you, he can't hit you." Kate swung her hand wide. Mariana ducked. Kate expected her to move, so she swung her other arm and caught Mariana on the shoulder. "Always be prepared for the attack to come on all sides."

Kate worked with Mariana for an hour, teaching her to move, punch, and kick. Most of all, she taught the girl that escape didn't mean defeat. She hoped that lesson sank in, because at Mariana's five-foot-nothing height, a grown man could do some damage. Her father had done enough.

Mariana breathed heavily in front of Kate. They circled each other on the mats. "Enough. We'll work some more tomorrow."

"No. One more time. I'm getting better."

Ah, confidence. Kate loved it. She swung her arm wide, palm open to smack Mariana on the side of the head. Mariana ducked and sidestepped under it, avoiding her other hand coming the other way. "Good job. You are getting better. We'll work on it tomorrow."

"Come on, Kate, one more lesson."

Kate backed Mariana into the corner of the room and stood in front of her, blocking her escape. "You're cornered. What do you do?"

"Be smart, don't let you get your hands on me before I get free."

"How?" Kate moved in and reached for the girl.

Mariana smacked her left hand away and ducked under her right, diving out from the corner to get past Kate. She shoved between Mariana's shoulder blades and knocked her to the floor. Mariana twisted to her back, ready to protect herself with her hands. Kate landed on top of Mariana, straddling her hips, and held her hands down on the mats.

"Got you. What did I tell you?"

"Never let him pin me down. I'm too small and weak to fight in this position."

"Exactly. So be smart."

"You said girls are stronger in the legs than in the arms, so I kick and try to get you off."

"Men are vulnerable in their private parts. You get a shot at their groin, you take it and make it count."

Mariana kneed her in the back and bucked to dislodge Kate.

"What is going on?" Ben demanded.

Surprised Ben arrived early, Kate looked up. Ben stood in the doorway, a fierce look in his eyes. Mariana bucked again, sending Kate up on her knees. Mariana used her speed to get her feet up and through Kate's legs. She planted her feet on Kate's hips at her thighs and pushed. Kate went flying backward, letting go of Mariana's hands. She stumbled into the wall and hit hard with a thump.

Ben rushed forward to help Mariana up from the mat by her hand.

"I got you," Mariana shouted, and pointed her finger straight at Kate, triumph lighting her eyes.

Despite the sting in her back, Kate smiled, infected by the girl's enthusiasm. "Yes, you did."

"What is going on?" Ben asked again, his voice more bewildered than upset now.

"I'm teaching Mariana to protect herself."

"Be smart. Never be a stationary target. Keep moving. Hit him where it hurts. Retreat isn't failure, it's survival." Mariana bounced on the balls of her feet, fists at the ready to fight.

Kate laughed under her breath and nodded. "That's my girl. We'll do some more tomorrow."

"Will you teach me some of those cool kicks you do?"

"Yes. I promise. Now, if I'm not mistaken, you're on kitchen prep for dinner tonight. Go wash up and get to work."

"I don't even know how to cook."

"Learn. You'll need it when the choices become your own. First rule, be smart. That means learning everything you can about taking care of yourself and being independent. School will take you places you never thought possible."

"School is boring."

"School is the key to a prosperous life. Find something you love and learn everything you can about it. Get a good job, one that makes you happy and fulfilled. Never let yourself be stuck in a job or a life you don't want because you limited yourself and think you don't have any other options. There is always another choice, but it takes guts and work. You've got the guts. Now work hard to achieve the dreams you think won't come true. They never will if you don't try."

"You think I've got guts?"

"And so much more. You're smart. You work hard. You're hungry for more in your life and willing to accept help to get it. You even impressed Ben, besting me in the fight."

"I did?" Mariana stared up at Ben, so much hope in her eyes.

Ben didn't miss a beat. "Are you kidding? That was a great move. You've got the makings of becoming a real badass."

Mariana's eyes went wide with surprise that Ben

would use that word in front of her, but then the smile bloomed on her lips and she eyed Kate. "Maybe I'll be as good as you someday."

"I have no doubt. Now, go. Punctuality shows you have respect for other people. They'll respect you for doing the right thing."

"On it. What time do you want to work out tomorrow?"

"When you get back from school, come find me."

Mariana nodded and turned to go, but spun back around and threw her arms around Kate, hugging her close. "Thank you."

Kate hugged Mariana back. "You're welcome, sweetheart. It's going to be okay."

Mariana let her go and ran out the door.

Ben stared after the girl. "That's not the same angry girl I've seen these last weeks."

"More than being angry, she's scared. She feels vulnerable and that she doesn't have a say in her life. For the most part, she's right. She can't keep her mother from going back to her father. She feels helpless. I've been there. I used to be her." Kate put her hand on his chest over his pounding heart. "Your approval means a lot to her."

"Because I'm a man."

"Yes. You're a strong, good-looking man who is nice to her and isn't her rotten son of a bitch father. She needs to learn the difference. Your approval of her learning to fight and protect herself reinforces that you think it's okay for her to stand up for herself when her father has taught her doing so will only lead to pain. He makes her feel weak and vulnerable. You made her feel strong and capable. What you think is a small thing to praise her for, she thinks is huge."

Ben bent and kissed her softly. "You're amazing."

"For teaching that girl to be a badass."

Ben laughed. "Yes. And for understanding why she needed you to teach her how to fight. If she'd been a boy, I'd have thought it the perfect idea, but hesitated to encourage a girl."

Kate smacked him on the arm. "Girls can fight."

"I knew that in the abstract, but you showed me the girls who come here need to fight. Not just to protect themselves, but to build their self-esteem. To know they can."

"The people who come here are beaten down in body and mind. Their bodies heal, but it takes a long time to build back the mind and a person's sense of worth. Little achievements—"

"Like shoving you into a wall."

Kate smirked. "Yes. Those small victories change the way you think about yourself. You're not stupid, or worthless, or unlovable."

"I'm sorry if you ever felt that way, Kate. It kills me that anyone could ever make you think those terrible things." Ben cupped her face and kissed her again with a tenderness that brought tears to her eyes. "You are smart." He kissed her forehead. "You are kind." He kissed her cheek. "You have a beautiful heart." He kissed her other cheek. "You are lovable." He kissed her on the lips, taking the kiss deep, sliding his tongue along hers. "I missed you today." He kissed her again to show her how much.

She tried not to read too much into the comment about her being lovable. She got that he liked her and wanted more than friendship between them. She wanted the same. She loved the dinners they shared these last two days, the easy way they talked about their day, their past, and hints about what they wanted in the future.

Her hands fisted in his suit jacket and pulled him close. She rose up on her toes and pressed her body to the length of his. Each day, every kiss brought her closer to him, until she dreaded his absence and anxiously awaited his return.

Someone cleared their throat behind them. Ben placed his lips on hers in one last searing kiss, then hugged her close with his head pressed to the side of hers. He dipped his lips to her ear and whispered, "You make it so damn hard to remember why I'm here."

"This little one is hungry," Jill said to get their attention.

Kate reluctantly released her grip on Ben's suit jacket and smoothed her hands over the wrinkled material. "Sorry."

"I'm not." His smile and the heat in his eyes fanned the flames of desire licking across her nerves.

She stared at his chest, resisting the urge to pull him back in for another sultry kiss. "This is so not like me."

Ben touched his finger to her chin and made her raise her gaze to meet his. "This is who you are with me." Ben eyed her for a long moment, making her take that simple statement into her heart.

Is this who she wanted to be? Someone who can't take

a breath without thinking of a man. Well, not just any man. Him. It had never been like this for her. The thought of pulling away, taking more time to think about what being with him meant to her life, left her cold. She liked spending time with him. He made her laugh. He made her think. She glanced down at Margo's engagement ring. He made her believe in dreams.

Ben walked over to Jill and scooped Alex up with his hands under Alex's arms. He raised Alex up into the air over his head. "Hey, buddy, how was your day?"

Alex smiled and squealed with delight. Ben brought him down and held him close to his chest. Jill silently left them alone. Kate stared at Ben with Alex safe and secure in his strong arms. He leaned down and planted a kiss on Alex's head, took his hand, and held it with his big one.

Kate's heart swelled and filled with so much warmth it spread to every dark corner and lit it up with joy. A voice inside her called her a fool for ever thinking about giving Ben up and not at least trying to build something with him. Good guys like him didn't come along often.

Ben caught her staring. "Are you okay?"

Unable to put her intense feelings into words, she closed the distance between them and walked right into his open arm. He held her close with Alex in his other arm. She buried her face in his chest and inhaled his spicy, woodsy scent. She held Ben and Alex close, feeling something she hadn't felt in a long time. Lucky. Blessed to have both of them in her life. Now all she had to do was hold on to them.

Ben kissed the top of her head. She looked up at him, but he stared down into Alex's smiling face. "Should we tell your mommy our good news?"

"What good news?" After everything that happened these last days that had her hiding out at Haven House, she needed some good news.

"I got a call this afternoon from the clinic. This"—Ben hugged Alex close—"is Alex Faraday."

"Donald is his father." The relief that washed through her made her sigh.

"One hundred percent. The clinic didn't make a mistake."

"But the lab report Donald had in his papers. They never put through the adoption with the courts."

"You said Margo saw you struggling to let Alex go. Maybe they wanted to wait and give you time to really decide. As much as Margo wanted Alex, she loved you and wouldn't want to make you miserable the rest of your life."

The words rang true, but she had a hard time believing that after everything they'd been through to have Alex, Margo would give him back.

"Is it so hard to believe that after you did this amazing thing for Margo that she wouldn't do something that selfless and amazing for you?"

Kate had to admit the truth. "No. I hate that she died thinking I'd take him away from her."

"I don't think she thought that at all. I think you two would have come to an arrangement. Shared custody. When she married Donald, Margo would have been

Alex's stepmother. If she couldn't have a child of her own, maybe that was enough for her. Alex is a piece of the two people she loved the most."

That sweet sentiment hit her right in the heart. "You always know the right thing to say."

"It's simple when it's the truth. Stop beating yourself up over this."

"So, this is why you came so early."

"In addition to wanting to see the two of you, yes."

She liked that he included Alex. In fact, he never seemed to mind that it was always the three of them. Of course, it had only been a couple of days. That might change over time.

"I also came to pick you up. Detective Raynott has some information. He asked us to come down to the police station so he can fill us in."

"Did they arrest Evan?"

"Unfortunately, no."

Alex began to cry. Ben touched her back to move her toward the door. "Where are we going?"

"To get this one a bottle before we go."

She followed Ben into the kitchen. He didn't hesitate to go to the counter, pour some water into the mug, and set it in the microwave to heat the water. He grabbed the can and dumped three scoops of formula into the bottle. The microwave dinged. Ben grabbed the mug and poured the water into the bottle. He twisted on the nipple and stirred the bottle around and around to mix the milk, but not add a bunch of air bubbles. Alex fussed, sucking on his fingers, fat tears trailing down his chubby cheeks.

Ben used his pinky to move Alex's hand and stuffed the bottle into his mouth. Alex settled comfortably into Ben's arm and sucked away, staring up at him with nothing but love and gratitude, like, "Hey man, thanks for helping a guy out."

The silly thought made her grin.

Ben glanced at her on the other side of the counter, his eyes narrowing when he caught her staring at him in fascination. "What?"

"You."

"What about me?"

"How do you know how to do that?"

"I read the instructions Margo left at your place. It's no big deal."

She held his gaze. "Yes, it is to me."

One side of Ben's mouth tilted down. "I really need to step up my game if you think my feeding Alex is impressive."

"I don't know, you seem to be scoring a lot of points just for being you."

He swayed side-to-side with Alex in his arm. "I'm not trying to score points, Kate."

"Which makes the sweet things you do all the more appealing."

"How about after we see the detective, you and I go out for dinner?"

"I can't leave Alex."

"Who said anything about leaving him? You met Elizabeth a couple days ago. We'll go to Decadence. She'd love to see this one again and you."

"She works at Decadence. It's one of the best restaurants in the city. The desserts are legendary."

"She owns the place. She'll stuff you full of treats, I promise."

"You don't have to do this."

"I want to take you to dinner and spend more time with you. I hate leaving you here each night."

"Ben, this is all so . . ."

"New. Different. Exactly what I want. It's a date, Kate. We'll set aside everything that's going on, eat a meal together, and get to know each other better. There will be chocolate."

"How do you know I'm a sucker for chocolate?"

"Never met a woman who wasn't. I don't want to meet the one who isn't. That's just not natural."

"You're teasing me."

"Bribing is more accurate."

She laughed. She couldn't help herself. It made it all seem so easy. Maybe it should be. At least with the right person.

"Okay, dinner."

Ben's smile made her insides flutter. She felt like a silly schoolgirl, unable to control her reaction to the popular boy paying attention to her. But Ben was no boy. The way he looked at her, all that intensity and smoldering heat in his dark eyes, drew her in and made her want to leap into the flames of desire licking at her insides.

"The promise of chocolate took it over the top, right?"

"No, it's just you. The chocolate is a bonus."

Yep, that smile might make her do anything he asked . . . and enjoy every second of it.

"Come on, let's go. I want to hear what Detective Raynott has to say about the case."

Ben grabbed a dish towel from a drawer, draped it over his shoulder, and put Alex up against him and patted his back. Alex cooed and patted Ben's shoulder with his hands, then let out a huge burp.

"That's my man," Ben said, rubbing his hand over Alex's back in gentle circles.

Kate used the towel to wipe the spit-up from Alex's mouth. When had the numbness inside disappeared? That warm, comfortable feeling that came over her every time she was with Ben washed over her. Impulse and need made her wrap her arms around Ben. She pressed her face to Alex's side and Ben's shoulder and hugged them close. She glanced up at Ben, hoping he saw all the things she had no words for in her eyes. "Thanks."

He reached over, threaded his fingers through her hair, and held her head. "Anything for you, Kate."

"Evan on a platter," she suggested.

"I'm working on it."

He'd keep working on it. He'd never stop. For her.

She squeezed him tighter, holding on, thanking him for all he'd done and was trying to do, loving him for sticking by her side and taking care of her. Love? Wait. When did she ever use that word? With her sister and Alex, yes, but never a man. Was that the warm glow pulsing in her chest? Maybe.

Chapter Fourteen

BEN PARKED THE car in the police station parking lot, but didn't make a move to get out. He held Kate's hand in his, their fingers linked. She stared out the window, lost in her own thoughts. Quiet. He wondered what she was thinking and how she really felt about him.

She responded to his touch and the kisses they shared with a warmth and openness he'd rarely felt from a woman. When they lost themselves in a kiss, it was all he could do not to drag her to the floor and make love to her. He wanted her more than he'd ever wanted a woman and the waiting was killing him. As much as he felt he knew her, from past encounters and especially these last few days, this was all new. He needed to take his time. She needed time to grieve, figure out the next steps in her life, and decide if what she felt for him now went beyond the need for compassion and companionship during this

difficult time. It went deeper. For him. But did she feel
the same way?

She smoothed her free hand down her leg and over
the black slacks for the fifth time in ten minutes.

"What is it?" he asked.

"I didn't pack very many clothes when you moved me
to Haven House. I . . . Do you think this is okay to go to
dinner at Decadence?"

"It's perfect."

"It's just, I'd have liked to wear a dress, something
pretty. For you," she whispered, her words filled with a
shyness he'd never heard from her.

"Kate, while I'd love to strip you out of those tight
black pants you wore to work out in, and see those stun-
ning legs in a dress, that's all for my selfish enjoyment. I
really don't care what you wear. You're always the most
beautiful woman I've ever seen."

Her lips pressed together. She didn't look at him, but
stared at her lap. "I don't think anyone has ever said I'm
beautiful."

"Maybe they never said it, but it's what they thought.
Anyone with eyes can see how pretty you are. Anyone
who's ever spoken to you knows that beauty goes deep.
You hide it well, but I see how deep you feel things every
time you look at me."

Her head snapped around, her eyes went wide, and
she stared at him. "You can't know that."

"I think you feel things so deeply you try to hide it so
you don't have to feel it, but it's there. It's always there,

isn't it, Kate? Whether it's your work, your sister's death, Alex—you take it all in and want to make it right and perfect. You work really hard to be everything to everyone. With me, you want something for yourself. It's okay to take it. Accept it. It doesn't mean you aren't still working to make things right for Margo and Donald and providing for Alex."

"I want this to be over. I want to bury them with a clear conscience that the person responsible paid for what he's done. I want to love and raise Alex and know he'll have a happy life. I want . . ."

"What?"

She met his gaze. "To have dinner with you. And more."

He brought their joined hands to his mouth and kissed the back of hers. "Let's go take care of this so we can enjoy the rest of our evening together."

Kate released him and got out of the car. He got out and went to the backseat to retrieve Alex, who smiled up at him. The little guy was really growing on him. He actually liked spending time holding and feeding him. His initial nervousness and awkward moves with the kid dissipated. The way the kid looked at him, so trusting and open, touched something deep inside of Ben. He'd never really thought of himself as a father. Not when he'd had the father-fuck-up-of-the-year for a dad. He needed to stop looking at his life through that lens and picture himself as the man he'd become and how he'd be as a husband and father. The picture didn't seem complete or worthwhile without picturing Kate and Alex with him. Maybe that's the picture Morgan saw. He didn't know, but he liked the one in his head. He liked the way taking care of them made him feel.

"Ben."

God, that sultry voice did something to him.

He turned to face her with Alex in his arms. "Hey."

"Are you okay?"

"Fine. Just getting my buddy out. Let's go."

"I'll take him." She held out her hands for him to hand over Alex.

Ben kept Alex in one arm and wrapped the other around Kate's waist as he turned her to the door. "I've got him." *I hope I've got you too.*

Detective Raynott spotted them when they entered the building. He waved them over to his desk. "Figures you'd get the girl. Why did I even call you?"

Ben smiled, ignoring the detective's remarks for Kate's sake. "What do you have to tell us?"

"Is the woman with Evan in that office Christina Faraday?" Kate asked, her gaze locked on the two people sitting behind the glass windows past all the cubicles.

"They arrived about fifteen minutes ago. They're talking to my boss with their lawyer," Detective Raynott explained.

"Did you get the warrant for a DNA sample from Evan?" Ben asked.

"No. Thanks to the lab results from the knife and kitchen floor, I won't get a warrant for him at all."

"What do you mean?" Kate asked.

"The blood is not a familial match to Donald Faraday. It can't be Evan's blood."

"Are you saying that Evan didn't kill my sister and Donald?" Kate asked, shaking her head in denial.

"That's what it looks like."

"He may not have done it, but he was there," Ben said. "I saw the guilt and remorse same as you when we went to the Faraday house."

"I don't know what to say. I really thought we had him," the detective admitted.

"If it's not a familial match, then maybe Christina Faraday is the one who got stabbed," Kate suggested. "They were in on it together. Both of them were at the house. Evan shot them, but Christina confronted Margo and her blood is on the knife and floor."

"If that's what happened, it's going to be an uphill battle to prove it. We have nothing that links her to the scene. I can't get a warrant for her DNA without something to tie her to the murders. Yes, she's got motive, but that's not enough to compel a judge to sign a warrant."

"They're still covering for each other, is that it?" Ben asked.

"Lawyered up and sticking to their lame story. They've got too much to lose to slip up."

"Someone's been trying to break into Haven House to get to Kate," Ben pointed out. "That's anything but smart."

"No, it's not, but Evan has a temper. Let's hope it lands him in more trouble, but not too much." Detective Raynott eyed Kate, knowing Evan probably wanted her dead and out of the way, so the Faradays controlled Donald's estate and Alex's inheritance.

"There's something you need to know. Once Evan and Christina find out about it, it will make them even more dangerous."

"Here they come," Kate warned, touching Ben's arm to get his attention.

"It's Kate Morrison, right?" Christina said, stepping close. Too close to Kate for Ben's liking.

"That's right."

"It's terrible what happened to my husband and your sister."

"Yes, it is." Kate bit out the words like each one tasted bitter.

"Donald's funeral is tomorrow at noon. Family and close friends. Although the circumstances of Donald's death are unseemly, I'd like his son Alex there."

"Murder is unseemly?"

"Their affair, dear. I mean, I want Alex there, but I don't want to flaunt my husband's indiscretion."

"Really? Which of your boy toys will be by your side? You never minded flaunting your affairs right under your husband's nose. I'd think Donald's friends would want to know that Donald died happy with the woman he loved in the home he shared with her and their son. I think they'd all like to know he asked you for a divorce the very day he died. I bet they all come to the same conclusion I did when I found them lying dead on the floor."

"You don't know anything about my marriage and the terrible way he treated me."

And the Oscar goes to Christina Faraday. Ben didn't believe the sheen of tears in her eyes. From the scoff Kate huffed out, neither did she. Evan stood beside his mother looking bored, though his gaze never left Kate's beautiful face, pissing Ben off.

"Donald and I were friends. He loved my sister. He was happy with her. Happier than he'd ever been he told me too many times to count. You stole that from him. From my sister. I won't let you steal everything he left behind too."

"I'm his wife. I have rights." Christina shot her lawyer a look.

"Miss Morrison, I'm the Faradays' attorney, Daniel Cagney."

"I know who you are, Mr. Cagney," Ben interrupted. "Donald Faraday fired you two months ago. I believe the termination letter stated he was tired of you sleeping with his wife while representing him."

Kate shot him a sideways glance. "Really? Wow, you do get around."

"Shut up, bitch," Christina fired back.

Kate opened her mouth to shout back, but Ben interrupted again. "What does your client want?" he asked Mr. Cagney.

The man pulled a large envelope from his briefcase and handed it to Kate. She pulled out the papers. He read over her shoulder.

"You want custody of Alex," she scoffed, then let out a fake laugh. "Never going to happen."

"Mrs. Faraday feels that Mr. Faraday's son should be raised with his brother."

"His brother is twenty-five and not about to spend his time playing with a baby when he'd much rather be out drinking himself stupid and getting into fights." Kate smiled insincerely at Evan with nothing short of revulsion filling her eyes.

"Alex should be with his immediate family. That includes his brother, Evan," Christina chimed in.

"No, Alex should be with his mother," Ben shot back.

"His mother is dead," Christina spat out.

"No, she's not. Kate is Alex's mother."

"She's his aunt," Mr. Cagney pointed out. "Just because her sister died, doesn't make her custodian over Alex."

"No, but the fact Kate gave birth to him does." Ben smiled when Christina, Evan, and Mr. Cagney exchanged confused looks. "You really should get your facts straight before you start filing papers with the courts about custody. Kate and Donald are the biological parents of Alex Faraday. Alex was conceived by artificial insemination because Margo was unable to conceive and carry a child. Kate loved her sister very much and had Alex for them."

"Then she gave up her rights to the child when she turned the child over to Donald and Margo to raise," Mr. Cagney pointed out.

"No, she didn't. She never signed her rights away. Donald had the papers drawn up, but they were never filed with the courts. Margo never officially adopted Alex."

"This can't be," Christina said. "She can't gain control of Alex's inheritance."

"She can and she will," Ben said, handing Alex over to Kate. Alex fussed and cried, feeling everyone's upset.

Kate bounced Alex and he settled against her shoulder, his face pressed against her neck.

"No judge will side with you and take Alex from his mother." Ben hoped this would be the end of it. Should have known better.

"Alex isn't even named in the will," Christina said in a desperate attempt to hold on to the upper hand.

"You mean the will your lover Mr. Cagney drew up years ago?" Ben asked. "No, Alex isn't named in that will, but he is in the will Donald set up nearly a year ago after Alex was conceived and updated weeks before his death. Your prenup is in place. Donald filed for divorce and served you the papers. We will go to a judge and ask him to uphold both the prenup and Donald's will."

"I want to see this new will. You can't do this. I'm still his wife."

"He made his wishes perfectly clear the day he died. He didn't want to be married to you anymore. He invoked his right to execute the prenup. His new will has been in place long before he asked you for a divorce. His estate goes to Alex."

"No way. He may have left my mother out of it, but Alex and I will share it, right?" Evan asked, speaking up for the first time.

"He set up a trust fund for you with a set amount of money."

Evan's hands fisted at his sides. "How much?"

"One million. You are unable to touch the principle.

You'll receive a monthly income from the investments on a quarterly basis. Upon your death, the money goes to Alex in full."

"That little brat gets my money." Evan took a menacing step forward.

Ben stepped in front of Kate and Alex and planted his hand on Evan's chest. Evan didn't step back, but glared down at Ben's hand, then back at him.

"Get your hand off me."

"Back off."

Ben waited the ten seconds it took Evan to decide that throwing a punch in the middle of a police station might not be a good idea. Detective Raynott stood close, eyes trained on Evan, waiting for him to be that stupid.

"Those were your father's wishes. I will work with Donald's new lawyer to see that the will is upheld."

"We'll fight it," Christina vowed.

"Try it and Evan gets nothing."

"What about the business?"

"That will depend on what a judge decides about the prenup and the divorce Donald asked for but didn't live to see through. Alex is his sole heir for the bulk of his estate. Kate is Alex's mother and guardian, so she will be in charge."

"No fucking way." Evan shook his head, his eyes filled with hate and disgust.

"Did you really think you'd get away with this?" Ben asked, meaning the murders and trying to take everything Donald left behind. He shook his head. "You did all of this for nothing. Had Donald lived, he might have softened his stance and paid you off to keep you away from the family he really wanted to be with and protect. Now he's gone and Kate and I will do everything possible to see that Donald's last wishes are carried out and Alex gets everything his father left him."

"I will see that you pay for killing my sister," Kate vowed, staring down both Evan and Christina.

"I'm sure you've heard. We had nothing to do with their murders," Christina said. "The blood on the knife isn't a match to Evan. You'll stop accusing him of this heinous crime." Christina turned to Detective Raynott. "Maybe now you'll start looking for the real killer."

"I'm staring right at them." The hate in Kate's voice made even Ben turn to look down at her. "We don't have the evidence yet, but we will find it."

Christina glared at Kate, then locked her gaze on Alex. "I see Donald in him. Too bad he'll never know his father. Let's hope the person who killed Donald doesn't go after him."

Christina reached out to touch Alex's head. Kate smacked her hand away.

"You scratched me," Christina shouted, holding her wrist, the diamond tennis bracelet sparkling in the light.

"Don't you dare touch him." Kate held Alex close and turned him away from Christina.

"Let's go," Christina ordered Evan and Mr. Cagney, walking away without another word.

Ben waited for them to leave, brushing his hand up and down Kate's back to soothe and reassure her.

"What a piece of work," Detective Raynott said when the group was out of earshot.

"Yes. But she gave me just what I wanted," Kate said.

"What are you talking about?" Ben asked.

Kate held up her hand. "Her DNA. I scratched her."

"I'll call one of the lab guys to come up and collect it." Detective Raynott went to a desk and picked up the phone to make his call.

Ben smiled down at Kate. "Nice work. I'd have never thought to do something like that."

"She made it easy. Now we'll know exactly whose blood is on the knife."

Ben cocked his head and stared off in the distance. "I don't understand. I really thought it belonged to Evan. I mean, he had the bruises on his torso and face, a limp I thought meant he'd been cut or stabbed in the leg. Christina doesn't have a mark on her. She doesn't exhibit any signs she got hurt."

"Blood will tell."

Chapter Fifteen

KATE SAT ACROSS from Ben in the elegant restaurant suddenly wary after their encounter with the Faradays at the police station. What she thought would be easy to prove turned out to be a complicated mess.

"I feel like I'm missing something."

Ben reached across the table and covered her hand. "We'll find the evidence and put him behind bars."

"I thought the blood would be the last nail in his coffin. We know he did it."

"Christina had a lot to do with it too." Ben frowned. "I'm not so sure she was actually there."

"But the blood?"

"It could be hers, but it doesn't make sense. If they both went there and Margo kicked Evan's ass, why doesn't Christina seem to have a mark on her?"

"Did you see the odd look in her eye when Evan was cleared because the blood didn't match him? It's like she got something over on us. I could almost hear her taunting us that they got away with it."

"We'll figure out how."

"Maybe she paid someone off in the lab to falsify the results."

Ben linked his fingers with hers and squeezed. "Maybe. Let it go for now. You need to eat and get some rest."

"Let's hope it's uninterrupted. I swear, between Alex getting up in the middle of the night and the security alarms going off at odd times I've barely slept."

Ben frowned and looked away before turning back to look her in the eye. "Now that they know Alex is Donald's sole heir and you control everything, or at least you will once everything is settled, they'll come after you even harder. I'm worried."

"They can't get into Haven House. They've tried. I'll be fine."

"If something happened to you or Alex . . ." Ben's gaze fell on Alex sleeping in his car seat atop a high chair beside the table.

"Ben, you're sweet to worry about us. I'm worried, but I can also take care of myself. I've been doing it a long time."

"I've seen your skills. Well, some of them. They didn't help your sister."

No, they hadn't. That thought turned her insides cold. A man determined to see another person dead would stop at nothing. Evan knew how to fight. He'd been in enough skirmishes to not be deterred by her abilities.

He'd come after her. He'd keep coming to get back what Donald gave to Alex and not him.

"He won't stop, Kate," Ben said, echoing her own fears. "Besides . . ."

"What?" she asked when he didn't continue and looked away.

"I want to protect you and keep you safe. I want you to trust that I will."

She covered their joined hands with her free one and squeezed. "Ben, you are doing so much for us. For me. Letting me stay at Haven House . . . it means so much. Alex and I would be vulnerable at my condo without all the security you have at the shelter."

"You're safe there for now, but how long can that last. I can't hide you there forever."

"One thing at a time. Let's focus on the investigation. Donald will be laid to rest tomorrow. We'll settle the estate with Christina."

"Are you up for a fight with her?" Ben asked.

"Not really. Do you think a judge will uphold Donald's wishes and enforce the prenup?"

"It's kind of a gray area. She had multiple affairs. His lawyer has the evidence to back that up to substantiate Donald's claims that she violated the terms of the prenup. However . . ."

"Donald was having an affair with my sister. They had a child," Kate finished Ben's thought.

"Exactly. So, you and I can work with Donald's lawyer to either fight hard to keep everything, or negotiate a settlement."

"Maybe if I pay her off, she'll go away."

Ben pressed his lips together. She'd gotten to know him well enough to understand that small gesture meant he didn't really think so.

She let out a deep sigh, resigned that she'd have to fight. Her whole life had been a fight. What she wouldn't give to turn this whole thing over to Ben and let him handle it. Huh, she trusted him to handle it. That was certainly new. But Christina and Evan wanted her dead. She couldn't let her mind go to that dark place that she believed they'd try to kill Alex too. Still, that ominous thought disturbed her thoughts and filled her nightmares.

"Kate?"

She gave Ben a halfhearted smile. "I'm okay. Just tired." She raked her fingers through her long hair and pushed it over her shoulder to lie down her back.

"What are your plans for Margo? Will you hold a service?"

"Alex and I are her only family. Her coworkers sent a card and flowers to the house. I'll have to go to her office and clean out her desk."

"Kate, honey, the funeral home contacted you today. Her ashes are ready for you to pick up. You need to say goodbye."

"I can't. How am I supposed to do that after everything we've been through together?" The tears flooded her eyes and spilled over, but she didn't completely give in to her grief. She held it at bay for long periods, but thinking about scattering Margo's ashes as she wanted left

Kate's insides cold. The sense of loneliness she felt since her sister died amplified inside of her, making her heart ache too much to bear.

"Kate, honey, breathe."

"I can't. Not without her. She was my best friend. The one person I could count on always. She promised we'd grow old together."

Ben slipped from the booth, came around the table, and sat beside her. He hooked one arm around her back and pulled her into his chest. She leaned into him, trying to stop the flood of tears and emotions. He smelled fresh—soap and a light, crisp aftershave, like a cold dawn in a meadow. She focused on him and the warmth he enveloped her in, safe in his arms. The hesitancy she felt with other men to get close and share her true feelings didn't exist between them. It never had, since the night he stayed at her place and held her while she wept, then fell asleep in his arms.

"This is not at all what I expected." She never thought she'd fall for a guy, but if she did, she expected it to be exciting and tumultuous, filled with fun dates and ups and downs that proved they could work through anything. She never expected that falling for a guy meant she'd simply just fill with this overwhelming need to be with him and know everything about him. She never thought that it meant she'd feel like she knew the most basic things about him without even asking. Like despite him being a lawyer and needing to win, he knew how to compromise. He'd shown her that when he suggested they come to a settlement with Christina. For her safety

and Alex's, he'd give up the fight and have her pay off
the woman responsible for taking the most important
person in her life. Well, besides Alex. Ben wanted her
to do that for her son, so he didn't lose his mother. Kate
didn't want that to happen. She wanted to make a life
with Ben.

Oh, God, how did this happen? She loved him.

At least, she thought she did.

She pulled back and stared up at his handsome face.
His dark eyes stared back at her filled with concern and
something she didn't quite recognize. Maybe she just
didn't want to admit that she saw it there. Lurking behind
his own fear.

She brushed her hand over his soft, dark hair and
touched her fingers to his cheek. She confessed something she'd never let anyone know. "I'm scared."

Ben didn't say a word, just leaned in and kissed her.
His lips were warm and soft against hers. He held her
close, wrapped her in his warmth and that something
she didn't want to name but felt all the same. Without
words he told her how he felt, shared his fear, and the
same certainty she felt that she needed him in her life.

Yes, she could face down the Faradays, taking on the
responsibility of overseeing Alex's inheritance, being a
mother, learning to live her life without her sister. But
she couldn't face a future without Ben. Without her
son. They meant more to her than she ever thought
possible.

Told you so, she heard her sister's voice in her head.
Okay, maybe Margo was right about finding someone to

love and being happy. Her sister found it. Why couldn't Kate have the same thing with Ben? Did he want to build a life with her and Alex?

The second the thought entered her mind, Ben answered it with a hungry kiss, sliding his tongue along hers, tasting and tempting her to pay attention to everything he didn't say with words.

"You two are about to set this place on fire," a woman said from behind Ben.

Ben ended the kiss and pressed his forehead to Kate's. "Settle into it. We have all the time in the world."

Not giving her a chance to say anything, he turned and smiled up at Elizabeth. "Hey, we missed you when we came in."

Elizabeth cocked up one eyebrow. "That's because you only have eyes for her."

Ben tilted his head and a lopsided grin made the dimple in his right cheek appear. "Busted. You remember Kate."

"It's nice to see you again." Elizabeth set two plates of chocolate cake in front of them, then stared down at Alex. "I hoped he'd be awake."

"He had a long afternoon at the police station," Ben said, brushing his fingers over Alex's hair. The sweet gesture touched something deep inside of Kate.

"What did he do to end up in custody, steal your heart?" Elizabeth teased.

Ben chuckled. "Well, he did that. His mother too," he said with an easy smile. "We went to exchange information with the detective working the case."

"If you need Sam's help, he's ready and willing any-time."

"He's not working undercover?"

"Not these days. The kids hate it when he's gone for days and weeks. Me too. Sam doesn't like it as much any-more either."

"He wants to be with his family," Ben guessed.

"Yes."

"I'll give him a call if things heat up. Right now, we're waiting on some lab results and to see what the Faradays want from Kate."

"Money," Kate said. That simple and that complicated. With so much at stake, she needed to figure out what Donald would want her to do—how far would he want her to take this? He'd want her to protect Alex.

"People always think money will make everything better. All it does is make things more complicated. It's not so much the money, but the greed. That's what makes people do things without thinking about the conse-quences or who they hurt." Elizabeth spoke like she knew exactly what she was talking about.

"Elizabeth was almost kidnapped and ransomed a few years ago. Sam stopped the guy before he could take Elizabeth and . . ."

Kill her, Kate finished Ben's last words in her mind.

"Sam is an FBI agent. He was assigned to protect me after a serial killer shot him in front of my house and I became the only witness who could identify him."

"Wow, that makes what I'm going through with the Faradays seem tame by comparison."

"They're just warming up, Kate," Ben warned.

"I have the same feeling myself."

"Eat cake. Chocolate makes everything better. If that doesn't work, go back to kissing. Ben, you look happier than I've ever seen. You two make a great couple." Elizabeth glided away, saying hello to her other customers in the restaurant.

Ben forked up a bite of cake and stuffed it into his mouth, avoiding looking at her.

"Why haven't you been happy, Ben?" She couldn't help but ask. She hated to think some woman broke his heart and he'd been pining away for her. The thought of him with another woman burned her gut and cracked her heart.

"My friends think I work too much and don't take enough time for myself."

"Are they right?"

"For the most part. Work is great. My business has expanded over the years. I've built Haven House and sustained it with donations and city, state, and federal funding. It's a legacy that will live on without me. I'm at that point in my life when I want more. My friends want me to have more."

"They're all happily married with families, so you're the odd man out, and they want you to join the club."

Ben laughed. "Basically, yes. The thing is, I want to be a part of that club. Not going to a club and meeting women who only last for a flicker of time instead of becoming a flame that lights up my life."

She didn't know what to say to such deep and meaningful words.

"You know that moment we shared a few minutes ago?" he asked.

"Yes."

"I want more of that. With you. The way you looked at me. The way it made me feel. The honesty of it."

"This feels like it's going too fast and too slow all at the same time. My head spins whenever you're near and my heart . . ."

"What?"

"Wants more. Of you, of everything you make me feel, even when I try not to feel it. Everything seems so complicated for me right now. It seems so easy for you."

"It's not easy leaving you each night, trying not to call you ten times a day while I'm at work, giving you the time you need to grieve, settle into being a full-time mother, and figure out what you want from me. Just my help. A few fun dates. Something more and permanent."

"That's the part that scares me."

"A relationship?"

"No, how much I want something more and permanent with you."

"Good to know. We're on the same page. We can both relax."

"That's the last thing I can do around you."

"That's because you want to sleep with me, but we haven't known each other long—at least in this way—I get it."

"Are you always this blunt, or are you teasing me?"

"No. And no. I just don't see any reason for us to do the whole half-truths and flirting thing to know what we each want and will happen. Soon."

"Soon?"

"God, I hope so. You're killing me just being this close." He leaned in and kissed her softly. "Kissing you makes me dizzy. Making love to you will probably kill me, but I'll die happy."

Kate reached for him, planting her hand over his thumping heart.

"Want to feel it jump?" He didn't wait for her answer, just leaned in and kissed her again, taking the kiss deep.

She lost herself in the pounding of his heart against her palm, the feel of his lips pressed against hers, the slide of his tongue into her mouth. He tasted like chocolate and need. So addictive she forgot where they were, what she wanted to say, everything but him.

"You two need to get a room." Elizabeth's words and the truth in them made her smile against Ben's lips. It's just what she needed to break the coiling tension inside of her. She was making too much out of this. Fighting the inevitable. Worrying that Ben wanted more—or less—than she did when they wanted the same thing.

Ben's hand cupped the side of her face. She leaned into it.

"Are you okay?"

"I'm good. I'm with you."

"Right where I want you."

Alex cooed and giggled, drawing their attention.

Elizabeth stood by the table with Alex in her arms. She bounced him and made silly faces to make him smile. "I so want another one of these."

"Does Sam know that?" Ben asked, toying with a lock of Kate's hair, much the same way Alex did, like he couldn't let go of her.

"We've talked about it. Can I get you guys anything else? A room at the Four Seasons down the street?"

Ben pulled Kate closer and tilted his head to touch it to hers. "We're good for now, thanks. I might ask you to babysit, so I can take Kate out on a private date."

"Anytime. I'd love to have this little guy. Grace and J.T. will have so much fun playing with him."

"You don't have to," Kate said.

"Nonsense. I'd love to. Jenna and Marti too. We're family. We help each other out, don't we, Ben?"

"Yes."

"It's amazing how you've all included each other as family when most of you aren't related."

"Family, love, these things go beyond blood," Elizabeth said, smiling down at Alex. "Like Margo's love for her son, for you."

Elizabeth's understanding touched her. She understood the bond Kate shared with Margo and that bond extended to Alex. The two of them would have raised Alex with so much love. He'd have had two mothers. She accepted that now. Margo hadn't worried she'd take Alex from her. She'd wanted Kate to accept being a mother and loving Alex and sharing those two things with Margo.

Overwhelmed again, she sought out Ben's comfort

and understanding and buried her face in his neck and held him close. He hugged her back, brushing his hand down her hair. She didn't like this weakness in her. She'd always stood on her own or leaned on Margo. Now Margo was gone, and she had Ben. She mourned one friend and welcomed another into her life. She didn't want to be alone again. Not like she'd been before she met Margo when they were kids. In some way, Margo had brought Ben to her.

"Hey, honey, it's okay."

"I know. I'm tired and letting things get to me." Kate sat back and gave Ben and Elizabeth a weak smile. Alex squirmed in Elizabeth's arms. Kate took him and cuddled him close, rubbing his back. "He's hungry and ready for bed too."

"Come on, let's get him back to Haven House. It's late. He's missed his bath time."

"Elizabeth, dinner was delicious. The cake was outstanding. I can see why your customers rave about this place."

"Come back. Anytime. Bring this one with you. He doesn't show up nearly enough."

Ben slid out of the booth and hugged Elizabeth, kissing her on the cheek. "Thank you."

"I like her. She makes you smile."

"Now, if I can just get her to smile more often."

"You're up for the task. You never quit." Elizabeth waved goodbye and let them secure Alex back in his car seat and collect the diaper bag.

"You guys seem close."

"I see Elizabeth more than everyone but Jenna. I bring clients here all the time."

"I can see why. This place is amazing. The food . . . oh, my God."

Ben swung his arm around her shoulders, pulled her close to his side, and carried Alex in his other hand, and led her out of the restaurant and down the parking garage ramp toward his car. They'd parked in his cousin Cameron Shaw's spot, since he was the CEO of Merrick International and Decadence was on the first floor of the building.

They rounded the corner and Kate stopped in her tracks and gasped. Ben shoved her behind him, scanning the parking area and between all the parked cars.

Kate recovered and pulled her cell phone from her purse. She only got two bars and hoped the call went through to the police.

She hit speaker and dialed. "Nine-one-one. What is your emergency?"

"My name is Kate Morrison. I'm at the Merrick International Building parking garage. My friend's car has been vandalized. All the tires have been slashed and every window has been broken."

Ben kept watch over the surrounding area while she made the call. All the while, he kept a tight hold on Alex and stayed close to her.

"Are the vandals still on scene?"

"No. I don't think so."

"We'll send an officer." Kate hung up.

Ben pulled out his phone, but didn't let her listen to

the other side of the conversation. "Jenna, it's Ben. I'm at the Merrick Building. Call security and have a couple of guards sent down to the parking garage. I'm here with Kate. I'm parked in Cameron's spot while he's out of town. Someone trashed my car." Ben listened to whatever Jenna said. "Thanks. I've got this. I'm waiting for the cops to arrive, but want to be sure we've got some protection in case the asshole comes back."

Ben hung up and stared at her.

"Evan." That's all she had to say for him to sigh and cock up one side of his mouth in a grim line. She reached up and touched his cheek. "I love this dimple. It comes out when you smile."

"Well, I'm not smiling right now."

"I see that. I hope you've got good insurance."

"I don't give a shit about the car. He came here. While we ate dinner."

"He's gone now." She tried to soothe him, but it didn't work. He continued to scan the garage for any threat.

The elevator dinged in the distance. Within moments, two security guards appeared.

"They're checking surveillance now. If we caught this guy on any of the cameras, we'll nail him," the dark haired guard said to Ben.

"Cops should be here soon." Ben pointed to one of the guards. "Keep an eye on her and the baby. I want to check out the car."

Kate took Alex from Ben and moved toward the wall, some fifteen feet from Ben's car, with the guard. Ben swore several times as he rounded the car. She had to admit, the damage looked extensive. New tires and windows would cost him a fortune.

Kate glanced back up the ramp and sucked in a startled breath when a woman who looked shockingly like her sister walked past the entrance. The wind blew her long blond hair into her face, so Kate didn't get a good look at her as she disappeared out of sight. A trick of the mind?

"I'm sending you back to Haven House in a cab." Ben's deep voice startled her and made her turn to him before she ran up the ramp to get a better look at the woman. Why? Her sister was dead, not walking the downtown streets in San Francisco.

"Kate, I can't drive you and this is going to take a while. The guard will go with you and see you back safe. I'll call you later."

"What aren't you telling me?"

"He slashed all the seats with a knife and left a note."

"What did it say?"

"You don't want to know."

"Ben, you can't keep me out of this. I'm the one he's after."

"That's the point. I'm trying to keep you safe." Anger filled his words, but behind that came a deep need to protect her.

"Ben, please, I need to know what I'm up against."

"That bastard killed your sister. He shredded the leather seats and left a note saying next time it will be you. What you're up against is a man who will stop at nothing to make sure he doesn't lose everything. Do you get it? Do you understand why I want to surround you with guards and lock you in a room?" Frustration at the lack of an enemy to fight made him shove his hands into his slacks pockets and glare past her at the wall. He wanted to fix this, make it right and safe for her to go home and be on her own.

"Okay." Her easy answer made him frown even harder.

"Okay? Just like that. Okay?"

"If I only had myself to look out for, I'd fight you on this and win, because let's face it, I don't like being told what to do. But I have to think about Alex. He needs me. So I won't be stupid about this. I'll take the guard and go back to Haven House and wait for you to call me."

"Thank you." He pulled his hands free from his pockets and reached for her face, cupping her cheeks in his warm palms. He stepped close, blocking her from view of the two guards. "You forgot one thing in that nice but totally unbelievable statement."

He got it. She'd said the words, but didn't really want to leave him here to deal with this mess alone. She didn't want to take a backseat and let others handle things for her. Not her way, but the safest way in this case. "What's that?"

"Alex does need you. And so do I." He pressed her back against the wall as he leaned in for a kiss. She expected there to be all heat and need scorching her lips and insides. Instead, he kept the kiss light and filled with warmth that spread through her in a wave of heat. His hard body pressed against hers. She slipped her hands inside his jacket, around his lean waist, and up his back, pulling him close. He held himself against her with one arm braced at the wall next to her head; the other hand held her face, his thumb pressed under her chin to tilt it up for him to take the kiss deeper. His tongue traced her bottom lip. She opened for him and he slid his tongue along hers in one long sweep. Sexy as hell. She moaned, and he did it again. Slow, controlled, every movement of his mouth over hers was meant to get and hold her attention. He had it. She wanted more. She wanted to lead him deeper into the fire and watch him burn. She wanted to see him lose control. At the moment, she barely had her desire to rip his clothes off leashed. They were in public, being watched by two armed security guards. Alex sat on the floor right next to her feet. Still, the man knew how to kiss and make her melt.

"Cops are here," one of the guards called out from further away than she expected. They must have moved back to give her and Ben some space. Either that or the heat coming off of them might scorch the bystanders.

Ben ended the kiss with a brush of his lips to hers, then he kissed the tip of her nose. His thumb pressed her lips and rubbed across them. "You taste so damn good." The words came out rough and filled with the passion still riding through her own veins.

"I want to stay with you." To prove it, she fisted her hands in his shirt at his back and held on.

Ben pressed his forehead to hers and closed his eyes. "You. Are. Killing me." He opened his eyes again and stared into hers. How he found the strength to be tender, she didn't know, but she appreciated it so much when he caressed the side of her face with his fingertips. "Please, Kate. Go back to Haven House where I know you'll be safe."

Kate slid her hands back around his sides and up his chest and over every strong muscle. She pushed him back as she stepped away from the wall. "Okay. You win. I'll go."

"Kate, honey, it's not that I want you to . . ."

She pressed her finger to his lips. "I know. It's okay. Call me when you're done here. I'm going to put Alex to bed."

"You need to sleep." He swept his thumb along the dark circle under her eye. At this point, she probably looked like a raccoon.

"I will. After you call me and let me know what they find here and that you got home okay."

"Worried about me?"

She pressed her hand to his over her face, turned, and kissed the inside of his palm. "Yes."

Ben let out a sigh, his chest heaving under her other hand. He moved aside and gave her space to reach down and grab Alex. "Get moving before I can't let you go."

Kate walked away with the security guard and left Ben to deal with the police and the building's security people. His parting words stuck with her because what she wanted to say back was, "Don't let me go."

Chapter Sixteen

THEY STOOD IN the shadows a block from Haven House. The man stared at the money, trying to decide how bad he needed it. Bad enough to commit a crime.

"Look, if you're not up to the task, just say so. All I'm asking is that you bring me the baby."

"No one gets hurt?" he asked again.

"That's up to you. I don't care how you get the baby, but you don't get the twenty-five grand unless you bring him to me."

Parked outside the gates surrounding the small play yard at the back of Haven House for hours, opportunity finally arrived. A way into the heavily secured shelter. The coconspirator talked to his wife through the bars. The man wanted his wife back, but needed the money to pay his legal fees and provide for his family. Easy enough to talk him into doing this with the right amount of cash as incentive.

"You said you could do this for me. If you can't, well, I'm sure I can find someone else who needs the cash."

"No. I'll do it." He narrowed his eyes and strode off like a man on a mission.

Finally, someone who understood how to do a job. You get it done. The alarm system at Haven House proved its worth, keeping people out. The stunt with Ben's car had been a half-baked idea to get back at the cocky lawyer. A complete waste of time. The lawyer didn't matter. Killing that woman and the kid gained them the total inheritance.

Victory.

Chapter Seventeen

KATE CLOSED THE door to her room, ready to crash for the night. In the five days since Evan destroyed Ben's car and got away with it because the only thing on tape was a dark figure in a mask, she'd barely slept, worrying about what Evan would do next. Would he go after Ben to get to her? The thought nearly stopped her heart.

Ben turned on the romance these last few days. He called her several times a day to talk. Really he called to assure himself she was okay. She found it sweet and charming, because he filled up those phone calls with snippets of his day and stories from his past. Out of the blue he'd say, "Did I ever tell you about the time I went fishing at the creek with Jimmy? We played Indiana Jones. Jimmy fell off this fallen log we tried to cross the stream on and I had to fish him out of the water. Biggest catch of my life."

This inevitably led her to tell him about something

she and Margo did when they were young. Like boosting two teenage boys' bikes when they were eleven and fourteen, riding down to the grocery store to pick up two jugs of chocolate milk, and hiding out in the branches of their favorite tree at the park. When those boys came looking, those bikes were still at the grocery store two blocks down, and they never looked up. Just called out a dozen gruesome threats while they beat all the bushes looking for them.

It took her four of those phone calls to figure out that when he asked her a direct question about her growing-up years, she blew him off each time. But if he told her something about himself, she inevitably tried to top his story with one of her own. She scolded him for tricking her. All he said was how cute she sounded when she was mad. Which made her hang up on him.

So he sent her a gorgeous bouquet of flowers. She leaned down and smelled the sweet spring blooms. Roses, lilies, daisies burst in red, pink, and white and made her ridiculously happy every time she came into her room and saw them.

Kate pulled her shirt off over her head and tossed it on the chair by the window. She undid her bra at the back and sighed when it landed on her shirt. She snapped up her favorite cotton nightgown with the spaghetti straps, white with little blue flowers. She smoothed her hands over the material, straightening the skirt over her jeans. She pulled it up just enough to unbutton and unzip them and slide the denim down her legs. Free of her day clothes, exhausted, she went into the bathroom to scrub her face clean. The warm water helped relax her. So did the cup of tea she'd shared with Jill and Mariana in the dining room. Thank God Mariana begged her to take Alex for the night to earn some extra cash. With assurances from Jill that the teenager had babysat for other babies, Kate gave in and let Mariana take Alex. He'd had a good day. Played a lot during their sit-down tea. He'd sleep well and probably would only get up once in the night for a bottle. She'd made Mariana swear to come get her if Alex woke up more than once, or Mariana couldn't handle him. She tried to remain relaxed after washing her face and using the toilet, but something nagged at her. She blew it off as missing Alex.

Kate climbed into bed, but grabbed her phone off the side table when it chirped a text message. She smiled before she even swiped the screen to read Ben's message.

BEN: *Sweet dreams.*

KATE: *Sweeter when you're in them.*

BEN: *Then dream of me.*

Okay, so maybe she liked cheesy lines. She must, because her heart did that flutter thing she'd gotten used to since Ben became a real part of her life.

Kate settled into the blankets and let her tired body relax into sleep and a dream filled with Ben and the passion that had been building since the moment she saw him again at her sister's place. In her dream, those sultry kisses they shared weren't enough anymore. She needed him close. And naked.

He joined their bodies and made love to her. With his body pressed to hers, his hand clamped around her thigh, his hungry mouth pressed to her lips, he loved her into oblivion.

She woke with her heart pounding against her ribs, her breath sawing in and out, and sat up, wondering what made her freeze with fear. Something pulled her from that dream and alerted her to danger.

Muffled whispers in the hall drew her attention. This late at night, most of the residents, if not all, were fast asleep. No alarm sounded, so it must be someone who lived here. Still, the tightness in her gut and the dread flowing through her veins made her slip from bed and her room, headed straight for Alex. The halls were dark but for the soft streetlights glowing from the hall windows.

Her thrashing heart refused to settle, even as she approached Mariana's door. Voices sounded through the wood.

"You can't do this," Valentina shouted.

"Don't tell me what to do," a man's voice shot back.

"He's just a baby."

"Papa, please, I promised to watch him."

"Let him go," Valentina wailed.

Something thumped and glass crashed to the floor and shattered.

Kate turned the door handle and threw the door wide open, ready to protect her son against whatever threat loomed. She spotted Valentina on the floor by the sofa. Broken shards of glass from the lamp lay spread around her. She struggled to get up, leaned on one hand, and pressed the other to her red, swollen cheek.

Kate glared at the man in front of her. Dark hair, even darker eyes, he stared back at her and sneered.

"So, you like to hit women. Well, come on," she taunted. "See if you can get past me."

The man reached down to take Alex from his playpen. Mariana grabbed at his back and pounded with her fists. "No, Papa. Leave him alone."

The man shoved Mariana aside, sending her sprawling to the wood floor. Mariana scrambled up and kicked her father in the leg, dropping him to his other knee.

Kate stepped in before the teen got hurt. The man stood up, ready to go after Mariana again. Alex wailed from the playpen, spooked when the man jostled it sideways. Kate jumped on the guy's back and wrapped her arm around his throat. She held her hand and pulled tight, choking him. His hands wrapped around her arm at his throat. He tried to pry her off of him, but she held tight. He spun one way, then the other, trying to throw her off. She used her thighs to hold on to his waist and keep her body stable. When he couldn't swing her off, he turned and backed into the wall. She banged her head and back, but didn't let go, not until he shifted and slammed her into the window, breaking the glass. They nearly fell through the window, but the man kept his feet and pulled her back into the room. She lost her grip, slid down his back, and shoved him with both hands the second her feet hit the floor. He swung his arm wide, spinning to face her, and clocked her in the side of the head. Flashes exploded behind her eyes. She squeezed them shut and opened them to help clear her vision.

The man plucked Alex out of the playpen. Mariana stood in front of him, her hands on Alex's torso, trying to pull him from her father's grasp. "Let him go, Papa," she screamed.

"Stay out of this, *chica*."

Mariana held tight to Alex and kicked her father in the knee again. He fell sideways, but caught himself. Kate punched him in the kidney, then the ribs under his left arm. He released Alex. Mariana pulled him close, spun around, and ran. Unfortunately for Kate, the man turned and threw a punch right at her face. She blocked the blow, but he wasn't done and came after her, rushing her head-on. He grabbed her around the waist, picked her up off her feet, and slammed her to the ground, landing on top of her. He punched her in the side three times, planted his arm across her throat, and scrambled up her body to straddle her hips.

"Who sent you here to take my son?"

"Fuck you, bitch. You hide my wife and daughter here, you get what you deserve."

"Is that right?" She punched him in the nuts.

"Fuckin' A," he wailed, grabbing his junk. She tried to buck him off her, but he smacked her across the face. She leaned up and punched him square in the nose. His head snapped back and he fell off her. She scrambled to her feet and kicked him in the jaw, knocking him out cold. Blood flowed out of his broken nose and down his face, pooling on the floor where he lay immobile.

"Fucking asshole." She pressed her hand to her face, hoping to ease the throbbing sting.

Valentina cowered in the corner, her back to the wall. The second she saw her husband lying on the floor, she scrambled forward and shook him. Her tear-streaked face rose up to her. "What did you do?"

"I gave him exactly what he deserved. Why the hell did you let him in here?"

"He loves me. He misses me."

"Yes, it's written all over your face how much he loves you." Kate tried to find her compassion, but couldn't. The asshole tried to take her son.

Three cops rushed into the room, guns drawn and at the ready. Kate put her hands up in front of her and froze.

"Kate Morrison?" one of the officers asked.

"Yes, where's my son?"

"Outside with the girl. He's fine."

Another officer subdued Valentina while they hand-cuffed her husband. "No, please, don't hurt him," she pleaded. "Don't arrest him. He didn't mean it."

The cops pulled the man up from the floor. Not quite awake after she knocked him out, he swayed. The officers held him up. "She broke my nose," the guy whined.

"You probably deserved it," the officer said, dragging him out of the room and out of sight but not earshot.

"Fucking bitch, I'll get you for this."

"Come and get it," she shouted back, still pissed off he'd gone after her son. Mostly, she felt guilty for leaving Alex with Mariana. He was her responsibility. She'd left him, and he'd nearly gotten kidnapped and, probably worse, killed if Evan got his hands on him.

"Miss Morrison, why don't you sit down," the remaining officer suggested.

She didn't so much sit as fall onto the couch cushion. The adrenaline wore off and she felt every cut on her back from the glass window, every bruise to her ribs, and the pounding ache in the back of her head where he'd slammed her into the wall.

She rubbed her fingers over the small lump. "Fuck, that hurts."

"Medics are on their way up. Tell me what happened."

The cop's gaze dipped to her chest. For the first time she realized all she wore was her skimpy nightgown, which got pulled down and nearly off her breasts. She righted it and grabbed a pillow to hold against her for comfort and warmth.

"I left my son, Alex, here with Mariana to babysit so I could get some sleep. Something woke me. I heard whispers in the hall and got out of bed to investigate. I heard that asshole fighting with his wife and daughter and came into the room to make sure they were okay. I needed to know my son was okay. He came here to take my son."

"Why would he do that?"

Her heart lurched again.

"Evan Faraday must have paid him to do it."

"Why?"

"My son is Evan's brother. Their father was murdered nearly two weeks ago. Alex is due to inherit everything, unless he's dead. Then the Faradays will get everything as Donald Faraday's surviving heirs."

"Are you serious?" the cop asked, skeptical.

"Call Detective Raynott. He'll confirm everything."

The medics rushed in, cutting off the officer from asking more questions. She'd let him get the answers from Detective Raynott.

Mariana stood in the doorway, Alex crying in her arms. Kate waved her forward and took Alex, despite the protests from the paramedics.

"We need to check you out."

"He's my son. He was nearly kidnapped. Work around him."

The head pounding she took made her woozy. She didn't fight the medics demanding she go to the hospital to get her head checked out. They settled her on the gurney on her side, thanks to the glass still stuck in her back and the bleeding cuts. She settled Alex next to her.

"Is there someone who can look after the baby?"

"No. He's coming with me."

"I can call Ben," Mariana said, tears shimmering in her eyes as she wrung her hands together.

"Go to my room. My phone is beside the bed. Call him, and bring my phone and Alex's car seat to me at the ambulance."

Mariana took off to do as she said. The girl met her at the ambulance and handed over her phone.

"Ben will meet you at the hospital. He's very worried."

Kate took Mariana's hand and squeezed it tight. "Thank you, sweetheart, for protecting Alex. You did so good."

Pride lit Mariana's eyes, erasing some of the embarrassment and regret that clouded them after what her father did. She squeezed Kate's hand back, then let go, brushing her hand over Alex's back before she stepped away.

Kate let the paramedics do their thing, taking her blood pressure and cleaning the cuts on her back. She snuggled Alex close, pressed her face into his sweet little body, and closed her eyes, hoping Ben hurried. She wanted to see him. As tough as she was in the moment, now she needed to feel Ben's arms around her. She needed him to reassure her Alex would be safe. Somehow they'd find a way to end this.

BEN RACED TOWARD the hospital, smacking his hand against his rental car's steering wheel when he got caught at another red light.

"Fuck."

He needed to get to her. He needed to see her. The second his phone rang in the middle of the night, he'd known something terrible happened. He hoped it was just another false alarm at Haven House. His hopes turned to fear when he heard Mariana's shaky voice on the line and not Kate's.

Mariana stumbled through telling him what happened. At this point, he could barely decipher her jumbled statements about her father attacking Kate and trying to kidnap Alex. There'd been a struggle. Kate got hurt, but what about Alex? Was the little boy okay? Kate would never forgive herself if something happened to her child. He'd never forgive himself for not protecting them better.

The light turned green and he rammed his foot down on the gas, squealing the tires as he raced the last half mile to the hospital. It was all he could do to muster the patience to park the car and not leave it outside the front doors. He ran into the emergency room and asked at the desk, "Where are Kate Morrison and Alex Faraday?"

"Room nine. Down the hall, last door on the right."

Ben ran, dodging an old woman pushing her husband in a wheelchair, sliding a pole with IV lines next to them. He nearly slammed into a nurse.

"Hey, slow down."

He didn't stop, just rushed to the room and pushed open the door, stopping in his tracks when he spotted Kate lying on her side, Alex tucked against her chest, and a doctor sitting behind her with a pair of tweezers in his hand. He dropped a piece of bloody glass into a metal tray. The clink of glass hitting metal snapped him out of his stunned state and made him move to the bed. He leaned down and kissed Kate on the forehead, pressing his lips to her skin and holding the sweet touch until his heart stopped beating itself against his ribs and settled down. Her hand came up to touch his face. It trembled against his skin. He leaned back and held her hand between both of his.

"What's the damage, Doc?"

"Mild concussion. Bumps and bruises. I'll stitch closed some of these cuts, the others are minor. Almost got all the glass out now."

Ben shook his head and ran one hand over his head.

"Kate, honey, are you okay?"

"Better now that you're here."

"And Alex?"

"Sleeping like a baby," she said, but without even the hint of a smile. Her lips began to tremble. Her eyes filled with tears that spilled over and ran down her cheeks and into her hair. "He tried to take my baby."

"He didn't. You stopped him."

"The way I heard it, she kicked some ass. Busted the guy's nose. Knocked him out." Admiration filled the doc's voice that matched the grin on his face.

"That's my girl." Ben brushed his hand over Kate's hair. "You're one tough chick."

"Don't forget it," she said, though it lacked the oomph he'd hoped for.

He held her hand and rubbed his hand up and down her thigh covered only by the thin hospital gown they'd put her in.

"What hurts the worst, honey?"

"My head."

"We gave her something to take the edge off. I'll give her a prescription for pain meds to take home."

"You're releasing her tonight?" Ben asked.

"As soon as I'm done here, she's free to go. Someone should stay with her. The concussion is mild. She'll have a headache for a day or so. She needs to rest and take it easy. She should refrain from carrying the baby around in case she gets dizzy."

"I'll take care of her."

"Ben . . ."

"No arguments."

"I was only going to say that I don't have anything to wear. They cut my nightgown off in the ambulance to check out my back."

"Oh, well, that's no problem. I'll get you something."

"You can wear the hospital gown home for now," the doc said, tying off another stitch in Kate's back.

Unable to help himself, Ben leaned over to see the damage. He hissed in a breath. "Damn, honey, that looks bad."

"Oh, good, I thought it only felt bad," she teased.

"Most of this is superficial. Looks worse than it actually is. In a few days, the swelling will go down and most of these cuts will heal. Stitches can come out in five to seven days," the doc explained.

"Okay. I'll make sure she sees someone about them."

The doctor worked for another five minutes. Kate flinched a couple of times when he pulled tight on a stitch, but otherwise she stared up at him. He kept her hand firmly in his and rubbed her leg to let her know he was there. Right beside her.

It took the emergency room personnel another half hour to finally get her paperwork together and discharge her. Ben hated to leave her, but he had to run out and bring the car around. A nurse wheeled Kate outside. He'd already secured Alex's car seat in back, though he didn't have the base.

He helped Kate out of the wheelchair and into the front seat.

"Nice car," she said.

"I rented it while mine gets a makeover," he teased.

"You have a thing for sports cars."

"So?"

"It's nice."

With her settled in the front seat, he ran around to the driver's side. Kate stared over her shoulder at Alex in back.

"That's not safe." The seat belt crossed over Alex's car seat. It would keep him from tumbling over if they got in an accident, but no, it wasn't ideal.

"We'll stop by Haven House and get the car seat base and your things before we go to my place."

Kate went quiet on him during the ride. Not surprising given the early-morning hour and all she'd been through. He called Jill at Haven House to pack up Kate and Alex's things. Used to late-night phone calls from women in trouble and in need of a safe place to hide, Jill didn't mind doing what he asked. By the time he pulled into the back parking area, she'd put all of Kate's things by the door. He grabbed them, stuffed them in the trunk, and resecured Alex's car seat with the base. Kate scanned the parking area like any minute an army would rush out of the shadows. He hated seeing that fear in her eyes. The second he got behind the wheel, she reached for his hand and held it tight.

"You're okay, Kate. We'll be at my place in a few minutes."

She nodded, but didn't say anything about his plan to take her home. Things between them had been heating up this week. They'd grown closer. So much so that he couldn't really imagine his life without her and Alex in it. He'd long ago stopped thinking that all of this, his feelings, was because of what Morgan predicted. All he knew is that getting that call tonight, the fear he'd felt on the way to the hospital not knowing how bad Kate was hurt, his mind spinning every conceivable "what if" that turned out worse than the next, made him understand one thing. He loved her. How that happened, he didn't know. But he didn't want to lose it. He wanted to hold on to her, make her happy, be happy with her for the rest of his life.

"Ben?"

"Yeah, honey?"

"I'm glad you came to get me."

Ben brought their joined hands to his mouth and kissed the back of hers. "I'm sorry you got hurt, sweetheart. It kills me to see you scared and in pain. I swear, you'll be safe with me."

She didn't say anything. He hoped he could keep that promise, but like him, she probably thought nothing would keep her safe so long as the Faradays wanted her and Alex out of the way.

Ben pulled up to the gate at his place and punched in the code for the security gate. Kate leaned forward to stare out the window and up at the luxury apartments.

"You live here?"

"Yeah. Why?"

"Nothing. It's nice. Expensive."

"I make a good living, Kate."

"I thought you'd have a house, that's all."

"This place has security, a pool, a gym, and a concierge service if I need it. I work a lot. I don't have time to take care of a house and property."

"Oh."

He heard so much in that "Oh." Like he didn't have the time for a wife and family. For her and Alex.

"To tell you the truth, I've gotten tired of this place. Well, not so much the place as being alone here. Which is probably why I work so much and avoid it. It'll be nice to have you and Alex here with me."

"For how long?"

He pulled into his parking space and cut the engine. He turned and faced her, her hand in his. "As long as you want to stay, Kate." He leaned in and kissed her softly. "As long as you want to stay."

She didn't say anything, just stared up at him, her eyes wide and round.

"Come on, honey, let's go inside. You're tired. You can take the meds the doc gave you. I'll fill your prescription in the morning. I'll take Alex, and bring your stuff in after I get you settled."

Kate got out, her movements stiff and automatic. He pulled Alex from the backseat, carried him, and led Kate to the lobby door. Steve and John, the two night guards, nodded to Ben when they entered. Kate punched the button for the elevator, holding the hospital gown closed.

"Everything okay, Mr. Knight?" Steve asked.

"This is my girlfriend, Kate, and her son, Alex. Kate had an accident. I picked her up from the hospital. They'll be staying with me."

"Welcome, Kate. Feel better," Steve said.

Kate gave the guards a halfhearted smile and stepped into the elevator. They rode up in silence. Ben walked out ahead of her and led her to his door down the hall. He unlocked the door, let Kate go in ahead of him, and entered the code into the security panel by the door.

Kate sighed with relief.

"You'll be safe here. The alarm system is monitored by security downstairs. We're on the third floor, so nobody can get in through the windows. Fire exit is three doors down the hall to the left."

She nodded and stood in the middle of his living room in her bare feet and the hospital gown tied at her back looking lost. She didn't see the comfortable furnishings or landscape paintings on the walls.

"Come on. Let's get you to bed."

He led the way down the hall past his office in the spare room. She stood in the doorway, staring at the king bed covered in a dark blue blanket.

"You and Alex can take the bed. I'll sleep on the couch."

"You don't have to give up your room."

"I don't mind. You need your rest, Kate."

"I want to stay with you." Her head fell and she stared at the floor. "If that's all right with you," she said to her pink painted toes.

This time Ben didn't know what to say. He wanted her to be with him. He'd never expected it to turn out this way. Still, this wasn't about seducing her into his bed. She needed him to comfort her. She needed him so she could feel safe.

He walked straight into the master bedroom and set Alex's car seat on the bed and pulled the blue comforter and white sheet down. He unstrapped Alex from his seat and gently lifted him out, trying not to wake the little guy. Alex sucked his pacifier hard and grumbled a bit, but settled once Ben laid him in the middle of the bed and tucked his baby blanket around him.

He turned to face Kate. She stood next to his tall dresser, her fingertip touching his law school graduation photo. The hospital gown, though tied, showed off her backside. A man could get used to seeing a woman in white-lace-trimmed blue panties. He could get used to seeing her in anything—and nothing.

Focusing on the task at hand, he went to his dresser and pulled out one of his college T-shirts. He closed the distance between him and Kate and stood too close to her just to see what she'd do. If she was half as nervous as him, well, they'd have to find a way to ease into this together.

Kate surprised him and walked right into his arms. She held him close, her face buried in his chest. "Thank you."

He closed his arms around her, the T-shirt hanging from his fingers down her backside, his fingertips pressed to her smooth spine where the hospital gown split. "Um, you're welcome."

"I mean it. I really appreciate this. I know it's weird. We haven't even . . . You know. And here I am asking to spend the night with you, but we have Alex, and it's not for the reasons you want, and . . ."

"Kate, stop." He cupped her bruised face and tilted her head back so he could look down into her worried blue eyes. "I'm glad you're here. I'm still so angry and upset about what happened to you. I want to hold you close and reassure myself that you're really okay. Let's start there, like we started this relationship as friends. Everything has to start somewhere. It doesn't have to happen all at once."

"I'd really like to . . ." She waved her hand toward the bed. "But . . ."

"We will when there isn't a *but*, just you and me and what we want and need from each other. Right now, you need me to comfort you. I can do that. I want to do that."

She hugged him close, then turned in his arms and reached up over the dresser to touch one of the silver framed photos of him as a boy with his trusted black Lab at his side. Ben had his arm hooked around his beloved dog.

"You were such a cute little boy."

"I think I was about eight in that picture. All big front teeth and gangly legs."

"That cute dimple in your right cheek when you smile."

He smiled behind her and felt the heat in his cheeks. He draped the T-shirt over his shoulder, placed his hands on her shoulders, and squeezed, massaging the tense muscles, knowing the worst of the cuts and bruises were a bit lower.

"What if he'd taken Alex? I might never have had the chance to see him grow into a little boy." The hitch in her words tore at his heart.

"Kate, honey, he's safe and sound. They didn't take him. They won't. You kept him safe. I'll keep you both safe."

She bent her head. He couldn't see her face or hear her cry, but he felt the shaking in her shoulders beneath his hands.

"You're tired. You need to take your meds and rest." He slid his hands over her shoulders to the first tie on the gown at her neck. He pulled it free and traced his fingers down her spine to the next one, and the next one. Finished, he pushed the gown off her shoulders and let it fall at her feet. He leaned in and kissed one of the cuts high on her shoulder. Maybe he got a glimpse of one rosy tipped breast, but he didn't stare or linger, but moved down her back to kiss a particularly angry red mark that would turn to a bad bruise.

"Ben." She sighed out his name.

"Kate," he answered, kissing another small cut, a bruise, the length of her puckered stitches running along her shoulder blade. Now that he had her attention, and she wasn't thinking about losing Alex, he continued to kiss the marks on her back and crunched up the T-shirt so he could pull it over her head. He kissed his way up her neck, draping her long hair over her shoulder. He hated to stop, but she needed comfort and time to settle into this part of things between them. He didn't want to take advantage of her vulnerable state. They could lose each other making love and forget for a little while the terrible things that happened, but he wanted more. He wanted to give her more than a distraction.

The T-shirt went over her head with no resistance. She pushed her arms through the sleeves and he pulled the material down her body to drape mid-thigh. He hated to cover up all that delectable skin, but did so for her benefit. And to save his sanity. A man could only take so much, and having a beautiful woman nearly naked in his room not five feet from his bed stretched the limits of his restraint.

Kate stood by and let Ben take care of her. She hadn't balked at him taking off the hospital gown. In fact, she didn't feel the least bit self-conscious. This was Ben. The man who showed up at two in the morning at the hospital in his wrinkled blue dress shirt and a pair of old worn jeans with his hair in disarray. He'd jumped out of bed and come running to her.

She turned to him, wearing his shirt, and looked him up and down.

"What?" he asked, wary of her perusal.

"How is it that you look seriously sexy in a suit and damn delectable in jeans?"

He chuckled, reached out, and hooked his hand around the back of her neck under her hair. "How is that you look so damn adorable in my shirt?"

"I like the shirt. It's my new favorite thing."

"I hoped I'm your new favorite thing."

"You're the very best thing in my life. You and Alex."

Ben pulled her close and walked backward toward the bed, pulling her along. She went willingly. She couldn't put up much of a fuss. The last of her energy dissipated as Ben turned and gently pushed her shoulders so she'd sit on the bed. He reached down, hooked his arm under her legs, and put them up on the bed, helping her roll to her side, facing Alex. He leaned down and kissed her on the head, making her feel even more special and loved.

Yes, he made her feel loved.

"I'll be back in a few minutes. Try to get some sleep."

She grabbed his hand before he walked away. "Wait. Where are you going?"

"To get your bags and Alex's stuff. He's going to need a bottle and diaper change soon."

"Oh. Okay."

Ben leaned down, planted his hands on both sides of her shoulders, and kissed her softly, taking his time, letting the kiss stretch out even as her nerves relaxed. His mouth met hers again and again with soft brushes.

"I'll be right back. Please, Kate, rest." Ben tucked the blankets around her. She tried to find a comfortable position, but she ached and the cuts on her back hurt. Ben's hand settled on her thigh, just like in the hospital. Just the feel of his hand, the reassurance that he was there, settled her. He walked out of the room, flipping the light off, but not leaving her in the dark. Light from the hall spilled into the room. She felt the loss of Ben and held her breath waiting for him to return, listening to every sound in the unfamiliar place. The fear of losing Alex and the fight she'd had with that man washed over her again as she thought about the night's events.

Alex stirred beside her. She couldn't help but think he sensed her unease. She rubbed his back, hoping to ease him back to sleep, but he let out a wail and cried. He needed a diaper and a bottle. She needed to sleep. All of a sudden her energy disappeared, but she scooted up on the mattress, put her back to the soft pillows, leaning to one side away from the worst of the stitches, and picked Alex up, settling him against her chest.

"I'll bring the diaper bag and a bottle," Ben called down the hall. The front door shut behind him with a thud.

Too tired to answer him back, she focused on her son. "There now, Ben's on the way."

Kate pressed the pacifier into Alex's mouth, laid him back on her up-drawn knees, and rocked him side to side with her legs. She softly sang "Twinkle, Twinkle, Little Star" over and over until Ben walked in, smiling at her.

"You've got a pretty voice."

"It's late. You're overtired and being nice because I'm a wreck."

Ben shook his head. "You are not a wreck. And I do like your voice." He spread the changing pad on the bed, picked up Alex, and laid him on it. He undid Alex's sleeper, changed his wet diaper in a snap, and folded the soiled diaper like an expert. He put Alex back on her lap and handed her the bottle. "Let me get rid of this"—he held up the diaper—"and I'll be right back."

Alex happily sucked on his bottle, his eyes bright and very awake. He held her thumb, squeezing tight like he didn't want her to go.

"I'm not going anywhere, baby. I'm staying with you forever."

"Are you talking to me?" Ben said, entering the room,

pulling his shirt off over his head. She swallowed hard and stared at his bare chest, six-pack abs, and gulp-worthy biceps. "Kate?"

"Huh? Yeah?"

"Were you talking to me?"

Eyes glued on his massive shoulders and lethal biceps, she said, "No. I was talking to Alex." But maybe she meant it for Ben too. The more time she spent with him, the more she wanted. The more she dreamed.

"You keep staring at me like that and I'm going to have to do something about it."

Her gaze shot up to his. The right side of his mouth cocked up, revealing that dimple she loved, and his eyes sparkled with mirth.

"I'm not used to seeing you not wearing a suit." The stupid statement only made him smile more.

"I'll work on that."

As in she'd get to see him out of his suit more often. Yes, please. She slid her gaze back over his broad chest to his lean waist and over the thick ridge pressed up the length of his fly.

He undid the button on his jeans. She gulped.

Her gaze shot back to his. "Don't. Have mercy on a girl in my condition. I can only take so much."

Ben's deep chuckle reverberated in her chest. He went to the dresser, grabbed a T-shirt, and disappeared into the bathroom. She let out a ragged breath and raked her fingers through her hair. What she wouldn't give to make love to Ben and forget about everything that happened. She wanted to lie in his arms, feel his strength, and take it in, because right now she felt weak. Afraid. Not for herself, but for her son. She'd do anything to protect him. The aches and pains she felt proved that. She'd lay down her life for his. She hoped it didn't come to that.

"Kate, honey, what's wrong?"

Ben stood beside the bed. He'd left the hall light on, the bedroom door closed but for a slim crack. He stood in the sliver of light. Concern etched lines in his forehead as he bent over her, hands planted on the bed beside her.

"Nothing. I'm fine. Tired."

"Give him to me. I'll finish feeding him and get him back to sleep." Ben scooped up Alex and held him tucked in the crook of his arm. Ben wore the clean T-shirt and black boxer briefs. Sexy. Relaxed. Comfortable, like they did this all the time.

Ben walked around the bed and climbed in beside her, leaning back against the headboard, much like her. Kate scrubbed her hands over her face and dug them into her tired, itchy eyes.

"Come on, honey, slide down and rest. I've got Alex. You sleep."

"You must be exhausted too."

"I'm fine. More worried about you than anything."

Kate settled into the mattress and pillow on her side facing Ben and Alex. She stared at her sweet boy, so lovingly held and cared for in Ben's strong arms. Alex stared up at Ben, so trusting and enamored with him. So awake. She feared he'd never get back to sleep now and keep Ben up all night.

Ben rearranged Alex in his arm, so he could hold the

baby and the bottle with the same hand. His other hand settled on her head. "Close your eyes, honey. Relax." He brushed his fingers over her head and down her long hair over and over again. The hypnotic caress eased her muscles, but her mind took her back to what happened, seeing Alex in that man's hands as Mariana pleaded with her father to let him go.

Tears fell from her eyes. Reliving those terrifying moments left her raw and unable to hold it together any longer. Ben's fingertips brushed across her cheek and back into her hair. She scooted closer and buried her face in his side, smelling the spring scent of his laundry soap on his shirt, feeling him breathe, and hearing the steady beat of his heart.

Alex finished his bottle. Ben adjusted him up and over his shoulder and patted his back, waiting for the inevitable burp.

How could this man be so sweet and kind? She'd never known anyone like him.

His deep voice broke the quiet. He sang "Row, Row, Row Your Boat" over and over again to settle Alex back into sleep. He never stopped running his hand over her hair and down along her arm, constantly letting her know he was there with her. He'd protect her. It was safe to let go, he'd be there for her.

She could get used to this. To him. She wanted more. Dangerous territory in her book, but with a man like Ben, worth the risk.

Chapter Eighteen

BEN WOKE UP with that damn nursery rhyme still in his head two days after Kate got attacked at Haven House. Alex stirred on his chest, and Kate snuggled up to his side. He loved having them here, but God, being close to her these last two days, spending all their time together at his place, seeing her making meals in his kitchen, made him realize he wanted to make her a permanent part of his life.

Hell, wanting her was killing him.

If he spent one more day in her company, one more night in the same bed without touching her the way he wanted, he'd go completely insane. All he thought about was stripping her bare and making love to her. They'd shared several hot make-out sessions on the sofa, but she pulled back, put on the breaks, and retreated behind the fog she lived in each day. With everything unresolved in her life, he got that she needed time to think about her future and Alex's. He needed to find a way to not only get her to consider him in that picture, but realize he had no intention of not being included in that future.

She wanted him. He felt it every time he kissed her. Yesterday, she'd actually walked into the kitchen after putting Alex down for a nap and kissed him. Just a "Hey, I'm here" quick kiss while he put together some sandwiches for them, but it meant so much that she'd come to him. She thought it was just attraction. They certainly shared that. The woman devoured him with her eyes and made him burn without even laying a finger on him. He needed to find a way to get her to acknowledge this thing between them went deeper than attraction, than lust. He was falling in love with her. He thought she felt the same, but she held herself back more and more. Except for that kiss yesterday. She'd done it without thinking.

So, if she wanted to believe all they shared was intense lust, he'd show her that they certainly had that, and oh so much more.

First, he needed to change the baby's diaper and get him ready for his sleepover. He dreaded Kate's reaction when she found out what he'd set up, but they needed this. A little time alone. And Alex would be safe.

Ben needed to figure out their living arrangement. Alex needed a schedule and his own bed. He'd work on that, too, this weekend. He'd taken Thursday and Friday off to see Kate through after she was attacked, but these next two days he intended to solidify their relationship and come up with a plan for their future. Okay, he meant to convince her they needed to live together. For her and

Alex's safety. He'd use that excuse for now. She'd see right through it, but would she admit she wanted to live with him? He didn't know. It all felt so new. He'd never even had a woman spend the night, and here he'd slept with Kate, but they hadn't even made love.

I'm losing it.

His body certainly thought he'd lost it. The horny teenager inside that left him in a perpetual state of arousal around Kate shouted for him to do something to stop the agony of wanting her. Now.

Alex gurgled and tried to raise his head, but only ended up face-planting on his chest. He grabbed fistfuls of Ben's shirt and dug his hands into Ben's tight muscles, trying to push himself up.

He couldn't lie in bed all day with Kate, but he wanted to. Giving in to his baser needs, he turned and looked at her lying beside him, her face tucked into his side, her legs down the length of his. He loved her long dark hair, the soft slope of her cheeks, and the way her nose turned up just a bit at the end.

"Are you going to feed him?" She didn't even open her eyes, which made him smile. She wasn't a morning person. She liked to wake up slow, cuddling in the covers. And into him. She rubbed her face against his side, then pressed her lips to his ribs and kissed him. She settled back into the mattress like it was the most natural thing in the world. Maybe it was when she was still half-asleep and not thinking about all that happened and all she had to do. Right here, right now, she could be the woman who wanted him, maybe even loved him.

He ran his hand down her arm and over her hip. "Sleep, honey. I'll take my best bud and get him squared away."

Kate wrapped her arm over his middle and hugged him close. "You are the best."

"I'll show you how good I am later."

"Promises, promises," she mumbled.

He liked they could tease like this, but she had to know he meant those words. To prove it, he squeezed her hip. "You'll see, sleepy head."

"Mmm. Can't wait," she whispered, falling back into sleep.

Ben shook his head. He swore she tortured him on purpose. He must love her if all these little things she did without realizing it endeared her to him more and more each day.

Yep, I'm losing it.

Ben rolled out of bed and held Alex high over his head like an airplane. Alex smiled and dropped his pacifier right out of his mouth and onto Ben's face. It bounced and landed at Ben's feet.

"Dive-bombing me so early in the morning, buddy."

Ben brought Alex down to his shoulder, bent and grabbed the pacifier from the floor, and carried Alex into the kitchen.

"So, do I have time to make the coffee, or are you starving?"

Alex stared up at him, his blue eyes bright and full of happiness this morning. The kid woke up happy and ready to go, while his mother slept the daylight away.

"Coffee, it is." Ben rinsed the pacifier in the sink first, then pushed it back into Alex's mouth to keep him happy for the next few minutes. He set Alex in his bouncy seat on the kitchen floor and got to work on what they both needed.

Coffee brewing, Alex's bottle ready. He sat on the sofa, turned on the morning news, and sat feeding Alex, thinking about the day and how he was going to convince Kate to go along with his plans.

He stared down at Alex propped up on his legs staring back at him, happily eating. He liked this time they spent together. He'd grown close to the baby this week. So much so that the thought of not having him around made Ben a little sad. He liked playing the dad, helping Kate with Alex, and playing with the baby.

"I want to be your dad," he admitted on a surprised whisper.

He wanted to have more kids with Kate. Alex felt like his. He loved the little boy. Every time he looked at him, he saw Kate. He saw Alex grow in his mind. All the things Ben would like to do with him. Teach him to play baseball and swim. Take him to his first day of school. Help him with homework. Talk about girls. See him graduate and become a man.

He looked at Alex and saw his own future with Kate beside him, their children the joy of their lives. He loved his work, the accomplishments he'd had over the years, but nothing would be more satisfying than having a family. Not like the one he or Kate grew up in, but the happy one they'd make together.

By the time he fed Alex, the coffee was ready. He poured himself a mug and carried it down the hall to his bedroom door. He stared at Kate, lying asleep in his bed. Damn, but that was a pretty sight. Her hair spread over the pillow. The splash of sunlight coming from between the curtains highlighted her face, but didn't streak across her eyes. Good. She needed her rest. He'd wear her out later.

He grabbed his jeans off the chair and pulled them on. He'd shower in a little while. After he made breakfast.

Alex played on the floor in the living room on his play mat. Ben smiled down at him, sipping his coffee. Alex liked it here. He'd certainly taken over the place. Toys littered the floor around him, a stuffed dog and bear sat on the couch. Baby bottles, nipples, and extra pacifiers sat on a dish towel next to the sink. A book about baby's first year sat on his dining room table. Kate read it often, tossing out odd tidbits and facts to him as she read. Yep, they'd made themselves right at home. Now to figure out how to get them to stay. Well, maybe his other idea would work better if Kate agreed. He'd have to wait and see.

With Alex settled on the floor, playing with a rubber duck that squeaked every time he gnawed on it, Ben went into the kitchen to make breakfast. He pulled out a frying pan, grabbed the eggs and other fixings for Kate's favorite omelet out of the fridge, and began cooking.

By the time the hash brown patties he had under the broiler browned, she walked into the room, rubbing her tired eyes. She raked her fingers through her hair, pulling the mass away from her pretty face.

"Morning, beautiful. Hungry?"

"You are the best boyfriend ever."

Ben went still. He didn't look at her, just planted his hands on the counter and stared down at the omelet in the pan. The tension in the room built, until he raised his head and stared at her over the island.

"I thought I'd try it on, see how it feels."

"And?"

"I like it," she admitted shyly. "Too much? Too soon?"

"Not enough. It's about damn time," he answered, making her laugh.

"You've been really sweet these last few days. Well, since the night my sister died, really. You have the patience of a saint. For Alex. And me. You've gone out of your way to take care of me and Alex. I can't tell you how much I appreciate it. How much it means to me that I can count on you."

She trusted him now without hesitation, or a second thought. Finally. Hallelujah. "I want to take care of you," he assured her, because though she'd said the words, she still needed the reassurance.

"I know. I see that. I've been kind of muddling my way through, trying to figure things out. I still don't know what to do with everything that's happened. The one thing that is clear, the thing I see clearly, is you."

Ben didn't know what to say.

"I need to start making decisions. I'm starting with you, because although I could get through this on my own, I don't want to. I'm always the tough girl. The one who has to do everything on her own. When I was lying in that hospital bed with Alex while they stitched me up, all I could think about was you. I wanted you there with me. I needed you with me."

"You scared me half to death. It's bad enough that guy hurt you, but if something happened to you . . ." He hung his head and shook it back and forth. "Kate . . ."

"I know. I see it, Ben. I feel it between us. So instead of doing what I normally do, what I've been doing with you all this time, holding back, I'm doing what my sister wanted, what she was brave enough to do, and so am I. I'm taking that leap of faith because I believe that what we have is something special. It's not my grief pushing me toward you and the comfort you give to me. It's so much more and it's rooted in my heart. It grows every time I see you with my son. Every time you kiss me. Every time you look at me and I see what I saw when Donald looked at my sister."

He pushed away from the counter, turned off the stove, and pulled the hash browns from the oven before they burned to a crisp. "I wanted to take this weekend to talk to you about what comes next. Your sister's house. Donald's company. Everything."

Kate rounded the counter and joined him in the kitchen, stopping a mere six inches away from him. "Yes, we've let that all simmer on the back burner. If we don't take care of it soon, it'll boil over."

"You said *we* need to take care of it."

"You and me. That's how it works, right?"

Kate rose up to her toes, pressed her body down the length of his, wrapped both her hands around the back of his neck, and pressed her forehead to his. She stared into his eyes, hers filled with intent and regret all at the same time.

"Every breath I take, every beat of my heart, is for you and Alex. I don't have one foot out the door. I'm not looking for a way out. I was scared of what I felt for you, but I'm not holding anything back anymore. I want to be with you. I want to make a life with you. I never want to spend a single day without you."

Overwhelmed by the depth of her words and the emotion she put into them, he crushed his mouth to hers, sliding his tongue deep, taking possession of her mouth. He held her tight to his chest and lifted her right off her feet.

Ben had the woman he loved in his arms. All he wanted to do was take her down the hall to his bed, but if Alex saw her, he'd want her. Ben needed her more right now. He needed to see her, touch her, worship every square inch of her.

He backed her toward the table. The backs of her legs hit, and he leaned down and laid her out on the solid wood. His lips left hers, but only so he could trail kisses down her neck. He inhaled her sweet floral scent and went dizzy with a lust that nearly sent him to his knees.

Not a bad idea.

He worked his hands under the T-shirt she liked to sleep in. His shirt. He slid his hands up her sides, grabbed hold of the shirt, and tore it off over her head.

"Ben."

His name on her lips came out as a demand he had every intention of answering. Right now. He stared down at her creamy skin, dark hair spread across the table and spilling over, soft pink nipples that hardened beneath his gaze, and down her smooth stomach to her waist and strong legs that wrapped around him, holding him close.

"God, but you are so damn beautiful."

She grabbed a fistful of his shirt and pulled him down to her. The kiss rocked him and drove him on to show her how much he wanted her. Desperately.

He kissed a path down her neck, over one plump breast, to her hard nipple. He took it into his mouth, sucked hard, then licked the tip with his tongue. Her sweet honey taste quickly became his addiction. She arched her back and moaned for more. Her fingers dug through his hair and pulled him back down. He took her other nipple into his mouth, circling his tongue. He took her other breast into his palm, squeezed, and brushed his thumb over the wet nipple.

"Oh, God, Ben."

Yeah, he thanked God for bringing her to him.

Her arched back fell to the table and she sighed out her pleasure. God, how he loved those sweet sounds she made.

He kissed his way down her belly. She tensed and giggled when he licked her skin from her belly button down to the waistband of her black leggings.

"Ticklish?"

"Only when you do that."

"Oh, I'm going to do a hell of a lot more of that."

He hooked his fingers in her pants and panties and dragged both barriers down her legs and out of his way.

"Ben? We're in the kitchen."

"Yes, I know. You're breakfast."

To prove it, he leaned down and kissed her belly again, his hands sliding up the outside of her thighs to relax her again. Her fingers combed through his hair, over his head, down his neck, and over his back. Her fingers dug into his muscles, rubbing and massaging, holding him to her. He licked his way from her belly button down to heaven. He took her in his mouth, sank his tongue deep into her wet core, then he sucked hard. She nearly came apart beneath him, but he wanted to take his time. Love her right.

He sank to his knees, slipped his arms beneath her legs, and drew them up and over his shoulders. He buried his face between her thighs and licked and laved at her sweet center. Her taste on his tongue, the musky smell of her, went to his head. He sank his tongue deep again, loving her with his mouth. He swiped his thumb over her slick clit and rubbed soft circles that made her rock her hips and moan.

Her nails bit into his shoulders, and she came apart beneath him. He rode out her orgasm, then laid his tongue flat against her and licked his way up to her belly, setting off another round of aftershocks through her system. Her legs fell off his shoulders and wrapped back around his waist as he kissed his way up her ribs, over her breast, up her neck, and to her sweet mouth.

Her arms wrapped around him, hands sliding down his back. She dragged his shirt up and over his head. He stared down into her bright, dancing eyes.

"My turn."

She might just be the death of him. Loving her had nearly sent him over the edge more than once. He hoped he could pull it together and hold back the orgasm riding him hard, begging him to sink his dick deep inside of her and let go.

"Come here, I need to feel you against me," she begged.

He didn't want to be anywhere else. He leaned over her, pressed his chest to her hard-tipped breasts, and kissed her again, rubbing his body over hers. She made one of those sweet moans again, so he pushed down hard over her, smashing her breasts against his chest. Her softness against his hardness did something to him. Her, this close, only made him want to be closer.

Her hands never stopped roaming over his skin. Her fingers dug into muscles, massaged over his shoulders, and raked down his spine to his hips. She slipped her hands around his sides and between them, though he hated to put any space between them. She worked the button and zipper free on his jeans, slid one hand down the length of his hard shaft over his boxer briefs and back up. He nearly disgraced himself when she wrapped her fingers around him and rubbed back down and cupped his balls.

Unable to stand the sweet torture, he stood in front of her, intending to pick her up and take her to bed. She had other ideas. She sat in front of him, dragged his jeans and boxers down low enough to free his swollen flesh. Her small hand wrapped around him, and she worked her hand up and down. She kissed his chest, then sank her teeth into his pec. Her tongue smoothed over the small hurt, and his dick jumped in her hands. He stared down at the top of her head, her mouth moving over him, her hand wrapped around his hard cock. Damn, but he'd never seen anything sexier.

The doorbell rang. Alex cried out in the other room at the startling sound. Kate's head fell back and she stared up at him, her mouth parted, lips swollen, and begging for a kiss.

A fist pounded on the door. "Ben, FBI, open up."

"Fuck."

Kate's eyes went wide.

Ben turned and yelled at the door. "Be right there." He cupped Kate's face in his hands. "I'll explain in a second. Go get dressed."

Kate released him. He missed her warmth, regretted the interruption, and anticipated being alone with her all at the same time. She jumped off the table. Before she shot past him, he grabbed her shoulders and stopped her. He stared down at her, dragged his gaze up all those naked curves, and met her gaze. "We are not done."

She smiled, but ducked her head, grabbed her clothes from the slate floor, and ran down the hall. Ben pulled his pants and boxers back up, sucked in his gut to get the zipper up over his hard length, and dragged his T-shirt over his head and pulled it low over his jeans. He walked toward the front door, stopping to pick up Alex from his play mat. The little guy stared at him wide-eyed and worried after his mother ran past him. He didn't seem to like the doorbell.

Ben opened the door and let it swing wide. "You're early."

Sam stepped in with Tyler right on his heels. "We're right on time."

Ben glanced at the clock. He got so caught up in his conversation with Kate and making love to her, he'd lost all track of time.

"Sorry. My fault. Thanks for coming. I really appreciate you guys doing this for me."

"You sure you don't want me to go with you?" Tyler asked.

"I'll take care of her. You two take care of this one."

Sam held out his hands. Alex leaned over to go to him, so Ben handed the baby over.

"Come here, little man. You want to come to my place for a playdate? I can't guarantee Gracie won't dress you up and paint your nails, but you'll have fun with J.T. He's more your speed probably."

"You sure Elizabeth is up for keeping him overnight? He gets up around three or four for a bottle."

"We're all good, man. No problem."

Kate walked into the room. Ben closed the front door and walked to her, putting his arm around her shoulders. "This is my girlfriend, Kate."

Her head went back and she stared up at him. He looked her straight in the eye. "I don't need to try it on. It fits for now." He hoped she understood that soon they'd outgrow the whole boyfriend/girlfriend thing. He wanted her to be his wife, now, but he'd give her time to settle into it. One step at a time.

"So, Morgan was right," Tyler said, smiling like a lunatic.

"Is Morgan ever wrong?" Ben shot back.

"No. I'm happy for you."

"Uh, you still haven't told me what this Morgan said to you. And who are they, and why does he have Alex?"

Kate stared at the two men, both armed with guns on their hips and badges on their belts. Unsure what was going on, she pulled free of Ben's embrace and took Alex from the handsome blond man.

"Kate, these are my friends Sam and Tyler. They work for the FBI. You met Sam's wife, Elizabeth, at my office and Decadence. Tyler's wife, Morgan, is pregnant and about to burst, so she's at home."

"She doesn't like to come to the city," Tyler explained. "Too many people and bad vibes."

Kate eyed Tyler, then Ben.

"You'll understand when you meet her," Ben explained, without telling her a damn thing about the mysterious Morgan, who made a prediction about them.

"What are they doing here? Did something happen on the case? Are you going to arrest the Faradays for my sister's and Donald's murders?"

Sam shook his head. "We've been monitoring the case for Ben, but there's no new information. The blood results aren't back from the lab. The gun used belongs to Donald and only your sister's prints are on it."

"My sister did not kill the man she loved."

Tyler touched her shoulder. "We never said she did. The evidence is what it is, but doesn't tell the whole story. We know Evan killed them. The police will prove it."

"You sound so sure."

"Well, Morgan won't give me any of the specifics, but she would warn us if the outcome isn't what we expect."

"She will?"

Tyler shook his head and frowned. "Maybe. She believes things happen for a reason. Trying to change an event doesn't guarantee you change the ultimate outcome. We'll have to wait and see."

"I really don't understand anything about your Morgan."

"You'll like her. She can't wait to meet you. You'll come with Ben to the next family dinner," Tyler said.

"Like the one Ben attended the night my sister died."

"We're Ben's family," Sam said. "We're here to help."

"What are you going to do?"

"We're taking Alex for the weekend. He'll be safe with us."

Kate held Alex tighter and turned him away from the men. "No. You can't just take him."

Ben took Kate's hand, but addressed the guys. "Give us a minute."

"Take your time," Sam said, sitting on the sofa in the living room. Tyler did the same.

Ben plucked Alex from her arms and handed him off to Tyler. "Here, practice for when Noah decides to join us."

Tyler scooped Alex up under the arms and raised

him up, flying him high. "Hey, buddy, want to have a sleepover at Uncle Sam's place? He's got all kinds of things for you to play with and drool all over."

Alex cooed and smiled.

"Alex is fine. Come with me." Ben dragged her into the kitchen behind him. Not much privacy. "Hear me out before you say no. I meant to tell you about this earlier, but I . . . we got distracted." He gave her a smoldering look and she got his meaning. She tamped down on her roiling emotions, the need to keep Alex close and safe, and listened to Ben.

"Why are they taking Alex for the weekend?"

"Sam and Elizabeth have two kids. Grace and J.T. They know how to take care of a baby. Sam is FBI. Anyone tries to hurt Alex, he'll shoot them dead."

"That still doesn't explain why he's taking Alex."

Ben raked his hand over his already disheveled head. She'd never seen him nervous like this. "I like having Alex here with us."

"But?" Her heart sank. Alex made things difficult. Maybe Ben wasn't ready to take on the responsibility of having a child. A child that didn't belong to him.

"Wipe that hurt look off your face. I'm not sending Alex away because he's in my way, or it's too hard to take care of him and try to get closer to you. Damn it, Kate, haven't I proven to you that I think of that kid as mine? I would do anything for him."

Kate's heart grew heavy in her chest.

"I asked Sam to take him, yes, because I want to be alone with you, but also because it's time for you to make some decisions. We need to make plans. We need to go to your sister's house and either get more of Alex's things, or move you both in there permanently."

"Would you rather we not stay here with you?"

Ben swore again. "I want you with me always. We need to decide what we are going to do next. I didn't want to risk taking Alex with us to your sister's place. Now we know he'll be in safe hands, and we can do what we've put off."

Kate stared at Alex lying on the sofa beside Sam. His hands and feet up in the air as Sam held his favorite stuffed puppy over him. Alex gurgled and laughed when Sam brought the puppy down to tickle his belly. He'd be okay with the FBI agent. He'd be okay without her for a couple of days.

Ben's hands landed on her shoulders and squeezed. "I know you're scared to let him out of your sight. We can't hide here, hoping this blows over, or Evan does something stupid enough to land him behind bars. We need to settle matters with the estate, where you're going to live, and getting Alex back on a schedule. Soon, you'll need to take your sister's ashes and say goodbye."

Kate's gaze shot to the metal urn on the sideboard in the dining room. Ben picked it up for her from the mortuary, but she couldn't decide what to do with it, or where to scatter Margo's ashes. She didn't know what to do about the house, the money she now had, the business, anything. Ben was right. She'd been hiding. She'd sunk her head in the sand and waited for all the bad to go away, so she could live her life free of this fear that she'd lose Alex and Evan would eventually get what he wanted and kill them both. Nothing had changed since her sister's death, except now she had two more reasons to put Evan in a cage or in the ground.

She wanted to build a life with Ben and Alex. She wanted to have everything her sister lost and so much more.

Kate walked out of Ben's grasp to dig through her purse on the counter. She found her cell phone and walked over to Sam. "Mind putting your number and address in there for me, so I know where he is and I can call him later to say good night."

"Sure thing." Sam took the phone and started tapping in the information. "I'm putting Elizabeth's numbers in here too." Once he finished, Sam tossed the phone to Tyler. "Put yours and Morgan's. Ben can add the rest of the family later."

"Good idea." Tyler punched his numbers.

Neither of them seemed to mind she'd hesitated to hand her son over to them. They were FBI, Ben's friends, not crazed lunatics. Still, she felt better having their information just in case she needed them and Ben wasn't with her.

"Honey, go pack up anything you think Alex will need. Extra clothes and stuff. I'll put the bottles and formula in a bag for Sam."

Kate left to do as he asked. Ben waited for her to enter their bedroom before turning back to his friends.

Sam popped the back off Kate's phone and put in a transmitter. "Here I thought it might be difficult to get her phone, and she just hands it over."

"You're sure you can track it with that thing?"

"On my phone, Tyler's, and if you give me yours, I'll set you up too. If that bastard takes her and she's got her phone, we can find her," Sam said.

"Unless someone shuts off the phone, which is why we'll put this one in her purse," Tyler said, putting words to action.

"Put the bottles and stuff together before she comes back and catches us," Sam said.

Ben tossed over his phone and let Sam do his thing. Alex lay on the couch next to Sam playing with Sam's keys. Every time they jingled, he smiled and squealed.

"Hey, I need those back, kiddo, if we're going to drive home." Sam pretended to try to take the keys. They jingled more, delighting Alex.

Kate stood just inside the living room watching Sam, her shoulders tense, her grip on Alex's bag so tight her knuckles went white. Alex kicked and squealed at Sam, loving the attention. Kate relaxed, and Ben let out the breath he'd been holding, hoping she agreed to go through with this.

"I have his bag. He'll want his stuffed dog and that purple ring he loves to chew on."

Sam grabbed both off the sofa and tucked them in the bag. Kate walked to the counter and grabbed a pen and the pad of paper next to the phone. She sat at the table writing, while Ben finished putting Alex's food together.

"Ben, what time did he eat this morning?"

"Seven-thirty."

"He'll need another bottle about ten-thirty. I've written down his schedule, how many ounces of milk he eats, the general routine we've got him on. His new favorite song to fall asleep to." Kate smiled at Ben.

"It's still playing in my head." Ben smiled back.

"Which one does he like?" Sam asked.

" 'Row Your Boat,' " Ben said. "Over and over again. He bobs his head to the words as he eats his last bottle of the night. It's very cute."

Sam and Tyler both smiled and laughed.

"No problem. I know that one. J.T. will be happy to sing it over and over again. He's been on this nursery rhyme kick for weeks." Sam picked Alex up from the sofa and handed him over to Kate. "Say bye-bye to Mommy."

Kate held Alex close and kissed his face several times. Alex grabbed fistfuls of her hair and held on. "You be a good boy. No playing with guns. Say please and thank you. Try not to wake up more than once so Elizabeth can get some sleep."

"He's going to be fine. We've got a playpen for him to sleep in right next to our bed. The alarm system on our place is the best you can get."

"If that's not enough, Sam is armed," Tyler assured her.

Kate secured Alex in his car seat, tucked his favorite blanket around him, and handed him the stuffed puppy from out of his bag. She rose and looked at Ben. "You got the extra pacifier? He only likes those."

"I got it, plus the bottles. He's all set."

"What about extra burp clothes?"

"I put two in the bag. Kate, he'll only be with Sam until tomorrow night. I promise, he will be safe."

"I know. Of course he'll be safe. Sam has a gun. He's FBI. It's fine."

"You're rambling, honey. Say goodbye."

She turned back to Sam. "Bye. Thank you. I appreciate this."

"Not as much as Ben will." Sam winked. "Call anytime. As often as you like. I know how much I miss my munchkins when I'm working."

"It's fine." Kate leaned down and kissed Alex on the head again. "Be good. I love you."

Tyler stepped forward, carrying one of the bags and the base to Alex's car seat. He patted Kate on the shoulder. "Don't worry. He's got two armed guards."

"Thank you."

"See you soon," Sam said, stepping out into the hallway. Tyler took the lead to the elevator. Ben and Kate stood in the door until they got into the car and the doors closed. Ben pulled Kate back into the apartment and closed and locked the door.

"I miss him already."

"I know you do, honey." Ben took her hand and pulled her down the hall to their room. "Which is why I'm going to distract you from thinking about it."

"Don't we need to make plans and go to my sister's place?"

Ben walked into the bedroom and pulled her around.

She thumped into his chest. He wrapped his arms around her and stared down into her questioning eyes. "Later. We never finished what we started this morning." He slid his hands down her back and over her hips. He squeezed her ass and pulled her close. Her arms went up around his neck. He leaned in and nuzzled her neck, kissing her soft skin and inhaling her sweet scent.

"Well, when last we left off, I was naked and I had you well in hand."

She always made him smile. "Yes, you did, darlin'." Ben pulled her shirt up and over her head. He didn't waste any time, unlatching her bra and sliding it down her arms. After that, his clothes, hers, went flying until they were both lying in bed naked, their bodies pressed together.

Ben stared down at Kate.

She pulled him down for a kiss. He kept things soft, light, no demand. He lingered over her lips, pressing his to hers, slipping his tongue past her lips in a long glide. She settled beneath him, let go of her anxiety about handing Alex over to Sam, and gave herself over to making love to him. Her hands slipped down his neck, under his arms, and around his back. She held him close, hugging him tight.

Her feet skimmed up his calves, her thighs squeezed his hips. "I need you," she pleaded.

"What about your back? We can—"

"Shh. I'm fine."

He pressed his hard cock against her center, teasing her, tempting her. He kissed her neck, down over her shoulder, and back to her chest. He planted little kisses over her breast, then licked the underside in one long sweep ending at her hard nipple. He took the bud into his mouth and sucked hard. Her fingers dug into his back. Her hips rocked against his.

He kissed his way to her other breast and took it into his mouth. The one he left got lost in his hand. He squeezed. She moaned and went limp beneath him.

He reached down, wrapped his hand around her thigh, and squeezed. He slid his hand up her thigh to her hip, then pushed her thigh out wide and trailed his fingers over the sensitive skin and straight to her hot, wet core. Impatient to have her, he slid one finger into her slick center. She rocked her hips into his hand. He pulled his finger free, sliding it over her soft folds and up over her clit. Her nails bit into his back again. She sighed out his name.

Desperate to have her, he answered that call to action and leaned to the side and snagged a condom out of the drawer beside the bed. Kate took advantage of his position and slid her hand down his taut belly and over his hard shaft. She wrapped her fingers around him and he bit back a groan. Her mouth pressed to his chest, her teeth sank in and nipped at his pec. She liked to give him love bites. He wanted her to do it again. "Ah, God, Kate. The things you do to me."

She bit him again and raked her nails down his side. The combination of the small hurt, the tingling that spread over his side, and her hand working up and down his cock nearly undid him.

He pried her hand off his dick and held it down above her head. He took her nipple and sucked hard. Her free hand slid over his head and gripped his hair, holding him to her.

He couldn't take any more of her sweet torture. He sucked her nipple and rose up until it pulled free of his lips. He tore the condom wrapper with his teeth and sheathed himself. All the while Kate never stopped touching him. Her hands rubbed up his chest, her lips pressed kisses to his neck, her thighs held on to him, making it nearly impossible to get the condom on. Once he did, he plunged into her welcoming heat to the hilt in one hard thrust. Kate's head went back and a soft moan escaped her open lips. He took her mouth in a deep kiss, sliding his tongue along hers. Desperate, out of control, he pulled nearly free of her, then thrust back home. The sensations that swept over him lit a fuse on his restraint.

Kate planted her heels in the bed, raised her hips, and pushed against him as he thrust deep. She fell back to the bed and pushed up her hips, meeting him as he came back to her again and again. Her hands smoothed down his back and over his ass. She squeezed and pulled him to her. He didn't retreat this time, but grinded against her. She tilted and circled her hips, finding that spot that made her moan. He caught her rhythm, pulled out, then plunged back in, circling and rubbing against her clit.

Balanced on one hand, he used the other to stroke her breast, squeeze it into his palm, and pluck at her hard nipple with his fingers.

Kate panted beneath him, her body tightening, luring

him to the peak. He refused to leap without her and thrust deep again. She contracted around him, letting out a soft moan. He thrust into her hard and fast and followed her over the edge and into oblivion.

Ben collapsed on top of her, his breath sawing in and out at her neck. She wrapped her arms around him and held him close. She didn't know what possessed her to be so aggressive, but he didn't seem to mind. In fact, it seemed to set him off.

Now, all she wanted to do was softly caress his back and run her fingers through his hair to soothe him. She wanted him close. She traced her fingers up his spine, featherlight. She made circles on his shoulders, then retraced the path back down his back to his very fine ass.

"I like that," he whispered, planting a soft kiss on her neck.

"Yeah, I got a little rough. You might have some scratches on your back. I'm sorry."

"Don't be." He raised himself up on his forearms and stared down at her. "Don't ever apologize for giving yourself over to me, trusting in me to let you know what I want, what I like, and what I don't. You showed me what you wanted. I hope I gave you everything you needed. If not, all you have to do is ask, Kate. The time we share together like this should always be honest. I never want you to leave our bed unless you're happy and satisfied."

"I am. You . . . The way we were together. It felt so raw and open and . . . I don't know."

"Freeing."

"Yes. I wasn't worried about what you'd think of my

body, the way I touched you, the things I did. I just let go. I took in everything you gave me and I wanted to please you, but I also wanted to be a part of what you felt."

"First, your body is perfect. Made for me. We fit together, read each other, and complement each other. Never worry about the things you do, or the way you touch me. I loved it. I can't wait to do it again."

"Me too." She leaned up and kissed him softly. "I really never knew it could be like this." She pulled him down and hugged him close, loving the feel of his skin pressed to hers. She brushed her fingers through his dark hair again and again.

Ben kissed her neck, tilted his head back, and looked her in the eye. "It's only going to get better."

She hoped he meant everything in their lives, because right now everything besides the two of them together seemed out of control and unsettled. She longed to stay in this bed, in his arms, and happy the rest of her life.

Chapter Nineteen

KATE STARED UP at the massive house from the front yard. The deep green grass and cheerful spring flowers didn't take the edge off the sharp pain in her chest. Instead of the beautiful stone and wood home, all she saw was her sister and Donald lying dead on the floor in pools of crimson blood.

Ben's hands settled on her shoulders. His body pressed along the back of hers. His warmth eased the chill running up her spine. His presence made it easier to face going into this place again.

"A part of me thinks I'll knock on the door and she'll answer with a smile on her face. She'll hug me, and I'll feel that connection we shared that, no matter what, I always have her."

"I'm sorry, honey. Remember you still have Alex. You have me."

She placed her hands over his on her shoulders and took a bolstering breath. He was right. She needed to move on, think of her future with him and Alex. She couldn't continue to live in this limbo any longer.

She glanced over at the planting bed under the window. "We planted the pansies and ferns when I was pregnant with Alex. We sat in the shade, talking about all our wishes and dreams for him." She stared up over her shoulder at Ben. "It was such a good day."

Ben squeezed her close. "Let's go in," Ben coaxed.

"I don't want to see it again, but I guess I can't avoid it any longer."

"Kate, I hired the cleaning crew after the police released the house. The scene is clean."

"You did?"

"Yes. I couldn't let you walk back in there and see that again. I know you'll never forget, but I could at least do that for you."

She turned in his arms and hugged him close. "I don't deserve you."

"You have to keep me all the same. I'm only happy when I'm with you."

"That's sweet. You make a really good boyfriend. I'm surprised no one snatched you up before now."

"I was waiting for you." He kissed her on top of the head. He did that a lot. She'd grown to expect it. She loved it. "Took you long enough to show up."

"Sorry. I had some things to work out before I got here. I didn't believe in love until I saw Margo and Donald together. Now I get it. My heart unfroze and opened up when I had Alex. You saw the woman I was before. Distant. Reserved."

"I remember her. I kissed her once."

Kate frowned, thinking of the way she acted, running away from him like that. "It's probably better this way. Ask any guy I ever dated before you—I was cold."

"Can't. I'd only kill them for touching you."

She squeezed his middle tighter and smiled against his chest. "Now you're the only one who gets to touch me."

"You're damn right about that." His hands slid down her back and over her ass. He pulled her close. "You know we can't stand out here all day. Stalling won't change the house or what happened here."

Kate sucked in a deep breath, squeezed Ben's sides, and bolstered her strength to let him go and face her past and find a way to move on. She turned and walked up the path to the door and used her key to go in. She stood in the foyer like she did that night and took in the feel of the house. Instead of an ominous vibe, she felt the emptiness. The void of a happy family living here.

"You know, I never really got a look at this place when I came that night. It's nice. Open. Bright. Big," he said from beside her.

"She loved it here. We decorated it together. It seemed so unreal. Her living in this big house. I mean, we grew up with nothing but what we could fit in a suitcase to go to the next foster home, so having something as grand as this, well, you can imagine we were overwhelmed at first. Then we really got into it. She picked the art on the walls. I picked out the sofas."

"She was the more artsy, make things pretty person. You're the practical one."

Kate nodded. "Yes. Exactly."

"Donald didn't help with the decorations."

"Sure he did. He paid the bills, smiling at Margo like the money didn't matter, but seeing her happy meant everything."

"I know how he feels." Ben squeezed her hand.

"He'd come in, see us pouring over magazines and fabric swatches and give us this huge indulgent smile and shake his head.

"We laughed over ridiculous patterns that reminded us of things from our past long forgotten and better left in another era. When we'd hit an antique store or some boutique, we'd ooh and aah over things and bring them home and put them in their perfect spot."

"I've spoken with Donald's lawyer at length. This house is yours free and clear."

"You mean it's Alex's."

"No. Yours. Your sister left it to you. You said it yourself—you helped make this place the beautiful home you both always wanted. She made you a part of this home, included you in all the decorating decisions, because you were a very important part of her life."

Kate lived vicariously through her sister whether she wanted to acknowledge it or not. This house had been such a dream. The beauty and hominess they created here was exactly what Kate always wanted for herself. Now, it belonged to her, but how could she keep it?

"I can't afford to keep this place." The sadness engulfed her. She hated to think she'd have to sell the house and lose the tangible evidence of all her memories.

"You can use the money Donald left to Alex."

"No. That wouldn't be right. It's for him."

"I can afford the taxes and upkeep on this place." Ben stared down at her.

The softly spoken statement was filled with a longing she felt. Wishful thinking, or a chance for a real life. A happy life. "Ben . . ."

"Hear me out. I know what I want. To be with you and Alex. I think you want the same thing. My place is fine for now. But it's small. We'd have to turn the spare room from my office into Alex's room. I don't mind, but that means I have to move my office into the living space. I work from home a lot, especially at night. The building I live in is safe enough, but not really kid friendly. The nearest park is, like, five miles away. Parking sucks in the city."

"You seriously want to live with me and Alex, here?"

"Yes. You own the house. I pay the monthly expenses. You come to work for me at Haven House as the new director. You can take Alex to work with you every day. Eventually, I give you a ring, you say yes, we get married, and we raise Alex and however many more kids you'd like to have together."

Wow. All that. All at once. It overwhelmed her, but

settled quickly in her mind, like, "Oh, yeah, that's what I want too."

She shook off her jumbled thoughts and focused. "You want me to quit my job and work for you?"

He smiled.

"Why are you smiling?"

"You have no problem with the part where I ask you to marry me—you're worried about your job."

"Well . . . I . . . I worked hard to get where I am."

He only smiled more. "Keep your job. Live with me. Make a life with me."

Kate stared down at the ring Donald gave her sister now sitting on *her* right hand. A promise never fulfilled with a wedding, but enforced every day they were together by the love they shared.

"I don't need the ring, just your promise that we will love each other forever."

Not exactly the "I love you" declaration they'd both avoided until now, but close enough to reinforce they both felt and wanted the same thing.

"I promise, Kate. I swear, I'll spend the rest of my life trying to make you happy."

"You do make me happy. You're more than I ever thought possible for my life. You and Alex."

She scanned the rooms laid out before her and up the stairs leading to the second floor.

"What do you think? Do you want to live here? If not, we can sell it and buy another place."

The thought of selling tightened her gut. As much as the ghosts in this place haunted her, they comforted her more. She eyed him, her practical side taking over for her whimsical heart. "You'll have to commute to work."

"It's not that far. If I have you to come home to each night, I don't mind."

She took a deep breath and mentally leaped for that happy life her sister had and wished for Kate to embrace too. "Okay. I think this will work."

"You think? Of course it will work."

His enthusiasm sparked hers even more. "I'd like to change a few things. Make the house feel more like us, but still have those things Margo picked out and put together here and in Alex's room that I can share with him. We'll make new memories, but I can hold on to some of the old ones too."

"Whatever you want to do, we'll make it happen."

"I'll move my things from my condo. Sell it. Alex will have his room back. A backyard to play in when he's bigger. You can set up your office in there." She pointed to Donald's office.

"We'll get rid of whatever you don't want. We'll bring our things here. You'll have them and us. Right now, it's just a place with a bad memory. We'll make it a home again." Ben wrapped his arm around her shoulders, pulled her close, and kissed her on top of the head.

Her heart lightened. She couldn't wait to live together, here, as a family. She leaned into him, loving the solid feel of him beside her. She smothered out the nightmare in her mind with dreams of what their life would soon be like.

"So, when do you want to do this?" Kate asked, allowing herself to set aside her pain and look forward to her future.

Ben couldn't believe this went so well. He thought he'd have to do some fast talking and a whole lot of convincing.

"We can hire a crew to pack up your place."

"I think we should go through this one, decide what stays and goes, then we'll know what to bring from our places. We are definitely bringing your bed."

That made him laugh. "Well, now that we've christened it, we have to bring it."

"I think that's the best bed I've ever slept in."

"It's the last bed you'll ever sleep in," he warned, eyeing her.

"Then you better uphold your best boyfriend status."

"Is that right? Didn't I treat you good this morning?"

"We never did eat breakfast."

"I did." He winked at her, remembering having her laid out on his kitchen table. He loved the blush that spread from her neck up to light up her cheeks. "You're so pretty when you're embarrassed."

She pressed her hand to her red cheeks. "Stop."

He laughed, but inside he recognized those walls she'd erected had come down. He slid his hand behind her neck and pulled her close for a sweet kiss. He loved that they could be like this. Her resilience and strength shined through when she stopped living in the past and her grief and saw their future here in this house. She turned to him to give her strength to see this through. They'd wipe the slate clean and start building their own memories in this place.

He pulled her close and hugged her tight. His phone rang. He groaned, hating the interruption.

Kate pressed her hands to his chest and leaned back, staring up at him. "It might be Sam. Something about Alex."

He kissed her forehead, then stood tall and pulled his phone out of his back pocket. He frowned at the caller ID. "It's Haven House." He swiped the screen to accept the call. "Hello."

"Ben, it's Jill. You need to come to Haven House now."

"Whatever it is, can it wait until Monday?"

"Someone tossed a rock through the day care window. There's glass everywhere."

"Did anyone get hurt?"

"No. A couple of children were in the room, but they're okay. The cops are on their way."

"Take the kids outside and organize a game. I'm on my way."

Ben stuffed his phone back in his pocket, stared at Kate's worried face, and at the open rooms around them. He reached out and traced the side of Kate's face. "More trouble at Haven House."

Kate grabbed his hand and pulled him toward the door. "Let's go."

After a few steps, Ben dug in his heels and held her back. "No. Wait. What if Evan set this up to get to you? I can't take you there. What if something happens? I'll take you back to my place first."

"Nonsense. I want to help. I need to help. I can't stand to be cooped up in your place alone another minute. I'm not letting you go there alone. You said we stick together. We face whatever happens together."

"I don't want anything else to happen to you."

"I took care of myself the last time. I can do so again if I have to, but I won't, because you'll be with me."

"Stay here. Lock the door. Turn on the security system. I'll call Sam to come and get you. Better yet, I'll drop you at his place in the city before I go to Haven House. You can stay with him and see Alex."

"No. Alex is safe with Sam. If Evan's coming for me, I'm not leading him to Alex."

Kate held the door wide, waiting for him to make up his mind. Everything in him wanted to make her stay here—better yet, lock her away somewhere out of state, out of Evan's reach. Ludicrous. Evan wouldn't stop. Not until she was dead and the Faradays took everything. He needed to settle the estate, get everything into Kate and Alex's name, and end this madness.

Chapter Twenty

BEN STOOD AT the back of the building staring at the damage to the massive six-foot-by-twelve-foot-wide windows. He'd purposely made the room the day care because of the brightness the windows provided for the children.

"I'll go into the office and start making some calls to replace the glass," Kate said.

Even with the cops standing beside him, writing their report, Ben hated to let Kate out of his sight. "Kate, come right back. Don't go anywhere else."

Kate gave him a soft indulgent smile, but he read the underlying message. She could take care of herself.

Maybe so, but that didn't mean he didn't have to take care of her.

"Mr. Knight, any idea why you've been targeted?"

Ben rattled off the same tired story about Evan, Donald, and Margo mixed with the threats from Christina toward Kate and Alex. He hated this mess, this unyielding threat against them, Evan's constant pursuit of Kate. It had to end. He needed to find a way to stop it. Them.

The police officer folded his notepad and walked back to his patrol car.

Ben turned to Jill and the other staff members who'd set up a kickball game to distract the children. He needed to clean up the glass and board up the window.

"Jill, keep everyone out here until I finish inside."

She waved to let him know she heard. He walked back toward the building, but caught a movement outside the gates. He turned and caught sight of a woman walking on the other side of the street. She looked his way for a second, then dashed into the alley between two other buildings. She wore large dark glasses that obscured her face. Long blond hair hung down over her shoulders and chest. He swore she looked just like Kate's sister.

A cold shiver raced up his spine, warning him of danger.

Ben ran for the back door of the building. It slammed against the wall as he burst through and ran down the hall, calling, "Kate!"

He ran through the dining room and stopped short when Kate ran toward him, her expression dark with concern.

"Ben, what is it?"

He smelled it first, but the surprise and fear registered on Kate's face a second later. He turned and scanned the kitchen, saw the line of emergency candles all lit up on the counter, and beyond to the broken gas pipe just over the restaurant-size range.

He ran for Kate just as a whoosh split the stunned silence a second before the explosion. His body flew into Kate's. He took her down to the floor, shielding her with his body, blocked from the brunt of the blast by a low stone wall wrapped around a bank of booth seats. Debris hit his back along with a blast of heat, but the wall held. He didn't look back, just grabbed Kate by the arm, scrambled to get up and pull Kate with him to get away from the crackling flames consuming the building. They stumbled over pieces of wood and metal and ran out of the room, along the wide hallway where the windows had blown out along with part of a wall. They pushed through the door that led to the lobby and out the front of the building.

Kate patted her hands all over his back as they ran; she didn't stop when they got outside. He finally registered what she was screaming at him. "You're on fire."

Ben tore off his heavy coat and dumped it on the concrete, thankful the thick material hadn't burned all the way through to his shirt and skin.

"You're okay. You're okay," Kate said, checking his back, then launching herself against him, wrapping her arms around his waist. "You're okay."

"I'm okay, but what about you?" He had to yank her arm to bring her around his body. He checked her out from head to foot. She seemed fine. He brushed his thumbs over the redness on her hands from trying to put out the flames on his back. She hissed and pulled her hands away.

"That stings." She held her palms up and studied them. "They're okay."

"Oh, God, I can't believe we made it out of there alive." If he hadn't gotten to her in time, that blast would have killed her. The office Kate used to make the calls sat right behind the kitchen. Judging by the flames and damage to the building, she'd have been blown to bits.

His stomach soured. He leaned over, planted his hands on his knees, and dragged in several deep breaths, trying to erase the disturbing images in his mind. He coughed to clear the clog in his throat. His heart clenched at just the thought of what could have happened to Kate.

She rubbed her hand over his back. "Just the gas and smoke. Breathe, honey."

He did, but it wasn't easy, knowing how close he'd come to losing her.

BEN STARED AT the wreckage of all he'd built. The south side of the building survived the fire, but the north side smoldered, sending up plumes of smoke. Firefighters continued to pour water on the hot spots. He'd have to close the place until he could rebuild. He'd have to find a place for the displaced families living here. All twelve of them. The task seemed monumental, but Jill was already speaking to the Red Cross workers who'd arrived moments ago.

Kate stood by his side, her hand in his, their fingers linked. The paramedics gave her some salve for the minor burns. They didn't seem to bother her at all. She squeezed his fingers to get his attention. He hadn't really moved or said anything since this happened an hour ago.

"I'm so sorry, Ben. Everything you've worked for to do for this community. Those women and children who needed your help."

He gritted his teeth and shook his head. "The place is insured. I'll rebuild."

"I know you will. I'm sorry, this is all my fault."

Surprised she'd say something so stupid, he glanced down at her. "What? No, it's not."

"Yes, it is. If I hadn't stayed here, none of this would have happened. I heard what you told the police. Someone intentionally set this fire. They wanted to kill me. Now they've destroyed this place."

"Kate, none of this is your fault. You can't take the blame for what the Faradays do." He pulled her into his side. "I don't blame you for this. I blame them."

"Ben . . ."

"No. We are not going to let them win by putting a wedge between us."

"Then I guess my first order of business as the new director of Haven House is to work with the insurance company to push through the claim. I'll need to hire a contractor. Once we know the extent of the damage, I'll figure out what we need to replace and what we can do better this time. I'll let Jill handle finding places for the current residents. The rest of the staff will be on paid leave until we are up and running. Once we have a new structure, they can help with the decorating and furnishings."

Ben stared down at her, dumbfounded she'd made the decision to take the job, especially now that it was so much bigger than just running the place.

"What?" she asked. "I'm your girlfriend. Your partner. This place is important to you. It is to me too." She squeezed him tight. "We'll fix it, Ben. Together."

Ben crushed her to him and kissed her hard, then settled into it and the comfort she offered. He broke the kiss and pressed his forehead to hers. "I like the sound of that."

"You know what else? I'm tired of reacting to everything the Faradays do. It's time we made things happen."

"What do you have in mind?" he asked.

"Well, if Alex owns the majority share in the company, then someone should be heading it like Donald did that has Alex's and the employees' best interest at heart."

"You want to hire someone to run the company?"

"Yes. Someone we can trust. Someone who doesn't have an agenda, or can be bought or manipulated by the Faradays."

Kate pressed her lips together and considered the one thing she hated to do, but realized needed to be done to stop this madness. The heaviness in her heart wouldn't go away. What if someone got killed today? What if Ben got killed because the Faradays wanted all that money? She'd never live with herself if she didn't at least try to put an end to this.

"I also think we need to make Christina an offer. Settle the estate once and for all. End this before someone else gets hurt." Kate's gaze shot to the burned-out rubble. A sickening chill ran up her back. "It's pure luck no one got killed here today."

"Whether luck or design, I'm glad everyone got out."

"You don't think they meant to hurt anyone?"

"The fire started in the kitchen. Breakfast was over long before the fire. No one was in the dining room. All the residential rooms are on the other side of the building." He left off that she was the only one close to the fire's origin.

"Makes sense. Still, you can't count on everyone staying clear of that part of the building. The rec room and day care are on that side of the building."

"Except all the kids were outside playing games Jill set up because of the broken window."

"A distraction to get me here and do this." Kate shook her head. "We can't let anything like this happen again. If we take away their reason for coming after us, then we end this."

"That's if the Faradays accept a settlement."

"What alternative do they have? Spend the next several years in court fighting over this. Christina will lose. Her lawyer has to have told her that it's futile. Plus, we still have the murders. If they're convicted, they'll get nothing."

"We still don't know whose blood was on the knife. If they hired someone to do the crime, we might not ever find that person," Ben pointed out.

"You've turned into a real pessimist, you know that?"

"You're right. Let's start doing something to stop them, rather than waiting to see what they'll do next."

"There you go, lawyer man. What do we do first?"

"Call my cousin, Cameron, and arrange a meeting with the executives of the company."

"Why Cameron?"

"He's the president of Merrick International. He'll know what we need to do to run Faraday Electronics."

"Excellent. And he's family. You trust him, so I'll give him the benefit of the doubt."

Ben laughed. "Look at you all optimistic and trusting."

"I'm turning over a new leaf. Enough is enough. I want to take them down. Short of that, I'll settle for taking away their reason to come after me and Alex. Whatever it costs."

"Let's hope we can make a deal."

"We will. We have to. I've had enough cruelty and people taking things from me my whole life. I won't let them. We have to stop them."

Ben hugged her tight. She'd been so strong, but the cracks in her armor showed. She let them show to him, because she trusted him to help her make this right. To see her quest through to the end and keep her and Alex safe while he did it.

"Let's take that bastard down."

Chapter Twenty-One

KATE AND BEN met Cameron and his associate Bill Pratt outside the Faraday Electronics offices. They'd spent all day Sunday studying the company papers she dug out in Donald's office, the company literature, and everything they could find on the internet. Kate had no idea how to run a company the size and scope of Donald's. She didn't have the technical or engineering expertise. She didn't have the business acumen to pull it off well, at least not without a huge learning curve. So she took Ben's suggestion and made the call to his cousin, Cameron, herself. They spoke for an hour on the phone Saturday night. Cameron made some calls to colleagues within Merrick and Knight Industries, which he held a huge stake in, and found the perfect candidate to take the job at Faraday.

"Ben, so good to see you." The dark haired man with the gorgeous blue eyes held his hand out to Ben.

They shook and Ben pulled the man in for a quick back-smacking guy hug. "Is this your girlfriend?"

"Kate, meet Cameron Shaw, my cousin."

Kate shook his hand. "Nice to meet you in person. I really appreciate you doing this on such short notice."

"My pleasure. Anything for family. Besides, Bill owes me a favor, but I seem to be doing him one."

"Yes, you are." Bill stepped forward and shook her hand too. "Thank you for trusting me with this job. I won't let you down. I'll look out for Alex's interests."

She liked Bill right away, but when he said those words, she liked him even more. Still, that part of her that remained guarded warned her to beware. If protecting Alex's interests became second to Bill's interests, she'd fire his ass. She'd give him the benefit of the doubt because she needed someone on the inside at the company, but she'd watch him.

Cameron and Bill headed for the double doors leading into the building's lobby.

Ben squeezed her hand, leaned down, and whispered in her ear. "Stop glaring at him. He'll do a good job. He won't steal you blind. Cameron and I will be overseeing everything too."

Yes, they would. She took a breath, told that suspicious voice in her head to relax, and walked beside Ben into the building. They stopped short when they saw Christina and Evan Faraday talking to three gentlemen across the large open space.

"What are they doing here?" she asked Ben.

"Someone from the company must have contacted them about this meeting."

"But they don't have a say in what I do. Donald's will left everything to Alex."

"We're still waiting for a judge to rule on the prenup and divorce that Donald filed for before his death. Kate, they may get to keep a large stake in the company and gain most of Donald's assets if a judge rules in Christina's favor. That's why it's important to get Bill situated in the company now, so that Christina and Evan don't undermine what Donald built."

"Do you think she'd do that?"

"What I don't want her to do is sell the company out from under Alex. I don't want her to decide that she doesn't give a shit about the people who work here, the customers, and she just shuts this place down."

"She can't be that stupid. This place makes a ton of money. They made over a twenty percent profit last year alone. That was in a bad economy."

"And because Donald knew how to run a business. Christina and Evan have no idea what to do with this place. Unless they appoint someone like you're doing to oversee the operations, they'll drive this place into the ground. A company needs leadership and vision. Donald had both. Bill can fill that slot. He'll work with the executive team to keep things moving in a positive direction."

"Let's go see what they want." Kate scowled openly at the Faradays.

"You know, it really pisses me off to see that asshole still walking around and not locked behind bars after everything he's done." The fierce look in Ben's eyes surprised her. He always seemed so in control of his emotions. The attack on her and the fire at Haven House upset him, but the look in his eyes said a lot more. He feared that if Evan wasn't locked up soon, they might not be so lucky the next time Evan came after her and Alex.

The hairs on the back of her neck stood up and tingled. She shivered and shook off the eerie sensation.

"If you think you can take over my husband's life work, you're wrong. This is my company now. You can't call meetings and put someone in my husband's place," Christina spat out.

"No matter what happens with the estate split, Alex has a stake in this company. Bill will take over where Donald left off. He will ensure the company is run well and Donald's legacy continues and thrives for both his sons."

"I say what happens to this company and the estate. I'm Donald's wife."

"The only reason he stayed was for Evan's sake. He didn't love you, but he loved his children."

That something strange that came into Christina's eyes in the police station flashed in their depths again. Kate didn't understand it, but wished she knew what Christina feared, or was hiding behind that look.

"Yes, he did, which is why I am looking out for my son."

"As you should. As will I. So if you want to attend this meeting, let's get it started." Kate looked to the gentlemen standing by watching the whole sordid exchange.

One of the men swept his arm out toward the elevator. "This way, please. We'll use the conference room on the third floor."

Kate followed behind everyone. Bill and Cameron walked in front of her, blocking her from Christina and Evan. She wondered if Ben put them up to that with some silent signal to protect her. The three executives from Faraday Electronics, Christina, and Evan all stepped into the elevator. Bill, Cameron, and Ben held back, blocking her from entering.

"We'll take the elevator up next and meet you there." Ben's words came out casual, but his posture sure wasn't; he looked ready to strike down any threat that came her way.

The second the elevator doors closed, she grasped Ben's shoulder and turned him toward her. "What was that all about?"

"You think I'm going to give that guy another shot at killing you?"

"What's he going to do here, in front of so many witnesses?"

"He shot his own father, tried to kidnap a baby, and burned down Haven House, hoping to kill you. I wouldn't put anything past that murderous asshole. They won't quit, Kate. Never turn your back on them. Never give them an opening to hurt you."

Kate wanted to dismiss the warnings, but couldn't. Still, something about Evan's behavior today, holding his mother back, tweaked something in her mind. She couldn't put her finger on it, but it circled her mind with other thoughts she couldn't quite grasp or put together with their odd behavior.

"When will the DNA tests come back on Christina and the knife?"

"The lab is backed up. Detective Raynott is hoping to have them soon."

"Something doesn't add up."

The elevator doors opened. They rode up to the third floor in silence. As usual, Kate's thoughts were a jumbled mess with her grief taking center stage. She wanted to avenge her sister, but so far all she'd done was hide and hire a business executive. She needed to come up with a way to prove Evan committed the crimes. She needed to figure how big a role Christina played in all the events.

"Kate, we're here." Ben stood with his arm out, hand on the door, blocking it from closing on them.

"Sorry. Lost in thought." She walked out ahead of him.

"Ways to kill Evan and get away with it?" he asked.

"Something like that," she whispered back as they approached the conference room.

Everyone took their seats. The Faraday executives sat at one end of the table facing them. Christina and Evan sat on either side of the execs. Ben, Cameron, and Bill sat at the other end, facing the other side. Just to piss off Christina, she sat right next to her, but turned her chair to square off with everyone on that side of the table.

"Miss Morrison," the man at the head of the table began.

"It's just Kate."

"I'm Pete. I've worked at Donald's side for the last fifteen years. I knew him better than most."

"Did you ever meet my sister?"

Pete glanced at Christina, then met Kate's gaze again. "Yes. I met her several times. Donald seemed very happy with her."

"Seemed happy?" Kate pushed.

Pete eyed Christina again, sighed, and answered, increasing the tension in the room. "He was happier than I'd ever seen him."

"This is ridiculous. We're here to discuss business." Christina glared at her.

"She's right, Pete, so here is the deal. Donald left everything to Alex. Now, because of a legal muddle between Alex, Christina, and Evan the company may be split. I want Alex's interests protected and the company is lacking a president. So, I've hired Bill to fill that slot."

Pete frowned. "Kate, it's not necessary to bring someone else in. We can run the company as we've been doing. Everything is running smoothly without Donald here. I don't say that to be callous of his absence. Believe me, it's felt by everyone here and in every facet of the business."

"I'm not inserting someone because I don't believe you can do the job you've done exceptionally well these last years. I've read over all of Donald's papers, including the financials on the company."

"Then you understand that we will continue in Donald's stead and ensure this company remains as successful as it was when Donald ran it."

"I believe you, Pete. I have no cause to think otherwise. Bill has experience running a company of this size and scope. While he's got the business background this company needs, he's an engineer at heart. He can bring a fresh perspective on both fronts of the business."

Kate turned to Bill. She appreciated that the men allowed her to take the lead. After all, Alex owned the business and it was her duty to oversee it. "Bill, if you wouldn't mind giving these gentlemen a synopsis of your background and what you bring to the table. I'm sure once you start working together, they'll see what an asset you'll be to the company."

"Of course. Thank you, Kate." Bill ran through the jobs he'd held over the years and the degrees in business and electrical engineering he'd earned. He spoke of other projects he'd worked on, most of which went straight over her head, but the Faraday execs, including Pete, all perked up at many of the things Bill elaborated on, using technical language she just didn't get. To be truthful, she didn't really understand what Donald's company did, but by the end of the conversation it was clear that Bill got it and had several ideas he'd like to implement. Pete and he went back and forth for twenty minutes talking about a project that had been stalled for weeks.

Kate took the opportunity to study Evan. While he listened to the conversation, it was clear he didn't understand all the technical jargon tossed back and forth. He did add a few comments when they discussed sales and revenue. She didn't give him too much credit. She figured out what they were talking about in that respect as well.

Still, Evan didn't object to Bill working at the company. He didn't demand to take his father's place.

Evan lost focus on the people around them and stared back at her. If they were wild animals, they'd be circling each other. Kate didn't turn away from his intense stare. Instead, she tried to see past the nonchalant facade to the real man beneath.

His gaze swept down her face to her chest. She'd been checked out before. It didn't bother her. Much. He did it to piss her off and make her feel like she was just an object. His eyes filled with lust, but she saw past that false and practiced gaze to the calculating man who wanted the money but not the business. Certainly not the work that went with running the company. He wanted his life to remain as carefree and filled with luxury as it had always been. She wouldn't put it past him to try to make her an ally. He seemed the type to keep his enemies close.

Ben's hand settled over hers on the table. A show of possession that Evan didn't miss. His gaze shot from her hand beneath Ben's to her eyes. A slow smile spread across his handsome face. If looks could kill, the one Evan sent Ben would see Ben bloody on the floor. She caught Ben's glare out of the corner of her eye. Yep, he was much better at this silent conversation. While Evan's glare said he'd like to kill Ben, Ben's cold eyes said, "Bring it on. You'll lose."

She loved the air of confidence he wore as easily as the shirt on his back. When they'd worked together in the past, she'd thought him cocky and arrogant. Now, she understood he'd earned it. He only wielded it against those who deserved it. The people who needed his help got it. Evan deserved Ben's ire.

She'd made up her mind recently to set aside her grief and bring Evan to justice. Now, that compulsion to end this grew within her, blocking out everything else.

She couldn't sit here any longer. She'd leave the business to those who knew what they were doing. She needed some air.

"Please excuse me," she said, interrupting the group.

Ben held her hand, preventing her from leaving when she stood. She squeezed his hand to let him know she was okay.

She walked out of the conference room and down the hall, glancing at all the offices along the way. She stopped outside Donald's closed door and traced her fingers over his name. She stared through the glass window. The office remained dark. Pulled in by some unseen force, she turned the knob and walked into the dim room. Light from the outside windows spilled in and across his desk. Files, a discarded pen, and a half full cup of coffee sat on his desk. No one had touched anything since his death. She walked around to his chair and smiled at the photos of Margo and Alex. She picked up the picture of Margo holding Alex in her arms, a bright smile on her face.

She didn't so much see Evan come in as sense him standing by the door.

"You have no idea what you did when you killed her. She was warm and kind and gentle. She loved your father in a way I'd never seen someone love another. Your father soaked up that love and returned it. I don't know how you grew up in that house with your parents living their separate lives, hurting each other rather than admitting it was over and going their separate ways."

"You have no clue who my father was, or what he wanted." Evan stepped closer, his hands fisted at his sides.

"What angers you more? That he found happiness with a woman who wasn't your mother, that he had another son he adored, or that he meant to cut you off?"

"I'm his son. He can't just push me aside and start over with some other kid."

"He gave you everything. Spoiled you. Let you get away with your tantrums and fights. Protected you when you hurt others. He didn't want to start over with Alex, he wanted you to finally grow up and be an adult. He wanted you to take responsibility for your life and your actions. Instead, you lashed out without any thought to the consequences. How did it make you feel to see your father lying on the floor in a pool of blood?"

"I wasn't there. The blood on the knife proved that." The fear and distress that flashed in his eyes told her he lied. She knew he lied, but how to prove it. That bloody knife didn't make sense.

"You were there. You pulled the trigger. You killed them. I won't let you get away with this. Your mother thinks she can take whatever she wants. Face it, she always has, Donald's feelings be damned. She certainly doesn't think of you. I mean, she ordered you to do this, right? She pushed you, used your volatile temper and needled your sense of entitlement until you believed the only way to handle this situation was to kill him."

His gaze shot to hers. Bull's-eye. She'd gotten it right.

"You lost sight of who your father really was. Kind. Decent. Always on your side, even when you did the most heinous things. He wanted to teach you a lesson, but he'd have given in if you really needed help. You knew that deep down, but it's just so much easier to take him out, get rid of him so you could have what you really cared about. The money."

"Fuck you. It wasn't easy."

The admission stunned her. She didn't actually believe he'd admit in not so many words that he'd killed his father.

"Living with it must be hard. Knowing you're going to pay for it one way or another, that jail sentence hanging over your head, it must eat away at you."

"You don't know shit, lady. Shut the fuck up, or I'll make you."

"Bring it on, asshole. I'm not someone you want to fuck with. I will put you down and not think twice about it."

"You're some tough chick, is that right?"

"You already got a taste of it when I put you on the ground. I'm like no woman you've ever known. You killed my sister. For that, I'll make you pay and I won't stop until you do. So you keep coming. You're stupid enough to think you'll get away with it, but you're impulsive and make mistakes. Everything you do, I will use against you. You don't have your father to bail you out. With the estate in limbo, you don't have all that money to hire an attorney to get you out of the hole you just keep digging."

"You've a real mouth on you. You don't know when to shut up." Evan closed the distance and planted his hands on Donald's desk and leaned forward, trying to intimidate her.

"I'd think by now you'd get the message. Back off, or someone is going to get hurt."

Kate matched his pose, letting him know he didn't scare her.

"You come after me or Alex, I'll hurt you."

His eyes narrowed. One side of his mouth cocked up in a grin that made her want to grind her teeth. Arrogant jerk. He still didn't see her as a threat. He didn't see the threat closest to him either, so she pushed, hoping he'd see this had gone too far and had to stop.

"When are you going to wise up and realize your mother is using you? She doesn't care if you go down, because then the money will be hers. She'll be sipping margaritas on a beach while you're rotting in a cell and she won't think twice about it. She won't spare you a moment's thought while she's living the high life, fucking every cabana boy and waiter from here to Monte Carlo."

That flash of fear she saw earlier filled his gaze.

"You know what I'm saying is true."

In an instant that fear turned to fury. Evan only knew how to lash out when a problem presented itself. He whipped his hand out and clamped his fingers around her neck, giving her a shake. "You don't know anything. Give up the company and the money, keep that damn house and walk away before you really get hurt."

Kate opened her mouth to answer, but the words

were cut off when Ben's arm slammed down on Evan's, breaking his hold on her. Ben grabbed Evan by the back of the head, his fingers gripped tight in Evan's hair, and slammed him up against the wall. Evan tried to push away, but Ben punched him in the kidney and slammed him back against the wall.

"You ever fucking lay a hand on my girlfriend again, you'll be begging me for a cell over what I'm going to do to you."

"Get the fuck off me. I'll have you arrested for assault."

"Go ahead and try. You threatened Kate. You had your hands on her. You're a murderer and a menace with a record."

"What is going on in here?" Christina said, stepping into the office.

Cameron and Bill stood just outside the door.

"You and your son are leaving. We've settled the business for now."

"Let go of my son."

Ben pulled Evan from the wall and shoved him toward the door. Evan immediately turned to go after Ben again, but Christina jumped in front of him and planted both hands on his heaving chest, holding him back. He tried to shake her off, but she held tight.

"Don't give them the satisfaction or a reason to take this further. We still have the estate to settle. We can't resolve anything like this, not in public."

"Yes, Evan, not with so many witnesses." Kate pointed out what his mother was really trying to say.

"You may have gotten your way today, but don't think

I won't be watching everything your man does at this company. These people know me. They'll keep me informed about even the smallest change."

"If these people know you, they know all you care about is the bottom line."

"Yes. It's a business. A very lucrative business. Their job depends on the bottom line. Alex's future depends on it."

Kate reacted without thinking and stepped out from behind the desk to lunge at Christina. Ben blocked her at the last second.

"Don't."

Christina's mouth pulled back into a feral smile. "I heard about what happened at that shelter. Terrible thing, really. First you're attacked by some madman, then almost killed in a gas explosion. It's a good thing Alex didn't get hurt."

Kate fumed, but held her temper. "I kept him safe then. I will continue to keep him safe. No matter what I have to do to ensure his future."

"As any mother would do for her son." Christina took Evan's arm and pulled him toward the door.

"You keep telling yourself you're doing this for Evan, but we both know you want it for yourself."

Christina and Evan kept walking.

"She's one cold bitch," Cameron said, watching them leave.

Ben cupped her face and made her look up at him. "Are you okay?"

"I'm fine. Just pissed."

"What did he say to you?"

"He admitted he killed his father and my sister."

"He told you that?" Cameron asked.

"Not in so many words. He feels guilty about it. I taunted him. Baited him."

"Why would you do that?" Ben's concern came through beneath his angry words.

"Because I wanted to know the truth. He didn't go after them on his own. His mother pushed him. She's using him to do her dirty work. Like just now, she claims she's doing it to protect her son and ensure he inherits, but it's all her."

"I didn't like her comment about the attack on you and the explosion at Haven House," Ben said.

"You weren't looking at Evan when she said that. I don't think he did those things. You can see everything on his face and in his eyes. No wonder he's such a shitty poker player."

"Then they'll both go down for all of this."

"They've gotten away with everything so far. The fire burned up any evidence either one of them was there. The guy who attacked me refused to say who hired him to kidnap Alex. Valentina and Mariana disappeared."

"Valentina probably took the money her husband was paid and left before anyone could take it back." Ben frowned, as frustrated as her that nothing had been resolved.

"Are we at least all set here at the company?"

"Yes," Cameron said. "Bill will start work tomorrow. You'll get a weekly report, plus a quarterly update from all departments."

"Christina agreed to this?"

"For now. She said once she inherits the full estate Bill will be out."

"Never going to happen," Ben assured her.

"Then make her the offer to settle. What are you waiting for?" Kate feared Evan would come after Alex again. Or her. Or Ben. She didn't want anyone to get hurt over this. Donald wouldn't have wanted that either. He'd understand that she wanted to hand over part of what he'd left behind to keep his son safe.

Ben's frown deepened. "Kate, you knew I planned to make the offer after we got things settled here at the company."

She raked her fingers through her hair. "I'm sorry. He pissed me off, and I'm taking it out on you."

"Relax. We're almost there."

"Almost isn't good enough. I want results. I want my son safe."

"I want you to be safe, not meeting with a murderer in an office alone. What were you thinking?"

"That I want this to be over. That I want him to pay for everything he's done."

"This isn't the way to do it. Pissing him off so he'll come after you is not the way to end this. If I hadn't come in when I did . . ."

"He'd have a broken nose right now. I can take care of myself."

"That's not the point."

"Then what is the point?"

"You scared the shit out of me seeing him with his hand wrapped around your throat. You just stood there, like it didn't mean anything if he hurt you."

"I wanted him to keep talking. When he's upset and angry, he makes mistakes."

"Yes, and people get hurt. People die. If something happened to you . . ."

"Nothing happened to me. I had him right where I wanted him."

"I bet your sister thought the same thing when she fought him. That she could take him, but he got the upper hand and he killed her. Don't you get it? He wants you pissed, so you'll make a mistake. Then he'll have you, Kate. He'll kill you. What will happen to Alex then? What am I supposed to do without you?"

"I'm doing this for Alex."

"You're acting out of anger. You need to be smart."

The wind went right out of her sails. "You're right."

Ben leaned back, his eyes wide. "I'm right."

"Don't look so surprised. Look, I needed to know what I'm up against and how he thinks. I've got a read on him now. He's all brawn and ego. He doesn't think so, but he's easily led. Christina is the mastermind behind all of this. I clued Evan in to that fact."

"You don't think he knows his mother is pulling the strings."

"I think he doesn't want to admit that his mother is using him. Having me, his enemy, point it out pissed him off. If I can pit him against her, maybe he'll turn himself in and make a deal to take her down."

"I don't see that happening."

"Me either. But I do think Evan will think twice before he blindly follows his mama's orders again. He won't be so easy to manipulate anymore."

"Well, I guess that's something."

She stepped close to Ben, needing his comfort now that this was all over. She tapped him in the gut with her fist. "I can't tell you how sexy it was to see you thump Evan into the wall. His head bounced."

Ben pressed his lips together to hide a smile and shook his head. "You're not the only one who can kick ass."

"Where'd you learn those mad skills?"

"You know how I grew up. I feared my father, felt inadequate to protect myself or my mother. Once he was gone, my mother enrolled me in some self-defense classes and boxing to build my confidence. She wanted me to know how to protect myself and direct my anger in a more positive way."

Kate ran her hands up his flat belly to his hard chest. "You still work out, don't you?"

"Four days a week at the gym. Sparring matches once or twice a week to keep my skills sharp."

"So, not just a smart guy, a tough guy."

"When I have to be." Ben swept his hands over her shoulders and down her back, pulling her close. "You didn't say anything about what I said."

"That you can't live without me?"

"That's not what I said, but it is what I meant. You've got to stop, Kate. Let the cops do their job."

"The cops can't even tie them to the murders or the gas explosion."

"Damnit, Kate. Give them time to sort through the evidence and make their case."

"That's what lawyers do. Someone needs to take him down now."

"It doesn't have to be you."

"Who, then? Who will see justice done? Who will make them stop?"

Ben touched his fingertips to her cheek, wiping away the tears she hadn't realized ran from her eyes. "We'll get them, Kate. I promise. But we'll do it without putting your life on the line. Alex needs you. I need you."

His lips met hers for a soft kiss. His way of soothing her and dampening her building ire. It worked. Whenever he touched her, she melted. The tension in her eased away with every featherlight kiss. She sighed against his mouth and he took the kiss deeper just for a moment. Just a taste of what they'd shared last night. A promise of what was to come when they were home and alone. A vow of what they'd always have in the future. If she lived to see it.

"Okay, I'll stop pushing so hard."

"You'll stop poking the lion before he takes a bite out of you. I'm the only one who gets to bite you. Right on your gorgeous ass. Maybe the inside of your thigh before I lick my way up to your . . ."

Kate pressed her fingers to his lips. "Stop, or we'll never leave this office." She squeezed her thighs tight to ease the ache he'd created with those suggestive words that evoked images of them naked and in bed together. He knew just how to distract her. Very creative and lovely ways to erase everything from her mind but him.

Remembering where they were and who they arrived with, she looked behind Ben. "Where did Cameron and Bill go?"

"Back to work probably. Bill will be here tomorrow. He'll take over Donald's office. If there's anything you want from here, get it now. Otherwise, Bill will pack up the other personal belongings and send them to Christina."

Kate went to the desk and picked up the photographs of her sister and Alex. She sat in Donald's chair and went through his desk drawers, looking for any other personal effects that would mean something to Alex. Any small reminder of Donald.

"Alex will never remember his father."

"He'll know me." Ben's confident assertion went straight to her heart.

"Will he? Are we moving too fast? When this is all over, will everything change again?"

"Kate, it is what it is. Not everything has to be so hard and complicated."

"That's what you think. Nothing has ever been easy in my life. Or normal."

"Who wants normal?"

"After all that's happened, a little normal might be nice. For Alex."

"We'll get there. If you stop needling the Faradays. We want them to take the settlement, not keep fighting for everything."

Kate rolled her eyes. "I know. I just can't help myself sometimes. Their arrogance annoys me."

Ben rummaged through the credenza drawers and pulled out a tote bag with the company logo. He handed it to her to carry the photographs. She stuffed them inside, careful not to break them. She hated to leave all of the other items behind, but the trinkets would hold no memories or value for Alex.

"It's strange that all the things a person uses every day, the things we can't seem to do without, are rendered meaningless to others when you die."

"Kate, Bill will use nearly all this stuff. It's not meaningless or useless." Ben took her hand and pulled her up out of the chair. She went willingly, feeling her grief rise up and block out the happiness she'd felt in Ben's arms but moments ago.

"Come on, let's get out of here."

"I'm sorry I kept you from work this morning. I'll go over to Sam and Elizabeth's and pick up Alex."

"We'll get him together, then I'll take you back to my place."

"I thought I might go to my sister's again."

"No. I don't want you going there alone. It's dangerous for you and Alex to be in that big house with no protection."

"How long do you expect to keep me locked up? I need to go to the grocery store and buy diapers and formula. If you want me to work at Haven House, I'll eventually have to go there and do actual work. What about my place? My things? I can't keep wearing the same five outfits. I need to pick up my mail."

Ben held up his hand. "I get it. I don't know, Kate. All I know is that I worry about you every second you're out of my sight. So much so that I get nothing done and all I want to do is get back to you."

"Ben, I don't know what to do with that. No one has ever made me feel the way you do. I feel so much for you. It confuses me and doesn't seem real sometimes. I understand the threat against me and Alex, but I still need to live my life. I want that life to include you, but I can't live with you treating me like I can't take care of myself."

"I'm not saying that at all. They want you and Alex dead, Kate. You want to just walk out the door and right into their hands."

"Ben . . ."

"Don't. You're not going to change my mind about this."

"Then compromise."

"Fine. I'll stop at the store and pick up whatever you and Alex need. You can contact the post office and have your mail forwarded to my place, or your sister's. Give it a couple more weeks for the cops to put their case together and take it to the DA."

"Lie on your couch and watch soap operas and reruns of *Full House*," she suggested.

"Whatever you want. Netflix all day, every day."

"Cook dinner for you. Wait for you to come home every night, wearing nothing—"

"I'm all for that."

She smacked him on the arm. "Of course you are."

"You don't have to sit around and do nothing. Help me with the contractors and rebuilding Haven House."

"I give up. You're not going to stop being overprotective, or making me a permanent part of your life and work."

Ben cocked his head and eyed her. "I thought that's what you wanted."

"An overprotective boyfriend." Not what he meant, but she had a hard time believing what they shared would last, or survive any more turmoil.

"Here I thought we wanted the same thing."

"I'm sorry. We do."

His gaze narrowed on her. He stuffed his hands in his pockets and stepped back. Great, she'd done it now. Pushed him away for no reason, except her need to protect her heart and do what she wanted to do.

She closed the distance he put between them physically but she'd put there emotionally, and placed her hands on his chest over his thumping heart.

"I'm being a pest, pushing you away when that's not what I want at all. I'm frustrated. I want my life back."

Ben pulled his hands from his pockets and cupped her face. "Give it time, Kate. We'll get there."

She hugged Ben close. She hated to keep her plans

from him, but he'd never approve what she wanted to do next. She didn't want to wait for Evan and Christina to make their next move. She wanted to go after them. If the police needed proof Evan killed her sister, she'd get it for them.

Chapter Twenty-Two

"FIVE MILLION DOLLARS." The outrage in his mother's voice seemed misplaced with that sum of money.

Evan stood near the fireplace and rolled his eyes. His mother paced back and forth along the windows on the other side of the seating area. He tried to focus on the sprawling lawn, flowers, and trees outside past the pool, but his mother drew his attention. "For what?"

"That's how much she's offering. I get to keep this house, and she'll pay me five million dollars."

"Take it."

"Take it! That's nothing compared to what the estate and business are worth."

"Taking it to a judge means you might lose everything and wind up with only one million. The house and five million is a huge sum of money."

"She only offered you a million plus the trust your father set up."

Evan didn't know what to think. "It's more than I deserve after what I did. Five million is a hell of a lot more than you deserve after you cheated on Dad all these years. You set that shelter on fire. You could have killed someone. There were children there."

His mother waved her hand at him to brush all that aside, like it didn't matter. Like nothing but getting all the money mattered. "It's ours. She doesn't get to decide who gets what."

"You'd rather a judge decided. That clause in Dad's will states that if I fight it, I get nothing. I'll take the million and the trust and be done with this whole damn thing."

"You'll let that bitch run your father's company."

"She can have it. I never wanted it."

"The money it makes means you'd never have to work a day in your life. You'll run through that million as fast as you do a bottle of booze and a woman."

"Well, you've got a real high opinion of me. Maybe she's right. You're just using me to do your dirty work. You want her and Alex out of the way, so you can have it all. But where will I be, Mother? Rotting in a cell. Dead too. Burned alive in my apartment."

"For God's sake, Evan, we're fighting for our lives here. Don't let her turn you against me. I've always been on your side. I protected you when you killed that man. I will always protect you."

No, she'd use the information that he killed that guy against him if it came down to her or him going down for this mess. He was in too deep. Nothing would get him out of this now, but that didn't mean he had to sink deeper into the muck his life had become. If he took that settlement, left town, maybe he'd have a chance to do something with his life before it was too late.

"Take the money and the house. It's more than you would have gotten if I hadn't killed Dad. Let it be over. Move on. Find another rich husband and live off his money."

His mother stopped her pacing. A thoughtful look came into her eyes. Yeah, he'd planted a new pursuit for her to follow, but would she let go of this bone she'd held on to like a rabid dog?

"I spent almost my whole life with that man. If not for me, he'd have been nothing," his mother shouted.

Yep, a rabid dog who'd lost its mind. His father built that company. His mother didn't do anything but spend the money and fuck every guy who struck her fancy. She liked expensive things and meaningless sex with eager young men who wanted nothing more than the money and things she showered on them.

Evan tried to see a glimpse of the nurturing mother who gave birth to him and used to push him to be the best in school and sports. That woman disappeared long before he hit middle school. He sometimes wondered if she ever existed. The woman ranting about five million not being enough certainly didn't seem like the mother he remembered, or maybe just imagined he had, as a kid.

"Are you listening to me?" his mother snapped.

"What? Sorry, you were saying . . . you made Dad the man he was. Right. It was all you."

"Sarcasm is not helping."

"What do you want me to do? They've made an offer. Make a counteroffer and settle this thing before we both end up in jail."

"We aren't going to jail. I countered for fifty million."

Evan rolled his eyes. "She'd have to sell the company to pay out that kind of cash. She's not going to do that."

"She refused the counteroffer. She said her offer was final. Take it or leave it."

"Take it."

"No fucking way."

"You'll lose in court. If they prove I killed Dad and that lady, I'm going to jail. And so are you."

"Me. I didn't pull the trigger."

"No, but you planned it. You sent me there. You knew I did it and covered it up. In the eyes of the law, you're just as guilty as I am."

"You'd take your own mother down with you."

"You took me down when you pushed all the right buttons to get me to do it."

"Well, it wasn't far for you to fall after you killed that other man. The careless life you lead brought you down."

Yes. Careless of him to get into trouble in the first place. Even more thoughtless to let his viper of a mother know what he'd done and not expect her to use it against him someday. That's what she did, used people to get what she wanted.

"I'll be more careful from now on, which is why I'm letting this go. You'd be wise to do the same."

Chapter Twenty-Three

IT TOOK BEN nearly an hour to drive out of the city to Morgan and Tyler's place. He didn't mind the drive. It gave him time to think. Lately, all he thought about was Kate and Alex. Mostly Kate. The woman was driving him nuts with her impatience. No matter how much he tried to distract her from the lack of progress on the case with things to do and oversee at Haven House, nothing worked to cure her incessant need to call Detective Raynott for updates he couldn't provide and her desperate need to go after the Faradays on her own.

He finally got her to make them an offer. Their ludicrous counteroffer angered Kate even more. She'd taken to calling them "those greedy bastards." It made him smile and worry even more that she'd do something that would only lead to more destruction in their lives or her death.

She didn't seem to fear the possibility Evan or Christina might kill her. Probably because of the way she'd been raised, the threat of pain and death a constant fear living at home with her parents and later in a few of the foster homes where the people supposed to care for her would rather beat her or worse. At this point, he believed the only thing holding her back from seeking her revenge was Alex. Nothing he said or did seemed to make a dent in her stubborn mind.

She'd done something that took him off guard and asked Donald's lawyer to prepare her will. She didn't have any family or other close friends. With Margo gone, if something happened to Kate, the only person she wanted to take care of Alex was him. Smart of her to put her wishes in a legal document, but that little voice in his head nagged that she'd done it to ensure Alex's future because she intended to end this thing with the Fara-days once and for all. Oh, he didn't think she'd actually shoot them in cold blood, but she would confront them in hopes of getting a confession and evidence to prove what they'd done.

If the fucking lab would hurry up and send the re-sults of the blood test back to the detective, they'd have some kind of answer. Hopefully something that would put Evan behind bars and stop Kate from doing some-thing stupid.

Ben pulled into the driveway behind Elizabeth's and Jenna's cars. He picked up the flowers from the seat beside him, opened the door, and got out. He took the stone path up to the front doors of the sprawling stone and wood ranch house. Before he knocked, he turned and checked out the view. They'd really found the perfect spot. Isolated. A safe haven away from the city and other people. The perfect place for someone like Morgan.

Her prediction was never far from his mind. She'd been right. She was always right. Kate was meant for him. But how long would he get to hold on to her with the Faradays out to see her dead, and Kate anxious to take them down, making it too easy for them to get their hands on her?

Lost in thought, he jumped when the door opened behind him.

"Morgan said you were standing out here. Come in, man." Tyler shook his hand and pulled him inside.

"How is she?"

"Great. The delivery went well. She and Noah are perfect."

"I can't believe she had the baby at home last night."

"Me either, but with her gift, I can't exactly take her to the hospital. Blocking out all those feelings and thoughts from other people would have tired her out even more than the labor. Doing it here with a midwife and an ambulance on standby was the next best thing."

"Let me guess, you had the ambulance waiting outside."

"She swore we didn't need it, but I couldn't take that chance." Tyler led him into the living room.

Morgan sat in the rocking chair, Noah asleep in her arms. She looked beautiful. Radiant. He'd never guess she gave birth yesterday.

"Morgan, I'm so happy for you and Tyler. Congratulations."

Noah looked just like a mini version of Tyler with his dark hair. He pressed his hand to his mouth and blinked his pale blue eyes.

"Looks just like his dad, but got his mother's eyes," Ben pointed out.

"He got a few of his mother's other traits," Tyler said, slapping Ben on the shoulder.

"Oh, yeah? Your gift?" he asked Morgan.

"He's got a lot going on in his tiny brain." Morgan smiled down at her son.

Ben held up the flowers. "Where shall I put these for you?"

"They're beautiful. Thank you. Elizabeth, Jenna, Jack, and the kids are checking out Tyler's new barbecue out back. I just finished feeding this greedy little boy. He needs a change. Leave the flowers in the kitchen. I'll put them in a vase after I change this one's diaper."

"I'll help you, honey," Tyler said, taking his son from Morgan's arms. He held out his free hand and helped her up.

"I'm fine, Tyler. I gave birth. I can still walk on my own."

"The midwife said to take it easy. You need to rest and let your body recover."

Morgan shook her head.

"You know I can hear the names you call me in your head," Tyler said.

Morgan smiled sweetly at her husband. "I thought you'd like it better than me saying them out loud in front of Ben."

"Like he doesn't feel my pain. He's got a woman living with him, driving him nuts by not doing what he wants." Tyler gave Ben the you-know-what-I'm-talking-about look.

"Oh, honey, women will never actually do what a man wants when he wants it. What fun would that be?"

"Please, Morgan, sit down and rest."

Tyler and Morgan walked out of the room arguing, more like teasing each other, and took Noah down the hall to his room to change him.

Ben left the flowers on the counter by the sink in the kitchen. Elizabeth must have brought the cake and muffins from Decadence Bakery. He hoped to steal some of the cake before he left. He found the crew out on the patio. Jenna's and Elizabeth's little ones ran around the grass playing tag.

"Ben, how are you?" Jack said, stepping up to shake his hand.

"I'm good. How long are you and Jenna in town?"

"A couple of days. Once she found out Noah arrived, I couldn't keep her away. Cameron and Marti are on their way over. We're going to fire up Tyler's grill and toss on some steaks."

"Where is Sam?"

Elizabeth and Jenna stood by the patio edge with their backs to him, watching the children play.

"Elizabeth said he had the night off, but left at the last minute to check something out."

Elizabeth turned to him then, holding Alex in her

arms. "Ben, you're here. I thought you had dinner with a client tonight."

"I canceled when Tyler called me. What are you doing with Alex?" Ben took Alex when Elizabeth brought him over. Alex smiled up at him and rubbed his forehead on Ben's cheek.

"He's getting tired. Kate dropped him off an hour ago. She asked if Sam and I would watch him so she could go to dinner with you."

"What? She didn't call me." He'd invited her to come this morning. A chance for her to get out of his apartment. She'd said the walls were closing in on her. She declined, saying she didn't want to leave Alex with his friends again and put them out. No matter how many assurances he gave her that Elizabeth, Jenna, or Marti wouldn't mind, she'd said no.

His phone rang before he could call Kate.

"Hey, Sam, Elizabeth said you had to work tonight. I'm here with her at Tyler's place."

"Yeah, I'm chasing after your girl."

"What? What happened?"

"Nothing yet. I didn't believe her when she dropped off Alex. I didn't say anything to Elizabeth. I followed Kate just to be sure nothing was wrong. I thought maybe Evan set a plan in motion to draw her out. Looks like your girl is going after Evan."

"What the hell is she doing?"

"Drinking and playing poker."

"She's at a bar?"

"Evan's hangout based on the number of people who

know him, including the very talkative bartender and waitress working the back room."

Ben swore, trying to think through his immediate rage that she'd put herself in mortal danger like this. "Jones Joint. I know the place. It's where Evan goes to get in trouble. What the hell does she think she'll accomplish playing poker with him?" *Besides antagonizing the asshole into killing her.* He tried to set thoughts like that aside and think clearly.

"Well, as far as I can tell, she's trying to get him drunk and fooling him into believing he's winning. She's tossed in the towel on four winning hands. Either she's a shitty player, or she's lulling him into a false sense of security before she cleans him out."

"Is she drawing attention from the other players? Anybody else I need to worry about?"

"You mean the other two men hitting on her more than they're concentrating on the game? Unless she decides she likes them better than you," Sam teased, "they're no real threat. You should see what she's wearing. Damn the girl's got some fine legs."

"I'm standing next to your wife, would you like to repeat that for her?"

Sam chuckled. "Touchy, touchy. Leave Alex with Elizabeth and meet me down here. We'll keep an eye on her together."

"I'm going to wring her neck."

"She came here with a plan, let her play it out. Maybe it will amount to something."

"Do not let her out of your sight."

"I do this for a living, you know." Sam hung up on him.

Fear squeezed his heart and made it impossible to breathe easy. Not with her an arm's length from the man who killed her sister and Donald in cold blood.

Ben swore and tried to hold on to his temper.

"Hey, not in front of the baby." Elizabeth jabbed him in the shoulder.

"Sorry. Here, take him back." Ben kissed Alex on the head and handed him to Elizabeth. "I have to go meet your husband at a bar."

"What's he doing at a bar?"

"Staring at my girlfriend's legs apparently."

"Is that so?"

"Sorry, he followed her down there. She's playing poker with the man who killed her sister."

"Go. And tell Sam he's got a perfectly decent pair of legs at home to stare at all he wants."

Ben dropped his gaze to Elizabeth's gorgeous legs encased in a tight pair of jeans. "Yes, he does."

Elizabeth smacked him on the arm again. "Go." Her laugh followed him into the house.

"On your way to Sam and Kate, I see," Morgan said from the kitchen.

"Why didn't you warn me?"

"Well, it's not the most orthodox way to get evidence, but she'll get what she wants. She's got street smarts. She thinks outside the box. She understands human nature. She'll use that against Evan and his mother."

"Do you know what's going to happen? How this will all end?"

"You should go. You won't want to admit it, but you'll enjoy the show. She'll surprise you."

Not much surprised him. He'd seen the worst in people most of his life.

He'd wasted enough time. Morgan wouldn't tell him anything if she didn't want to because she'd learned that knowing the future didn't mean you could change it. Fate had a way of making things happen no matter what. If he was destined to be with Kate, he had to believe that in the end they'd be together.

Chapter Twenty-Four

KATE SAT ACROSS from Evan and tossed yet another winning hand onto the table, forfeiting the biggest pot yet. She hated to do it, but she'd noticed something about Evan. When you played poker, you didn't play the cards, you played the man across from you. The more Evan won, the more he drank. While she sipped at her Jameson, he downed shot after shot, slamming the glass on the table every time he won a hand, saying, "Hot damn, bitch. You lose."

She'd show him.

Handsy on her left slammed his hand down on her shoulder and dragged his hand across her back. "Better luck next time, sweetheart."

"Oh, I'll get him good in the end," she said under her breath.

Sideburn Sideshow next to Evan dealt the next hand. She had Evan right where she wanted him. Drunk. Feeling lucky and invincible. Now she'd bring him back down and leave him and his pockets empty.

"Evan, baby, you're back. I haven't seen you around here lately." Blondy Big Boobs slid her hand over Evan's shoulder, leaned down, giving him a full view of her rack, and kissed him on the side of the head.

Evan scooted back his chair, pulled Blondy Big Boobs into his lap, and tickled her. The high-pitched giggle fit the pert blonde to a T. "Mandy, God, how I've missed you."

Mandy raked her fingers through Evan's hair. "You always know where to find me. You also owe me from the last time you played here."

"You know I'm good for it." Evan pushed Mandy off his lap to stand beside him. "Let me work, darlin', then we'll have some fun. I always pay my debts—one way or another." Evan winked and Mandy giggled again.

Kate wanted to gag. "Are we playing poker or hide the Vienna sausage?"

Evan glared across the table at her. Handsy and Sideburn Sideshow laughed their asses off.

Evan tossed in a hundred-dollar bill. A little showing off for Mandy. A stupid, impulsive move. One Kate would exploit.

BEN WALKED INTO Jones Joint and spotted Sam by the far wall, sitting at the end of the bar. He made his way through the crowded tables, along the booths, and joined Sam.

"Where the hell is she?"

"Don't turn and look. Pretend you're only interested in me. Evan is looking this way. They're straight ahead in front of me." Sam looked him up and down. "At least you took off your suit jacket and tie. Roll up your sleeves so you blend in a bit better. This isn't the after-work crowd you're used to at Decadence. We're in a bar, man."

Ben did as Sam said, trying to tone down his appearance to look like he was meeting a friend for a drink. Sam fit in better with his worn jeans, black T-shirt, and leather jacket. Sam probably kept the jacket on to cover his badge and gun. Ben actually sighed with a bit of relief knowing Sam was armed and ready to help Kate if she needed it.

Ben didn't budge, but stared at the wall behind Sam and used the Budweiser mirror to check out the room tucked into an alcove behind him. Evan went back to playing cards and smiling at the pretty blonde beside him. Kate sat in front of Evan. He could only see the back of her dark head. The two other men at the table kept their gazes on Kate, leaving the blonde to Evan.

"What's going on?"

"Things turned around when the blonde arrived. Kate's won the last two hands. She's slowly bleeding Evan dry. He's distracted by the boobs beside him and too many shots."

"That's a two-hundred-dollar bottle of booze."

"Kate's got expensive taste. Good taste. We should get her to buy us a drink."

"Let's go get her before this all goes south."

"No."

"No?" Ben asked, his eyebrows nearly hitting the top of his head he was so surprised Sam took Kate's side in this.

"She's not doing anything but playing cards and pissing the guy off. Maybe that's all she wants, to sit across from him, letting him know she knows what he did. Give him a chance to look at her, knowing exactly what he took from her."

"You think she's here for a staring contest?"

"Ben."

"Fuck. I get it, okay. She wants him to pay, but this isn't going to make that happen. Taking his money in a card game, messing with his head, and getting him drunk won't change anything."

"It might make her feel better. So let her. No harm. No foul. She gets to taunt the guy and ease her conscience."

"She's got no reason to feel guilty."

"Maybe not in your mind, but we're talking about hers." Sam took a sip of his beer, then cocked his head toward the other room. "Your girl just cleaned up on that last hand. Evan is starting to sweat. The other two just want to get in her panties."

"Shut the fuck up," Ben snapped.

Sam laughed at him again. "You're lost, man."

"If something happens to her, I'm going to beat the shit out of you for letting this go on."

"You can try if it makes you feel better." Sam earned that cocky attitude.

Ben didn't really want to fight his friend. He wanted the woman he loved out of harm's reach. Out of Evan's vicinity and locked in a room. Safe. With him. He'd teach her a lesson for going behind his back. The only man getting into her panties tonight was him. Once he got his hands on her again.

"The blonde's headed for the ladies' room. Kate's following. Interesting."

"Why?"

"Well, if I wanted something from Evan and knew he'd never give it to me, I'd find someone he trusted and try to turn them to my side to get it for me."

"No way."

"We'll see."

Kate stopped to talk to a waitress before she disappeared into the restroom. Ben kept his eye on the door and jumped when the waitress touched his shoulder.

"Hey, Kate said to get a beer and sit in the empty booth over there before someone sees you. Follow me."

Sam smiled. "Shit. We've been made."

KATE STOOD IN front of the cracked bathroom mirror and dabbed on some rosy lipstick. She muted the dark color with the tip of her finger and wiped it on a paper towel.

Mandy flushed the toilet behind her and walked out of the stall. "I love that skirt. The gather in the back is super cute."

Kate smiled and smoothed her hand over the silky

material. Short in the front, longer in the back, with gathers that made it ruffle just below her butt and hang down six inches past the hem in front.

"Thanks. It's one of my favorites. Nice top. I love the sparkles." That were, of course, strategically placed over her boobs.

"Practically everything I own has sparkles on it. So, uh, how do you know Evan?"

"We met recently. I took over his father's company."

"Oh, I heard about his father's death. So tragic. I mean, I can't believe his mistress shot him, then killed herself."

"Don't believe everything you see on TV."

"Really?"

"I'm just saying, not everything is what it seems. Does Evan ever talk about his dad?"

"Not really. Evan isn't a big talker. We only hang out when he comes to the bar."

"So you two aren't close? You seemed real cozy in there."

"We like to hang, hook up. You know?"

"I do. Good-looking guy like him is probably great in the sack."

Mandy beamed a smile, her eyes filled with lust. "When he's not drunk like tonight, he can go forever. This one time, we stayed up all night. He did this thing with his . . ."

Kate held up her hand. "Details aren't necessary."

Mandy giggled. "Sorry. I tend to overshare."

"Yeah, like giving your money to Evan to gamble away."

"He's a good guy. He'll pay me back." Mandy pushed her fingers into her long hair and fluffed it up even bigger. She pulled out a bottle of hair spray and spritzed the mass of waves. "The thing is, my car broke down. Again. I need to buy a new fuel pump. I'm sick of taking the bus to work. I need my ride."

"I could help you out with that."

"Really? Why would you do that?"

"Because I need something from Evan. I think you can get it for me."

"Why don't you just ask him?"

"In case you missed it, he's not exactly happy I'm here tonight. We're not friends. More competitors."

"Oh, because of his daddy's business." Mandy nodded her head. "I get it. He doesn't like that you took over instead of him."

"Something like that. I'll give you a hundred bucks right now to take him someplace private and get him naked."

"You want to pay me to sleep with him?"

"I don't care if you sleep with him or not. What I want is a picture."

"Why the hell do you want a naked photo of him?"

"He's got a scar on his leg."

"No, he doesn't. Just the one on his neck."

"It's a new scar. You get a picture of him and the scar, so it's clearly him, I'll give you whatever I win in the pot tonight."

"You've barely won anything. Evan is up at least two grand."

"Trust me, he won't be for long. Are you in?"

"Is this picture going to get him in trouble?"

"Not at all. In fact, I'll give you the hundred now." Kate took the money out of her purse and held it out. "You leave with him. I'll follow you with the rest of the money. You do whatever you need to, to get the picture. If he's drunk enough, he'll probably pass out and never know."

"That could work." Mandy smiled, warming to the idea.

"Yes, it will. Once you have the picture on your phone, post it to your Facebook account with something cute like, 'Hot guy sleeping in my bed.'

"You meet me outside, show me the picture, and I'll give you the cash. You might even be able to buy a new used car. Something better than what you've got now."

"Okay." The smile turned up several notches. Mandy snagged the hundred out of her hand and stuffed it in her purse.

"You can't tell him about this," Kate warned.

"I won't. Promise. He's had so much to drink tonight, he'll probably want to crash at the Super 8 down the block. We've done that a few times."

"Perfect. Now let's go win you the money you need for a new car."

BEN NEARLY JUMPED out of his seat and stormed the bathroom it took so long for Kate to come out. When she did, she stopped short and dug through her bag for something, letting the blonde pass her. Once the blonde turned the corner into the small room, Kate looked up and glared across the two rows of tables at them.

"She is pissed at you." Sam took a sip of his beer, acting like none of this was his fault.

"She's probably pissed at you for following her and calling me."

"You'd have found her on your own with the tracking device in her phone."

"Let's not tell her about that."

"Did you know she went to her apartment today? Stayed about an hour. Packed up a couple of bags, picked up her mail from the manager, then went back to your place."

"You followed her?"

"No. I got pinged that she went out of range of the two-mile radius we set up around your place. I sent a local cop to sit on her while she was there."

"Can you do that?"

"I know a guy who owed me a favor."

"Thanks, man. I owe you big-time for this."

"You kept Jenna safe all those years. You got her to Jack. He's a very happy man. You don't owe me shit."

Ben sat quietly nursing the beer Kate sent to him earlier. He tried to be patient. Sam talked about his family, Tyler taking time off from the FBI to be home with Morgan and their new baby, and the drought in California. Ben finally focused on his friend and narrowed his gaze.

"Really, you want to talk about the weather?"

"You're not listening to a thing I say."

"I'm watching for Kate to come out of that damn room alive and well."

"Relax. There's no exit out the back of that room. She's going to clean Evan out, let him leave with the blonde, then follow him."

"How do you know her plan?"

"It's what I'd do. If she's not out in another half hour, I'll go up to the bar, buy another drink, and scope out the situation."

"Fine. Thirty minutes. By then, the beer you're drinking should be flat and warm."

"It already is."

"Why do you even bother?"

"It's for show. Like wearing the right clothes to fit the place and people around you. If I'm drinking water, I look out of place."

"I got it, it just seems so tedious."

"The definition of surveillance, my friend. This will be over soon. You'll have Kate back and can punish her all you want." Sam gave him a suggestive smile.

It lightened Ben's sour mood. "Drink your beer."

Ben tried to relax and tamp down the urge to walk into the other room and drag Kate out of this seedy place. Instead, he focused on his faith in Kate. A faith in her ability to see through people's facades to the real person beneath. She understood human behavior. She'd studied it in school and the reality she'd lived growing up. If she was in any danger, she'd alert them. He had to trust she'd come to him and Sam if she needed help.

He tried not to take it personally she'd left him out of her plans and gone behind his back. It didn't mean she didn't trust him. Still, it hurt.

Chapter Twenty-Five

THE POT IN the center of the table had grown over the last five minutes. All the men thought they had her on the run.

"I raise you a thousand." Kate tossed the cash on the pile.

Handsy side-eyed her and rubbed at his scruffy chin with his fingers. He tossed his cards down. "I'm out."

Sideburn Sideshow tossed in the cash, leaving him with a couple hundred dollars. "Call."

Kate met Evan's gaze and tried to keep her face expressionless, her breathing steady. An experienced card player, Evan would notice any little sign, indicating if she was bluffing or held the winning hand. She couldn't count on how much he'd drunk to make him go all in to beat her. She'd slowly bled him dry over the last hour. Now, she wanted to finish him.

"I'm all in."

Music to my ears.

Evan tossed in the last of his cash, picked up his drink, and downed the last of it. He blew out a breath and waited for her to turn her cards.

"Come on, sweetheart. Show us what you got," Sideburn Sideshow coaxed, a smarmy smile on his face.

Kate kept her gaze on Evan and turned her cards over one at a time. One king after another until all four faced up, along with the queen of hearts.

"No fucking way." Sideburn Sideshow tossed his three-of-a-kind down.

"You fucking bitch." Evan tossed his pair of aces on the table and leaned forward, arms braced on the edge. "You played me, bitch."

"You agreed to play the game. Don't pout just because you lost."

Evan reached for her neck like he'd done in Donald's office. This time she expected it. She grabbed his thumb and bent it and his wrist back.

"Fuck. Let go."

"Touch me again, and I'll snap you like a twig, asshole."

"Hey now, no one needs to get hurt here. She won fair and square," Handsy said, trying to defuse the situation.

She remembered why she was here and what she really wanted. Yes, a shot at taking Evan down off his high horse, but also to get the evidence she needed.

Mandy stood from her stool behind Evan and touched his shoulder. "Come on, baby, let's get out of here."

Evan tugged on his hand, which probably hurt more because she waited until the last second to let him go.

He leaned back in his chair eyeing her. She kept her gaze locked on his even as she raked in the pot and sorted out her cash.

Mandy rubbed her hand down Evan's chest and back up again. She leaned down and whispered something in his ear. The smile that broke out on Evan's face was nothing short of dirty. He snatched the bottle of Jameson from the table, stood, wrapped his arm around Mandy, and walked out with his hand on her ass.

"Thanks for the game, boys. Sorry I took all your money."

"Stay. Let us win back some of what we lost," Handsy pleaded as she stuffed the money into her purse.

"Sorry, boys. It's late. I've got work in the morning. You understand." Kate walked away, knowing the two broke card players stared at her ass as she left. She didn't acknowledge Sam at the bar, who'd stood there watching for the last twenty minutes. She caught Ben out of the corner of her eye still nursing a beer in the booth she'd sent him to. At least he'd stayed out of the way. She hoped Evan didn't see him on the way out, or all her plans would be for naught.

Kate walked out the doors just as Evan drove by in his Range Rover and glared at her. She caught the I-got-this look from Mandy. No doubt the amount of money in the last pot sprouted pretty dreams of a new car. One little picture, that's all Kate needed.

EVAN UNLOCKED THE hotel room door and dragged Mandy in after him. She laughed when he flung her in front of him and pulled her back into his chest. Her boobs bounced against him. He leaned in and kissed her, trying to forget that bitch's face and that he ever met her. Kate. Damn her. She'd shown up at the bar tonight looking to get a piece of him. She got it. He should have walked out the minute he saw her. Instead, he'd let her buy him a drink, thinking, "Why not?" For some unknown reason he wanted to tell her he'd take the deal. Back off, she'd never see him again. Instead, she used that sharp tongue of hers to tell him what she really thought.

"Does Mommy know you're out past dark?"

That's all it took for him to ask her if she wanted to play a grown-up game. He thought teaching her a lesson, beating her at poker, showing her he was good at something, would wipe that smug look off her face. Instead, she'd wiped the floor with him.

Fuck her. He had a woman in his arms and good booze in his belly. That's all he needed right now.

Mandy pushed him away, grabbed the bottle he'd taken from the bar out of her purse, and poured him a glass in one of the plastic-covered cups she unwrapped. He downed the booze, fell into the rickety chair next to the window, and kicked off his shoes. He wanted Mandy in the bed, naked, now.

"Take your clothes off."

Mandy poured him another drink. Bleary-eyed and off balance already, he didn't need another, but he drank it down. How did that bitch kick his ass? And what the hell was that move she pulled on him?

He stared down at his hand and rotated his thumb. It hurt. Without the numbing booze, it would probably hurt more.

Mandy took his hand, leaned down, and kissed his thumb. He stared at her breasts, his mouth watering just thinking about having her naked, his mouth on her skin.

"Does it hurt?"

"Not really. It won't stop me from fucking you good, baby."

"Off with this." She pulled his shirt over his head. The material got stuck on his watch, but he managed to wrench his arm free. He laughed, too drunk to do much else. This is what he needed. Some mind-numbing sex. Something to make him feel anything but the agony growing inside of him every second that he remembered what he did. The booze helped erase the bloody images from his mind, but they'd come back. Right now, he wanted to fill his mind with images of Mandy naked and writhing beneath him.

He stood and wrapped her in his arms. He tried to kiss her, but she leaned back, grabbed his belt, and used it to spin him around. His head spun. She pushed his bare belly and he fell back on the bed. The room spun around him like a merry-go-round. He pressed the heels of his hands to his eyes and tried to steady himself.

Mandy unbuckled his belt, undid his button and zipper, and pulled his jeans down his legs. "I guess I have to do all the work."

Evan was happy to let her.

"What happened here?" Mandy traced her fingertips over the scar that ran around the side of his right thigh.

"An accident."

"It looks like it got infected." Her fingertips traced the red marks.

"It did. I had to have it cleaned and stitched at the Emory Urgent Care after it happened." He'd cleaned and bandaged it himself, but after several days the deep wound got worse. He'd had no choice but to get a doctor to fix him up.

"Well, I'll make you forget all about that nasty cut."

"It doesn't hurt anymore. I wish it would go away," he slurred, sleep creeping in. He shook his head to clear out the cobwebs, but that sent the room spinning again.

"Give me a minute to clean up in the bathroom. I'll be right back."

" 'K." He stared at her ass and smiled back at her when she closed the bathroom door. His eyes closed along with it.

Chapter Twenty-Six

KATE PARKED FIVE cars over and one row back from Evan's Range Rover. She kept her eyes on the motel room door, waiting for Mandy to come back out. Sam parked behind the building and stood in the covered space between the office and the rest of the building by the ice and vending machines. He blended into the shadows. Ben parked two cars over. He kept his gaze trained on her. It burned into her like a brand. She felt his anger and knew she'd have to answer for her actions. He wouldn't be happy. He may not understand, but she had to do this.

It seemed like hours passed before the motel room door opened. Mandy walked out only twenty minutes later and stared at all the cars, looking for her. Kate stuck her hand out the window and waved. Mandy spotted her and trotted over.

"He passed out when I went in the bathroom. I got it," she said, leaning down to stare at Kate through the window.

"Let's see."

Mandy held up her phone. Sure enough, she'd captured Evan sprawled on the bed, a long angry red line across his thigh. It seemed like a long time for that cut to heal.

"It's a nasty scar. He said it got infected. He had to have a doctor fix it up."

"Did he say where he got medical care?"

"Emory Urgent Care."

"Did you post this to your FB page?"

"Oh, yeah. I forgot that part."

"Make the picture public, so anyone can see it. If he asks why you did it, just say you thought he looked cute."

"He does, doesn't he?"

"Don't forget to tag it with his name and put the caption we talked about."

"Okay, done." Mandy turned her phone to show Kate.

"Perfect. Thanks, Mandy. I hope you enjoy your new car." Kate handed over the forty-five hundred dollars.

Mandy counted it quickly, smiling and holding the stack of cash to her ample chest.

"Can I drive you somewhere?" Kate didn't want to leave her stranded.

"No, thanks. I'm going to walk to the Denny's on the corner and get something to eat. I'm starving. I'll catch a cab or call a friend to take me home."

"You're sure? I hate to leave you here alone."

"Evan and I have stayed here a few times. I'm good. Thanks for the money. This will really make things easier."

Mandy waved and walked away, down the driveway and sidewalk toward the corner.

Kate found the picture on her phone and emailed a copy to Detective Raynott with the information for the clinic Evan used.

Sam and Ben met at her car, staring down at her through the window. She held up her phone, showing them the picture.

"He's injured," Sam said.

"My sister sliced him open. The blood on the knife has to be his."

"But the results came back, Kate. It's not a match," Ben pointed out.

"They never tested it against Evan's DNA. The test was to see if the blood found on the knife was a familial match to Donald. It's not."

Ben swore, put his head back, and looked up at the night sky. Morgan's words rang in his head and came out his mouth. "The truth is in the details." He stared down at Kate. "Evan isn't Donald's son."

"Christina cheated on him from the very beginning of their marriage. She passed Evan off as Donald's son. That's what he found out. That's what prompted his sudden move to divorce her and cut off Evan."

"The DNA test you found in his papers," Ben said. "Not to find out if Alex was a match, but Evan."

"Exactly. Evan killed them to ensure he got his inheritance. I've sent the photo to Detective Raynott. Let me leave him a message. Hopefully, when he gets the DNA results back they ran to see if Christina's blood was on the knife, it'll show that the blood is a familial match to her. That will be enough to get a warrant and arrest Evan."

She called the detective and hoped to leave him a message, but he answered on the second ring.

"Raynott."

Kate put her phone on speaker for Ben and Sam to listen in. "This is Kate Morrison. I'm sorry to call so late."

"Don't worry about it. I caught a break on one of my cases and stayed late to see it through. What can I do for you?"

"I have some information on my sister's case. Check out the picture I sent to your email."

"Got it. Is that Evan Faraday?"

"In the flesh."

"Nice scar. So your sister did cut him."

"You're staring at the proof. I sent the name of the clinic. You can get the medical records from the doctor who worked on him."

"Got it. I'll contact them in the morning."

"You do understand what this means?" she asked.

"The blood on the knife is Evan's. He's not Donald's son, which gives him the perfect motive to kill his father before that fact came to light and Evan lost his big, fat inheritance."

"We're on the same page. How long until you get the DNA results?"

"I expect them Monday morning. Once I've got that plus what you sent me, I'll have all I need to arrest Evan. We're almost there, Kate."

"Thank you, Detective. Keep me and Ben posted."

"Will do. Try to have a good weekend."

Kate said goodbye and hung up. She gripped the steering wheel and stared straight ahead, wishing the wheels of justice didn't grind along so slowly.

"Elizabeth and I will keep Alex for the night. I'll drop him off at your place first thing in the morning. You two good?"

"We're fine." Ben bit out the words.

"I'll say good night, then. Kate, nice work tonight."

Kate stared up at Sam from her front seat. She didn't miss the scowl on Ben's face. "Thanks, Sam, for watching my back and taking care of Alex."

"You've got an outstanding backside to watch." Sam winked and walked away.

Kate laughed under her breath.

Ben glared down at her. "Are you okay to drive?"

"I'm fine."

Ben opened his mouth to say something, but closed it before he uttered a single word. He stuffed his hands in his pockets and continued to stare down at her. The anger rolling off him washed over her, making her chest tight. She'd really pissed him off with this stunt.

"Shall we go home to your place, or would you rather I stay at mine?" She held her breath, hoping she hadn't screwed everything up.

"I don't care where the fuck we stay, so long as we do it together."

"Okay, so we'll go to your place, since Sam will bring Alex there in the morning."

"If that's not where you want to be, Kate, then say so right now."

Unexpected tears filled her eyes. She hadn't just made him angry, she'd hurt him. Deeply. The thought of losing him made her stomach sour and her heart crack and bleed.

She pushed her car door open, stepped out, and threw herself into his tall body. She held on with her arms locked around his neck. "I know you're mad, but please don't end this. Don't push me away."

"You did that tonight by leaving me out of your plans and sneaking around behind my back." Despite the harsh words, he held her close with his hands banded at her lower back.

"I'm sorry. I'm so sorry. I knew I shouldn't have done it, but I did it anyway. I've never had anyone but Margo to rely on."

"That's bullshit, Kate. You know you can count on me. Haven't I proven that to you by now?"

"Yes. But you would have tried to talk me out of doing this. You wouldn't want me to put myself in danger."

Ben's hands clamped onto her hips. "Because that asshole has proven he's willing to kill to keep what he thinks is his."

"I had to do it. No one ever stood up for Margo and me the way we did for each other. I owed her this."

"Tell me something. If you hadn't gotten the woman to get Evan naked, did you plan to do it yourself?"

She tried not to smile, but it came anyway. She leaned back in his arms and looked him in the eye. She owed him that. "No. In my younger days, I was known to haunt a lot of bars just like that one."

One of his eyebrows cocked up.

"I was a messed-up girl, looking for love in all the wrong places. I thought my self-worth was tied to a man's devoted attention. A hard lesson to learn my worth is only calculated by me."

"You are one in a million, Kate." Ben reached up and traced her cheek with his fingertips. The soft gesture belied the frustration and anger still in his dark eyes.

"In any given bar, there is always a woman willing to earn some cash. I didn't need Mandy to sleep with him, though she's done that plenty in the past. That worked to my advantage."

"You didn't feel right about her taking the money and sleeping with him, so you made sure to get him drunk enough to pass out."

"You get that about me, which pisses you off more, because I left you out of this."

"If you'd told me your plan, I might have actually gone along with it and watched your back."

She smoothed her hands up and down over his shoulders, trying to soothe him. "You did. It worked out just like that."

"Just because Sam caught you in a lie and followed you, and I ended up here, doesn't make you right."

"I'm not right. What I did worked, but making you mad wasn't my intention."

Ben's grip on her hips tightened. He let loose his frustration and gave her a little shake. "Do you have any idea how I'd feel right now if you got hurt or killed tonight pulling this stunt?"

She kept her gaze steady on his. "Ben, I'm sorry."

"Right. Sorry you got caught."

"No. I'm sorry this has torn a rift between us."

"Kate, I'm angry, but I'm not leaving you."

"You think I don't trust you."

"You trust me to a point. That's not enough for me."

She pressed her hand to his jaw. "The thing is, I do trust you. I trust you to be you. To be the kind, caring man who will take care of my son if anything happens to me. To be the voice of reason when I'm unreasonable."

One side of his mouth drew back in a grim line. "Like tonight."

"Yes. I didn't want you to talk me out of this. I didn't want to hear all the reasons I shouldn't have done this, knowing you'd be right. Tonight, I had to set Margo free. Let her rest in peace knowing the man who killed her will pay for his crimes."

"Why tonight?"

"It's my birthday."

His grip went loose. One hand came up and rested on her chest; his fingertips lightly rested on the base of her neck. "What? Why didn't you tell me?"

She covered his hand and held it tight to her skin.

"Not my actual birthday. Margo and I celebrated two, the day we were born and the day we were set free."

"This is the day you killed your father."

"Yes. All I thought about all day is that I'd freed myself from my past, but Evan held my future hostage. Locked up in your apartment, a prisoner, unable to even go to the grocery store without worrying that he'd do something to me or Alex. I can't live like that. Never again." She hoped he understood her past had come back to haunt her. Living every second of her young life in fear of her father wasn't any different than doing the same now, only it was worse because she had to protect Alex. If something happened to him, no telling how far she'd go to avenge his death, no matter the cost to herself.

Ben cupped her face and tilted it up to meet his gaze. "I know you've been struggling."

"I've been falling apart little by little on the inside, Ben. I'm not the kind of person to sit back and let others do the dirty work. My grief for my sister wages war against my feelings for you. The happiness I feel when I'm with you and Alex adds on to my guilt that Margo isn't here to experience the same. My anger builds that all this death and devastation is over something as stupid as money. I want to just give it to them to make them stop, but know that doesn't really solve anything. I'm frustrated and feel completely inadequate to end this, be the mother Alex deserves, and find my way past all of this to be the woman you both need me to be. Look at how I fell short today with you."

Ben crushed his mouth to hers. His anger vanished

with every word she spoke with such honesty. He thought he understood her frustration and feelings, but to hear her admit how much she struggled with her emotions and trying to be everything for everyone in her life made his heart ache. He didn't want to be one more burden, but the person who held her up, the soft place she fell, the reason she endured and was happy.

He admired her strength. So much so that he figured there wasn't anything she couldn't handle. Just because she could, didn't mean it was easy for her.

He softened the kiss, brushing his lips over hers again and again to settle her and him. He tasted her tears and wiped them away with a brush of his thumbs over her damp cheeks.

"I'm not a crier. Lately, it seems I have no control."

She pressed her forehead to his chin and gripped his shoulders for support. She never lost it in front of anyone else. She held it together, but with him she let her guard down, trusting that he'd comfort her.

Maybe he'd overreacted tonight. Not about what she'd done, but that she'd done it with no regard for how it would make him react and feel.

"I'm sorry, Ben. I really am."

"Promise me you won't pull a stunt like this again, and I'll forget the whole thing."

Kate stepped back and stared up at him. "I'll tell you first the next time I need to pull a stunt like this, and I'll listen while you try to talk me out of it."

He couldn't help the smile. "Damnit, Kate, you just can't help making me crazy."

"Are you still crazy about me?"

"If it's crazy to want you the way I do, then I should probably be committed."

"I'd bust you out." The soft, seductive smile on her face did him in.

He pulled her back into his arms and kissed her softly. "Let's get out of here before that asshole wakes up and catches us."

One side of Kate's lush mouth tilted down. "He drank so much he won't wake up for hours. When he does, I hope his head feels like it's going to split open."

"You've got a mean streak in you, Kate."

"Only for those who deserve it. For you, I've got a soft spot that keeps growing."

He leaned down and kissed her on the neck, exactly where he'd learned made her shiver and melt in his arms. "Like right there." He slid his tongue up her neck and pressed a kiss behind her ear. "Or right there."

"Ben, take me home."

"I'm taking you to bed and keeping you there until you're too exhausted to plot behind my back."

"Oh, well, that's going to take a while. I have a very active imagination."

"Use it for good and come up with ways to make tonight up to me."

That seductive smile he'd grown addicted to bringing out in her spread across her face and brightened her eyes with mischief. "Oh, I'll come up with something."

"I'm counting on it."

The drive home seemed to take forever. He kept his

thoughts on how much he loved Kate and wanted to make love to her tonight. He put this whole incident in the back of his mind, knowing that once their lives were back to normal and the threat the Faradays posed was eliminated, Kate and he could finally settle into a normal life.

Kate parked beside him at his place. He tugged her out of the car and to the elevator. They held it together in front of the security guys, but the minute he had her alone in the elevator car, he kissed her the whole way up to his floor and had her panting when the elevator doors opened. She giggled and ran after him as he pulled her down the hall to his door. Once inside, he spun her around and pressed her against the back of the door and buried his face in her neck, kissing a trail down to her breasts, peeling her purple blouse aside to taste and lick her soft skin.

Her nimble fingers worked the buttons open on his dress shirt. Impatient toward the end, she dragged the material over his head and tossed it away. Her palms pressed to his chest and slid up over his shoulders and down his back.

He cupped her breasts. She moaned and arched her back, pressing her breasts into his hands. He wanted to tear her clothes off, but gave himself the pleasure of sliding his hands down over her body and around her hips to her gorgeous ass. He squeezed and kneaded. She pushed her hips forward. He slid one leg between her thighs and pulled her against him. She rocked against his leg, rubbing herself against him. Her thigh rubbed against his aching cock, making him groan in sweet pain. Her fingers dug through his hair and grabbed on. God, but he needed to be inside of her now.

He held on tight to her ass and pulled her up as he stood tall. She wrapped her legs around him and he turned and headed for the bedroom.

"You have been driving me insane in this skirt all fucking night." He dipped his fingers low and skimmed her bare bottom beneath the silky material. He held her with one hand as he walked and used the other to slide over the swell of her bottom, down to her wet center covered by the thin strip of her lace thong. "Fuck, you drive me crazy."

"You swear a lot when you're turned on," she said against his lips.

Right now he couldn't speak anymore. His knees hit the end of the bed and he fell on top of her. Their bodies bounced on the mattress. He planted his knees, hooked his hands under her arms, and hauled her up higher on the bed. She giggled, but he made her moan when he cupped her in his hand and swept his fingers roughly over her soft folds. He hooked his fingers in the lace and pulled it down her long, strong legs. Her heels fell off as he dragged the material off her feet. Anxious for him, she tore off her flimsy blouse, revealing the black bra he'd caught hints of beneath the sheer material all night. She unhooked her bra and tossed it away. His gaze feasted on her pretty breasts. His mouth watered to clamp onto her hard pink nipples. It was all he could do to tear his pants, boxers, and socks off. He landed on top of her the second she kicked off her skirt.

His skin pressed to hers and she sighed. Her sweet taste filled his mouth as he licked her breast and sucked hard on her nipple. Her nimble hands roamed over his heated skin, driving him to the brink.

She reached for the condom next to the bed. He kept right on kissing her breasts, licking, tempting her into the fire. He slid one hand down her side and over her hip. She tilted to make the grab into the drawer. He took advantage and squeezed her ass, then pushed her thigh wide, smoothed his hand over her toned muscles, up her thigh, and dipped one finger into her slick heat. Her hips rocked against his hand, riding his pumping finger. She tightened around him, but didn't let herself fall over the edge. Instead, she pushed his hand away and used her body to push him over to his back.

Her lips kissed a path over his chest and down to his belly. Her warm lips tickled his side and made him flinch. She smiled against his skin and nipped with her teeth, then licked his heated skin. He pulled her long, thick hair across her shoulder and draped it over his thigh, so he could see her face and the long slope of her back all the way to her pretty bottom up in the air. He lost all thought when she licked the head of his dick and took him into her mouth. He bit back a curse, it felt so damn good.

Her hands glided up his chest as her mouth slid up his hard cock. She squeezed his pec and raked her fingers down his chest as her mouth sank down on him again.

"Oh, God, Kate, come here." He hooked his hands under her arms and drew her up to him. He took her mouth in an urgent kiss, his tongue sinking deep. He wanted to push her down on top of him and thrust deep, but held back.

Kate broke the kiss, straddled his hips, sheathed him in the condom, and followed through on his last and only thought. She rose above him and sank back down on top of him, her head back, hair hanging over her shoulders and covering her pretty breasts. He smoothed his hands up her sides and covered the soft mounds, squeezing her nipples between his fingers. Her hands covered his and squeezed tight. She rocked her hips against his, slid her hands down his arms, and grabbed his biceps. She sighed and lowered her head to stare down at him. Her eyes smoldered. The heat and intensity in them sent a scorching wave of lust through his system. He grabbed her hips and pulled her up, then slammed her back down. He thrust deep, rocked against her, then pulled her up and brought her back down again. All the while, her gaze remained locked with his.

He felt connected to her in a way he'd never felt. He couldn't hide from her. She didn't hide anything from him. He saw the pleasure building in her eyes and felt it in her body. She tightened around him. He held her with one hand and found her slick clit with the other, brushing the pad of his thumb against her as she rocked against him. The need to let go hit him fast and hard, but he held back, every muscle in his body tight as he thrust deep, and she shattered, her body demanding he follow her over that sharp edge into sweet ecstasy.

Ben came back to himself in increments. First with the feel of her body lying atop his, her warm skin pressed down the length of him. Waves of her hair covered the arm he kept banded over her back holding her close. He used his other hand to trace circles on her bare bottom.

"Mmm, I love that." Her husky voice made him smile. He'd worn her out.

Because she liked him touching her, he covered her ass with both hands and skimmed them up and down her back in soft strokes, circling, tracing, loving the feel of her smooth skin against his fingertips.

"Don't ever stop."

"I'll never get enough of you."

"Are we good?" she asked, a hint of uncertainty in her voice.

"I thought we were better than good. That was fantastic."

She smiled against his chest and squeezed his shoulders. "Ben."

"One little argument isn't going to change the way I feel about you. But feel free to make it up to me again if you feel the need." He wanted to keep things light, to show her that even when they disagreed they could make up and not dwell on what happened.

He maneuvered her enough to pull the covers over them and still keep her tucked against his side. He settled into the mattress and held her close. To let her know he meant what he said, he kissed her softly and tucked her head beneath his chin and held her. It took several minutes for her to relax and fall asleep. He understood her need to hold on to him. With Margo gone, she didn't have anyone else. Still, he didn't like the trace of desperation he felt in her embrace. It left him feeling like there was a possibility he might lose her. The thought left him cold. He held Kate close, ready to protect her from anything, everything. He wished he understood why the need to do so seemed so urgent when they were on the cusp of finishing this and finally having a nice, safe, normal life together.

Chapter Twenty-Seven

KATE THOUGHT SHE'D wake up Monday morning to the
news that Evan had been arrested for her sister and Donald's murders. Instead, she woke up to more excuses. The
test results weren't back from the lab. Thanks to the picture of Evan's injury, they had probable cause to bring
him back in for questioning, but they couldn't find him.
Christina refused Kate's settlement offer and her counteroffer. A judge would hear the case on Thursday. Ben
assured her the judge would side with Kate and Alex.
Christina could lose everything if she didn't settle. Ben
warned Kate again how dangerous that made her and
Evan. With Evan missing, the cops closing in, Ben worried for her and Alex's safety more than ever.

Trapped in Ben's apartment, the guards downstairs,
her life on hold, Kate focused on Alex. She loved being
with her son. The pang of guilt dulled each and every day
she spent with him. Margo would want her to be happy.

Kate lay on the sofa, Alex on her chest. He raised his head and smiled at her. She tucked his arms up under him so he could hold himself up. She made silly faces and popping sounds with her mouth to make him laugh. He babbled and tried to mimic her.

A strange crack and hiss sounded just outside the door. Kate turned her head and tried to peer past the chair and table. The smell of smoke hit her seconds before it billowed up and into the apartment.

Scared, her heart thundered in her chest. She rolled up, holding Alex close. The fire alarm above her squealed, startling Alex. He bellowed in her arms. She set him on his mat on the floor, low and out of most of the smoke.

Kate ran for the kitchen behind her and grabbed her purse and phone off the counter. She pulled the dish towel off the oven handle and covered her mouth and nose. She picked up Alex's diaper bag by the front door and put the strap over her shoulder along with her purse. She placed her hand on the wood. Not hot. Good. She tested the handle. The metal remained cool to the touch. She didn't know where the fire burned, but hoped she could get down the hall to the stairwell and out of the building with Alex before the flames filled the hallway.

Cautious not to pull the door open wide and let any flames flare inside, she unlocked the bolt and knob and opened the door a slit to peek out. The door burst open, hitting her in the side as she jumped back to avoid getting hurt. She caught herself and stared at the person standing in the doorway, someone who looked eerily like her sister though most of her face was hidden by the fall of blond hair and oversized sunglasses.

Mesmerized by the sight of her sister, she didn't understand the loud pop or why she fell onto her butt and back until the pain exploded in her chest and shoulder. She stared up at the woman standing over her, a gun in her hand pointed straight down at her.

Kate held up her hand. "No. Don't. I have a baby."

"Exactly who I came for." The woman's voice sounded familiar, but Kate's mind raced too fast for her to catch any one thought, except to save Alex. She rolled and tried to press herself up, but her left arm gave out and she fell flat again. Adrenaline pumping, she scrambled across the floor in an odd crawl, but was too late to grab her son. The woman held him in one arm and pointed the gun down at her.

"I know you can fight. That gunshot should slow you down. Get up. Let's go. You scream, make any sound at all, and I'll shoot you dead right after I kill him in front of you."

With the barrel of the gun pointed at Alex's stomach, Kate planted her feet under her and stood on wobbly legs. The straps of the diaper bag and her purse tangled around her wrist. She freed them and pulled them up on her shoulder with her good hand.

"Please, the smoke. It's not good for him. We have to get out of here before the fire spreads."

"There is no fire. Just a couple cheap smoke bombs from Chinatown. Effective. Now move." The woman waved the gun indicating Kate walk out ahead of her. "Wait. Put that jacket on to cover the blood."

Kate pulled Ben's coat up her arm and draped it across her back. She didn't want to lose her purse with her cell phone in it or the diaper bag so she pulled the coat over her other shoulder. She moaned in pain and bit back a squeal. Ben's scent engulfed her. She inhaled and tried to stay calm. Kate tried to think. She needed to call the police, Ben, get someone's attention before this nutcase got them out of the building. Security downstairs would stop them. They had to.

"Careful, Kate, you hold your son's life in your hands. One false move, and I'll kill both of you."

The voice finally penetrated her fear-clouded mind. She saw past the pathetic disguise and saw the evil beneath. "Christina."

"Move or he's dead."

Kate walked out of Ben's apartment and headed for the elevator.

"Other way. Take the stairs along with all the other residents."

Not too many people were home at this time of day in this building. Most of the tenants were businesspeople who spent more time at their offices than they did at home. The few residents they saw in the stairwell were older people and women. She tried to get someone's attention, giving them pointed looks. Since everyone was in a panic, no one noticed hers was for any other reason than the fire.

At the bottom of the stairs, security and police officers ushered residents out of the heavy metal door that led down an alley.

"Don't say a word." Christina crowded close to her, pushing her through the door quickly and past the tenants gawking up at the building. Fire trucks screamed to a halt in the front of the building. Christina pushed her in the other direction. In the chaos, no one noticed. As much as she wanted to alert the cops, she believed Christina would shoot Alex.

"Take a left at the end of the alley."

Kate did as she said, stumbling along. The adrenaline waned and the pain in her shoulder intensified. Blood ran down the front and back of her shirt. She needed help. Fast. If she passed out from blood loss before she saved Alex . . . The thought didn't bear thinking about.

She kept her focus straight ahead and dipped her hand into her purse. She found her cell and swiped the screen without looking down. Ben's coat hung over her arm, so she hoped the woman didn't notice what she was doing. She needed to dial, so she stumbled, fell against the building's wall, and hung her head. Quickly, she dialed 911, then took a few unsteady steps when Christina shoved her from behind.

"Keep walking."

"The fire department is here." She spoke as loud as she could without alerting Christina that she wanted the dispatcher to overhear them. "They'll see us. You'll be arrested for kidnapping and attempted murder. Murder if I die from this gunshot wound."

"Shut up and get into the car."

Alex cried, startled by the sharp words.

"It's okay, sweetheart. You're going to be okay."

"That's what you think. Now get in the car."

"Which one? The white Ford Taurus or the silver Mercedes?"

"The Mercedes." She held the key fob up and unlocked the doors. Alex continued to cry out his distress. Kate wanted to comfort him, but held back the urge to reach for him, afraid Christina would hurt him.

Kate pulled the handle on the back door and turned to slide in. The coat fell open and the woman shoved the gun in Kate's face. "Toss it. Now." The fury in her voice made the words vibrate out.

Kate sighed and tossed the phone on the sidewalk, hoping someone found it. She'd done all she could. For now.

"I'm putting him on the floor in front. You make one wrong move, and I'll shoot him."

Kate believed her. Dizzy. In pain. Kate sat in the back and rested her head against the seat. Christina slid into the driver's seat and closed her door. She leaned over and set Alex on the floorboard in the passenger's side. He quieted and settled, which made it easier for Kate to focus and not feel the gnawing need to comfort him to stop his crying. Christina held up the gun for Kate to see she still had it ready, and set it down beside her to start the car. They drove off. Kate wondered if she'd ever see Ben again.

BEN PICKED UP his cell phone from his desk and answered Sam's call.

"Why is your girl traveling down 101 toward Redwood City?" Sam asked without even a hello.

"What?"

"My phone alerted me that she's out of the two-mile radius I set around your house. The tracking device in her purse is moving down 101. Her cell phone is still at your building. So either someone stole her purse, or she left her phone at your place and is going somewhere."

"She wouldn't leave my place. Not without telling me."

"She did."

Ben's phone beeped with a text message. "Hold on, I'm getting a text." Ben pulled up the text message and swore. "The building manager just sent out a message to all residents that there's been a false fire alarm at the building. The third floor filled with smoke, but no fire."

"That's your floor," Sam pointed out, even as Ben stood and headed for his office door to get into his car.

"They fucking staged a false fire alarm to get Kate and Alex. Where are you?"

"A block from your building. Let me check it out, then we'll go after your girl."

"Forget my place, follow the tracking device on your phone." Exactly what he planned to do.

"Mr. Knight, your four o'clock is here," his assistant called as he headed for the elevator.

"Reschedule it. I have an emergency."

The elevator doors closed on his assistant's surprised

face. He didn't care about anything right now, except getting to his car and finding Kate.

"You still there?" he asked Sam.

"Found her phone outside your building. She dialed 911."

Something in Sam's voice alerted him. "What aren't you telling me?"

"Nothing."

"Sam, you need to tell me everything."

Sam sighed. "The phone is covered in blood. There are drops leading back around your building."

"She's bleeding. How bad?"

"It's not good. Hold on, cops are coming my way."

Ben nearly lost his mind trying to decipher the mumbles coming through the phone. He almost yelled at Sam when he came back on the line.

"Firefighters found blood splatter on your door and on the floor of your apartment. Kate and Alex are missing. Cops checked surveillance. A blond woman wearing dark glasses set off the smoke bombs and walked Kate out of the building. They followed the blood trail out here to me."

"Does the video show how Kate got hurt?"

"No. Nothing conclusive."

"What the hell does that mean?"

"They think the woman had a gun."

"Kate's been shot?"

"Look, Ben, this is taking time we don't have. I'll follow her signal and see if I can catch up to them."

"What about Alex?"

"The blonde carried the baby. They got into a silver Mercedes."

"Margo drove a silver Mercedes. We got a call about a false alarm at Margo's last night. Cops checked it out, but found nothing. Maybe Evan stole her car."

"I'll have the cops put out a BOLO and send them in the direction I'm headed."

"I've got Kate's signal on my phone. I'm pulling out of the parking lot right now. Don't wait for me. Just find her. Save her and Alex. Please, Sam."

"On it."

Ben broke every speed law on his way out of the city. He raced down Highway 101. By the time he hit Redwood City, he knew exactly where to find Kate. The pulsing red dot on the map on his phone sat right on top of Margo and Donald's address. Ben's mind sprouted one nightmare after another. He prayed he got to them in time.

Chapter Twenty-Eight

KATE BARELY MADE it out of the car without passing out on the garage floor. She stumbled into Margo's kitchen, desperate to find a way to get Alex out of Christina's clutches.

"Figure it out yet?" the woman taunted. She leaned against the counter with Alex held carelessly in one arm, the gun in her free hand.

Christina pulled off her sunglasses and tossed them on the table. She pulled the blond wig off next.

"That you're jealous of my sister and that Donald loved her and not you that you ordered your son to kill them, then you set the fire at Haven House. It's so easy to figure it out."

"Hard to prove though, isn't it?" Christina smirked. "You didn't have the good sense to die in that blast. That damn do-gooder saw me leaving and ran in after you.

Now, we're here. This time, you won't walk out of here alive."

"Are you out of your mind? You're never going to get away with this."

"Yes, I will. I always get what I want. It's the one thing I learned about having money. You can pretty much buy your way out of anything."

"You can't buy your way out of killing an innocent baby."

"Oh, honey, I didn't kill him. You did."

Kate's vision blurred, but she made a grab for Alex anyway. A last-ditch effort to take him away from this madness. The world fell away and the last thing Kate knew for sure as her head thumped on the floor was that she hadn't saved her son, and she'd never see Alex and Ben ever again.

"WHAT THE HELL did you do?" Evan slammed the door behind him and stared at his mother, taking in the blond wig draped over the couch, the baby sleeping against a pillow in the corner of the sofa, and Kate leaning heavily to the side in a chair, her hands tied behind her back. Blood soaked the front of her shirt all the way down to her jeans. An angry red splotch marred the side of her head.

"Me? What the hell were you thinking letting someone take a picture of you nearly naked?"

"What are you talking about?"

"You're wanted for questioning in your father's murder

because some girl took a picture of you that showed the scar on your leg."

Mandy. Damn that stupid bitch. He bet Kate paid her to do it. She was fun in the sack and out, but he couldn't believe she'd sell him out like this.

"That's circumstantial. They don't have anything, since you fixed it that the blood on the knife didn't match me."

"She didn't fix anything for you. She lied." Kate's head bobbed as she tried to sit back.

"Shut up." His mother smacked Kate in the side of the head. It snapped back. Kate couldn't bring her head forward again.

"Did you shoot her?" He couldn't believe his mother would do such a thing.

"There was no other way. She knows how to fight. I couldn't take any chances."

"But you brought her here? Are you crazy?"

"She's devastated by her sister's death. Grief can make you do stupid things, like smother your baby and take your own life."

"Yeah, that explains why I shot myself in the shoulder." Kate let out a derisive snort. "She's lying to you, Evan." The words came out slurred and barely more than a whisper. He feared she'd die right before his eyes. "She brought you here to pin this on you."

"Shut up." His mother turned her hard gaze on him. Her eyes filled with pleading. "We're so close to having everything."

"I thought you were going to take the settlement. I told you to take it. This has gone too far."

"And let that bitch and this baby have everything? Never."

"You're actually going to kill my brother?"

"He's not your brother," Kate mumbled.

BEN GOT STOPPED at the end of the street by the police roadblock. Sam grabbed him before he tried to wrestle his way through five cops to run up the street to save Kate.

"Ben, wait." Sam fisted his hands in Ben's shirt and held tight even when Ben pushed against him to get to Kate.

"She's in there with both of them. You've got to be fucking kidding me—you want me to wait?"

"Listen to me, man. They've got a sniper on the roof next door. Christina and Evan are both in there. They have Alex and Kate. We have to handle this carefully. You don't want them to hurt Kate and Alex."

"How is she? Did that bitch shoot her?"

An ambulance pulled up. The police moved aside to let it park inside the police line. At the front. Where they could get to Kate fast.

Ben swallowed the lump in his throat.

"She's in bad shape. Alex appears to be fine."

"I need to get them out of there."

"SWAT is coming up with a plan."

"SWAT! Are you crazy? You want to have bullets flying with a baby in the middle of everyone, not to mention Kate. No. Make them let me go in there. I can talk to Evan and Christina. I can make a deal. They want the money. I'll make them believe Kate and I will give it to them."

Sam grabbed him tighter. "I'm not letting you walk right in there."

"We'll go in the back. You cover my ass."

"You have no training for talking down lunatics."

"Morgan said she's meant for me. She's mine. I want her back. It doesn't end like this."

"Shit." Sam ran over to the group of SWAT officers and spoke fast. After a lot of head shaking and some yelling, Sam came back with a bulletproof vest. "Take off your shirt and tie and put this on. We don't want them to see it. Put your jacket back on over all that."

Ben did as Sam said. Sam pulled the gun from his holster and held it at his side. "We go in through the side door to the garage. Evan's Range Rover is in the driveway. The Mercedes must be in the garage. Let's hope they kept the inside door unlocked and we can walk right in and take them by surprise."

Ben started walking toward the house.

Sam caught up and swore under his breath. "I can't believe I let you talk me into this."

"You know it's the best way. You and Tyler are always talking about how it's not the size of the force but the smarts of the man inside."

Sam grimaced and tilted his head. "Yeah, well, let's hope you're smarter than them."

Ben grinned, confident he had the upper hand. "Oh, I am. I know something Evan doesn't know. It will turn him against his mother."

"That might not be the best way to go," Sam pointed out.

Ben tried to hold back his doubt and think about how this could all go wrong in a second. "It's our only hope of ending this thing."

"WHAT DOES SHE mean I'm not Alex's brother?" Evan asked his mother, knowing the answer but hating what it meant.

His mother waved her hand. "She's babbling, trying to turn you against me."

"You should listen to Kate." Ben stepped into the room. His fucking nemesis. The one man who'd stop at nothing to take Evan down.

Evan glared at Ben. "Where the hell did you come from?"

Ben held out his hands to his sides. "I came for Kate and Alex."

"How do you know I'm not Alex's brother?"

"The DNA test of the blood on the knife came back a familial match to your mother, but not Donald."

"Shut up," his mother yelled, shaking the gun at Ben.

"Let them go, and I'll give you the fifty million your mother asked for."

"You refused my offer. This is what happens when you're greedy."

Evan stared at his mother, wondering when the irony of her statement would hit home. It didn't. She held the gun pointed straight at Ben's chest.

"So, what is the deal?" Ben asked his mother. "You blame this all on Evan. He shot Margo and Donald, now he's shot Kate. It's your word against a man who's already proven he'll kill his own father to get his inheritance. What about Alex? You going to shoot him too?"

His mother slid the pillow out from under Alex. Startled out of sleep, the baby cried out. His mother put the pillow over Alex's head and pressed down. The baby kicked his little feet, but he was no match for Christina's strength.

"Mother, no!"

Ben lunged two steps forward but stopped short when his mother shook the gun at him.

"Stop right there."

"Mother, don't do this."

"Shut up, Evan. It has to be this way." The baby's muffled cries grew quieter. "They can't leave this room alive, or all our plans, all we've done, will be for nothing."

Evan rushed his mother and grabbed the pillow out of her hand. She turned the gun from Ben and pointed it at his chest.

"It doesn't matter." Her eyes were filled with a strange brightness and a desperation he'd never seen in anyone. "She'll be dead soon. We'll kill the damn lawyer and burn the house down. We'll be gone before they investigate and discover they've been shot. We can leave the country." His mother wiped her sweaty forehead.

"You've really lost it, Mother. It's over. If you'd left it alone maybe I'd have gotten away with the murders and had my life. Now, after the fire, you kidnapping them, bringing them here to kill them . . ." Evan shook his head, knowing he'd never spend another day free in his life. Hell, he hadn't been a free man since he killed that man in the alley and she'd helped him cover it up. He'd never suffered the consequences of his actions, except in the form of the nightmares and dark thoughts that haunted him every second. He deserved this fate.

"Don't you see? I did this all for you. To fix what you screwed up, always fighting and getting hurt. That damn car accident really riled your father. Then the doctors spoke to him. You needed blood."

Evan traced the long scar down his neck. "Let me guess. He discovered my blood type didn't match his. The doctor told him I couldn't possibly be his son, because let's face it, you like fucking every man who isn't your husband." Evan shouted the last, pissed beyond words she'd lied to him his whole life. "Do you even know who my father is?"

"Donald Faraday was your father. He raised you. He loved you. Then he wanted to take it all away. From you. From me!"

"You deserved it. Then you sent me over here to kill them. You wanted me to get caught so you would get everything."

"No. I didn't think you'd get caught at all. But with your father out of the way, we'd have all that money. He couldn't tell us what to do anymore."

"He wasn't my father," Evan shouted, the pain that truth meant ripping him in two. He'd always hated his mother for her lies and manipulations. He'd lived with it because she'd always been good to him, but in reality, he was her biggest lie, used to manipulate a man who'd been too good to her for far too long. She didn't deserve it. She didn't deserve anything from his father.

"You knew about his fiancée. Did you know about the baby?"

"What I know is that he had that little brat to replace you. He wanted a child of his own."

"He loved you, Evan. He h-hated what she d-did, but he l-loved you," Kate slurred.

"He cut us off. He wanted to set up house with that blond bitch. She made him do it. She got what she deserved."

"Margo l-lov-ved your f-father, Evan." Kate didn't even open her eyes, but still she tried to make him see.

Evan shook his head. "All of this because you were jealous of her," he accused his mother.

"Jealous. I stood beside him for the last thirty years. I was there for everything he built, and he wanted to spend the rest of his life with that bitch and their son and live happily ever after with my money."

"It wasn't your money. He earned it. He worked his ass off to build that company." Evan spit out the words, wishing she'd get it. "You never loved him. You wanted him to worship you, but still be able to do whatever the hell you wanted with other men. God, how I hate you for manipulating me. I hate myself for being so stupid and taking the bait. You drove him away. Then you drove me to kill him. That's what I'm going to tell the cops. I did it. I killed them. But you made me do it. I'll go down for it, but I'm taking you with me."

The gunshot rang out. He had but a flicker of a second to think past the surprise and reach understanding. His mother wanted him dead so she could blame this all on him. His whole life had led to this moment where all his past deeds came back to haunt him and his mother used them against him.

Evan fell to his knees, blood pumping down his chest. He locked eyes with Ben. "Don't let her get away with this."

Chapter Twenty-Nine

BEN COULDN'T BELIEVE Christina shot her own son. The cold glare she leveled on him spoke to how far she'd go to finish this and get what she wanted. He glanced at Kate. She had nothing left and leaned heavily on her side. She'd lost so much blood. He hoped she'd passed out again. He prayed she hadn't died.

Alex sucked on this hand. He'd wedged himself into the back of the sofa. Christina took a step toward Alex.

"The police have this place surrounded. It's over, Christina. You killed your son for no reason."

"He did it. He did everything."

"That's not true, is it? You hired the man who attacked Kate. You wanted him to kidnap Alex."

"Without him I get everything."

"You set the fire at Haven House."

Christina shook the gun at Kate. "I almost had her that time." The hysterical giggle sent a chill up Ben's spine.

"Your plan almost worked this time, setting off the smoke bomb and getting Kate to come with you."

"All he had to do was kill them, but she turned my son against me."

"You did that all on your own. Evan may have done some terrible things, but he had a conscience. This was tearing him apart. He didn't want to hurt anyone else. I don't think you want to hurt anyone else either." Ben hoped to turn this all around and calm Christina down before she went too far. She'd stepped into the realm of delusion, thinking she could get away with this. He hoped to pull her back to sanity and reason.

"All I need is that little brat to get out of here." Christina held the gun trained on Ben and stepped closer to Alex and reached down for him.

Ben reacted without really thinking. He rushed Christina, shoving her back and away from the baby. The gun came up and a flash sparked a second before the bullet plowed into his chest, sending a shock wave of pain radiating through him. She turned the gun toward Kate. Ben caught his balance and pushed himself over Kate, wrapping his arms around her to protect her. Another shot blast echoed. The hit to his back made him jerk. The pain seized control of his body. Unable to hold on to Kate, he fell backward to the ground.

"Ben!" Kate's scream blasted through his ears.

Christina's chest bloomed with blood and her head exploded in a violent red spray of blood and brain. Sam and the sniper took her down.

Ben landed on his back on the floor. The slow-motion

scene before him erupted into real time as Sam rushed forward to check on Kate, cops flooded the house, and Alex bellowed from the sofa.

A female officer picked up Alex and rushed him from the room. Ben tried to catch the breath that had been knocked out of him from the bullet hitting his vest. Damn, it hurt to breathe, but he was alive.

"We need a helivac now!" Sam's words sent a rush of adrenaline through Ben. "Where are the paramedics?"

A pair of medics rushed through the door, carrying their gear.

Ben rolled to his side and managed to get up with the aid of another officer.

"You okay, man?"

"Fine. The vest saved me."

Sam gently laid Kate on the floor and started chest compressions. "Come on, Kate. Come back to us."

Ben rushed over and held Kate's head. He leaned down and kissed her forehead. "Come on, baby, you can't leave me now. I need you. Alex needs you. Please, honey, come back to me," he begged.

Kate sucked in a breath. Sam stopped CPR. The paramedics pressed bandages over the bleeding wound and started an IV line.

Ben kissed her head again. "That's it, baby, hold on. Stay with me."

"Alex," she whispered.

"He's safe. He's fine."

"Time for us to go," one of the paramedics said.

They lifted Kate onto a backboard and strapped her

down. Ben stood back helpless as they wheeled her outside. So lost in touching her and watching every rise and fall of her chest to be sure she still breathed, he hadn't heard the helicopter land in the neighbor's massive backyard. They loaded Kate and took off without him.

Sam grabbed his arm and pulled him back out to the street and the waiting ambulance. "Get in."

The medic held Alex. He screamed and cried uncontrollably.

"Is he hurt?" Ben asked, hoping nothing had happened to his son. That's how he thought of him. Nothing was going to happen to Kate, but if it did, Ben swore he'd be the best father to Alex. He'd be everything she'd want Alex to have in a dad.

"He seems to be fine. Scared. Maybe hungry."

The female officer who'd taken Alex from the house tossed Alex's diaper bag into the back of the ambulance. Ben dug through it and found a clean bottle and the formula. Kate always kept a bottle of water inside. He made quick work of mixing the formula. It wasn't warm, but Alex took the bottle and sucked greedily around his fits of cries and hiccups as he calmed down.

Ben sat on the gurney and took Alex from the medic. He held him close and sighed, feeling everything that happened over the last fifteen minutes hit him hard. Tears welled in his eyes as relief swept through him. Kate and Alex were alive and safe.

"Take them to the hospital. Check out Alex and Ben. Ben was shot twice. I bet his ribs need to be X-rayed. Make sure nothing is broken." Sam closed one of the ambulance doors and stood in the opening of the other. "I'll take care of things here with Detective Raynott. I'll be by to check on you and Kate in a little while. She'll be in surgery for a couple hours, so don't stress."

"Yeah, right." All he did was think about Kate and the desperate need gnawing at his insides to get to her. Holding Alex helped keep him calm. He wouldn't stop worrying until he had his whole family back in his arms.

Chapter Thirty

KATE WOKE UP by degrees, aware of the whir and beep of machines, a dull pain in her shoulder that radiated through to her back, light on her face, and someone holding her hand. Alex cooed nearby. Her heart eased just hearing his tiny voice.

The nightmare that plagued her last night came back, filling her mind with the sound of gunshots and Ben falling to the floor. Her eyes flew open. She stared at Ben beside her bed, Alex in his arms against his chest, his hand covering hers on the bed. The connection she felt to that man pulsed through her in a wave of relief and love that filled her heart. She exhaled, holding her breath when that made the pain in her chest shoot out like a starburst.

"Breathe, Kate. You're okay." Ben leaned forward and brought her hand to his warm lips, kissing it. He pressed her hand to his beard-roughened cheek and stared down at her. "Hey, you finally awake?"

She let her gaze drop from his gorgeous face to his chest. "Are you hurt? I saw you get shot."

He raised his hand and traced her forehead. "I'm fine. Sam made me wear a bulletproof vest before I went into the house. I've got several severely bruised ribs and muscles. Nothing some painkillers and having you back can't cure."

"How did you find me?"

"I put a tracking device in your phone and purse."

"What?"

"You refused to let the authorities handle things and stay out of it. You provoked Evan and Christina at every turn. I needed to protect you. I needed to be able to find you if they took you."

"You saved my life."

His eyes filled with a fear she never thought she'd see in him. His gaze narrowed with a touch of anger. "You died on me, Kate. Don't ever do that again."

She reached up and touched his scruffy jaw, laying her hand against his face. His warmth seeped into her skin. "I'll try." She pressed her hand to Alex's back. "I have so much to live for."

"I can't wait to take you home."

"I hate hospitals. How long have I been here?"

"Two days. You lost a lot of blood. Surgery took seven hours to repair your shoulder."

She ignored the pain and focused on Ben and Alex. "When can I go home?"

"Two more days. My apartment and Margo's house are crime scenes. Haven House is under construction. We'll have to stay at your place."

Kate hated all the destruction left in her path since she and Ben started this journey to protect Alex's inheritance and get justice for Margo and Donald. Ben's life had been turned upside down.

"I'm sorry, Ben. You must regret the day you ever agreed to help me."

"Never. None of this is your fault. I don't care what's happened or where we stay as long as we're together, Kate. I love you."

Tears welled in her eyes. "I love you too."

"Good, then marry me. I can't live without you. Those seconds I thought you were dead and gone forever were the worst of my life. I promise to love you and make you happy the rest of your life. I promise to be the father you want for Alex. I love him like my own. Say yes, Kate. Say yes to that happy life Margo wanted for you. Make that life a reality with me by your side. Will you marry me?"

"I never thought I'd want a family, but I do. So much. I always thought something was missing from life, but I had no idea what it was until now. It was you. I thought I had everything I wanted. You and Alex are what I need. Yes, I will marry you."

Epilogue

KATE STARED UP at Ben and said the words she never thought she'd say to any man. "I do."

The smile that spread across his handsome face lit her from within. She felt his love in that smile and the twinkle in his eyes. The love between them grew each and every day over the last six months.

Ben held Alex wearing his tiny tux to his chest, bouncing him up and down. At one, Alex had changed so much and was starting to walk. "Da," he said, staring up at Ben. It warmed her heart each time she heard him call Ben that, because Alex had the perfect dad. A man who would always protect and love him. Ben would show Alex how to be a good man.

"Do you have the ring?" the preacher asked Ben.

Alex clutched the red velvet box in his hands. Ben pried it open, despite Alex not wanting to give it up. Kate smiled when she saw the sparkling diamond eternity band that perfectly complemented the enormous diamond engagement ring Ben gave her a week after she got out of the hospital and they escaped for a weekend getaway. Morgan and Tyler babysat Alex, who became Noah's new best friend. The babies loved being together. She, Ben, Morgan, and Tyler had become quite close these last months, which is why they ended up here, in Morgan's sprawling garden for their wedding.

Kate held her hand up. Ben slipped the ring on her finger and recited the vow. He'd truly outdone himself. She still wore her sister's ring. One day, she'd give it to Alex to propose to the woman he loved. A symbol of the love that blessed Margo and Donald's lives entwined with hers that brought them Alex.

"And your ring for Ben," the preacher said.

Kate pulled the gold ring from her thumb and held it up for Ben to see. She repeated the vows and slid the ring onto Ben's hand and traced the two bands woven together encircling his finger, adding, "My life is tied to yours. Without you, I'm incomplete. My love for you is endless."

Ben reached out and slid his hand along her cheek and held her face. He glanced at Morgan, standing behind her as her matron of honor, then met Kate's gaze again. "You were meant for me."

She finally knew what Morgan predicted for Ben and smiled. Nothing Morgan said anymore surprised her. She'd gotten used to the cryptic messages, the visions she shared about Tyler's work and the family.

"You were meant for me," she said back to him.

Ben leaned in and kissed her softly. They lost themselves in the simple but emotion-filled moment.

"I guess you can kiss your bride," the preacher teased, ending the ceremony.

The crowd of over a hundred guests, mostly Ben's "family," including his mother and her husband, and his colleagues and friends, along with the few people she'd worked with at social services and now at Haven House, cheered when the preacher pronounced them husband and wife and introduced them. "I present . . . Mr. and Mrs. Knight."

Funny how it hit her all at once. She was Mrs. Knight. His wife. She had a husband. A son. The family she never had but always wanted even if she had tucked that dream away deep in her heart. She had happiness and love like she'd never experienced in her life. She'd lost so much, but gained infinitely more when her life shattered and Ben helped her put the pieces back together and opened her heart to a life filled with joy.

Ben held his wife close and kissed her on top of the head. He held his son in his arms and couldn't wait to have more children with Kate. He used to fear being a husband and father, thinking that someday his father's bad blood running through his veins would turn him into a monster. That fear evaporated when he fell in love with Kate.

His future once seemed dark, filled with nothing but work to satisfy him and get him through each day. He loved what he did helping others, but it didn't compare to being with Kate and Alex. They filled his life with a deeper meaning than he ever thought possible.

Love saved them from the loneliness engulfing their lives. Love made them see the truth. They were meant for each other. Love entwined them and made their lives brighter.

Keep reading for a peek at
New York Times bestselling author Jennifer Ryan's
next book in her sexy and suspenseful
Montana Men series,

STONE COLD COWBOY

With their hearts' desires on the line
Nothing can stop the Montana Men

Sadie Higgins has a bad habit of bailing her brother out of trouble. But when he rustles a herd of cattle from the tough, honorable Kendrick brothers, it's Sadie who's in for it. Because the cowboy tracking them down is big, silent, and forbidding as hell.

Rory Kendrick is on the hunt to find out who's been stealing from him. When he stumbles upon Sadie in the woods, he barely recognizes the quiet, vulnerable beauty who has always taken his breath away. His mission shifts in an instant: He will do anything it takes to keep her safe . . . and make her his.

Sadie has always protected her family—no matter the price. But when Rory ropes her heart, she's forced to take a look at her life and make a dangerous choice—one that could cost, or gain, her everything.

Available February 2016!

An Excerpt from
STONE COLD COWBOY

SADIE CRESTED THE rolling hill and spotted her target: her missing horses and a herd of cattle that didn't belong to her reckless brother. She didn't waste a hope he was saving them from some predator. Not with two of his miscreant cohorts right beside him pushing the mooing and bawling animals further along the valley. Leave it to her brother to make trouble with no regard for the consequences. If he got caught rustling cattle, he'd expect her to get him out of it. She'd been saving his butt since he hit a rebellious stage at thirteen that turned into his way of life, escalating from pranks to petty theft and drug dealing. What happened to the sweet boy who loved to swing the highest at the playground? The one who cried at their mother's funeral and brushed his hand over Sadie's hair that same night while they cried themselves to sleep on their mother's side of the bed. At twenty-one Connor had changed from a sensitive boy into nothing short of a hoodlum numbed by drugs with no regard for anyone else. One day she feared he'd end up in jail for the rest of his life . . . or dead.

If whoever owned those cattle didn't kill him, she might.

A soft pat on the neck and a nudge with her heels sent her horse, Sugar, down the hill in a trot. Sadie loved to ride, but chasing after her brother took the pleasure right out of it. The cold wind scented with pine, grass, and rain from the storm last night that had left the ground muddy whipped her hair out behind her and burned her cheeks. Her lips dried and cracked in the bitter cold.

Her horse's fast approach startled several cattle. They broke off from the herd and scattered. She rode straight up the middle and split the herd in two, hoping to discourage the animals from following the rider up front and the two flanking them. Her brother spotted her and reined his horse around to meet hers. She pulled up short and stopped beside him, glaring at his ruddy face, red from the cold. His intense gaze collided with hers. His pupils were the size of saucers. High. Irritated he'd been caught, his eyes narrowed on her.

"What the hell do you think you're doing?"

Her lips drew into a grim line. "Saving your ass from making another mistake."

"Get out of here before you get hurt." Connor scanned the area, avoiding looking at the two guys with him, who closed in on them. "You have to go now."

Sadie sighed out her frustration. The cows had stopped walking down the valley and milled around them, chomping at the new grass just beginning to grow

after the last of the snow melted. The cold temps remained even as spring pushed in to take winter's place.
She stared at the poor, tired animals. Her brother and his
buddies had pushed them hard and brought them a long
way. One steer turned and she caught a glimpse of the
brand on his hide.

She sucked in a surprised breath. "These are Kendrick
cattle. Are you crazy? Those guys will hunt you down and
beat the living shit out of you. If Rory comes after you,
you'll wish you were never born."

She'd gone to school with Colt Kendrick, but didn't
really know him. The last time she saw him, he'd been sitting around a table with his two older brothers at the bar.
She'd gone to drag her brother home after the bartender
called to let her know Connor was playing pool and looking for a fight. He'd nearly got one when he stumbled into
Colt and dumped beer down his front. Sadie stepped in
just in time, blocking her brother from the punch Colt
threw and almost landed straight in her face, until Rory
grasped his brother's wrist and stopped his swing inches
from her nose. When her brother tried to go after Colt,
she'd tried to hold him off, but he got around her. Rory
grabbed him by the shirt and held him off the ground
in front of him like he didn't weigh more than a puppy.
He'd looked her brother in the eyes and shook him hard
to get his attention. He didn't speak. Didn't have to. The
ominous look in his eyes made her brother quake in his
boots. Rory set her brother down with a thud, and Connor
ran for the door. Sadie chased after him, but not before
she turned back and caught the feral look in Rory's eyes.

The same kind of look she'd seen weeks earlier when she plowed into Rory's big, solid body in the feed store. The man was hard and unyielding, physically and mentally. You did not go up against a Kendrick, and especially him. Her stupid brother got off free and clear that time.

Connor scratched at a scab on his chin. "If you keep your fucking mouth shut and get lost, they'll never know."

"You don't think they're going to know an entire herd of cattle is missing? You've lost your mind, little brother."

He puffed out his thin chest, his bony shoulders going back. "I'm not little. I can take care of myself," he whined like the child he acted like most of the time.

"You have yet to prove that in any capacity. If it weren't for me, you'd have been locked up in juvy at fourteen. All these years later, you're not proving to be any smarter than that punk kid who cried and begged me to save him. You promised me on our mother's grave you'd do better, you'd quit drinking and doing drugs. But you didn't keep that promise to me, or her."

"I warned you." The words belied the sad, resigned look that came into his eyes.

A split second later, she had the blink of an eye to understand what he meant. A fist slammed into her face, sending her off her horse and into the mud, grass, and darkness.

"STOP TOUCHING HER. Let's just go and get the damn cattle to the trailers before we get caught." Connor stared down at her, lying on the ground practically naked.

What the hell? Her gaze locked on the man crouched beside her, his hand gripped around her upper arm, keeping her from scrambling away. Fear tore through her body. The cold bit into her skin and froze her bones. She clamped her aching jaw down tight to keep her teeth from chattering. She pushed up to sitting, her knees drawn up, and covered herself with her hands. Her cheeks heated with embarrassment. She scanned the area for her missing coat, jeans, and shirt. At least the asshole hadn't gotten her out of her panties and bra; still, it wasn't enough coverage to make her feel safe, or keep her warm.

"Give me back my clothes." Her sharp words didn't hide the fear shaking her voice.

"Shut up, or I'll clock you again."

Scott and Tony, Connor's so-called friends, stood over her smoking cigarettes. The three of them collectively added up to one brain. None of them came up with a good idea, but they sure could turn a bad one worse one-upping each other. Now that she was awake, their gazes shot from her breasts to her face, then off to the scattered clouds overhead.

Connor pushed away the guy beside her, someone she didn't know. "You don't need to strip her. You fucking lay another hand on her and I'll kill you."

She appreciated her brother's bravado, but the big dude with long greasy dark hair, devil tat on his neck, and the wicked knife in his hand he whipped out from behind him could probably kill her brother with a look from his cold eyes. Her throbbing jaw attested to the guy's powerful right hook. If he'd hit a woman, no telling what he'd do to her brother.

The devil dude, as she immediately thought of him, stood and took a menacing step closer to her brother. "Your sister has one hot body. She'd look damn good in lace." He raked his gaze over her prone figure, grimacing at her cotton bra and panties. "I say we teach her a lesson about butting into my business." The devil dude smacked Scott on the shoulder, trying to get his agreement.

Scott and Tony continued to look uncomfortable, shaking their heads and toeing at the dirt, avoiding looking the devil dude right in the eye. They probably needed another hit of whatever they were on. Despite the cold, sweat broke out on their faces. Her brother didn't look much better.

"She's not going to say anything. The last thing she wants to do is get me in trouble." The assurance her brother tried to put into his words fell short, making him sound more like a sniveling child.

"You do that all on your own," she snapped, glaring at all of them. She stood up, realizing too late she didn't quite have her head on straight yet. Dizzy, she stumbled a step, then caught herself. She spotted her clothes tossed a few feet away and rushed toward them, hoping to grab them, her horse, and get the hell out of there before things got worse. She definitely didn't want to get hit again. The fear building in her gut that the devil dude might make good on his ominous threats both spoken and unspoken made bile rise to the back of her throat. She needed to get away now before it was too late.

She wrapped her arms around herself, warding off another round of shivers, not all of which resulted from the cold, but the bone-deep fear they might not let her go.

"Where do you think you're going?" The devil dude grabbed her arm and spun her around. She took him by surprise, stepping in close, and kneeing him in the nuts. He fell to his knees, his hands on his balls, the knife sticking out toward her.

"Sadie, no," her brother shouted.

"I'll make you regret that, bitch." The devil dude lunged for her.

She expected him to grab her, but she couldn't get out of the way fast enough. His hands clamped onto her shoulders. The knife handle dug into her arm, but fear for her life made her act. She brought her arms up and broke his hold. Surprise showed in his eyes, but they narrowed with determination. He grabbed her wrist and yanked her forward. She plowed into his chest with a thump. His cold leather jacket chilled her skin even more. He wrapped his arms around her back, squeezing her close. She head-butted him right in the face, hitting him more on the chin than nose than she'd like. He shoved her back to the ground and swiped the back of his hand over his face. Slumped in the dirt and grass, she stared up at him, trying to clear the haze from her aching head and vision.

She tried to think fast, but the guy came after her again, falling to his knees, straddling her hips. His heavy weight pushed her butt into the soft earth and a jagged rock dug into her spine. He pressed the knife to her neck. The menacing smile on his face reinforced the dangerous look in his eyes. He'd do it. He'd kill her and not think twice about it.

Cold fear washed through her, stealing her every thought and breath. Her heart slammed into her ribs and stopped for a brief second. Her whole world halted as she stared up into eyes that held nothing but death.

"Kill her and I won't make any more meth," her brother yelled.

Startled by her brother's admission, Sadie glanced at Connor, caught the apologetic look, then stared back up into the devil dude's flat eyes.

"You'll cook, or you're dead. You owe me more than the price of those cattle."

"If I'm dead you get nothing. Don't kill her."

The devil dude smiled. It frightened her more than anything he'd done so far.

"Okay. I won't kill her."

The easy acquiescence didn't ease her mind.

"Grab that wire and rope from my saddle," he ordered Scott.

"We should get out of here. Those Kendricks come for their herd and we're dead." Scott tried to talk reason with the irrational.

"Get it now." The devil dude bit out the words. Scott jumped to do his bidding, beaten without ever really getting in the fight to save her.

The devil dude clamped his hand on her aching jaw and shook her face. "No one fucks with me. If they do, they get what's coming. You're going to get your due."

Sadie wanted to run, but he had her on the ground, that damn knife at her neck, pressed so hard to her skin she felt a trickle of blood run down her throat where he cut her. His gaze fell on the blood. The slow smile that spread across his face disturbed her, but not as much as the lust that filled his dark eyes.

Scott dropped the coiled barbed wire and rope next to her. Connor stood off to the side, pacing, biting at his thumb, his eyes filled with worry, but he didn't come to her rescue, just kept gnawing on his already raw skin.

"This is going to hurt, bitch." The menacing words held a note of anticipation and enthusiasm that soured her stomach.

He used his grip on her face to hold her down. He slid the knife into the sheath at his back and pulled a pair of wire cutters from his back pocket and snipped a long length of wire from the coil. He held it up in front of her, set the tool down, took both her hands, and pulled them up in front of him. She bucked her hips and tried to pull free, but nothing worked to dislodge the big man from her body.

"Let me go, asshole." She tried to put as much bravado in her voice as she could conjure to hide her fear, but the tremble in her voice gave her away.

"You asked for it."

He wrapped the wire around her wrists and in between. The harder she tried to pull free, the tighter he wound.

Panic rose in her chest, making it difficult to take a

deep breath. Her chest heaved in and out. In another minute, she'd be hyperventilating. "Stop. Please. You're hurting me."

"Ah, music to my ears." The amusement in his eyes told her how much he enjoyed her fear and pain.

"You sadistic son of a bitch."

"Yes, I am." His eyes went bright with delight.

The barbs bit into her skin. Blood trickled down her arms from multiple punctures.

"Go get the horses while I finish here," he ordered her brother.

Tony and Scott scurried away without a word. The dread in their eyes when they snuck quick glances back told her how much they feared this man.

"Leave her. You taught her a lesson. Let's go," Connor pleaded, pacing back and forth not even five feet away.

"I thought letting her walk home in her underwear in the cold would have taught her a lesson about sticking her nose into things that don't concern her. But your sister had to go and fuck with me." The devil dude leaned down close and stared her in the eyes. "You kick me in the balls, bitch, I'll make you bleed." The whispered threat didn't lessen the ominous reality that he meant it. He turned back to her brother and yelled, "Go get the horses. Hers too. We're leaving."

Connor backed up several steps, then turned and walked away without sparing her a single look, let alone an apology for his cowardice. She expected it, but it still hurt, leaving a pit in her stomach and an ache that squeezed her chest tight. Tears threatened to spill from her eyes, but she blinked them away. Her brother had proven more times than she could count he'd cover his own ass over anyone else's, including his own sister's.

Her heart ached worse than her face, jaw, and bloody wrists combined. How could he just leave her here? How could he turn his back on her like this and live with himself?

A wave of terror overtook her. Against her will and knowing it wouldn't change her brother's mind, she gave into her growing fear and screamed, "Connor, help me."

The devil dude laughed. "He owes too much money to go against me and help you. You've got some guts trying to fight me, but here's the thing, unlike your brother, I handle my business and any witnesses. Now I said I wouldn't kill you, but I never said I wouldn't let the cold do that for me."

The tears she'd kept at bay filled her eyes and spilled down the side of her face into her hair. She lost all her bravado and begged, "Let me go. I won't say anything. I just wanted to keep him out of trouble. That's all. Please, let me go. I'll walk home like you said. I won't tell anyone about this."

He cocked his head to the side and smirked, though it wasn't reassuring. "Nice try. I might have believed you, but then you had to go and take a shot at my nuts. Now, I'm going to teach you a lesson."

He pulled the rope close and tied one end to the wire around her wrists. She tried to pull free and scramble away, but she only ended up hurting worse when he wrestled her into submission, her hands crushed under his punishing grasp. Once secure, he finally rose and took his weight off her middle. Finally, she could breathe easier, but her breath stopped when he walked right over her head, yanked the rope, and dragged her over the mud and grass. She rolled to her stomach, pulled back on the ropes, squealing out in pain when the wire dug into her skin, and rushed up to her feet. Better to trot after him like a dog on a leash than get dragged over the ground.

"Please, let me go."

He didn't respond, just walked right up to a big tree. She pulled back, not wanting to get tied to the trunk, but he had other ominous ideas. He held the rope close to her by one hand and used the other to toss the other end of the rope up and over a high, thick limb. He pulled the slack tight, then pulled again until her toes barely touched the ground. She wiggled to get free, but it only hurt her wrists more. Fresh blood trailed down her arms. She kicked out her feet, trying to get him to let loose the rope. He anticipated her move, drew his knife again, and slashed at her legs in a wide arc, catching her across her left thigh and right knee. She yelled in pain and stopped struggling, stunned he'd cut her. The sting burned like fire.

"Keep it up. I like it when you bleed." The menacing note of truth in his words sent a bolt of fear through the denial in her mind that he couldn't be serious. But he was.

Afraid that all her fighting would only lead to more pain, she hung there, trying to think of anything she could say to change his mind about leaving her strung up in the biting cold. Even now, her skin felt like ice. She wiggled her numb toes hoping to restore circulation. Thanks to the wire around her wrists, she couldn't feel her hands.

He came toward her again, this time with his eyes on her breasts that were now at his eye level. He reached out to touch her. She pulled her knees up to her belly, planted her feet on his chest, and shoved him away. "Don't you dare touch me." The order didn't hold as much weight when she ended up swinging back and forth from her hands, grunting in pain as each movement made the wire bite into her skin deeper.

He moved forward again. She kicked at him again and again, her body swinging and twisting from the rope. She ignored the excruciating pain. Too soon she tired and swung back and forth unable to pick up her legs and strike out at him again. Defeat tasted vile. She swallowed the sour taste, hoping she didn't disgrace herself more and vomit.

He smiled and laughed, planting a hand on her belly and pushing, sending her swinging yet again. He'd been taunting her, tiring her out so she couldn't fight him off anymore. She'd played right into his hands. She needed to be smart, think, find a way out of this despite the reality staring her in the face—she was well and truly screwed.

"If I had more time, and those assholes weren't so fucking stupid and could finish this job on their own . . ." He left the rest unsaid. He didn't need to finish. The leering gaze he swept over her body said everything. Her mind conjured one gruesome thing after the next; all of them made her stomach pitch, bile rising up her throat.

After so many minutes holding her up, he struggled to hold the rope and tied off the end around the trunk of the tree, leaving her dangling in the wind. The devil dude grabbed the bundle of barbed wire and brought it back. He wound one end around the wire at her wrists to anchor it, then wrapped the rest around both her arms, down over her shoulders. The sharp edges dug into her skin like little bites of pain.

She couldn't help the tears anymore, or the pleading in her voice she hated. "No, please don't do this."

"I like it when you beg, but seeing you bleed gets me off." He rubbed his hand over his crotch and leered at her again.

She met his lust-filled gaze, unable to watch him stroke the bulge in his jeans, knowing at any second he could change his mind, dump her back on the ground, and torture her a whole other way. "Please. The cold is enough. I can't get free. You don't have to do this."

He cocked his head and grinned. "I don't have to. I want to."

He put the truth in his words to work and pulled the wire around her back and across her chest, once, twice, and over her breasts. To punish her even more for getting in her licks earlier, he pulled the wire on both sides of her tight, making the barbs pierce her thin bra and skin.

"No." She bit back another yelp when he pulled the wire even tighter.

"Uh, the trucks will be at the meeting place in an hour. We need to go if we're going to make it in time and before it gets dark," Tony said from behind the devil dude.

"I'll be right there. Gather up any strays and start pushing the herd down the valley again."

Tony left without another word and without bringing his gaze up from his toes.

The devil dude glared at her. "You've cost me a lot of time." He wound the wire around her hips, then around one thigh several times and across to go around the other. The wire bit into the knife wound, making it bleed even more. Tighter and tighter he bound her legs until he had her feet wrapped so tight her ankle bones ground against each other.

He tossed the rest of the wire to the ground at her feet. He pulled the knife out again and held it up in front of her. The waning sunlight glinted off the already bloody blade. Her heart stopped. She didn't dare breathe or take her gaze from the deadly weapon and the man who liked to use it.

He jabbed her in the gut with his fist and the air whooshed out of her. She tried to suck in a breath, but ended up coughing before she could refill her lungs. She prayed he didn't hit her again.

"If you somehow manage to get out of this, you say one word to anyone, I'll hunt you down and make this"—he pointed the knife up and down her bloody body—"feel like a hug compared to what I'll do to you next time."

"Please, let me down. You can't leave me here."

The sharp point of the knife dug into her side between two ribs, piercing her skin but not sinking deep. Damn, those shallow punctures hurt like hell. Exactly his intention. He pushed, sending her swinging and the knife slipping free. Lucky for her, he didn't hold the knife there for her to swing back into.

"Pray the cold gets you before the wolves." The devil dude lived up to his wicked tat with that parting shot.

"You can't leave me here," she screamed at his retreating back. "Help me! Connor, you can't leave me here," she bellowed. "Connor!"

She waited, hoping he'd do the right thing for once. For her. She'd saved him so many times. This time, she needed him.

The wind whipped up again, pushing against her back. Not a sound reached her. From her place on the hill and behind the cover of trees, she couldn't see the valley, the cows, or even her brother.

No one came.

He didn't come.

Tears spilled down her cheeks. She shook with the sobs racking her body.

I'm going to die here.

Not one to give in easily, she wiggled, trying desperately to get free. Her toes barely touched the dirt. The more she moved, the more dirt she displaced until she hung with no purchase on the ground. If he wanted to torture her, he'd picked the perfect way to do it. The more she moved, the worse things got. The wires bit into her skin, sending fresh dribbles of blood down her body. The cut on her side bled freely down her stomach, soaking her panties. She couldn't hold up her weight, so her body dragged her down, making her wrists and shoulders ache.

A branch snapped. Her gaze shot up. The devil dude

stood ten yards away with her clothes tucked under his arm. He shook his head and smiled. He liked making her crazy, seeing her struggle, and knowing she didn't have a chance in hell of getting out of this alive.

She stared him down, not letting him see the fear growing inside of her anymore. She used what little strength she had left to curse the bastard. "I hope those Kendricks find you. I hope Rory Kendrick finds you. Then you'll be sorry. You'll see. He'll make you pay."

Yeah, Rory would make him pay for the cows. Who would make him pay for what he'd done to her? No one. She'd die here abandoned by her brother and alone.

The World of

THE HUNTED

If you haven't read the rest of The Hunted books,
what are you waiting for?
Check out the rest of this bestselling series,
available now from Avon Impulse!

SAVED BY THE RANCHER

Book One: The Hunted Series

FROM THE MOMENT rancher Jack Turner rescues Jenna Caldwell Merrick, he is determined to help her. Soon, he is doing more than tend her wounds; he is mending her heart. Jenna is a woman on the run—hunted down by her ex-husband, David Merrick, from the day she left him, taking part of his company with her, to the second she finds herself in the safety of Jack's ranch. More than just a haven, Jack's offering the love, family, and home she thought were out of reach.

Jack's support will give Jenna the strength she needs to reclaim her life. The hunted will become the hunter, while David gets what he deserves, when they have an explosive confrontation in the boardroom of Merrick International. But not before Jack and Jenna enter into a fight . . . for their lives.

LUCKY LIKE US

Book Two: The Hunted Series

The Hunted series continues as
Special Agent Sam Turner discovers that
protecting the FBI's star witness is
more difficult than he thought!

BAKERY OWNER ELIZABETH Hamilton's quiet life is filled
with sweet treats, good friends, and a loving family. But
all of that is about to turn sour when an odd sound draws
her outside. There's a man lying unconscious in the street,
a car speeding toward him. Without hesitation, she gets
the man out of harm's way before they're run down.

Unwittingly, Elizabeth has put herself in the path of a
serial murderer, and as the only one who can identify the
FBI's Silver Fox Killer, she's ended up in the hospital with
a target on her back.

All that stands between her and death is Special Agent
Sam Turner. Against his better judgment, Sam gets emotionally involved, determined to take down the double
threat against Elizabeth—an ex desperate to get her back,
despite a restraining order, and a psychopath bent on si-
lencing her before she can identify him.

They set a trap to catch the killer—putting Elizabeth
in his hands, with Sam desperate to save her. If he's lucky,
he'll get his man . . . and the girl.

THE RIGHT BRIDE

Book Three: The Hunted Series

HIGH-POWERED BUSINESSMAN CAMERON Shaw doesn't believe in love—until he falls head over heels for beautiful, passionate, and intensely private Martina. She's perfect in so many ways, immediately bonding with his little girl. Martina could be his future bride and a delightful stepmother . . . if only Cameron weren't blinded by his belief that Shelly, the gold-digging woman he's promised to marry, is pregnant with his child.

No matter how much his friends protest his upcoming marriage to Shelly, Cameron knows he has a duty to his children, so he's determined to see it through.

Will he find out in time that Shelly's lying and Marti's the one who's actually carrying his child? It'll come down to the day of his wedding. After choosing Shelly over Marti at every turn, will he convince Marti she's his world and the only woman he wants?

CHASING MORGAN

Book Four: The Hunted Series

FBI AGENT TYLER Reed trusts only facts and evidence, until the day a beautiful blonde delivers a life-saving warning . . . based on nothing more than a vision.

Five years later, the mysterious Morgan Standish has used her talents to help Tyler and the FBI bring down countless criminals. Still, Tyler knows next to nothing about her. She contacts him by phone—and by some sort of psychic connection he's not prepared to admit exists—but has not shown herself once. Until now.

Morgan's gift may let her see things others can't, but it comes at a price. Getting too close to anyone is dangerous, especially the gorgeous, moody Special Agent Reed. For she's seen the future: if they meet again too soon, an innocent could be lost.

But when Tyler's latest case forces Morgan out of hiding, she is the one thrust into the path of a serial killer, the Psychic Slayer, who will stop at nothing to protect the secrets only Morgan can see.

JENNIFER RYAN is the *New York Times* & *USA Today* bestselling author of The Hunted series and the McBride series. She writes romantic suspense and contemporary small-town romances featuring strong men and equally resilient women. Her stories are filled with love, friendship, and the happily-ever-after we all hope to find. Jennifer lives in the San Francisco Bay Area with her husband and three children. When she isn't writing a book, she's reading one. Her obsession with both is often revealed in the state of her home and in how late dinner is to the table. When she finally leaves those fictional worlds, you'll find her in the garden, playing in the dirt and daydreaming about people who live only in her head, until she puts them on paper.

Discover great authors, exclusive offers, and more at hc.com.

Give in to your Impulses . . .
Continue reading for excerpts from
our newest Avon Impulse books.
Available now wherever e-books are sold.

DIRTY DEEDS
A MECHANICS OF LOVE NOVEL
by Megan Erickson

MONTANA HEARTS:
SWEET TALKIN' COWBOY
by Darlene Panzera

An Excerpt from

DIRTY DEEDS
A Mechanics of Love Novel
By Megan Erickson

After a devastating relationship left her reeling,
mechanic Alex Dawn swore off all men. She's got
a chip on her shoulder no man will ever knock
off, so she's content to focus on her family and her
job at Payton and Sons Automotive. But all the
defenses she's worked to build are put to the test
when British businessman L.M. Spencer rolls
into her shop late one night, with a body like a
model and a voice from her dirtiest dreams.

He followed her outside, the clack of his expensive shoes a contrast to the clomp of her boots. She was hyper-aware of his gaze on her back, like fingers down her spine. When they reached her truck, she reached out to open the door but the next second, a hand spun her around and a body pressed her up against the side of her truck.

She looked up, up into the face of one turned-on Brit. Her knees nearly buckled.

When they'd arrived at the bar, the sun was still setting, so she hadn't thought to worry about where she parked. Now she realized she'd chosen a spot that the dim lights outside the bar didn't reach. They were mostly in darkness, and she probably should have been afraid. Spencer was much taller than her, broader. His forearms were muscular and she could see the roundness of his biceps under his shirt.

But for some reason, she wasn't worried. The only part of him that touched her was his chest brushing along hers. She'd worn a push-up bra today and she cursed the padding that was separating her from rubbing her hardened nipples against him.

His hand was braced on the side of the truck, the other hanging at his side in a loose fist. His entire body was tense as he stared down into her eyes.

Slowly, very slowly, he lifted the hand at his side and settled it on her hip. Her tank top had ridden up so a strip of skin was bared between it and the top of her jeans. He ran his thumb along that strip of skin, watching her face. She got the impression he was waiting for her to say stop, or keep going, and she appreciated that.

Although what did she expect from a man named Leslie Michael Spencer?

She curled her tongue around her top teeth and lifted her chin. "You too posh to take what you want?" she whispered.

He barked out a laugh. "I have to make the first move, do I?"

She swallowed. "I'm pretty sure my invitation to stick your hand up my shirt was the first move." She was proud of her chest, always had been. Dawn girls were blessed in the boob department, that was for sure, despite their small statures.

His eyes dipped to her chest, then back up. "Hm, I guess you're right."

"Your move then, Posh."

"This *was* my move. Not letting you get in the car, pressing my body to yours, showing you that I want you." He emphasized that with a slight roll of his hips. "So, actually, it's now your move, Sprite."

There were a lot of things about a man's body Alex liked. Hands were one. Legs and ass were another. She'd seen glimpses of the muscles in his thighs flexing in his pants, the perfect shape of his ass, so now she decided she needed to feel too. She reached down with both hands, running her fingers up the back of his thighs, then cupped his ass. She pressed his hips to her, and he exhaled roughly. "Your move now," she whispered.

An Excerpt from

MONTANA HEARTS: SWEET TALKIN' COWBOY

By Darlene Panzera

If it wasn't for an injury to his leg, Luke Collins
would be riding rodeo broncos all day, every
day. Until he heals, he's determined to help
his family's guest ranch bring in money any
way he can. But when a cranky neighbor gets
in the way of his goal, Luke turns to the only
person he knows can help: the gorgeous,
rodeo-barrel-racing spitfire next door.

Sammy Jo froze as he met her gaze, and it seemed as if he could see right through her. But could he see the love she had for him swelling her heart? Sometimes when they stood this near she thought her chest would explode with the emotion she fought so hard to restrain. But if she gushed like a schoolgirl and told him how she really felt, he'd never believe her. Not that he did now. And she'd only shown him a quarter of the affection she'd been hiding.

"Okay," Luke relented, "you can help. But keep your eyes on the job."

"Where else would my eyes be?" she teased.

Luke shot her a look of amusement, but didn't reply and she didn't dare push the subject any farther. Determined to show him she could be of value, she shot out her arm to retrieve the bucket of paint he'd placed on an upper rung of the ladder.

Except Luke reached for it at the same time and the double movement made the bucket wobble, tip, and then . . . dump the five gallons of thick, clover green liquid right over both their heads.

Sammy Jo let out a screech, jumped back as the bucket hit the ground to avoid another splash, and brought her hands up to her face to keep the paint from streaming into her eyes. The chalky latex enamel substance smelled as bad as it tasted and she had to spit several times to get the wretched stuff off her lips and out of her mouth.

She glanced down at her white t-shirt and denim cut-offs coated in green, as were her arms, legs, and what used to be her blue, canvas shoes.

Then her hands flew to the top of her head where gobs of the green goo weighted down her long dark curls and left them hanging limp over her shoulders. She tried to separate the icky green strands with her fingers and let out another cry. Returning her hair to its natural color would be no easy task. No easy task at all! Maybe next time she'd think twice before offering to help for the sake of spending time with him.

She glanced at Luke, also covered in green, except she'd been right—his clothes hid the paint better. Holding her breath, she waited for his reaction. Would he be mad? Blame her for wasting the gallon of paint?

No . . . he grinned. As if this was funny. As if . . .

"Did you do that on purpose?" she demanded.

"Of course not," he said, inspecting the new color of his cane. "If I had, I would have stepped back so the paint didn't get *me*."

"Then why are you laughing?"

"I'm not." He broke into another grin. "Although you *do* look a lot like the wicked witch from *The Wizard of Oz*."

Sammy Jo sucked in her breath. "And you look like a cow has spewed all over you with a whole day's worth of green cud!"

This time Luke *did* laugh. He laughed for several long

seconds, harder than she'd ever heard him laugh since he'd been back home.

"You know that Emerald Isle shade becomes you," he teased. "Matches your eyes."

"Not funny," she shot back. "How am I going to get all this paint out of my hair?"

"You can't. You'll have to cut it all off."

The thought of styling a bald head didn't hold much appeal. She'd rather sport her clover green curls until the color grew out, although that image too, was almost enough to bring her to tears.

Then his amused expression made her realize he wasn't serious and she pointed her finger at him. "Now who's playing games?"

Luke shrugged. "It'll wash out with a good shampoo. You'll just have to scrub real good. For now, we can rinse off with the hose in the wash room."

She patted the front pocket on her denim shorts. "I hope the paint didn't go through to my cell phone. What if I lost all my contact numbers? Or my photos?"

"Would be a shame," he said with mock concern.

Luke did not appreciate the finer aspects of having multiple apps available at one's fingertips 24–7. A fault she could easily forgive him for if he'd only pick up the phone to call her for a date.

A real date. Not just hanging out at the barn, or attending a rodeo together with the rest of their friends, or even roasting marshmallows by the fire with his sisters. But one-on-one time with just the two of them.

Luke led her toward the open double doors of the stable

to the large cement wash room where they usually gave the horses a bath. When she envisioned a date, this setting had never come to mind either.

"Stand over the drain and I'll hose you down," he said, turning on the water.

She took her phone out of her pocket and set it on a shelf holding the horse shampoo, a sponge and squeegee. Then stood ready to embrace the oncoming shower.

"Tip your head back and close your eyes," Luke instructed.

"So you can kiss me?"

"No," he said, shaking his head. "So I can do *this*."

Join Avon Impulse and celebrate the holiday season with our three, brand new romances about love, laughter, and those cold December nights.

LORD DASHWOOD MISSED OUT

A Spindle Cove Novella

By Tessa Dare

A snowstorm hath no fury like a spinster scorned

Miss Elinora Browning grew up yearning for the handsome, intelligent lord-next-door . . . but he left England without a word of farewell. One night, inspired by a bit too much sherry, Nora poured out her heartbreak on paper. *Lord Dashwood Missed Out* was a love letter to every young lady who'd been overlooked by gentlemen—and an instant bestseller. Now she's on her way to speak in Spindle Cove when snowy weather delays her coach. She's forced to wait out the storm with the worst possible companion: Lord Dashwood himself.

And he finally seems to have noticed her.

George Travers, Lord Dashwood, has traveled the globe as a cartographer. He returned to England with the goal of marrying and creating an heir—only to find his reputation shredded by an audacious, vexingly attractive bluestocking and her poison pen. *Lord Dashwood Missed Out*, his arse. Since Nora Browning seems to believe he overlooked the passion of a lifetime, Dash challenges her to prove it.

She has one night.

BURNING BRIGHT

Four Chanukah Love Stories

By Megan Hart, Stacey Agdern,
Jennifer Gracen, and KK Hendin

This December, take a break from dreidel spinning, gelt winning, and latke eating to experience the joy of Chanukah. When you fall in love during the Festival of Lights, the world burns a whole lot brighter.

It's definitely not love at first sight for Amanda and her cute but mysterious new neighbor, Ben. Can a Chanukah miracle show them that getting off on the wrong foot doesn't mean they can't walk the same road?

Lawyers in love, Shari Cohen and Evan Sonntag are happy together. But in a moment of doubt, he pushes her away— then soon realizes he made a huge mistake. To win her back, it might take something like a Chanukah miracle.

When impulsive interior designer Molly Baker-Stein barges into Jon Adelman's apartment and his life intent on planning the best Chanukah party their building has ever seen, neither expects that together, they just might discover a Home for Hannukah.

All Tamar Jacobs expected from her Israel vacation was time to hang out with one of her besties and to act like a tourist, cheesy t-shirt and all, in her two favorite cities. She definitely was not expecting to fall for Avi Levinson, a handsome soldier who's more than she ever dreamed.

ALL I WANT FOR CHRISTMAS IS A DUKE

By Valerie Bowman, Tiffany Clare, Vivienne Lorret, and Ashlyn Macnamara

The holidays are a time for dining, dancing, and of course—dukes! Celebrate the Christmas season with this enchanting collection of historical romances featuring the most eligible bachelors of the ton . . .

A childish prank may have reunited the Duke of Hollingsworth with his estranged wife, but only the magic of Christmas will show this couple 'tis the season of second chances . . .

Sophie Kinsley planned to remain a wallflower at the Duke of Hollyshire's ball. Yet when a dance with him leads to a stolen kiss, will the duke be willing to let her go? Or will Sophie's Christmas wish be granted at last?

To the Duke of Vale, science solves everything—even marriage. When the impulsive Ivy Sutherland makes him question all of his data, he realizes that he's overlooked a vital component in his search for the perfect match: love.

Patience Markham never forgot the fateful dance she had with the future Duke of Kingsbury. But when a twist of fate brings them together for Christmas Eve, will the stars finally align in their favor?